The Aliens of Summer

of

Summer

CALVIN ROSS

DISTANT STAR

Napa, California

To Sandy Koufax, a Giant
of a Dodger.
Before I saw him, it was
baseball; after, magic!

This is a tale. Resemblance to
anyone living or dead is completely
unintended. There are, naturally,
some allusions to historical figures.

ISBN 0-9642658-9-3

Part One

1

ANCHOR:

Well, the Planetary Council has made it official: it has come out squarely against biofashion. And to lead the charge, First Councilor Tarn has had himself retrofashioned in a very public way, as you'll see in this holoclip.

REPORTER:

The leading biofashion house of First City, StarFaces, was abuzz today as the First Councilor made a surprise visit here to make known what many of us had already guessed: the Planetary Council believes biofashion has gotten completely out of control and has to slow down a bit or risk being regulated, a step which the Council is of course loath to take. What surprised most observers was the way that the First Councilor chose to make his point.

FIRST COUNCILOR:

I called this press conference on the steps of StarFaces to emphatically demonstrate the seriousness with which myself and the whole Council view this disturbing situation. In spite of numerous studies that repeated biofashioning can lead to cell damage, there are still many people who will change a self for *one day*, just to make a splash at a party! So that no one mistakes my feelings on the subject, I'm getting retrofashioned to my original self today here at StarFaces. And, although I have enjoyed this self for over fifteen years now, I pledge to refrain from biofashioning in the future.

REPORTER:

Whether or not he can keep that pledge remains to be seen, but, sure enough, one hour later First Councilor Tarn emerged from the doors of StarFaces with a look that many of us can barely recall. He looked fit, although a bit short and certainly not as stylish as before!

ANCHOR:

Well, the First Councilor sure has style in the way he makes policy statements! Who knows, maybe I'll consider retrofashioning, ha, ha, maybe it'll be a trend...

CO-ANCHOR:

Yeah right, that'll be the day! Personally, I thought the First Councilor's new look is kind of cute!

ANCHOR:

You would, Taza! Show some *respect*, ha, ha. Anyway, turning to the world of baseball, there's trouble brewing on the First City Sluggers' pitching staff, and here's Jevv to tell you all about it.

SPORTSCASTER:

Thanks. That's right, folks, the Sluggers' right-handed ace, Hohallen, pulled one open minder too many as the Seaview Captains took advantage of the gaffe to pull within four games of the league-leading Sluggers with a 12 to 2 pounding of the champs. Bisrotare of the Captains started it all off in the second inning with his 19th home run of the season. I caught up with him at the end of the contest...

BISROTARE:

Well, I read fastball, and jumped on it and I knew it was out the second I hit it. As I was rounding the bases I thought, wow, that was Hohallen, I mean you're used to open minders from rookies, but guys like Hohallen usually make you earn it. And it was Hohallen's open minder too, I mean the catcher's mind was white rock.

SPORTSCASTER:

Hohallen's mind was anything but white rock as he committed his tenth acknowledged open minder of the season. And as anyone in baseball will tell you, open minders will always come back to haunt you, and it sure seemed to put a damper on the Sluggers' usually prolific offense as they were held to four hits. And Bisrotare's homer started a party that didn't end until 14 hits later. Concerned manager Samfor of First City had this to say about his erstwhile ace...

SAMFOR:

We haven't lost faith in Hohallen, he's just had a couple of rough outings, and our pitching coach has been working with him. We think a little time with the team counselor might do him some good but, you know, it's a long season and we're still four up on the Captains and you can't panic over one loss. Our pitching staff is holding up pretty well and we're sure Hohallen will contribute before this is all over.

SPORTSCASTER:

Well, in spite of Samfor's kind words, Hohallen had better turn it around or, ace or no ace, he just might find himself in the moon leagues! We'll just have to wait and see.

ANCHOR:

Thanks, Jevv. In other news today...

Tarn threw the doors of the Council Chamber open and walked a bit bruskly over to take his seat in front of the already assembled Council.

Second Councilor Semptor rose in traditional greeting.

"The Planetary Council welcomes the First Councilor, and I know I speak for the whole Council when I commend you on your new, or should I say *old*, appearance. If I hadn't served with you on the First City Board of Governors twenty years ago I daresay I might not have recognized you."

"I barely recognized myself at StarFaces this morning after the retrofashioning, Semptor, but it had to be done. Hopefully this will somewhat abate the biofashion madness until we can convince the public to quell this, this, decadence. This obsession with Earth styles has completely gotten out of hand. Why, half the male population of Ball Four must look like Earthling ballplayers! I myself have run into a least a dozen Steve Garvey's! I half regret making those holographic reports from Earth about Operation Universe Series public. But back then who could have foreseen the reaction?"

Third Councilor Niver rose for recognition.

"Unfortunately, First Councilor Tarn, the perfection we have achieved in Ball Fourian society leads to such a malaise from time to time that the people will find, against *our* better judgement, new and unusual ways to have their fun. Surely, your gesture will have a profound impact on the people. But, of course, this is not why you have called this special session of the Council."

"No, it isn't, Niver. Gentlemen, I received a report yesterday evening from Earth. And it appears that, finally, this is the year!"

"Whatever do you mean, First Councilor?" said Semptor amid the general murmur.

"I mean that, with the addition of Buck Nichols to the roster, the entire team is Ball Fourian. Gentlemen, we *are* the Cleveland Indians. And, if all goes as expected, this year's Earth World Series will be the Universe Series we've been waiting for."

The Council chamber slowly began to fill with the low, rumbling huzzahs of approval but, this time, it reached a peak not elicited by the usual mundane issues. This indeed was a splendid moment for Ball Four, and it only remained to be seen which statesman would seize the opportunity.

Niver, as Third, was never at a loss. "Surely, this is a glorious day for Ball Four, and everyone who was part of the Operation is to be commended for the incredible speed at which this was accomplished. I recall with some chagrin that I was among those at the beginning who doubted the whole design. That a successful, peaceful and, more importantly, clandestine infiltration was accomplished in a mere nine years is a credit and, shall I say, a glory to the Baseball Commission."

"A feat which the Baseball Commission will be only too happy to revel in at the proper time and place," interposed Tarn.

"But, certainly, as you *are* First Commissioner of Baseball as well as First Councilor, you will accept our congratulations in this chamber?" asked Niver.

"Although I subscribe to the ancient wisdom that one should never mix important things like baseball with trivial matters like politics, I will gladly accept your congratulations. I will, however, insist that you amend your claim of doubt for the project to open hostility."

Niver protested. "I was not in fact hostile. I strongly believed at the time, as I still do, that the whole idea flew in the face of the Technology Non-proliferation Act which has stood us in good stead for centuries, and should not have been toyed with lightly."

"At which I refer you again to the aforementioned ancient wisdom," said Tarn. Low huzzahs filled the chamber. "In any event, the issue was settled when infiltration was chosen over open challenge. Although I was not yet First Councilor at the time, I *was* First Commissioner and I let my views be known concerning the Non-proliferation Act, and the Council concurred. But this is old news, Niver, and we are wasting the Council's time when there is so much to do and enjoy. Let's forget old battles and move on to new business."

"With pleasure, First Councilor."

"All right. In light of the news from Earth, I am immediately calling a meeting of the Baseball Commission. Those in this chamber who are also members of that body please plan to attend forthwith. I am dismissing the rest of the Council to committee work. Councilor Jerve, I have accepted your proposals for the changes in the climate parameters of First City, and I have recommended only minor alterations in your overall global plan. They're all in the report I gave you, and I authorize you to proceed to implementation through your Weather Committee. By the way, we had a brief rain-out at Seaview Stadium last week. Whatever could you have been thinking?"

"Oh, that was the boys at WeatherCon, First Councilor. Apparently they were watching the game instead of monitoring. They've been reprimanded and fined a substantial number of gambling credits. It won't happen again."

"I have no doubt. Okay, gentlemen, to your committees. We have exciting work to do. Council adjourned."

A half an hour later the Baseball Commission convened. Tarn, as in the Council, sat at the head console.

"Commissioners, I understand we have much to celebrate and much to do. I've seen the report and duly announced it to the Council, but I've not had time to fully digest it. Have you gotten a good look at it, Semptor?"

"I have indeed, First Commissioner, and with your permission I'd like to share the more salient points with the Commission."

Tarn nodded.

Semptor continued. "Very good then. Gentlemen, we have reached a goal that we've striven for these nine years. With the announcement of Bolnici, or Buck Nichols as he's known on Earth, as a starter, Ball Fourians now comprise the entire starting lineup, starting rotation, key pinch hitters and stoppers on the Cleveland Indian roster. A couple of utility players and a few in the bullpen are still Earthling, but we agreed that we could start the "Year" once we'd achieved this. And manager Evan has guaranteed that not much of the season will go by before we've taken the whole team. Of course, public announcement will be delayed until we've agreed."

Tarn rose. "Based on that information, I should think we're ready to vote. Gentlemen?"

The room fell silent and movement ceased. After a moment, Tarn sat down.

"I sensed no opposition, the agreement is declared. Semptor, prepare to issue the announcement in the usual way. This should shake up the planet! Hopefully, this will curb interest in biofashion. This whole project, when it began thirty years ago was meant to breathe fresh air into a wilting society, and to a certain extent it has. It hasn't had much affect on biofashion abuse yet. Hopefully, it'll calm the gambling down. What else have you got?"

Semptor went on. "There's still the fine tuning to do. We've got sociologists constantly watching for ways to prevent detection. To avoid scrutiny we've got to continue to look for inconsistencies. I'll give you an example. According to the report, one problem we're still having trouble with is the 'bench-clearing brawl.' Although we've gotten better at arguing with umpires, we haven't managed to fight very much. Earthling ballplayers fly into a rage at things all the time, and our guys on the Indians have trouble duplicating it. We did have one good brawl last year, but there were still a substantial number of Earthlings on the squad and they instigated it. We tried to start a 'bench-clearing brawl' in the Cactus League this spring but with mixed success. We'll continue to work on it."

"We should. Any other problems?"

"Only minor ones. The usual thing in restraining talent. Since the Indians were 80-82 last year and 65-97 the year before, we've been having trouble keeping the boys from crushing the Cactus League. Various problems, nothing big. Nothing to call a meld meeting over."

"The principal thing that I wonder about, Semptor, as I'm sure the entire Commission as well as the fans do, is: is this a fair contest?"

"We have no reason to believe that it isn't, First Commissioner. Of course we're confident of victory, but that's what the Universe Series is all about — to find out if we're the best in the known universe after all. I tend to doubt that there's a Ball Fourian alive who'd think the Earthlings had a chance given our mental advantages. That's what this year will prove. I look forward to it with relish, First Commissioner."

"As do I, Semptor. And the betting line will let us know what Ball Four makes of all this. The damned betting line! It's another thing that hasn't been generated by Operation Universe Series. It has yet to divert interest away from the gambling houses. Why, people have bet on how many years it would take to find a baseball-playing planet, or if it would be found at all. They've even bet on the quadrant in which it would be found. One can only imagine the novel wagers the public will now contrive."

"Well, as the old saying goes, if you can't beat 'em, bet on 'em. Let's enjoy this Earth season and hope all of Ball Four does as well."

"Sound advice, my good Semptor. We should all heed it. And now, gentlemen, copies of the report have been downloaded to all your consoles. I urge you all to give it a good study and welcome any recommendations. A message to Earth containing new instructions will be sent as soon as I get your input. And the last supply ship is being loaded and prepared as we speak. So with that, all I have left to say is, see you at the game!"

Belteron ambled along the narrow walk among the trees that meandered across the center of Seaview City Gardens. He knew there was a cafe at the far end of the walk and, at the leisurely pace he was traveling, it would be a nice time for lunch when he arrived.

He often spent time here, being his favorite spot for relaxation in Seaview and not far from both his home and Seaview Stadium, and now that he wasn't playing baseball he found himself here more and more. Not playing baseball! Belteron shuddered at the thought. Being from a family in the baseball caste, there hadn't been a generation in memory that didn't possess a player, a star player at that. His father had been the star of his era, just as Belteron was of this one. The brightest star in the game, and I'm not playing!

He understood why and knew he had made a good decision. Being bumped from the Earth team when he was the best on Ball Four was something he just couldn't abide. Other players had been bumped and had gone straight back to their teams, but with him it was different, deeply and philosophically different.

Belteron was now wandering in the lowest, shady central basin of the Gardens, and the refreshing cool always centered his thoughts. He understood the case against him well. The fact that in recent seasons he had taken to playing open mindedly on offense was a minor point. Of course he never did it on defense, that would risk giving away the pitches, and would never be tolerated or considered sportsmanlike. No, it was his way of having fun, of challenging the pitchers, it was his *style*, go ahead, *read my mind*, I'll knock the cover off the ball! That rankled the other players, brought on petty jealousies, but it gave him flair. There wasn't enough flair in baseball, but nobody seemed to miss it.

This was all minor, in fact the news media liked it, made his star a little brighter, and the First Commissioner had never reprimanded or chided him about it. Secretly, he had a feeling that Tarn was amused by it, if no one else was. No, Belteron knew why he was deselected from the Earth team. He had argued that using the white mind, mind projection or any mental advantage at all would make the contest against Earth unfair and a little meaningless. What got him in trouble for good was going public with it. That got the Commission riled! But putting it before the public and getting their opinion was good for the whole enterprise. First Commissioner Tarn himself had declared that the purpose of Operation Universe Series was to have *fun* and that who actually won was secondary. But that was a bit of political mumbo-jumbo, because everyone was taking this very seriously, the public and the players and the Commission alike. Ball Four wanted to *win*.

So did Belteron. He loved to win, winning was the thing, any other way and games were meaningless. And on Ball Four, games and gambling were all there was left to do, except for the odd maintenance task. And that was for the maintenance caste to take care of. No, games had to mean something to bring value to life. Was he odd for feeling so deeply about it? Perhaps so.

The argument against his case was clear. For all they knew Earthlings had some advantages of their own and if Ball Fourians didn't use theirs, who knows what would happen? And Evan, manager of the selected team and already active on Earth with the infiltration of the Earthling Cleveland Indians, had made it clear that he welcomed no dissent on his squad and had gone on to suggest that Belteron might, with his reckless ways, risk discovery by Earthlings with his open-mindedness. This was absurd, for research had shown that Earthlings couldn't read minds. But the view had prevailed and Belteron, one of the last players scheduled to infiltrate, was deselected. He was off the team.

The whole business deeply disturbed him. What a grand adventure, the Universe Series to determine the champion of the known universe, and the great Belteron was not playing! A team was assembling on Earth that was sure to win. And Belteron would not be there to win with them, to return home the conquering heroes. All he had done was to insist on fairness and giving Earth a fair chance. By the holy pantheon of baseball immortals, he was not going to stand idly by! Something had to be done, and he knew he was the man to do it. He had made his mind up some time ago, he knew what he had to do, but how? That was the question.

In the meantime he was idle, not even playing baseball, and it was a new experience for him, a good experience for him. At least it gave him the leisure to work on a plan, and bide his time.

The walkway through the trees was coming to an end at the foot of a rise and, on a grassy, little knoll in front of him, was a cozy garden cafe, the Octurus. Belteron knew the host, Fendreck, and always enjoyed his visits. He felt like seeing a friend.

"Belteron, good fellow, it's been a while! What brings you here?"

"Nothing more unusual than lunch, Fendreck."

"Of course, it's only that I'm not used to seeing you this time of the season, but then, you're not playing. It's hard to get used to the idea."

Belteron sighed. "No harder for you than for me, believe me. I confess I'm enjoying the break."

"That's a bit hard to believe," said Fendreck, "the greatest in baseball at the height of his powers, that he would be content to be out of the game. But then, I've come to realize, you're not like lesser men."

Belteron chuckled. "I appreciate your sarcasm, Fendreck. My family, friends and teammates are taking this so, so gravely. But you know what they say, a ballplayer has fifty, maybe sixty good years. My father played eighty. I figure I can take off a season and still have seventy left. So, what's for lunch?"

"You *are* a confident man! Oh, today we've an all-Octurian special. Care to try it?"

Belteron considered. "Is it fresh or duped?"

"You forget that cafes in the Garden are only equipped with duplicators. But it's as good as fresh and comes with mead of the region."

"I'll take your word for it. You rarely steer me wrong."

"Very well."

Fendreck was right. Belteron relished Octurian cuisine and this offering was splendid. And this cafe, with its garden freshness, gave a freshness to the food.

Fendreck came by to see if all was well. "And how is everything?"

"Delightful, this mead is really lifting my spirits."

"I suppose after losing your spot on the Earth challenge team you might be a trifle gloomy. Yes, I heard about it. Some time back. It made quite a splash on the news. You certainly manage to be quite controversial, don't you?" Fendreck stopped abruptly. "Oh my heavens!"

"What is it, my good man?" asked Belteron.

"Why, the news! The lunch rush had me so occupied, I'd forgotten." Fendreck was animated. "It was on the morning news. Didn't you see it?"

"I've been out walking. What was it?"

"It's finally here, it's official, they've made the announcement. Infiltration is complete, an Earthling team is now completely Ball Fourian, the championship Season has been declared! First City is in a flurry. They said a last ship was being readied, and..."

"*What?*" Belteron bolted upright.

"Oh, it was something about supplies and such. Isn't it exciting? What fun! Oh, how thoughtless of me, you must feel somewhat disappointed."

"Don't worry about me. Listen, I'm afraid I must be going. You have my account number, don't you? You can debit me?"

"Certainly, but..."

"Well, then, I'm off. Lunch was delicious. See you soon!"

"Oh, yes, well, my dear Bel..." Fendreck's voice trailed off as Belteron vanished through the door.

Third Councilor Niver stepped gingerly out of a side door of the "Sure Thing" gambling house and rapidly rounded the corner. It was the only gambling establishment located in the fashionable section of First City in which he resided, and Niver had only entered it as a last resort. He thought it has gone reasonably well and, quite possibly, that he hadn't even been recognized. It was a risk he had decided he must take.

If he was to profit from the Universe Series, then he must bet. Early bets would mean longer odds, which would be locked in. Timing was often everything. Bets placed at a gambling house could be discreet, whereas bets placed through his account by console could be made public in the event of an official probe. He had to profit by this opportunity but he could ill-afford discovery. The official policy of the Planetary Council was against gambling abuse and, if found out, Tarn could turn it to his advantage and most certainly stifle Niver's political advance. He had mulled it over, had judged it a worthy risk and had wagered all his available gambling credits and his lawfully allowable limit of investment credits as well. Every credit he could risk, he had bet on the Ball Fourian team.

Niver strolled briskly back toward his home, his breathing more relaxed now. He was walking down a broad boulevard of greenway with two-story dwellings on either side. His home was at the end of it, three blocks farther. He had passed up a transport booth, preferring to walk. He slowed his pace. Tarn *would* press this anti-gambling stance, he thought cynically. As much as the prevailing view was that wealth had nothing to do with political success, Niver felt the opposite. Sure, the people had virtually everything they could ever need and surplus credits were often never used, but the public was quite impressed by mass wealth. Tarn's family was fabulously wealthy and Tarn himself was known to have greatly added to his fortune on his own. Surely this lay behind his political power. Niver could never forgive Tarn's maneuvering to keep him off the Baseball Commission. Imagine, the Third Councilor of the planet and not on the Commission as well! It stung just to think about it. Yes, it was worth the risk. Ball Four will defeat the Earth and a fortune would be his. Try denying him a Commissionership then. And Tarn won't be First forever, Niver thought. My hour will come.

It was early afternoon, and pleasantly temperate on the veranda of Second Councilor Semptor's residence atop City Center Towers. He sipped his cool drink and took in the alabaster of the city buildings against the pattern of greenways that framed them; he allowed his gaze to rise up to include the green, red and purple hues of the hills and mountains to the east. This was a pleasing ritual in which he indulged daily after returning from the Council meetings. It gave him a sense of the value of his work, his service to First City and all of Ball Four.

The Second Councilor bathed in the breezes that wafted gently through his rooftop garden. Even twenty stories above the city the wind was always just right, unless of course a cleansing storm had been scheduled. When young he had studied the ancient weather patterns of prehistoric Ball Four, knew their unchecked power and never ceased to marvel at the WeatherCon network's ability to constantly fine tune and manipulate the delicate balance between high and low pressure systems. He still believed, almost like a schoolchild, in the saying learned as a youth: Marvel always at the gifts of Science.

Semptor gathered his mind back to the morning's events. He had seen to it that the announcement of the Season to begin on Earth had been holocast around the globe, and here in First City one could already sense the growing excitement. He had checked with the Preparedness Group at Spaceport and was reasonably assured that the flight to Earth would omit nothing vital to the Ball Fourians' needs there. Another trip wasn't foreseen. This voyage was to be the last until the team began its return after the Series. He was certain everything was in order and he had carried out his responsibilities as executive director of Operation Universe Series.

Semptor was gratified that Tarn had given him the appointment. He had supported Tarn when he had first put forth the idea twenty-seven years ago; he understood what Tarn had wished to accomplish. The odds were very high against even finding a planet which played baseball, but Tarn felt the search alone would be stimulating and scientifically valuable and he was right. Semptor had speculated as to whether or not Tarn had ever believed such a planet could in fact be found. But Operation Search did uplift baseball and did stimulate society in general, and all speculation was made moot by the discovery of Earth. An almost mystical awe had enveloped the planet when the implications began to be understood and a powerful curiosity about the natural laws spread throughout the people, affecting most profoundly those of the scientific and political castes. After the amassing of so much data through the centuries, Ball Fourians had developed a deep confidence in the thorough and complete manner in which the natural laws of the universe were understood; it was commonly accepted that everything was known about how the universe functioned, leaving nothing left to do but witness the endlessly diverse ways in which these laws were obeyed. But two planets from different solar systems at opposite ends of the galaxy had evolved not just a similar game, but the *same* game of baseball! Why? How? The most powerful minds on Ball Four were awakened by these questions.

Semptor smiled to himself. These afternoon muses never failed to take on an almost poetic glow. But he had more work to do, reports to check and reports to send, odds and ends. He went inside to his console and back to tasks more concrete and less lofty.

ANCHOR:

> There was a flurry of activity at Spaceport today as final preparations were underway for the voyage of a transport ship to Earth. Of course, Holovision One was there.

REPORTER:

> This class B transport you see behind me has been taking on fuel and supplies for the past few hours, and everything seems to be going smoothly. With the number of flights to and from Earth these past few years, the procedures for readying a ship have gotten pretty routine. But the preparations for this flight, thought to be the last until after the Series, have been exceptionally thorough. We've been told by Fleet Central that there will be no significant personnel aboard, as this is mainly a supply ship to bring needed goods to the support group that has overseen the infiltration. Our baseball boys are said to be well taken care of by their unsuspecting Earthling friends! They're more or less on their own now, but the support group will be very vigilant in case of any problems. And these supplies are for them.

ANCHOR:

> Liftoff will be in two days time and WeatherCon has planned a perfect open window for the event. It was announced that WeatherCon's work in preparation for the flight will have no effect on First City's cleansing rain scheduled at about the same time. The technicians have guaranteed that they'll keep the two weather systems independent. Oh, they said don't forget to check your schedule and keep your umbrellas handy!

Belteron clicked the set off. His holovision unit had a built-in recorder which automatically recorded the most recent one hundred hours of programming, a feature Belteron rarely availed himself of. He wasn't much of a viewer. But he was glad for it now.

After leaving the Octurus he had rushed to the nearest transport booth and gone straight home. He immediately punched up the newscast Fendreck had spoken of, and of course it was all true. The Season was here. But more importantly, the break he had been waiting for had arrived. This ship was his ticket to Earth, his only ticket.

Belteron had planned for this eventuality but they had thrown him a curve. He had expected more lead time, more time to prepare, more chances to go to Earth. Instead, he had two days.

Actually, there really wasn't much to do. Disappearing shouldn't be hard. But he lacked a role model. He couldn't recall anyone ever having done it before. Well, I'm about to do something no one ever does, Belteron thought. I suppose it would be called breaking the law, if we had laws anymore.

His first priority was getting biofashioned. He'd never done it, it held no appeal. If he was going to Earth, he'd have to look like an Earthling. Okay, no problem. Well, yes, there was one. If he was going to disappear, there could be no record. If he walked into StarFaces and got biofashioned using his credit account, the transaction would be recorded at both his bank and his console. Anyone looking for him would surely check that. The fact that he had gotten biofashioned earthling-style just before disappearing would certainly be a clue to his whereabouts. Belteron wanted lead time. There was a way to avoid detection but it was a longshot.

Belteron had been a rookie when Earth had been discovered. The Baseball Commission had spent a year planning the operation and player selection didn't begin until the next. Belteron was in his third season and already a big star when he was chosen. The next three years he spent in intensive training and education which took all his spare time when he wasn't playing baseball. He had learned English, studied Earth history and culture and had been provided with an identity he was to assume when it came time to infiltrate, an identity he had to study and practice until he felt he was becoming that very person. He had been scheduled to infiltrate early, but as his status as a star rose higher and higher there was a lot of pressure from his manager in Seaview to let him remain playing. Season after season Belteron got better and better, and infiltration was delayed again and again. This gave him lots of time to prepare for Earth but, unfortunately, it also gave him time to open his mouth and get deselected.

Early on in the preparations it had been arranged at StarFaces that all ballplayers and support personnel would come in to get biofashioned one by one, as the time of their journey to Earth approached. A roster had been provided to StarFaces with the names of everyone they should expect to see, and the total fee was paid in advance. This was Belteron's longshot.

He had been deselected, but what if his name had never been removed from the original roster? Since people on that roster had been dropping in one by one to get biofashioned until very recently, one could assume that the roster was still at reception. It was quite possible that it never occurred to anyone that there was a need to remove his name, never suspecting that Belteron or anybody, for that matter, would ever consider using such a situation to advantage. And what was more, StarFaces wasn't allowed to reveal the nature of anyone's visit there because of medical ethics. Biofashioning was, however mundane the practice had become, a medical procedure. It would take a personal visit from the First Councilor himself to have a medical record opened, something Belteron had reason to believe Tarn would never do.

The woman at reception was elegantly beautiful, but then the whole staff at StarFaces resembled the cast of a holodrama. Belteron acted casually, an easy feat for a ballplayer trained so thoroughly in mind discipline. He hoped only a gambit or two would be needed. As a catcher he had run many a gambit on weak-minded batters, and he prayed that the principle worked the same in other arenas of life.

"Why, you're Belteron, aren't you? It's a pleasure to meet you. What brings such a fabulous star to our establishment? It's well known you don't favor biofashion." Her voice was syrupy and seductive, as he might have guessed.

"You must be quite a baseball fan."

"Who *isn't*! What can I do for you?"

"I've come to get biofashioned, of course. It's for Operation Universe Series."

The receptionist was taken aback. "Excuse me, but didn't I hear that you were dropped from the team?"

Belteron smoothed all ripples from his mind. "You have an Operation roster, don't you? Check it."

The woman punched a few keys on her console. "Why, there's your name. Are you going to Earth after all?"

Belteron coolly smiled. *Don't be so nosy.*

"I shouldn't be nosy."

Belteron steadied his look. *I am on the roster.*

"You are on the roster..."

Everything is as it should be.

The woman's face turned a bit quizzical, then she smiled. "I suppose everything is as it should be." She looked down at the console. "Do you have a style in mind? The roster style entry for you says Lou Gehrig."

Of course. A style had been selected for each person destined for Earth. Coincidental look-alikes had to be avoided. Lou Gehrig, hmm. Belteron had studied Earth baseball history intensely. The Iron Horse of baseball. It had been intended as a subliminal support for his Earth identity. Perfect.

"That would be perfect."

"Very good, sir. Roster style entries are already on file. Biotemplates for your style are in memory in each biosalon. Please inform your technician of the style name as you enter. You may go in immediately, roster clients have priority status." She looked at Belteron questioningly. "Are you sure this is, ah, appropriate?"

He smiled and answered good-naturedly, "Of course!" *Everything is in order, isn't it?*

The receptionist smiled back. "Why of course, everything is in order, isn't it? Enjoy your new self!"

Tarn sat at his console in the executive office suite of the First Councilor's official residence near the summit of Mount Superior, high above First City. From his vantage point at the console he could see all of the City and, though a bit too distant for detail, he imagined he could just make out the outline of Semptor's rooftop garden. He anticipated a call from his Second Councilor at any moment. What a loyal assistant he is, thought Tarn. He's been invaluable in so many ways through the years.

Tarn had spent the last couple of hours, as he often did, walking with his wife through the woods which surrounded the official residence. He had brought her up-to-date on the current events and consulted her on various issues. Then he had called his son and daughter to enjoy their reaction to the news from Earth. His son, recently appointed to the First City Board of Governors, was elated and reported that the feeling was shared by the entire board. And his daughter, a member of the board of directors of Holovision One, had said that everyone in the media was delighted and looking forward to all the news that was going to be generated by the coming Season on Earth. Tarn held a special affection for his daughter. She was the first member of the family in generations to jump castes, in this case from the political to the business caste. Lateral movement between castes had become increasingly rare in recent centuries and was yet another sign of the decay of Ball Fourian society. Tarneen had for a long time seen mind-to-mind with her father and, in a wonderful show of support for his anti-decadence campaign, had of her own accord decided to move between castes. Tarn was exceedingly proud and grateful for this, as it set a great example for the planet to have a member of the leading family make such a move. Since its occurrence eight years ago lateral movement between castes had increased two percent. This strengthened his campaign on yet another front.

Thirty-two years ago when Tarn had been promoted to First Commissioner of Baseball he began to consider that there might be something, well, inappropriate, for a society's second most powerful position to be that of commissioner of a sport. Of course, baseball and wagering on it were the favorite pastimes of a planet of citizens with such a preponderance of leisure time on their hands. He himself had been a terrific fan of baseball, and his dedication to it early in his political career had led to his eventual election to such a high post. Tarn kept his thoughts to himself and held on to the First Commissioner's position and approached his responsibilities with zeal; for power was power, and with it the power to enact change.

Ever since his youth Tarn had been fascinated with the historical and cultural anthropologies of the various worlds Ball Four had established contact with during its centuries of exploration and commerce with alien worlds. The Technology Anti-proliferation Act had put an end to that. Tarn had majored in alien anthropology at the University and one theme seemed to run through his studies of the more advanced worlds. At the peak of a world's advancement some form of decay would bring on a decline which in some cases led to outright destruction. The number of worlds out there that were ash heaps was startling. At the core of Ball Fourian scientific philosophy was the belief that the advanced state of the science of mind discipline was what would hold Ball Four forever above and apart from the fate of these other worlds.

Tarn didn't think so. An advanced practitioner of the scientific art of mind discipline himself (many on the planet regarded Tarn as the most disciplined mind on Ball Four) Tarn believed that the isolationism of the Anti-proliferation Act was the turning point leading to the decay and possible eventual collapse of Ball Fourian society. How could one get around the Act without challenging its basic tenets? Propose a universal search for another baseball world in hopes of participating in a Universe Series. However unlikely that such a goal could be achieved, the obsession with baseball had led to the Planetary Council's approval. And now that contact with Earth had been established, however discreetly, Tarn's plan was working.

Tarn felt from his studies that all cultures could decay, even one as advanced as Ball Four. Games and gambling were too rampant, and Tarn suspected that although the society looked healthy on the surface, underneath it was rotting. And it was this more insidious decadence which could bring down a culture without its being aware. Games, gambling and biofashion would be fine if life could be stimulated from below, by giving the society new aims and new challenges and new dreams, not to mention new questions. Ball Fourians more than anything had stopped questioning. That was unhealthy. Involvement with Earth had already stimulated all the castes and communities of Ball Four, and who knows what could happen between now and the last out of the inpending Universe Series?

The holocom at Tarn's console chimed. That would be Semptor. Tarn pressed a button and Semptor, seated at his own console, quickly materialized above and in front of Tarn's.

"Ah, Semptor, I've been expecting you. What do you have to report?"

"Not a lot, First Councilor, and most of it routine. Firstly, all is being prepared for the launch from Spaceport. And First City is coming alive at the announcement of the impending Season. Unfortunately one of our worst fears is being realized: half the population is at their consoles placing wagers."

"Old habits die hard, Semptor. Anything else?"

"Yes, I have two surveillance reports. The first will interest you. Sensors picked up Third Councilor Niver near a gambling house, undoubtedly attempting a discreet bet. Subsequent checks revealed he had exhausted his gambling credits and dipped into investment credits."

Tarn chuckled softly. "Not an entirely unexpected act by a politician passed up for promotion, grasping at the wrong straws, eh, Semptor? What's the other one?"

"Baseballer Belteron. He had lunch in a Seaview Gardens cafe, then went home by transport booth. An hour later, he took a transport booth to a location in downtown First City, destination not immediately clear."

"Very well, Semptor," said Tarn after a pause. "Let's continue the usual surveillance on Niver, although I very much doubt he has many tricks left. As for Belteron, switch off the surveillance on him."

Semptor looked surprised. "Do you think that's wise, Tarn? Belteron's a bit of a wild card after failing to return to baseball."

"Oh, he's suffered enough, what with the deselection and all. Let's give him some peace."

"Very well," sighed Semptor. "If we weren't on the holocom I'd be tempted to sense your thoughts, not that I'd have much success with you."

"Sorry, my good friend, but not likely. Surely you can trust me on this one."

"Of course, Tarn. But be on guard at tomorrow's Council! If there's nothing else, I'll be going."

Tarn smiled. "No, thanks, that'll do. See you tomorrow at Council. Tarn off."

An hour and a half after entering a biosalon at StarFaces, Belteron was back home standing in front of a holomirror. Unbelievable, he thought, someone else is staring back at me. But it's not Lou Gehrig, it's me. He ran a relaxation feedback loop through his mind to adjust for the slight panic he was feeling. He could only guess that people who got biofashioned often became used to it.

Well, I've got until dawn the day after tomorrow to get to Spaceport and get on that ship, he thought, and my work's cut out for me. Packing wouldn't take long. He had some Earth-style clothes left over from training, so he wouldn't have to shop. Good, that's one more way they can't trace me.

Belteron wished he could see his girlfriend, Filidane, once before leaving. But he dared not risk her knowing anything. Her standard mind training wouldn't be able to withstand even media questioning, and lying was not an art well-practiced on Ball Four. He would program his holocom to send her a suitably obscure yet reassuring message in a few days. He hoped to see her again when this was all over.

He would spend the rest of the time at his console, going over all the materials from his training days for the Operation. He had deleted nothing and a quick refresher course was in order. The most vital task remaining, however, was to access the console encyclopedia. Surely it contained a holomodel of a class B transport ship. The more he knew about the ship the better his chances of a successful stowaway. He'd better get to it.

Spaceport was situated in a small valley southeast of Mount Superior in the eastern reaches of the Superior mountain range. It was close, as the hovercar flies, to First City but the bulk of the mountains made it easy for WeatherCon to maintain separate weather systems. In its heyday, WeatherCon had kept the skies over Spaceport in pristine condition and, even after the bustling days of space travel had waned WeatherCon had held to the tradition. Over the centuries a new flora had evolved. Whereas nearby First City was green, Spaceport and the surrounding slopes were dry and desert-like. For this reason, through the doldrums after the demise of space travel, a small tourist trade had survived. People came for weekends to experience the dry climate, the odd-looking plants and to visit the space museums.

It had not always been so. After the meld teams had discovered Time Drive, Spaceport had grown up overnight and, during the height of the exploration and commerce period, two or three hundred flights came and went morning, noon and night. But the brief Zorkin War had put a rapid end to that, as the Technology Anti-proliferation Act brought two centuries of space travel to a grinding halt. For nearly two centuries more Spaceport had been reduced to a tourist attraction. Then Operation Search and the subsequent Operation Universe Series had changed it all yet again. Of course, not nearly so many flights as before were needed but Spaceport was back in the space business.

This night Spaceport lay in a dark and moonless slumber. In the predawn hours the only hint of activity were the soft lights around the class B transport that sat unattended under the calm, starlit skies. No one would stir for an hour and there was no security, for who was there to fear? Through this soft and secure twinkle of lights a shadowy figure crept up the open gangway and vanished into the shadows of the ship.

3

San Francisco Examiner

April 5th.

John Houser

GIANTS POISED TO
TAKE THE WEST

Every year at this time sportswriters everywhere engage in one of their favorite pastimes: predictions. And, year after year, Bay Area sportswriters dismiss the Giants with the usual phrase: Where is the pitching? I can tell you where it is in two words. Brad O'Nealy.

Except for pitching, the elements have been there the past three years for the Giants to take it all. General manager Hal Barnham has been making all the right moves that his predecessor hadn't been, and, contrary to all the historical romance of the game of baseball, the game is won or lost in the front office. Barnham knows this, and has spent his time developing the farm clubs. How many three million dollar free agents are on the club? None. How many minor league prospects has he traded away for a stopper in the bullpen? None. Why are the Giants going to win the West this year? Brad O'Nealy. Where did they get him? The farm system. Thank you, Mr. Barnham.

Yes, the Giants have the hitting. The outfield of Mitch Simpson, Rick Barker and Willie Washington are capable of 80-plus homers a year, and the pre-season showed it. They tore up the fences in Arizona and the Giants will take that momentum straight to the playoffs. Sure, the Cleveland Indians, a mediocre team at best, roughed them up a couple of times, but who didn't pitch in those games? Brad O'Nealy.

The infield is finally stable, and it's a credit to Hal Barnham again that he found something other than a headcase to put at shortstop. Sorry, Eddie Sandoval, but good luck in Seattle. We've got Archie Stokes. And where'd he come from? Double A ball. Thank you, Mr. Barnham.

If the Giants have any chinks in the armor, it's in two places: catcher, a perennial problem since Sammy Mathers retired, and, of course, don't tell me, right-handed pitching. But, aging though they are, Upton, French and Gonzales will hold up the right side of the mound. Who will hold up the left? Brad O'Nealy. Left-handed starters of quality have been absent from a Giants pitching staff for so long, we've forgotten they existed. O'Nealy will change that.

No, I haven't forgotten Lou Chambers. It's easy to take for granted a manager who's as even-tempered and good-natured as Lou, and he should be given as much credit as Barnham in bringing this team along. The tight infield is largely his doing.

Some might think me crazy to call a rookie a franchise player, but the kid from Harvard has all the right stuff, for a left-hander. Brad, you're the franchise. Crazy me is just going to sit back and enjoy.

The Giants are going to win the West. Thank you, Mr. Barnham. Oh yeah, thanks, Lou.

Jimmy Strongbow sat back in the empty dugout and looked out at the broad expanse of earth and grass, so neatly manicured and ready for play. A few groundskeepers were finishing up with the infield while Jimmy's eyes scanned the vast emptiness of Candlestick Park before coming to rest on the pitcher's mound. It looks good, he thought with absentminded pride; he had just finished recontouring, packing and watering the mound, his specialty. He had been "brought up" to the majors from Phoenix for that one reason, his expertise with the mound.

Lou Chambers stepped into the dugout from the clubhouse passageway and stopped to survey the field. He was wearing the look, and Jimmy had seen it on the faces of all Giants since he'd arrived a week and a half before. He'd given it a name. It was the 2-12 look, only now it was the 3-17 look. Same look, just a little longer.

"Hey, how you doin'?"

"Fine, Skipper. Guess I shouldn't be sitting here." Jimmy got up.

"Nah, sit down. You the guy they call Chief?" Chambers walked over and extended his hand. "Lou Chambers."

"Nice to meet you. Yeah, I'm Chief, or Jimmy, whatever. Brad calls me Chief, that's where I got it. We worked together down in Phoenix last year. I mean, he pitched and I took care of the mound."

"Yeah, I know. That's why you're up here. Actually, I had them call you up. The pitchers were blaming the poor start on the shabby mound, Brad mentioned the great mound in Phoenix and I said if it'll help them get the curveball over the plate, what the hell. Anyway, welcome to San Francisco."

"Thanks."

Chambers stroked his chin. "Jeez, no wonder they call you Chief. You Indian?"

Jimmy grinned. "Full-blooded Apache."

Lou grinned back. "Yeah, with that long hair you look like Cochise. I'll be damned!" He took a closer look. "Wait a minute, I've seen you before."

"You saw me pitch at the Phoenix camp a couple of years ago. I'm surprised you remembered."

"Me too. Strongbow, right?"

"Right, Jimmy Strongbow. Wow."

"Yeah, good fastball. Wild though. You scouted?"

"They don't scout the reservations much. No, I was in camp on a make-good basis. Giants camp wouldn't let me in. Phoenix took a look at me, and you were there checking prospects. Nothing came of it. Ended up groundskeeping."

"No wonder you know a good mound. Well, welcome aboard. I gotta go have a long talk with a line-up card. Shake these monkeys up. See you later."

Belteron stood in a ticket line outside Candlestick Park. It had become a ritual the last two weeks, getting to the Park with the early birds and milling around waiting to get in. These were the real fans, the die-hards, and he'd learned as much about the Giants listening to them as he had from reading the papers.

"Simpson's a wimp. Twenty-eight homers last year, what's he got, one, in the first three weeks? Chambers oughta bench him."

"Yeah right, who's he gonna play, Ramirez? He hit .063 in spring!"

"Upton and French suck. I checked it out. Combined ERA of 12.73. The whole right-handed staff has an ERA over 10!"

"O'Nealy's carrying the bums. He's 3-0, got all the wins on the team."

"God, and it ain't even June yet. Usually they wait till June to fall apart."

Belteron wondered if he'd made a mistake. He'd gotten to Earth two days before the season started and went right to work on picking the team to go after. It had taken a week of hectic research, but he chose the Giants for two reasons: one, they were picked by a few sportswriters around the country to win their division and, two and most importantly, they had the weakest catcher in the league. That was Belteron's position back on Ball Four and, although he knew he could compete at any position including pitcher, it was his best bet for influencing the outcome of games. It had been that way in Ball Fourian baseball and would be doubly so here.

It had been equally obvious that he had to get on a National League team. If he played in the American League, he risked discovery before he could have an impact on a team. This way he had most of a season and, hopefully, the playoffs to prepare a team to go up against the Indians.

Now the Giants had started out 3-17 and he was concerned. But the good news was that the catching position was in shambles. Chambers had even called up a no-name rookie from Phoenix to take over for the faltering Quigley but the rookie had gone 0-for-23, was back in Phoenix and the .097-hitting Quigley was back behind the plate. To make matters worse base runners were stealing on him with impunity. Yes, this was the place to start, but how to do it was the question. As far as he'd learned, signing unknowns was unheard of after the season started. He would have to find a way.

"What do you want, buddy?"

"Oh, lower box seat, best you got."

"Hey, Chief!"

Jimmy Strongbow looked over at the bullpen. It was Brad O'Nealy. "Hey, Brad!" Jimmy loped on over.

"Evening, Chief. Help me loosen up? Mitt's over there."

"Sure." Jimmy liked Brad, had since they met in Phoenix. Brad never talked down to him, always treated him more like a teammate. He never understood why, it was just Brad's way. Of course, Brad was friendly with everyone, cracking jokes, trying to kept the team and himself loose. Jimmy had helped Brad warm up down in Phoenix and was glad the tradition was continuing in San Francisco.

They'd been at it for about ten minutes when Brad said, "Care to burn a few?"

"Oh, I don't know, Brad, Chambers is already out and about this evening. Phoenix is one thing but this is the big time. He can't like you catching a wild man like me, especially on game day."

"Ah, don't sweat it. I still got my catcher's mitt somewhere here. Just don't smoke 'em. Let's work on your breaking stuff, you know, that cut slider we worked on before and maybe your change-up. That's the stuff you need to work on anyway. Your smoke is fine. Faster than anybody we got here, except me, of course."

Jimmy guffawed. "Don't make me laugh, O'Nealy. My fastball's great, sure, but it's never seen home plate. The only reason I was a star in high school was batters were scared to death of me. My team used to yell 'Geronimo!'

every time I dusted some poor bastard."

"Don't worry about that," chuckled Brad. "That'll come in handy. If they think you're wild, it'll keep 'em off the plate, and they won't charge the mound so often when you hit 'em. Okay, let's see that curve."

There was a special beauty to the vast emptiness of the Park as Belteron and the rest of the early birds began to trickle in. It was an exhilarating sensation for Belteron to enter an Earthling stadium; he'd been to four since his arrival on Earth and to Candlestick many times these past two weeks. Sure, the engineering was crude, very crude, compared with the ballparks back home. But the field, one look at the field, and he was awestruck anew. The dimensions were exact and even the grass was the same. He had seen pictures and holographs during training but it wasn't anything like being here. Our bodies function virtually the same, except for our minds, he thought, and we can eat Earthling food, breathe their air, survive here quite nicely. The Earth's mass perfectly matched Ball Four's, gravitational forces were the same, and therefore we walk, run and play the same as we do on Ball Four. Why, even these coincidences were perfectly reasonable given the natural laws.

What Belteron found nearly imponderable was that the game of baseball was played on another planet across the galaxy. During his training, the concept had retained an academic quality, like alien world studies at school. But being here in the flesh and seeing it for himself, this was something that shocked his normally placid mind. We don't know everything after all. This is not explainable. The thought shook him but delighted him, made him come alive.

Belteron brought himself back out of his reverie to the task at hand. He had gravitated through the stands down to the Giants' bullpen, as he had every day. It was a favorite spot for early-arriving fans. They lined the railing by the bullpen area and watched the pitchers as they took turns loosening up. Occasionally fans would yell out greetings to their favorite pitchers and often the players, after their workouts, would come over to the railing and chat with the fans or sign autographs. All in all it was a very friendly scene. It gave Belteron hope that this would be a likely access point for establishing contact. He had made a particular effort over the past few days to study pitchers as well as catchers, and the results were interesting indeed. The pitchers were good, as good as many on Ball Four. But, as he scanned them for random thoughts and feelings he could pick up, one general tone was clear. They were tentative, unfocused and unconfident. In short, they were losers. Except for that left-hander, the one called O'Nealy. Confidence couldn't describe what Belteron sensed in Brad O'Nealy. O'Nealy reminded him of himself. It was *here, suckers, try and hit this one!* That was the way Belteron had been challenging them back on Ball Four.

O'Nealy was scheduled to start today. Unlike the others, he had been warming up with someone out of uniform. Belteron had seen this guy before. He was hard to miss, with his tall, lanky frame and straight black hair well past his shoulders. He had appeared a few days before and had joined the groundskeeping crew. And now O'Nealy had switched mitts and was catching him! The fellow had pretty good stuff but seemed to lack control. O'Nealy offered bits of good-natured advice and it was obvious there was a camaraderie between the two. Belteron scanned the tall thrower's mind and was surprised to find such a clear, unaffected aura. He threw with a casual freedom and abandon which might explain why he was wild.

"Hey, O'Nealy, what the hell do you think you're doing?" Lou Chambers had come up on the scene unobserved.

"Oh, just playing a little catch, Skipper," O'Nealy said sheepishly.

"The hell you are, you're catching Strongbow here. Dammit, you're starting today and you're the only winner I got!"

The other pitchers in the pen looked up.

Chambers laughed. Looking around pointedly he said, "So far, anyway." He walked over to O'Nealy.

"Listen, son, you're my meal ticket right now and I've seen Strongbow's stuff. You're no catcher, you could break a finger. Frankly, you should know better."

O'Nealy stared down at his feet and pawed at the dirt. "Sorry, Lou, won't happen again."

Strongbow had drifted over to the wall below where Belteron was standing and fumbled with a hose, pretending to coil it up.

Belteron leaned over and said amiably, "He was angry, wasn't he?"

"Oh, I shouldn't have done it. I warned Brad. Hope they don't send me back to Phoenix."

"Phoenix? Why Phoenix? You work on the field, you're not a player, are you?"

Jimmy continued fiddling with the hose, watching out of the corner of his eye as Chambers headed back toward the dugout. Jimmy briefly told Belteron the story. "So, technically I could be back in Phoenix as quick as that catcher they had up for Quigley. Look, I gotta get back to work. Nice talking to you, ah, what's your name?"

Belteron stuck his hand out, trying the Earth handshake. "Bel...er, ah, Billy, Billy Icarus," he said, giving the name he used when he registered at the hotel he was staying in. He'd avoided using the name the Operation had assigned him. "Strongbow, right?"

"Yeah, Jimmy Strongbow, how'd you know?"

"Oh, I heard Chambers talking to O'Nealy. Listen," he said, grabbing for the opening, "I saw you pitching, and you're good. If you want to pitch, I'm a catcher, well, used to be. Maybe we could get together sometime."

Jimmy thought briefly, then shook his head. "Appreciate it, but better not right now. I'm gonna have a ton of work to do. The head infield keeper and his assistant just quit, some labor dispute or something. They say I'll be doing a bunch of overtime. Should just forget pitching for now. Hey, I gotta go before I get in trouble again. Enjoy the game. Later."

The whole time they'd been chatting Belteron had been mind-scanning Jimmy. Back on Ball Four mind scanning was impolite except on the ball field and futile against most well-guarded minds anyhow, but Earthlings were open books; he'd been amazed and felt a little guilty when he intruded on Earthlings' thoughts as he often had while trying to get around America since he arrived. Most Earthling minds revealed that they had something to hide. But this Strongbow fellow, he was different. He appeared pure of motive, guileless, and Belteron took an instant liking to him.

A sudden thought made him sit down in the seat behind him. Jimmy talks to the team, and he's a groundskeeper. There are openings on the grounds crew. He'd learned during his brief time on Earth that, to his surprise, people came and went as far as jobs were concerned. On Ball Four, most people had their jobs for a lifetime or at least evolved in the same line of work. That was the nature of the caste system. People rarely quit. But here on Earth they did, all the time, it appeared. This was his chance. He rose quickly, his body having decided at the same time as his mind.

Belteron stopped the first usher he saw. "Hi, excuse me, but where's the grounds crew office?"

The usher was taken aback. "Ah, well, let's see. Oh yeah, they're behind right field, but that's restricted. Ah, you might check at Personnel. That's located on the mezzanine level, over there, sorta between right field and first base." She eyed Belteron. "What's the deal anyway? You..."

"Thank you." He moved away at a brisk pace.

The secretary at the Personnel office was friendly but brusque. There was constant traffic in and out and telephones seemed to ring non-stop.

"I'm sorry, but I don't have time for this. As I said, we handle ushers, vendors, security, ticket takers and such, but groundskeeping's separate, as far as I know."

Belteron bathed his aura in good-natured warmth. "I can see you're busy. As I said, I was told the grounds crew is in an awful jam. I wouldn't take up your valuable time if this wasn't important." *This is important, I should see your supervisor. Help your team.*

The lady's face softened. "Well, I can see this is important. The Giants need all the help they can get! You should probably see the head of Personnel, Mr. Hartman. It's the first cubicle on the right. Go ahead, and tell him Mrs., ah, tell him Althea sent you in."

Mr. Hartman was all business. "Yes, I've certainly heard about the grounds crew's situation. Typical crap. But as far as I know, people don't ordinarily get hired for groundskeeping right off of the street. Say, this only happened yesterday. How'd you even know about it?" Hartman was very wary.

"A friend of mine on the crew mentioned it," Belteron said. "He said they were in a real mess."

Hartman smirked. "They're always in a real mess. But it's not my job, it's Burt's. You want a job, I'll give you a job. I need ten ushers, five security guards and twenty vendors. I'll put you to work yesterday if you want work. But I do not do grounds crew. You can't even get down there now."

Belteron leaned forward. *This is Burt's problem. Send me to Burt.* "You could send me down to the grounds crew office with an usher." *I'd be Burt's problem, not yours.*

Hartman stroked his chin. "Hell, I'm too busy for this. It's Burt's problem, I'll send you to Burt. Knowing him, he'll probably hire you! Do *not* tell him I said that. Yeah, I'll send you down with an usher." He buzzed Althea.

Burt hired him. Walking down with the usher, Belteron had been formulating his final push. It was unnecessary.

"If you were Satan, I'd hire you. Total of three actually walked, if you wanna know the truth. Go into the locker room at the end of that hall there, and ask Luis for a uniform. Get dressed pronto, and go straight out the back door of the locker room. Centerfield gate's open. Find Manny. He'll be around home plate. He's temporary infield chief." Burt, already an intense man, grew more so. "Icarus, you wanna find out how temporary you are, just screw up. You're doing infield. Infield's dirt, and dirt's dirt, for chrissake. My baby daughter could handle it. We need you throughout the game and tonight probably till lights out. *And*, tomorrow's a day game, so you gotta be back here at nine. Can you handle it?"

"No problem," Belteron said.

"I sure hope so. Just do what Manny says. You've got until tomorrow to prove yourself. If Manny likes you, maybe you can stay. Now hit it."

Twenty minutes later, Belteron walked through the centerfield gate. The Montreal Expos were having batting practice, so he carefully scrambled along the warning track over to foul territory. As he picked his way through the maze of activity in the Montreal bullpen, he hoped that he was taking the right path to making the team. At least he was on the field and could easily access the coaches and players. All in all, he was pleased at the odd turn of events. On the week-long space journey aboard the supply ship he'd had ample opportunity while in hiding to plot various strategies. This did not even vaguely resemble any of them. But he had assumed that flexibility and opportunism would be key elements if his overall goal was to be reached. This indeed was one way, and he was pleased with his luck.

He had also learned a couple of things about humans: one, that they could be mind-influenced almost at will. He could only imagine with what ease the Ball Fourians had taken over Cleveland. The number of years allowed for infiltration obviously had been used to establish plausibility, not because there were many obstacles in their path. And, two, many humans' motives were so convoluted that they were ready to give you what you wanted in spite of what was best for them. Burt, the grounds crew manager had taught him that. Burt didn't hire Belteron because he wanted a good worker; he hired him because he wanted to fire him. That was Burt's way of hitting a home run. No wonder the grounds crew was in tatters.

When Belteron reached home plate, none of the crew was there, naturally, because batting practice was in full swing. He glanced around and saw Jimmy Strongbow and another man leaning against the backstop.

Jimmy was startled as Belteron walked up. "Weren't you the guy I was just...did you say your name was, ah, Icarus? What are you doing here?"

"Needed a job. You told me the crew was short. I went to see Burt. And," Belteron raised his arms to show his uniform, "here I am. I'm supposed to look for Manny."

"You found me," said the other man with Jimmy. "You supposed to do infield?" Belteron nodded. "Good then. It's you, me and Jimmy. We're still one short. You do infields before?"

"No," said Belteron, lightly, "but dirt's dirt, right? Besides, I *know* baseball. Tell me what to do and I'll do it." *I'm a good worker who follows orders.*

Manny grinned. "I believe you, *hombre*, you look like a good worker. Just hang out with us here. When they finish batting, we bust tail and prep the infield."

Since they were to drag the infield every other inning and wet it down three or so times depending how windy it got, the infield crew spent the game behind the backstop. This suited Belteron just fine, as it was a perfect spot to observe the Giants, assess the performances and attitudes. The speed gun to measure the pitchers was located here and one could find out the speed of each pitch by discreetly glancing over the operator's shoulders (O'Nealy's fastball was almost uniformly 92 m.p.h.). Belteron verified at close range that the strategies of each world's game were very similar; the only real difference was the mental aspect of the game on Ball Four, and if one discounted the two to three per cent of the time that mental gambits, tricks and maneuvers were successful, then the games of both planets were virtually identical.

Belteron passed some of the time chatting with Jimmy, finding out about life on the Indian reservations (something very alien to Belteron and not covered in his training) and Jimmy's aspirations to pitch in the majors. Jimmy hadn't exactly given up his baseball hopes, he was just being practical about it. He was doing so much better than most Native Americans, he said, and that seemed to mean a lot to him. He was grateful to baseball in spite of his lack of success, for it had gotten him off the reservation. He wasn't pitching, but he liked his job.

Belteron did too. The infield work went smoothly, it felt good to work with his hands and Manny seemed to be quite satisfied. Belteron laughed inwardly when he realized that here he was on Earth with a *job*. He hadn't even asked what the pay was, not that he had an immediate need for money. He had plenty for now.

During a tortuous bottom of the fifth when the Expos gave up five runs and made two pitching changes, Belteron mused about how well events had transpired and how easy it had been to get to Earth in the first place.

He had expected his trip to Earth to be chancy at best and fraught with an ever-present danger of discovery. But, from the moment he had walked aboard the unguarded transport in Spaceport to the time he had beamed down from the space station which orbited high above the Earth, he encountered no such difficulties. In fact, the whole journey had been laughably unimpeded, and for one simple reason: Ball Fourians had no safeguards against intrigue from one of their own. Naturally, if Belteron had been an alien, alarms would have automatically gone off from one end of the ship to the other. The same thing would have happened on the space station. But, being Ball Fourian, he had triggered no such alarm. Furthermore, after creeping about the ship for a day or two, he came to realize that he had free run of large sections of the ship, had access to food duplicators and had found an unoccupied and delightfully appointed cabin in which to sleep. The two times he had accidentally come face to face with crew members in a corridor, they had smiled and moved on without the hint of suspicion. They apparently took him for someone who *belonged* there, for who would be there if they weren't supposed to be? Was it possible that he was at that moment the only Ball Fourian alive who was up to no good? Surprisingly, he found the thought amusing. He had been a bit of a rebel as a ballplayer and he was being a bit of one now, but he was satisfied that his motives were pure, and he felt, deep down, that what he was doing was in the best interests of baseball *and* Ball Four. Whether he would succeed or not seemed incidental. It was exhilarating that he was merely attempting it.

The orbital station, which was Operations headquarters, was a more dicey matter. It had whirled about the Earth for seven years now, safely cloaked from Earthen eyes. There was still a whirlwind of activity aboard, as a full staff was maintained in the unlikely event of a sudden need to evacuate the team and support staff from Earth. Belteron had no choice but to blend in and move about in full view. He was glad that biofashioning had made him unrecognizable on both the ship and station. His simple strategy to avoid detection had worked. He went about the station with a pleasant demeanor and a constant business-like bounce while projecting in all directions the thought, *Ah, another new arrival from the ship,* every few seconds or so. He was on board the station less than a day, for he only needed to discover two things: safe coordinates for landing on Earth and an unoccupied transport room for disembarking. Just as onboard the ship, there was no security in the absence of an alien intruder alert and movement about the station was unfettered. He discovered an unoccupied console in a room marked "Communications and Entertainment Lounge" where a few people were absorbed in either sending messages or relaxing in front of a holovision while off duty. The console had required no access codes and Belteron easily punched up maps showing a number of safe and secured landing zones on the surface. He chose a zone in St. Louis, a National League city.

Ah, there was one more thing he must think about. Getting to Earth appeared troublefree, but how to get back? Belteron theorized that some form of equipment must be necessary to operate transport units. Obviously, it would have been too risky to construct transport booths anywhere on Earth. They could be discovered. Hand-held devices might suffice to transport from Earthside. He scanned various files in the console until he located one entitled "standard-issue equipment." Among the list of equipment and devices was something called a "communications and transport control module." That would probably be it. If he were not to become stranded on Earth he must get one. Where? He asked the computer. The answer came in the form of a map locating the various storage compartments of the space station. There were two places one could obtain the module. One compartment was located adjacent to a transport room.

He hastened off in search of that equipment compartment. If he were successful, he could step into the transport room and be gone. But it was not that simple. Apparently the facility was in the main transport complex of the ship, for as he neared it he could hear a buzz of activity. It would not do to be discovered trying to leave the station. A pair of crew members came into view as Belteron went around a curve in the passageway. Instinctively he smiled and casually turned and returned the way he had come.

There had been the other storage area on the map, perhaps he'd have better luck. It took a few minutes to reach the area, as it was located on the other side of the station. When he got there he was relieved to find that it was an unmanned storage bay. Supplies that came from ships were apparently unloaded and stored here, then distributed throughout the station as needed. Dozens, perhaps hundreds of the control modules were needed, depending on how many support personnel might at any time be Earthside. Belteron had no way of knowing. But sure enough, there were open cases of the modules. There was a sign attached to the top case informing personnel that they were required to enter the module number in an electronic inventory unit located at the storage bay exit. Belteron grabbed a control module and exited quickly. He would forgo inventorying the device.

On his way to find a transport room, he quite by accident passed a room labeled "Financial Support." With no slight apprehension, he pressed the access bar and the door slid open to reveal a room empty but for a couple of machines that very much resembled duplicators, and stacks of small bundled paper, neatly arranged in bins. After a hasty examination, Belteron concluded that the bundles of paper were the medium of exchange called "money" which was used on Earth to secure goods and services. He was chagrinned that he hadn't anticipated the availability of money on board the ship or station. Of course, operatives would need fistfuls of it to avoid detection. All those plans to obtain money were another waste of time, he thought, as he happily filled his satchel.

The standing ovation at the end of the inning brought an end to Belteron's musings, and he and Manny ran out to water down the infield while Jimmy did a little fine-tuning on the mound.

The game ended 6-2 with another complete game for Brad O'Nealy. The Giants had looked good except for Quigley, who had gone 0 for 4. It's only a matter of time, thought Belteron, but I'd better not wait too long. If the Giants traded for a catcher, it would be a major setback.

"Hey Jimmy, Do you think they'll trade Quigley?" Belteron asked as they groomed the field after the game.

"No, it's a bit early in the season for a trade. But you never know, when a team's going bad they look around for someone to blame. Only trouble is, there's no one in the minors ready to take his place. Quigley had an okay season last year, my guess is they're hoping he'll come out of it."

Belteron for one was hoping that he didn't.

"Icarus, you did okay tonight," Manny told him as they finished up for the night. "I'll tell Burt to hang on to you. See you at nine tomorrow?"

"Thanks Manny, sure, I'll be here," said Belteron. Don't worry, I'm not going *anywhere*.

4

THE PLAIN DEALER

April 5th.

Lloyd Cronin

YOU CAN'T WIN WITH
SMOKE AND MIRRORS

Every year about this time I clean out a corner of my little cubicle at the paper for the sacks of mail that inevitably follow my annual predictions for the coming baseball season. So, readers, man your typewriters, grab your copies of *Foul Language Phrase Book* and coming out slinging.

All spring long we've been hearing what an improved club the Cleveland Indians are. The way they tore up the opposition in the preseason was awe-inspiring indeed, so who am I to disagree? The Indians *are* an improved team, so I'm predicting they'll improve their record this year. Last year they were 80-82, this year they'll be 81-81. They are ready for the big time: .500 ball.

What, not generous enough? Let's get *real*. A good preseason does not a great season make.

Four years ago, when Indians owner Elliot Edwards hired no-name general manager Abe Watkins, he said, "It's time for some new blood and, if I've got to hire outside of baseball, well, then that's what I'm damned well going to do!" Okay, so the team's record has improved every year since and I've got no argument with Edwards' decision anymore. He finally did something right for a change.

But there are concrete reasons for my prediction:

1) A team needs a leader on the field, a take charge guy, usually a veteran, to win through the course of a long season. But there isn't a player in the starting lineup that's been in the majors longer than three years (the average is 1.4 years by the way). Sure, there's Burton and Rodgers, but they're aging and nobody can lead a team from the bench. Jake Conrad is a respected, veteran manager but managers manage, players lead, that's why a team has a captain. So the team elects second-year player Alan Van de Kirk captain? Sorry, no leaders, no pennant.

2) The Cleveland Indians of today look more like an *expansion* team than a team with a proud century-long tradition. Who are these guys, anyway? They look like the product of an expansion draft, not a well-thought-out, well-crafted, properly

developed team. Preseason is the time for rookie phenoms to shine and that's why they looked impressive. When the real season starts we'll be reminded that teams like Detroit, Boston and Toronto chew up rookie phenoms for breakfast with their Wheaties. 3) Pitching wins pennants and these guys haven't shown us that they're winners. Where Abe Watkins found Warren Evans for pitching coach beats me, and once again I have to admit Evans hasn't hurt the team and may have even helped it. But Vance Bueller is the only winning pitcher on the staff. Congratulations on going 23-10 last year, Vance, but you can't do it by yourself. No way.

Sorry, Messrs. Edwards and Watkins, it may be a noble experiment but you can't do it with smoke and mirrors. And sorry, readers, be kind to my mail bag and I promise to pick the Browns for the Super Bowl. But as for the Indians, 81-81 is the best I can do.

Warren Evans flashed the signal for fastball to catcher Eddie Martin, and leaned back in the dugout to watch the result. Strike two. Okay, 1 and 2, let's try curve, low and away. Strike three. The scouting report is right, Richter is a sucker for low and away when he's behind on the count. One out. We can afford a walk now.

Martane, walk this one.

Yes, Evan.

What a luxury open-mind communication is, Evans thought, I'd better not get too spoiled. When I get back to Ball Four, I'll have to be retrained.

"Good call, Warren," said Jake Conrad, "you've been doing your homework. Vance can get this next guy easy."

"No problem, Jake." No problem indeed. Ball one, ball two, ball three, foul ball, ball four.

Vanbellen, Alverez must hit.

Yes, Evan.

"Dammit, what the hell's Vance doing out there? You wanna go talk to him?"

"Don't worry," said Evans, "he can get Alverez. Fork ball in the right spot and we got a double play. Watch." He flashed the sign for a fork ball, waist high. Bueller responded with a fork ball, all right, but the bottom dropped out of it and Alverez waved at it and missed. Evans didn't even flinch.

Discipline, Vanbellen! Alverez must hit.

Sorry, Evan.

On the next pitch, Bueller floated a fork ball and Alverez stroked it into right for a single. Men on first and third, one out.

"Jeez, Warren, go talk to him. Settle that boy down. This is getting out of hand." Conrad leaned away and spit, kicking up a little cloud of dust on the dugout floor. "It's the top of their batting order now."

Evans jogged out to the mound, Martin joined them.

"Okay, gentleman, we've got to let them score. But no home run. Just a single or double, we'll let them have one run. Otherwise, Conrad might start thinking about pulling you, Vance."

Vance nodded. "Sorry about Alverez. It's still hard to give up hits. Alverez is an easy strike out."

I know," said Evan. "But we've got to let Detroit score today. They're too good not to score. I won't stand in the way of a win today, Vance, but do your job. Davidson's up next. We'll try to go 2 and 2, and then hang a curve a little outside. He usually takes that pitch to left field, worst that will happen is a double up the gap. After that, we'll close them down. Agreed?"

The umpire came from home plate to speed them up.

Davidson singled to left, driving in a run with Alverez stopping at second. The next batter grounded into a double play.

"That's more like it! I'm telling you Warren, Vance is good but he sure makes me nervous when he goes south in the third inning."

Warren Evans just smiled.

As the Indians settled into the dugout Evans issued an order that he knew would be well received.

Hit at will, mind reading allowed.

Evans' mind felt a slight sting as nine minds said *yes Evan!* simultaneously. He smiled inwardly.

"Let's get 'em, Buck," said Conrad.

"Okay, boss."

Evans sat back to watch the fireworks. Ordinarily, he didn't interfere with the players' game, except to forbid mind reading, mind gambits or the like. If he allowed mind techniques every day, they'd never lose. But, if he banned them, he found that it somewhat leveled the playing field and they could lose from time to time. Humans weren't bad ball players; he actually wished he could take a few of them back to his team in First City. There was not yet enough data to know with any certainty that if Cleveland played the human game they would be assured of winning the division. It was Evans' job never to find out. Right now they were 16-4 and everything was going according to plan.

Today's game plan was in preparation for the time that might come in the season ahead where stricter control was needed to create the outcome of certain games. He needed to see, now that the whole Indian team was Ball Fourian, just how completely opposing teams could be manipulated and how disciplined his own team could be in carrying out his orders. So far, he liked the results.

During the spring he had mind-influenced Jake Conrad into letting him call the pitches. Jake had never let any coach call the shots in his whole managerial career, so his decision to let "no-name" Warren Evans call the pitching game caused quite a stir in the media. That rascal Lloyd Cronin had actually come out and criticized Conrad for it.

Now I'm in the driver's seat, as they say on Earth, thought Evans. He called the pitches and, because it was his place to sit or stand next to Conrad, he could easily mind-influence the signals Conrad sent to Hal Walker, the third base coach. For all practical purposes Evans was calling the whole game.

Buck Nichols had singled to center. Jimmy Fernandez was coming to bat. *Hit and run*, Evans projected.

Jake Conrad flashed the hit and run sign to Hal Walker who flashed it to Fernandez. Fernandez let the count go to 2 and 0 before grounding a ball between first and second.

Alan Van de Kirk came up to home plate. No reason to flash a sign now. Alan knew what to do. He'd wait and scan the catcher's mind until he read inside fastball and he'd take it downtown.

Which he did. 3-1, Cleveland.

Evans let the slugfest continue for four more runs before giving the order for two ground outs. The men responded and the side was retired. He continued to orchestrate throughout the game and was pleased to find that he was able to influence the outcome within a run on either side. He especially was happy with the results of the eighth inning Detroit rally. Using the scouting reports and Vance Bueller's control, Evans let Detroit come within two runs of tying up the ballgame. Conrad pulled Bueller and Spanky McTell put out the fire. Cleveland won, 9-6. Bueller's earned run average would recover. He was looking too unbelievably good.

Evans was walking around the Indians' dressing room chatting quietly with the players when Jake Conrad called him over to his office. Evans went in and shut the door.

Conrad sized him up before speaking. "All in all, a good game, Warren. You called it good and we won. But I've been watching Vance Bueller for two seasons now and I never seen him throw so many off pitches. He knows better, least I thought so. What the hell's up?"

Evans smiled. "Oh, I suppose it always hurts when you find out your ace is mortal. But, you know, Jake, Vance isn't our only ace anymore. We've got a crew of them. It's time to relax and let them do their work."

"Yeah, I suppose you're right," Conrad said. "I'm so used to frettin' all these years, I don't know when to quit. But I'm proud of these boys, they seem to be playing beyond their years. (They ought to be, thought Evans, their actual average age is fifty-one.) That's another thing that been buggin' me, Warren. They're so, you know, sorta quiet and assured, they never horse around in the dressing room. We just kicked Detroit's butt and it's like, I don't know, a library in there. And they never talk to the press. Rookies, in my experience, even three-year players, they're always mouthing off to the press, you wanna muzzle 'em sometimes. Not these guys. They don't even talk to *me*, for chrissake. You seem to get on with them more than me."

"You know how it is, Jake. You're the boss. They're still a little in awe of you. Heck, you've been with the franchise for thirty-seven years. To these kids you *are* the franchise. Give them a little time, they'll warm up to you."

Conrad considered. "I suppose you're right. But one thing's gotta start now. They've got to start opening up to the press. Edwards noticed it. A team needs publicity to draw, and we're the hottest team in the majors right now and we're last in attendance. He made a point of it to me. And it's gotta start with you. Cronin's in the media room and he asked for a word with you. Set a good example, Evans."

"I'll try."

This is the one flaw in the plan, Evans thought, as he made his way to the interview room. It was easy while we were losing, nobody was interested in us, but with this season's start everybody wants to know where we're from, which high school, where'd you play your college ball, and who did you emulate while you were growing up. And I know what Cronin wants to know.

Cronin was perusing the box score of the game when Evans came in.

"Good afternoon, coach. Thanks for coming. Listen, you called a helluva game out there today, discounting the eighth inning of course! Nah, seriously, I've given you a hard time in the press and I'd like to feature you in tomorrow's column. But I don't know a damned thing about you. Every time I ask I get the same thing."

Evans projected a casual, pleasant off-guardedness. "What else do you want to know? It's all in the team press notes. I was coaching in double A ball when Abe Watkins found me. I'm as surprised as you are that I'm here."

"That's not good enough, Evans, and you know it. What'd you do before that?"

"Well, maybe I'm a little humbled by my uninteresting past. Never made the majors, washed out of minor league ball. But I kept up with it, and made my way as a coach." Evans remained cool. "I'm sorry, Lloyd, but I've had a policy my whole career that the game comes first. You want to talk about the game, I'm all yours. I'm just a private person, that's all."

"This whole team's full of characters like you," Cronin scoffed. "Is that your final word, then?"

"Yep, that's my final word," said Evans. "There's your story for tomorrow, Lloyd. Tell them I'm a tight-lipped son of a bitch."

"Yeah, right, coach. Now, about that eighth inning..."

"Greetings, First Commissioner Tarn, this is the Week Four report. I'm happy to let you know that everything is proceeding quite well. What's most encouraging is that the decisions we've made in preparation for the Season are proving to have been largely correct and the little obstacles that have remained in our path are one-by-one being eliminated.

"Firstly, I commend you on your foresight regarding the manager and coaching positions. You know full well that I was quite opposed to your proposition for the last three years and I will tell you that I carried my doubts into this, the Season, as well. I couldn't conceive of allowing Earthlings to remain as manager and coaches, for I worried that, even with our mental capabilities, somehow they might retain enough control to negatively influence the outcome. I thoroughly understood that it was an impossibility to create characters with the twenty and thirty years of baseball experience and notoriety it takes to have credibility as managers and coaches under the scrutiny of the fans and the press. I only maintained my opposition in hopes that I would somehow find a way to overcome this last obstacle to complete infiltration. Your resolution to the problem that I become pitching coach has proved so successful, that I am again reminded why you are First Commissioner and I a mere manager. I am thriving in my present role and I happily stand corrected. The human manager and coaches are no threat to our eventual triumph, and I fully realize now that some of my more reckless suggestions would have risked discovery at worst and open hostility from a suspicious sports press at best. Thank you for your guidance in this matter.

"I am also happy to inform the Commission that we are nearing total infiltration of the team. Bill Burton, former right fielder, has been given his unconditional release after a few gentle mind-influencing sessions with owner Elliot Edwards, who remained stubbornly loyal to the first player he signed after buying the team. The two remaining pitchers will have departed by the time of my next report. The best of the two, thirty-four year old Mike Bolicki, still has a couple of decent years left, so we were able to trade him for Ellerban, who, as you know, has been infiltrating through the Houston farm system. Houston is in desperate need of starters and its management was shocked that we would trade a proven starter for a kid with a marginal record on the Class A level San Antonio team. The Cleveland press, as usual, were just as shocked. The mild tempest subsided after Ellerban threw a two-hitter in his major league debut. Since we've brought so many of our players through other teams' systems, we've gotten quite a reputation for shrewd dealing and, after the Ellerban deal, one *Sporting News* columnist wrote that the litmus test for prospects is whether or not Abe Watkins is interested in them! I'm grateful that, with Ellerban, we've brought in our last player who hadn't been in the Cleveland organization. It's taken one hundred agents in fifteen cities working night and day for four years to complete that section of the Operation. Their mind-influencing skills are so impressive that I have no doubt they could convince me to trade Vance Bueller for a player to be named later! Forgive my digression into Earthling humor.

"Two human players remain on the roster. The other aforementioned pitcher will probably be waived, as we've one too many on the staff as it is. Zaan is waiting down in Akron to take his place. The last human, Bertie Thompson, has been a difficult case. Our campaign to mind-disrupt him into retirement has taken unpredicted turns. Manager Jake Conrad has suspended him for ten days for an ugly incident in which he struck Vernanden, who had replaced him at second base. Our choice to use mind disruption is questionable simply because the results are the least predictable. However, I accept the necessity at this late date in the Operation. We've got agents working on all the principals in the situation and I hope that we can resolve it without further damage to Cleveland or Thompson.

"I am looking forward to a very enjoyable season and it is fascinating to observe the relative merits of Ball Fourian versus human baseball. These Earthlings play with a drive and spirit which is commendable and gives meaning to the challenge we have undertaken. And our boys are playing with a discipline undemanded of them back home. It is most inspiring to observe the grace with which the players who have been asked to moderate their talents accept their roles. They do understand that the whole team cannot hit .400 or win thirty games! The mind discipline of the baseball caste and how they've adjusted to life on Earth will inspire future generations, I have no doubt.

"I wish that I could conclude my report without bringing up anything worrisome, but I regret that cannot be the case. There is one area which threatens to disrupt the pleasant flow of events during the Season. We have not fully taken into account the zeal with which the news media delve into every element of the game and its personalities, and we risk discovery or, at the very least, disruption if we allow it to go on unchecked. Our original estimation that we could get through the Season before too much investigation took place may have been short of the mark. I will be instructing our team to open up to the media in a controlled way and I will monitor the situation carefully. And I will work with Abakin closely. As general manager, his is the most scrutinized position, but I myself am vulnerable and being pressed. The players are more secure but, I'm afraid, coaches are not allowed by the media to come out of nowhere. This, I suppose, is more in Second Commissioner Semptor's sphere than yours so I will prepare a report for him as we progress. I will keep you both informed on this delicate matter.

"That is all. I hope Ball Four is enjoying the reports and holoclips that the Holovision One team is sending home. As much as I have been thrilled and privileged to be here, I also regret missing the excitement back home. Thank you for your time, First Commissioner. Evan off."

5

San Francisco Examiner

May 3rd.

John Houser

AN OPEN APOLOGY

I will make no excuses. I won't even mention the names of the six other Bay Area sports columnists who picked the Giants to win the West Division. I won't even tell you that my mother picked them too. In telling you about the mistaken beliefs I held about the Giants a month ago, I'll try to muster more objectivity than I did then, and hopefully shed some light on the Giants' collapse.

Did I say collapse? That's an understatement. The Giants have gone so far south they're probably in Tierra del Fuego by now. Who bought the tickets for this flight to South America? The right-handed pitching staff, aided and abetted by me, who believed in them. Kiley Upton, Art French and Julio Gonzalez, do yourself a favor. Stop reading this column now. No? Okay, I won't insult you, then. I'll just say 0-15. Get the picture? French did offer us some hope Wednesday with his 1-0 loss. But impressive losses don't win titles.

The second miscall I made was to say that the Giants had two problem areas. I was dead wrong. They have more. I was right when I said they lacked a quality catcher. Ed Quigley is hitting .091 and the replacement for him they called up from

Phoenix for a cup of coffee went on the longest ohfer since the invention of waxed paper. And the Three Musketeers in the outfield must have left their muskets in their
lockers in Arizona. As for the bullet-proof
infield I so highly touted, somebody please
take them to Emergency before they bleed
to death. They don't make double plays,
they hit into 'em.

The only bright spot in the whole
show turns out to be my only correct call
as well: Brad O'Nealy. Brad, send me an
autographed baseball for my mother, she
needs some cheering up.

I spoke to Lou Chambers after the
loss on Wednesday and he, like me, makes
no excuses. Ever optimistic, he says it's a
long season and the boys will come around.
But when you add the usual Giants' June
Swoon to this year's Absent April, I doubt
the boys will come around for anything
except their paychecks. Sorry, Lou, the
season's just not long enough. There will
be no miracles this year, for miracles you
need more than Brad O'Nealy. I know it's
early, but it's time to start planning for the
winter meetings.

To the fans, to my readers, to my
editor and to my dear mother: my hum-
blest apologies for leading with my heart
instead of my head. I promise to write "I
will be more objective in my column" one
hundred times on the blackboard. And I'll
pray I don't find a pink slip in my mail box
at the paper. Maybe they need a sports
columnist in Tierra del Fuego. At least I'll
still be able to cover the Giants.

There were no immediate direct actions Belteron could take to get on the
Giants team; he had to bide his time and be watchful for any break or opportunity. There were, however, many little things he could do to prepare, to set the
stage, and he wasted scant time or energy on pursuits that didn't contribute one
way or another to his goal.

Through Jimmy he had met Lou Chambers and Brad O'Nealy. During the brief time he spent with Chambers he projected thoughts of confidence and credibility toward the manager's mind. He planned to do this whenever he encountered Chambers, knowing that Chambers was the key figure in his scheme. When the chance came, Belteron wanted Chambers already softened up. Chambers was of an easy and gentle disposition, a "player's manager" as the press might call him; but Belteron quickly realized that Chambers was no fool and a man of deep convictions. Belteron respected this and wanted Chambers to hold some positive convictions toward him ahead of the time when Belteron should have to convince Chambers that the team needed him.

Brad O'Nealy he liked instantly. Brad was apparently a rare commodity in human sports: a highly educated man and a superb athlete. Jimmy had made a big deal about the fact that Brad had graduated from Harvard which, as far as Belteron could tell, was one of the most highly regarded schools on Earth. Brad made light of it all, as he did most things, and Belteron enjoyed Brad's joviality. People were pleasant on Ball Four, but humans were *funny*, a difference Belteron, while not completely understanding, was really beginning to appreciate. And he felt with a growing certainty that O'Nealy would be an important ally in the struggle ahead. Belteron would need all the help he could get. He knew full well that he could never manage it alone.

Jimmy Strongbow he liked best of all. Belteron was charmed by Jimmy's humility. His wasn't a groveling humility but one based on a purity of character. Belteron wondered if it had something to do with Jimmy's Indian heritage. He intended to find out, not just because he liked Jimmy but because these were all new experiences for him; although his prime goal was to somehow challenge the Ball Fourian effort, he could not pass up the chance to learn about an alien culture first-hand. It might never come again. He also felt that anything he learned about the human culture would help his cause. In fact, he had to learn and learn fast, because somewhere out there in the body of human knowledge and history was a clue that would solve his dilemma, a clue which at present he was nowhere near apprehending. For now, Belteron was closest to Jimmy. He would start with him.

He had no illusions about his chances for success. He considered his cause hopeless, a feeling which his natural Ball Fourian mind-tuning had muted too quickly. He wanted to feel these human emotions, to understand them; though he was experiencing emotional pain for perhaps the first time in his life, there was a rich quality to it which he found stimulating. He felt more alive than at any time he could recall. There were no hopeless causes on Ball Four, few causes at all, for that matter. Operation Universe Series was the first real pursuit of any merit that Ball Fourians had been involved in within recent history. In that sense, Belteron suddenly appreciated what First Councilor Tarn was up to. He was providing a cause, a source of keen interest for his people. It was quite clever, really, of Tarn to take the favorite pastime of Ball Fourians, baseball, and utilize it in such a novel way. Ball Four was no longer isolated, no longer alone in a crowded galaxy. With a flash of insight, Belteron grasped that Tarn had broken the back of the Non-proliferation Act without assuming the political risk of having it repealed. A master politician, that Tarn.

Belteron could see Tarn's motivation, but what was his own? Was he only being vindictive for having been kicked off the team, or was he truly on a mission to singlehandedly uphold the honor of his planet? Or was he just doing what he had all his life: playing baseball and playing to win? If so, he was going to a lot of trouble in what was most likely a doomed effort. But it felt good.

Earlier that day after the game, he'd had a chance to put on a catcher's mitt for the first time in months. Of course it was made out of an animal product called leather, but the design was about the same as his own back home. Belteron had talked Jimmy into throwing a few. The groundskeeping crew had finished up early because the game, which the Montreal team had won 1-0, was very short. Jimmy had thrown well, though wild as usual. Belteron discovered that he had the makings of a good curve. He also threw three other pitches with varying degrees of effectiveness. His change-up was not convincing, his slider was, well, a slider and his forkball tended to float too long before dropping. Hitters had a name for pitches like that. They called them gifts. Jimmy's strength as a pitcher was his fastball, which blazed. But seeing that he had at least the beginnings of a large repertoire of pitches gave Belteron hope that he could help him. On Ball Four, pitchers were trained through a combination of visualization and mind focusing in addition to the usual mind discipline training. Being a catcher, Belteron had participated in the training of pitchers as a regular part of his duties. He had made a considerable effort to use these duties to enhance his overall growth as a player, even going so far as to ask his coaches to allow him to be trained as a pitcher in order to make him both a better catcher and hitter. Belteron grew to be the greatest star in the game, giving credence to this double-training technique and it was currently in vogue in both the major and minor leagues of Ball Four. How to use these techniques to train a human like Jimmy wasn't immediately apparent to Belteron. He would have to search to find a way. He had tomorrow off and he would use the time wisely.

Jimmy Strongbow finished grooming the bullpen pitcher's mounds, then walked over to get the hose to wet them down. He noticed that he'd forgotten the mitts on the bench outside the bullpen cage and hustled over to put them away before they got hit by the spray. He'd been keeping his glove in the bullpen box and nobody had said anything to him about it, probably because of his connection with O'Nealy.

It felt great to throw today, he thought, and it's great to have someone on the crew to play catch with. That Billy Icarus is a good catcher too. Jimmy felt oddly confident throwing to him and thought he had thrown better and more accurately than he had for a long time. By accurately, of course, he meant he hadn't thrown anything over Billy's head.

"Hey Chief!" It was Brad O'Nealy, calling from in front of the dugout.

" What are you still doing here?" asked Jimmy. "The game's been over for an hour and a half."

"Oh, I was just talking to Chambers. He doesn't talk about it much, but I gotta believe he's pretty down about the situation. Losing 1-0 is about as hard to swallow as anything in life, especially when it makes your record 4-18. He said at this rate I'll be 40-0 for the season and the Giants will be 40-122! I laughed but he didn't. French pitched a good game today and still lost. Right-handers can't buy a victory this year."

"You'll just have to carry them, Brad."

"Oh, sure," O'Nealy said. "I'm a rookie. Just wait until the scouting reports catch up with me, they'll start getting to me. Happens to rookies all the time, it'll happen to me. The second time these hitters see me they'll thrash me. I figure I've got another month of honeymoon, then it's down the toilet."

Jimmy grinned. "I know you, O'Nealy, you don't believe that for a minute. Anyway, just being aware of the problem is half the battle. You're probably saving a few tricks for them."

"I can say no more," O'Nealy said eerily as he hummed the *Twilight Zone* theme. "Say, you want to play catch?"

"No way, Brad. They'd lynch me. Besides, Chambers is right. You can't risk your hands."

Ah, you're right," O'Nealy admitted, "it's just that I want to see you keep working on your stuff. You're twenty, right? Well, I'm almost twenty-three. By the time you're my age you'll be ready for the big show."

"Brad, you had four years of college ball to perfect your stuff. The only time I competed was in high school. We didn't even have little league on the reservation."

"Baseball at Harvard was like one long boy's camp," countered O'Nealy. "If we were in each other's shoes, you'd be the star now and I'd be a bag boy at a grocery store. Why are you arguing with me anyway? I thought you wanted to pitch in the Majors."

"I do, and I'm not giving up, but I'm just trying to be practical about it. Hey, guess what, you know that new guy on the crew I introduced to you, Billy Icarus?"

"Yeah, what about him?"

"Well, he's a catcher, a good one too. We worked out today after the game. Gave me some good pointers too, he really knows his stuff. So save your hands, I got a new coach."

"Really? That's great. Where's he from?"

"I don't know, he never said," replied Jimmy. "Doesn't say much about himself, but I like the guy. Solid character, good worker."

"Yeah, I liked him too. I felt like I knew him when you introduced us, he looks familiar. He looks a little out of place, like he should be governor or something. I mean, what's he doing being a groundskeeper, for chrissake."

Jimmy shot him a dirty look. "Hey, watch it, Brad. Beats being a bag boy."

"I'm just kidding. Listen, you almost done there? I feel like pizza and beer. Tomorrow's an off-day, so what do you say? My treat."

"Great. Let me change and I'll meet you in the parking lot."

San Francisco had awakened Thursday morning in a sea of fog and mist and Belteron had awakened with it. He looked out of the window of his room on the thirty-third floor of the Hotel Meredith. The lights of the city around and below him blinked through the mist and began to merge with the growing dawn. There was magic and mystery out there, and Belteron could hardly wait to get out into it. He loved this constant weather. There were changes, unexpected changes that weren't announced by WeatherCon ahead of time. San Francisco had its own climate with its own will. Of course, this willful weather *was* predictably cold and damp, and the first thing that Belteron had done was to buy a coat. He now grabbed that very coat, picked up his map and, passing the dresser, he reached into a drawer and grabbed a small bundle of bills.

Though his training for living in that Earth country known as America had been thorough, Belteron was thrilled and fascinated by the never-ending parade of new experiences. Elevators and buses and traffic, noisy and smelly traffic, all these things assaulted his senses with an enlivening delight; it had, however, taken a bit of time for his nose to accept the fumes. He liked walking in the early hours before the fumes had had time to accumulate.

Coming out of the hotel he turned left and went up toward Market Street. He had determined from his map that walking to the San Francisco Public Library was feasible, and he looked forward to the exercise.

He cut a zig-zag through the maze of city streets, marveling at the hodgepodge of businesses that lined them, and stopped every so often to check his map. One such time he paused at the opening to a narrow alley and was unfolding his map when an arm suddenly reached around him and tightened on his throat. Before he could react he was dragged into the alley.

"Reach down and grab your wallet and hand it over your shoulder. Now! I'll kill you," the man breathed into Belteron's ear as he tightened his grip.

Time froze. Belteron gathered one focused thought and sent it straight back with force. *You can't feel your arms. They have disappeared.* The arm around his throat suddenly slacked and, with a pushing motion and a turn, he pivoted to face the man.

There is no money. I am dangerous. You will die.

The man began to back up slowly, hesitated for a half moment, then spun around and ran away into the mist.

Belteron quivered, then purposefully began to relax himself. He backed out of the alley and turned up the street in the direction he'd been going. His mind slowly cleared and returned to placidity with a final quiver. There it was, he thought, a crime! He was stunned. He'd read all the material the Operation had given him in training and yet, now that it had happened, he was filled with a dread that was as difficult an emotion to mind-balance as he'd ever in his life experienced.

He walked several blocks before his mind was fully clear. He now understood why the Operation had made such a fuss over the crime-aborting training and why it had been drilled so repeatedly. Though it had been a year since the last session, Belteron had instinctively performed the drill almost to the letter. He had embellished a bit, but the drill provided for that: react and embellish according to the situation. It had obviously worked, and he was grateful. He knew now that he must be more on guard. The thought saddened him.

After a breakfast of tea, bagels, cream cheese and smoked fish, Belteron entered the Public Library just as it opened.

"Pardon me, miss," he said to the lady at the main desk. "If I need specific information on a subject, where should I start?"

"Have you used a library before, young man?" she said curtly, looking over her glasses.

"Oh, yes, of course, I mean where do I start here at your library?"

"Well, you'll find the card catalogues over there. Authors and Titles on the left and Subjects on the right."

"Thank you."

On Ball Four, virtually the entire knowledge of the known universe was available at the household console. But Belteron would be content to wend his way through the human recording system if it would yield results. Knowledge was contained on paper in volumes called books, and to access these books one searched through these wooden cabinets full of cards. Yes, it seemed simple enough. He would start with A for "Apache," go to B for "baseball" and "brain" and on to I for "intelligence." He'd better get to it.

Belteron reported to work on Friday in high spirits, in spite of having to come in two hours early. Lou Chambers had "suggested" after the shutout Wednesday that extra batting practice could be "available" on Friday afternoon to all who felt they might "benefit" from it. Only fools or rookies would fail to understand what Lou meant by that. The still shorthanded grounds crew had its hands full with the extra work.

Belteron's day off was fruitful indeed. He was hopeful that he had found what he needed to help Jimmy, although he would have to wait until after tomorrow's day game to find out. He had also developed the beginnings of a theory which just might be what he was looking for to solve the larger question of how to beat the Ball Fourians should he engineer the impossible task of reaching the World Series. Fortunately, he had a while to work on that one. There were a few more pieces to the puzzle, but at least he now had reason to hope. In addition, he had organized a series of projects he could work on one by one. He had compiled a good deal of information on the various Giants from his vantage point behind the backstop and this extra batting practice was a perfect opportunity to make casual contact with the players.

After the early preparation of the field and the setting up of the batting cage for practice, he and Jimmy had little to do but wait to move equipment from time to time. They were basically free to move around if they stayed out of the team's way. It was not unusual for the players to chat with the grounds crew, because players from the various positions liked to confer about the conditions of their particular spot. Archie Stokes, the shortstop, for example, liked a hard surface and was always asking for extra wet-downs. The grounds crew was, in a way, considered part of the team.

Belteron and Jimmy were in fact talking to Stokes when Willie Washington, the left fielder, walked up to take his warm-up cuts next to the batting cage. Washington, a big brute of a man, had been the home run leader on the club the past two seasons but this year, like most of the team, he was off to a slow start.

Belteron slipped away from the conversation and walked up behind Washington.

"Excuse me, Willie?"

"Yeah, what's up?" he said, without looking up or interrupting his swings.

"I just wanted to tell you I noticed a little hitch in your swing this year."

Washington stopped abruptly and turned. "Say, who the hell *are* you?"

"Oh, I'm sorry, I'm Billy Icarus, just joined the infield crew a couple of days ago," Belteron said amiably.

"That's good, because for a second I thought you were the new batting coach or something," Washington said scornfully.

"Look, Willie, I may not be a coach, but how many home runs did you hit last year?"

"Thirty-seven," he replied.

"And how many so far this year?"

"Two. And I may not hit another one if you don't let me practice." Washington was getting testy.

"You may not hit another one with that hitch in your swing, either."

Washington halted in mid-swing. "Just what the hell you talking about?"

"You're double-cocking your swing, that's what. Here, can I show you?" said Belteron, stepping forward.

Washington leaned against his bat and rolled his eyes. "Sure, what the hell."

"Okay," said Belteron as he grabbed a bat. "Maybe because of your slump you're looking for extra power. So, when you swing you cock it a bit too early and take it back a little too far, like this. So, while you wait for the ball to come, you drop your wrists and that causes your bat to come around late and a bit low. You're not getting extra power, you're robbing yourself of it."

"Sounds kinda cock-eyed to me," said Washington skeptically.

"Maybe, Willie, but tell me, where in the park did you hit your home runs?"

Washington thought for a moment. "Off-field. In fact, one of 'em hit the right field foul pole."

"That's right, and did they feel good?"

"Nah, they were dead ducks, sounded like my hands flattening a hamburger patty."

"They were flukes, Willie, your strength carried them out, not your talent. Slumps will do it to anybody, don't take it personally. When you swing, cock the bat once, keep your wrists level and forget about the slump. Listen, you're turn's coming up. Give it a try. If it doesn't help, you've got regular practice later to straighten it out. Thanks for your time. Good luck."

Washington managed a smile and took a trial swing. "Like this, huh? What the hell, I'll give it a try."

Belteron smiled and nodded, then walked over to rejoin Jimmy. Washington stepped into the batting cage and awaited the first pitch. He smashed it into the left field wall. The next pitch cleared the fence in left-center. The next one he smashed into the left field foul pole. The one after that hit the bleachers in straight-away left. He turned around, found Belteron by the backstop and smiled. Belteron nodded.

"What were you talking to Washington about?" asked Jimmy.

"Not much," said Belteron. "I just told him to relax."

A couple of hours later, the teams were into their regular pregame workouts and the Philadelphia Phillies were taking their turn in the batting cage. Belteron had been helping Jimmy finish up with the Giants' bullpen and they were still over there as the pitchers came out to warm up. Kiley Upton, last year's best right-hander at 15-11, started to loosen his arm up. Belteron hadn't had a chance to see Upton start yet, so he paid special attention to every pitch. As Upton began warming up, he threw practically sidearm, but ten minutes later he was loose enough to try smoking it in there and his arm was coming straight over the top. The movement made him look tight.

Upton dropped a toss from his catcher and the ball bounced over to where Belteron was leaning against the fence. Belteron grabbed it and jogged it over to Upton.

"Hi, Kiley, new delivery this year?"

"What?"

"Over the top like that. Is it new, or the way you always threw?"

"No, it's something new I thought I'd try for a few starts. Say, I see you with Jimmy over there. You a friend of Brad's too?"

"No, I'm new on the crew," said Belteron. "Just getting to know everybody. Anyway, Kiley, over the top like that if you're not used to it will tighten your motion and you'll hurt yourself."

Upton put his hands on his hips. "Jeez, when the team slumps everybody's a coach. Why am I talking to you?"

"Let me take a guess, Kiley. The speed gun says you've lost about three miles an hour off your fastball and they've been killing your slider."

"You hit the nail on the head," admitted Upton. "But..."

"And you threw at about forty-five degrees until this year, right?"

"Well, yeah, but..."

"Okay, then," said Belteron. "Look, I may be wearing groundskeeper brown right now but I've caught a lot of pitchers in my time and here's the way I see it. Coming over the top when it's not your natural style will steal speed and movement from your fastball and flatten out your slider. Doesn't do your curve much good either. Throw your natural pitch, Kiley, it's what got you here in the first place. Hey, sorry to take up your time, and have a good start tonight, okay?"

Upton let out a long breath. "Thanks. You know, O'Nealy told me the same thing the other day, but who listens to rookies, even smart asses from Harvard. Okay, I'll ask Coach and see what he says. What's your name, anyway?"

"Billy," Belteron said, walking away. "Billy Icarus. Good luck tonight."

The crew had set up the field for play and Belteron, Jimmy and Manny were in their usual spot behind home plate. That went pretty well, thought Belteron, I got my points across. Now let's see what they do.

He took some satisfaction from another thing as well. He had decided that he didn't feel good about using mind-influencing on players of his own team (even if he wasn't on it yet), so he had foregone using any techniques on Washington and Upton during his talks with them. He'd been able to make his case directly and they'd listened. That was honest and straightforward, and it was the way he would have handled it with teammates back on Ball Four. If he were to try mind-influencing on Ball Fourian players it would have been considered an insult. He saw no reason to insult his human teammates even if they were unaware of it. Yes, he was right to respect them. He only hoped that they had taken it to heart. He didn't have long to find out.

It was immediately apparent in the top of the first inning that Kiley Upton had listened to him. He threw at about fifty-five degrees from level and looked quite natural. He gave up a lone single and no walks. He struck out the last batter on a slider and ran briskly from the mound to the dugout.

In the bottom half of the first, Giants second baseman Eddie Renker led off by swinging at the first pitch and grounded out to first base. (Swinging at the first pitch again, thought Belteron.) Third baseman Mickey Roberts struck out. Rick Barker, center field, managed a walk. That gave Willie Washington a chance at the plate.

Washington worked a 3 and 1 count. The Phillies' pitcher let an inside slider creep out over the plate and Washington sent it into the left field bleachers. As he touched home plate to the "high fives" of his teammates, he searched the area behind the backstop for Belteron. Seeing him, he flashed a quick smile and a thumbs-up as he trotted to the dugout.

The Giants won the game 4-3, with Washington driving in all four runs by adding a bases-loaded double in the sixth to his earlier home run. Kiley Upton, surviving a three-run uprising in the seventh, went on to win his first game. Chambers wisely and patiently left him in to allow Upton to savor a complete game victory.

Jimmy and Belteron were collecting the bases from their fittings when Kiley Upton came out of the clubhouse door and walked over to them.

"Hey, Billy," said Upton, "Lou made a point of giving me the game ball. And I'm giving it to you. Thanks for the tip."

"I can't take this, Kiley, it's your first win."

"I ain't taking it back," Upton yelled over his shoulder as he jogged away. "Don't worry, I'll win another one."

As Upton disappeared through the door Jimmy whistled and shook his head slowly. "Apparently, I'd better start calling you Coach! A groundskeeper getting a game ball. That could be a first, Billy."

"It was a nice gesture. We'll use this ball to work out with next week while the Giants are away."

"Yes sir, Coach."

This is working, thought Belteron as he smiled at Jimmy's mocking tones. Hopeless cause or not, this is great fun.

ANCHOR:

The authorities have made an official statement concerning Belteron, the great baseball player. It seems he is not missing, he's absent, a determination which has left many observers more than a little curious. The first man in a century to quit the game early in his prime re-entered the news a few days ago when manager Haverdine of Belteron's team, the Seaview Captains, announced that repeated efforts to find the man had failed. Here's a report filed from Seaview.

REPORTER:

Seaview Captains' manager Haverdine had attempted to contact Belteron several times in the last week to plead once again with him to return to baseball. When his repeated calls went unreturned, Haverdine became concerned.

HAVERDINE:

It just wasn't like Belteron. First, there was no message on his HoloCom. And, second, he didn't return any of my calls. So I decided to visit his home, which I've done often over the years. I was surprised to find that no courtesy message played when he didn't answer the door. It's just not like him. Belteron's a gracious and courteous man, always has been. So I went to Seaview Public Safety and reported a possible Missing Person. I see now my suspicions were warranted.

REPORTER:

Seaview Public Safety took very seriously the suggestion that something had happened to a ballplayer of Belteron's stature, and immediately issued an alert known as "Unusual Situation involving Possible Danger to a Citizen." This alert allowed emergency authorization of credit and transport records checks. These checks revealed nothing unusual in themselves, but led the search to Spaceport.

ANCHOR:

We have reporter Lestronek standing by live at Spaceport. What can you tell us?

REPORTER:

I'm at a tiny inn some twenty miles from Spaceport Center. This inn, called Desert Rest, is located on a picturesque rim of Space Valley. Beyond that rim is a desert that is renowned for its scenic beauty. Standing with me is Public Safety Official Cantel. What can you tell us, sir?

CANTEL:

Well, Belteron checked into this inn some three weeks ago and apparently stayed one night. Transport records show that he traveled here, and there is no record of his departure. The innkeeper said that the subject made a reservation for one night only, but informed him that he would be returning at a future date. This innkeeper said that this is consistent with the pattern of hikers who come to enjoy the beauty of the desert region. Based on that information, Public Safety has issued the following determination: Belteron is officially listed as a Person Absent Without Knowledge by Another, which is a downgrading from the original alert. Indications are that he may simply be on a nature quest, something quite popular in this area, and consistent with Belteron's present leisure status. The subject has been out there for quite a while, but with his known athletic prowess there's just no cause at this time for official concern.

REPORTER:

There you have it from official sources, Belteron at this time has not been declared missing. That's up to the minute live from the Desert Rest near Spaceport.

ANCHOR:

Thank you. That brings us to sports, and I suppose the baseball world is concerned about the disappearance of Belteron. What can you tell us, Jevv?

SPORTSCASTER:

Well, Ball Four has had to get used to the disappearance of more than one star baseball player in recent years, as more and more of them reported to their assignments on Earth. But the excitement about the long-awaited Season has more than made up for the loss. We've got some holoclips of recent action on Earth and the boys of Ball Four are really tearing it up out there! The latest transmissions will be holocast in their entirety tonight at eight, but here's a little preview of what's to come...

First Councilor Tarn sat down at his console in his office at Council Hall. Before the meeting of the Planetary Council began he had a final bit of business to attend to. He needed to talk to his daughter. He entered the number for her office at Holovision One Studios.

Tarneen's image appeared. "Why, Father, it's nice to see you. You're in your Council garb. Are you in session?"

"No, but we're about to commence," Tarn said. "I needed to talk to you before things got underway."

"You rarely seek my input before meeting with the Planetary Council, Father, this must be serious." Tarneen allowed herself a faintly amused smile.

"Not really, my dear, I just have a small favor to ask of you. I'll get straight to the point. I'm expecting some petty politicking involving the disappearance of the ballplayer Belteron. Some ambitious men are letting their imaginations get the better of them. They fear that something is going on and they're missing out on the fun. This is highly distracting from the real work of the Council. I think you can be of help."

"What could I possibly do to influence the Council?" Tarneen asked.

"It's simple. Let this Belteron story die out. The public, I imagine, is more interested in events on Earth than anything else, so if the media pays less attention to the Belteron affair it'll fade of its own accord. Perhaps you can point out to your colleagues that if Belteron wants time to himself his wishes should be respected. Can you help?"

"I do have editorial powers here, Father, but I don't recall using them to pull a developing news story. You wouldn't ask if it weren't vital. Yes, I can help."

Tarn smiled. "Tarneen, this matter should not be characterized as *vital*. But if public interest is absent, these petty political adventurists will have to get on to the really vital matters. I appreciate your help and support. By the way, I've seen the holocasts of the games from Earth. I can't imagine how you've done it. The coverage is almost as if the game were being played at First City Stadium. You're to be commended."

"Oh, I can hardly claim credit," she said. "I handle content, not technique, but thanks. We're all proud here of the job the news crew is doing on Earth. It must be dangerous."

"Well, Tarneen, we have the most capable people of Ball Four involved in the Operation and they've been able, I've been assured, to eliminate practically all risk. We've based this entire endeavor on that principle. Anyway, the whole planet is grateful to Holovision One for making this most exciting of times all the more enjoyable and entertaining. Ball Four may never see the like of it again. Listen, my dear, I must go. Council is due to start momentarily. Thanks again for attending to this small matter."

"I'll get right on it, Father. Keep Ball Four turning. Tarneen off."

Second Councilor Semptor waited until Tarn was seated to call the Council to order.

"Welcome, First Councilor. As this special session of the Council is at his request, Third Councilor Niver shall be accorded the right to speak first. With your approval?"

Tarn nodded. Third Councilor Niver rose to address the Council.

"Thank you, First Councilor. As all in this assembly are aware, the eyes of Ball Four are on the enthralling pursuits of our team across the galaxy and each day seems to bring yet another triumph for us to savor. It is not my intent to distract from these festivities, but events have intervened which deserve our momentary attention. I refer to the odd disappearance of the ballplayer Belteron."

Murmurs passed about the chamber.

"As leader of the Junior Council, I feel an obligation to ask for an explanation for this unusual occurrence. I must point out, First Councilor, that in your dual role as head of baseball you were highly influential in choosing the challenge team and equally influential in having Belteron, at such a late date, removed from said team. Having said that, I will get to the heart of the matter. Where is this Belteron, and has he been reassigned to the team? Surely these things should be done openly, if not in this chamber, then at least in that of the Baseball Commission. With all due respect, First Councilor, we of this Council have a right, an obligation, to know."

Tarn waited for a few huzzahs from the Junior Council to subside. "Firstly, I would like to thank the esteemed leader of the Junior Council for calling this matter to our general attention, but unfortunately, gentlemen, I cannot. This unwarranted waste of our valuable time is not only distracting us from the vital affairs to which we normally attend but is also detrimental to the citizens of Ball Four. I will, however, address the questions raised if for no other reason than to allow us to move ahead to our usually elevated matters.

"Yes, I was instrumental in the deselection of Belteron from the challenge team. And, yes, my actions appear to have precipitated the most unusual reaction that he has, at least temporarily, left the game of baseball. Belteron is obviously troubled by the turn of events and, assuming that the deductions of the officials at Public Safety are correct, is using the isolation of a nature quest to come to grips with his situation. Were I in his position I would no doubt do the same.

"No, Belteron has not been reassigned to the challenge team and, further, I have no particular knowledge of his whereabouts. I have not publicly discussed outside of the Baseball Commission chambers the original reasons for his deselection, but to clarify matters I will make those deliberations open to the Council. Briefly, Belteron's principles were at odds with those of manager Evan of the challenge team and the Commission concluded there was a potential security danger in such conflict. Belteron has, by his very style of play, demonstrated that he is of a differing mind from the average ballplayer, and absolute cohesion would be necessary for the safety of a team so far away from home. Thus he was deselected and thus he remains. Gentlemen, let's allow Belteron the time and isolation needed to process the extraordinary events of his recent life so that he can return to his vocation, as we all wish him to do. That, in essence, is that."

Niver rose, too quickly for proper etiquette. "I cannot promise, First Councilor, that your answers will satisfy the Junior Council. Moreover, I..."

"One thing you *can* do, Niver," Tarn interrupted, "is to inform them that it is a dead, I repeat, dead issue. And I'm sure you will set a good example by wasting no more of the Council's time. To insure this, though it pains me to utilize such a significant power on such a petty perturbation, I am ordering the proceedings of this special session to be sealed and I further order that its details not be discussed by any councilor, junior or otherwise, in the public ear. I would hate to have the present pleasures of Ball Fourians everywhere diminished by one iota because of our embarrassingly inappropriate quibbles. Are we in accord?"

Murmurs of reaction echoed throughout the chamber.

"Gentlemen, are we in *accord*?"

Slowly, a stony silence filled the room as everyone became still.

After a moment or two, Tarn announced, "I sense accord. This Council is adjourned."

Semptor strolled with Tarn as they headed toward their respective offices.

"You realize, Tarn, that sealing the Council records will prevent the public from learning about its contents but they will, however, nonetheless report your action."

Tarn smiled. "My dear Semptor, I learned a valuable political lesson from my father, namely, that it is sometimes better to appear to be sinister in the public's eyes than to allow an opponent to appear to be righteous. Though our politics of consensus are so much more advanced than any alien system I've ever studied, we do still require our ploys and gambits. I just used one."

"But all these machinations to protect the privacy of a baseball player? Surely, there's more to it than that."

"I have no doubt, Semptor. Niver is probably just nervous about the sizable number of credits he wagered on the success of our challenge team. Using the Planetary Council to hedge his bets is a bit much, wouldn't you say?"

"You're probably right," laughed Semptor. "But he's not the only one hedging his bets. The endless variety of new wagering going on around the planet is mind-boggling. Aren't you disappointed that your efforts to curb gambling seem to be yielding so few results?"

"Yes and no. We're up against many obstacles. In a society with eighty per cent leisure time the people need their amusement. Actually, the only citizens who do any real work are baseball players. That's why, if Belteron wants some rest and relaxation, I say let him have it. No, I'm by no means discouraged. Our overall program will benefit Ball Four, slowly but surely. And we are getting results. A recent Robustness report from Public Health shows that the General Health Quotient has surged since the Season has been underway and is approaching record highs. A healthy society is a happy one, and less susceptible to decay. We are making progress, I assure you."

"I'm sure you're right. Well, here we are. I'd better get some work done. The never-ending reports. So, what about Belteron?"

"Who?" asked Tarn.

7

BROADCASTER:

Hello, everybody, welcome to the San Francisco Giants' pregame show. I'm Bud Cummings, and it's another gray day here at Candlestick Park. But there's nothing gray about the mood around here after the Giants' Kiley Upton posted the first right-handed victory of the year, as the Giants won last night, 4-3. We'll be back to chat with manager Lou Chambers about it in just a moment. But first these words from Hanover's Big, Tall, Small and All, with five Bay Area outlets to serve you...

Welcome back to Candlestick, everybody, we're visiting with Giants' manager Lou Chambers. Lou, I think it was John Houser of the Examiner who all but wrote off the Giants and their right-handed pitching staff in his column yesterday. But it didn't look like Kiley Upton bothered to read the paper.

LOU CHAMBERS:

Well, you know, Bud, these sportswriters have a job to do and unfortunately sometimes they're a little quick to call a season over, but Kiley's got a job to do too and that's to throw baseballs, and I think he did a hell of a job of it last night.

BROADCASTER:

The Phillies must have thought so too as Upton was in complete control except for the seventh inning, but he went on to complete the ballgame for his first win of the season.

LOU CHAMBERS:

Well, Bud, I think Kiley's finally found his rhythm, it's just a shame it took him five starts to do it, but baseball's not always kind and sometimes you just have to be patient. Baseball can be a bit mysterious that way, who knows where your pitching or hitting rhythm goes and then, boom, out of the blue it comes back to you. I'm sure that's what happened to Kiley and like I told him last night, welcome back...

On Saturday morning, an air of general merriment filled Candlestick Park. It was as if a cloud that had been hovering over the stadium had lifted and the sun had come out. This was, in fact, not actually the case, for the weather was chilly and the usual fog was so thick that the light standards could barely be seen from the field. But last night's win seemed to have awakened the sleeping Giants, and everywhere a palpable cheeriness was in evidence. The groundskeeping crew had a lighter bounce to its step, absenteeism among the concessions and security staff fell off dramatically, twice the number of players' wives were making plans to attend, and Lou Chambers sat in his office and read the paper instead of staring moodily at a blank lineup card. Everybody connected with the Giants, the 5-18 Giants, was milking this one.

Belteron was no exception. He had extra reason to feel good, for last night's victory was more than a mere win; it was the first glimmer of real hope he'd had since his arrival on Earth. He thought it rather poignantly appropriate that the first real impact he'd had on the civilization known as Earth was to help a ballplayer out of a slump. He had his projects selected for today and, because the Giants were leaving on an eight-game road trip the day after tomorrow, he felt a particular urgency.

He, Jimmy and Manny were running around, this way and that, doing little chores and assisting in general with the infield warm-ups and batting practice. As the Giants' turn in the batting cage got underway, it was obvious that last night had given them a lift. They stood around the cage joking and shoving each other, and as each in turn took their cuts they drove into the ball with a decided *whap!* that had been absent. Baseballs banged off fences, rattled in the bleachers and shot up the power alleys. All the while, Belteron kept his eye out for Eddie Renker.

Scrappy, pugnacious Eddie Renker, second baseman and lead-off hitter, he was going to be a tougher matter, Belteron felt, and might require a peculiar tactic.

Belteron decided to approach him away from the cage and the others, and it was a while before he could catch Renker in the right spot. Finally, Renker had brought some gear out onto the grass in front of the dugout and was applying pine tar to a couple of bats when Belteron came up.

"Hi, Eddie, how're you doing? Say, I was watching you in batting practice and you were really banging them pretty good."

"Thanks. Feels good today," Renker said without looking up from his work.

"So, tell me, Eddie, why do you think you're hitting .183?"

The hackles rose on the back of Eddie's neck. His chin jerked up and squared off as his eyes scanned Belteron up and down.

"Dirt farmer, eh? You got your damned nerve talking to me on game day...say, are you the guy who talked to Willie about his hitting? I heard about you."

"Yeah," Belteron nodded, as Renker dropped his gear and stood up. He was bristling.

"Well, maybe you did Willie some good, but I'll tell you one thing: there's not a damned thing wrong with my swing!"

"I have no quibble with any of that," Belteron said right back at him. "Damned fine swing. Solid."

"Then why you throwing my batting average in my face? It's hard enough with the season the way it's going, with the newspaper jockeys telling everybody to dump me as leadoff, and now a goddam groundskeeper ribs me."

"I don't mean to rib you. Look, Eddie, I watched you last night. What'd you do, an ohfer with two ground-outs, a pop-up and a strike out. Don't you see a pattern here?"

"I don't get what you're driving at," said Renker.

"You swung at the first pitch every at-bat, Eddie. And after everybody left last night I went into the clubhouse and looked through the old score sheets, Eddie, and you've been doing it almost every at-bat since the second week of the season. If a groundskeeper can notice it, you can bet the opposing pitchers have. They're suckering you, Eddie. First pitch they throw you every time is a drop pitch of some kind, right in your favorite spot. You go after it and nub it to first. Or they'll zing a rising fastball in the same place and you pop up to the catcher. You never allow yourself the opportunity to get your timing with a pitcher. They're on to you."

"I hadn't noticed," Renker admitted, "really hadn't noticed."

"Don't tell anybody this," Belteron said quietly, "but where in the hell is your hitting coach? This is his job. In a way, it's not your fault. You start off slow and you get over-anxious. Tell me, how were your bases-on-balls last year?"

"Number one on the team." Renker stroked his chin for a moment. "Yeah, and I've got what, three or four this year? I see what you mean."

"Of course you do. Those pitchers have got you measured. Measure 'em back. Take a few. You'll get your walks and, don't worry, you'll get your cuts. Oh, there's Manny. I'd better run. Sorry I bugged you. Good luck."

Renker stood there shaking his head as Belteron hustled off.

Manny sent Belteron over to help Jimmy finish up the mounds in the Giants' bullpen. They made short work of it because the pitchers, including today's starter, Julio Gonzalez, were just walking up.

"Hello, Julio, I'm Billy Icarus. I help Jimmy with these pitcher's mounds. How do they feel?"

Oh, just fine," said Gonzalez.

"You ready to smoke 'em today?" asked Belteron.

"I'll give it my best shot. I could use a win, I'll tell you that much."

"Oh, by the way, Julio, there's one thing I noticed about..."

"Hey Billy!" It was Manny over by the batting cage. "We gotta move this *now*! Help me out here."

"Good luck today, Julio," Belteron said over his shoulder. I hope I get another shot at it, he thought, as he trotted over to help Manny.

With one thing or another, he never did get around to Gonzalez before game time, and had to content himself with the start he made with Renker. It seemed to go over okay and Renker was the kind of guy who just might take his advice if only to prove him wrong. He could hope, but he had to wait until after the Phillies' at-bats to see. This was not fun either, because the Phillies jumped on Gonzalez early for two quick runs.

Eddie Renker stepped in to lead off the Giants' half of the first. The first pitch was a slider that tailed away and Renker watched it fall out of the strike zone for a ball. He swung and missed at a fastball. He fouled off the next pitch to go 1-2. Eventually he worked the count to 3-2. He was expecting fastball and the pitcher did not disappoint him, as he smashed a hard line drive up the power alley in left-center. Unfortunately, it was a little closer to left than center, and the Phillies' left fielder reacted quickly to glove it on a dive.

A good at-bat, Belteron thought, I only hope Renker thinks so too.

The Phillies homered in the second inning and Gonzalez then gave up a hit and a walk before settling down. It was just in time, because a couple of men had started to warm up in the bullpen. They sat down quickly when the Giants got a double play and Gonzalez finished it off with a strike out. It remained 3-0 Phillies through the third inning.

The Giants were still hitless when Renker came up to the plate in the bottom of the fourth. He took the first pitch for a called strike. As in his first at-bat he worked the count to 3-2, fouling off anything in the strike zone. Once again he was thinking the fastball and once again the pitcher offered one. This time the rising fastball sailed a bit too much and Renker held back and took ball four. He sprinted up to first.

Mickey Roberts sacrifice-bunted Renker to second, Rick Barker flew out to right and Willie Washington was walked intentionally to set up the force play. Right fielder Mitch Simpson came up to the plate and ripped a double down the first base line, cleaning the bases. First baseman Bob Butterfield popped up to end the inning, but the damage was done. And it had all started with a Renker walk.

The rest of the game the Phillies and Giants took turns beating up on each other. Both Washington and Barker got home runs and even catcher Ed Quigley got into the act with an RBI double, his first extra-base hit of the year. Gonzalez was rocked for four runs in the sixth and left-hander Steve Lafite was brought in to put the fire out. After giving up a two-run homer in the eighth, Lafite had to give way to Rick Santiago, who set down the last four Phillies in order for his first save of the year. When it was all over the Giants had put together an eighteen-hit attack and won it 11-9.

Eddie Renker went 2-for-3 with two walks, scored three times and never once glanced in Belteron's direction.

When the grounds crew finished up for the day, Jimmy and Belteron grabbed their gloves and started to work out. Burt, the testy crew chief, didn't seem to care as long as the work got done. He even came over to the bullpen to say goodbye and to joke with them, telling them not to forget to lock up and turn out the lights when they went home.

Belteron let Jimmy loosen up in his own way, throwing the whole gamut of pitches until the fastball began to pop. When Jimmy was fully warmed up, Belteron stood up and walked up to the mound.

"Jimmy, I know you think you got what it takes to pitch in the Majors. I want to tell you that I feel the same way. I also know that you understand it was your wildness that kept them from taking a better look at you at the Phoenix camp. But they were right. You do everything almost correctly, and an almost correct pitch is another name for home run. Where the coaches and scouts made their mistake was in thinking it wasn't worth the effort to help you past a few things. I think it's worth the effort and so do you. But we're going to get nowhere just playing catch. If you want something badly enough, only hard work will take you the rest of the way. Do you want it, Jimmy?"

Jimmy didn't answer right away. He toed the rubber on the pitcher's mound, folded his arms and looked at Belteron as though no one had ever asked the question. A certain distant gleam came to his eyes as he straightened his lean, six foot, six inch frame.

"Yes," he said simply.

"Okay, good. Now, where I come from we..."

"Billy," interrupted Jimmy, "just where *do* you come from? We've talked a lot about my life. I don't know anything about yours."

Belteron smiled. "It's a long story and I promise to tell you some day. Trust me. But we've got some serious work to do today and I'll tell you now it's going to take some trust and acceptance to accomplish what we're setting out to do. Can you do that?"

"Sure, Billy."

"Okay. Where I come from I was trained as a pitcher as well as a catcher. We used a system called visualization to hone our skills, to direct and control them. Now, each player needs to visualize what they're doing in a way that particularly suits them. Jimmy, you're an Indian and the culture and history of your people have shaped you and produced you as you are today. Your strength and wisdom are in your blood. I spent last Thursday at the library and I don't presume to know much about your Apache forebears. But I think I discovered enough to get us started, and the rest will be up to you to fill in the blanks with images from your Indian tradition, as you feel and see fit. You follow me so far?"

"I think so."

"Good. The most important visualization for a pitcher is the strike zone. It is your best friend but, if you don't know it very well, it becomes your worst enemy. To trust a friend you must get to know him very, very well, in order to rely on him. Jimmy, we're going to turn the strike zone into your friend."

Belteron ran back to home plate.

"Can you visualize the strike zone?"

Jimmy peered at the space over the plate. "Yes, I think so."

"It's here, here and here," Belteron said as he traced a shape in the air above home plate. "Now, close your eyes. Visualize that rectangle known as the strike zone in your mind. Frame it in bold strokes, in any color you like. Burn it into the retinae of your eyes until you can imagine that it will never fade, but be there for the rest of your days. Concentrate. Now, open your eyes. Can you see it?"

"Yes."

"Good. Okay, place that rectangle right where it belongs over the plate here, and throw a fast one right through the middle of it."

Jimmy wound up, reared back and blazed one exactly through the heart of the strike zone. He straightened up and stared in quiet amazement as Belteron strode slowly up to him and handed him the ball.

"Perfect, Jimmy. But that's the last time you're going to throw one like that."

"What? I threw it right where you said."

"I know. Even Ed Quigley could hit that one over the fence," said Belteron with a grin.

The light bulb went on over Jimmy's head as he slowly matched Belteron's grin. "I see what you mean."

"That's right. Not all of the strike zone is your friend, and down the middle is definitely your enemy. But the point is you can do it. You can visualize the zone and you can pitch with control. Begin to believe it."

"I am," said Jimmy. "What's next?"

"All right, keep this visualization of the strike zone wherever you go for a while. Everywhere you look, sixty feet, six inches away, this shape will be floating. Burn it into your eye sockets, dream about it at night. But this is not just your strike zone. It is your Medicine Wheel, Jimmy. It is the Medicine Wheel of your tribe, it is the Medicine Wheel of the Apache warrior."

Jimmy gazed sixty feet, six inches toward the bullpen home plate and a slow, broad smile crept to his lips. "Yes, I like it. Billy, how on earth could you know of this?"

"From books, only from books."

"But it is right for me," Jimmy said softly. "You knew that."

"It's more important that you know it. Now, keep looking at this strike zone, your Medicine Wheel. It is not enough for an Indian to know only the west, or only the east. To be a complete man, to have a complete soul, the Indian must know east, west, north and south. Let's spend the rest of the day traveling around your Medicine Wheel, to the land of the buffalo, and that of the eagle, the bear and the mouse. Shall we?"

"I'm ready if you are," Jimmy said with glistening eyes.

Jimmy Strongbow climbed the long steps up Telegraph Hill from the bus stop down below. Clinging to the east side of the hill were a jumble of homes with lush gardens, all linked by shaded, twisting walkways. The walkways had street signs, probably going back to the days before there were cars. Cars could never make it up the steep slope in any event, so the residents parked their cars down on the Embarcadero side where Jimmy was coming from, or on the other side toward the heart of North Beach. Either way they had to hike in. It was classic San Francisco.

Jimmy lived in a small mother-in-law cottage behind a large, two-storied, wood-framed house. Brad O'Nealy had found this set-up for him and Jimmy loved it. The occupants of the front house were wealthy jetsetters who rarely used it and, technically speaking, Jimmy was caretaker and gardener. The fact that he was a groundskeeper at Candlestick Park had cinched the deal for him and, during the negotiations, he and Brad had kept it to themselves that he knew about pitcher's mounds but not a damned thing about gardening. The garden was relatively small and Jimmy liked fooling around with it. There was nothing like it back in the arid spaces of San Carlos Reservation in Arizona. The garden shed behind his cottage had a small library of gardening books and he was sure he'd learn enough before he killed everything. Brad told him that since he was an Indian, he should just plant a fish under every bush. Jimmy was not amused.

He sat down in the shade of the cottage's wisteria arbor and thought about the day's events. Billy Icarus, who was this guy? Jimmy looked over at the main house and there, hovering about a foot off the ground, was his Medicine Wheel. He'd thrown two hundred pitches at it back at Candlestick with Billy. He'd thrown rising fastballs into the land of the buffalo to the north, inside sliders into the land of the eagle to the east, curveballs into the land of the bear to the west and forkballs into the land of the mouse to the south. As he threw and threw, the strike zone had slowly taken on the colors of the Medicine Wheel: in the west, black for introspection; to the north, white for wisdom; in the east, yellow for illumination; and to the south, green for innocence.

Jimmy was grateful to Billy for more than just the coaching. When Jimmy was young, taking up baseball was, in a way, a rejection of Indian ways. It was the white man's game. His room on the ranch had no Indian shields on it, it had pictures of Ty Cobb, Christy Mathewson, Pie Traynor, Walter Johnson, Cap Anson, Babe Ruth. In the drawers of his desk there were no arrowheads, there were boxes and boxes of baseball cards. Not that his family was all that immersed in Apache ways. Like most Apaches on the reservation, his family raised cattle and, under the practical guidance of his father and uncle, they'd built a successful ranch. Jimmy had never endured the hardships known to the Indians of the Navaho Nation and other reservations where clinging to the Indian traditions was sometimes the only way to cling to sanity. Still, he had chosen a white man's sport to pursue, and it had always inwardly gnawed at him that it was a treacherous act. But Billy Icarus had changed all that today.

He had showed Jimmy his Medicine Wheel, and the treachery was dispelled. Baseball would from now on draw from his Indianness, not spit in the face of it. Baseball was no longer the white man's sport, it was Jimmy Strongbow's, it was the Apache's, it was everyone's.

Jimmy went back to the gardening shed and grabbed a pair of pruning shears. He thought he'd have a go at the camellia bushes; they looked overgrown. He snipped away at them here and there, unsure of what he was doing. But the work had a pleasant, relaxing quality to it, and, slowly the bushes began to have a neater look.

He'd had a definite breakthrough as a pitcher today. Oh, he was still wild and during the workout with Billy he was still missing on a lot of his tosses. But as he threw he felt himself drawing on some inward source of strength and control, a source that, the more he drew from it, the more it would give. He could begin to visualize how he could gain control, whereas before he never really had a clue. He pitched from desire, not knowledge. As in many small towns in and out of the reservations, his high school coach had been the social studies teacher, whose main job was to keep the kids from getting hurt. Actually the coach had done a remarkable job with his almost non-existent baseball experience and, through dedication and encouragement, had guided Jimmy's team to the state finals two years in a row. They lost both times to Phoenix teams, but it had been an accomplishment nonetheless.

Jimmy would never forget those days: the long hours on buses to towns like Globe, Safford and Seneca, playing on fields that looked more like rattlesnake patches than baseball diamonds. His favorite game of the year, though, was the annual match against the Navahos. They'd get up before daylight and meet at the school for the long bus ride to Holbrook where they'd borrow a field from the local high school. A team from a school in the Navaho Nation in New Mexico would make an equally long trek to meet them. There they would play what was informally known as the "Indian World Series." It was really only eighteen kids knocking a ball around a dusty field full of holes, but for one day they felt like the center of the universe and they were playing the most important game in the world.

Jimmy stepped back and took a look at the camellia bushes. They look okay, he thought, but I'd better quit while I'm ahead. Apache warrior dangerous man with pruning shears.

He felt more at peace about his Apache heritage today, also a result of finding his Medicine Wheel. He'd always been proud of being an Apache but the long history of violence and hardship, though only history for him, still evoked a painful tribal memory. He was a Chiricahua Apache, the direct descendant of Mangas Coloradas, the powerful chief who fought at the side of Cochise. At six foot, six inches, Mangas Coloradas towered above his contemporaries. Because Jimmy matched the height exactly, his father regarded his son as the reincarnation of the famous warrior. Jimmy's great, great grandfather Mangus, son of Mangas Coloradas, had joined Geronimo and other chiefs when they led a band of Apaches off the reservation and into the last and bloodiest of the Indian Wars. Mangus had, like Geronimo, died in internment, but his son had been allowed to settle on San Carlos Reservation. There, with remnants of herds stolen by Geronimo in raids against the Mexicans, the tribe peacefully pursued cattle raising. Jimmy's father tended the descendants of that herd to this day.

The spirit of his ancestors, although violent, was a pure spirit, because they had only fought to preserve the land that had been their home. Jimmy could live with that spirit, and tap it as he had today for the first time in his life.

"Excuse me, you're Billy, right?"

Belteron was bringing out the bases to mount them in their sockets on the diamond when Rick Barker came up.

"Yeah, I'm Billy Icarus. What can I do for you?"

"Er, I'm Rick Barker, center field," he said, extending his hand. "Word's kinda gotten around that you seem to have a hobby of watching batting stances and stuff. Willie swears you helped him out and, well, I was just wondering if you had noticed anything about my swing. Something's wrong, because my numbers are way off so far this year."

Belteron thought for a brief moment. "Rick, I *have* been watching you and, frankly, you've got a good swing. It just might be the most natural swing on the team. I have noticed one thing, though. During batting practice you're smooth and natural, like a contact hitter. But in the game, you're swinging for the downs. Which are you, a contact hitter or a slugger? Tell me."

"Well, a bit of both, I guess," replied Barker.

"Ideally, yes. Lou's got you third in the line up and that's the spot for a contact hitter with power. But, Rick, you're no muscleman like Willie. Your home runs come from solid contact, not brute strength. Which would you rather be, a .260 hitter with forty home runs or a .320 hitter with twenty-five home runs?"

"That's easy, no contest," said Rick. "I'll take .320."

"And you should. No, there's nothing wrong with your swing. It's a beauty. Relax and be yourself. Your talent will take care of the rest."

"Thanks, I hope you're right."

"Me too," said Belteron. "Got to get these bases installed. Good luck today."

Brad O'Nealy made his fifth start of the year and, with the help of the hapless Philadelphia Phillies, easily turned it into his fifth victory. Prominent in the box score was Rick Barker's 4 for 4, as he sprayed four singles and scored each time he got on base. He was aboard when Willie Washington got his fourth homer of the year. The final score was 5-1. With the two previous games, that made it three wins in a row, a nice end to what had been a depressing home stand. The Giants were now looking forward to the road trip, in spite of the fact that they were going to be facing the Mets, Pirates and Cardinals.

Belteron was pleased about Rick Barker. It was gratifying that Barker had approached him, even more so that the results were so immediate. Barker had tipped his hat to Belteron as he scored his final run.

From the time that he and Jimmy had arrived for work through all the typical chores and routines of the day, Belteron had sensed a profound change in Jimmy. Of course, they had joked and done their work lightheartedly, and wisecracks flew back and forth as Jimmy helped O'Nealy warm up. But there was a new assuredness in Jimmy's eyes. Belteron was sensing a growing bond with the young man, not just that of player and coach but one of friendship, the friendship of teammates.

After work, Jimmy was ready. Belteron told him to get his strike zone in focus for a few minutes before attempting even the first warm-up toss. Then, as they warmed up, he introduced a new concept.

"Jimmy, It's obvious that you're getting that strike zone more firmly in place. Now, here's a little extension. From where you are on the mound, there are two lanes running from you directly through the plane of the strike zone. They're about a baseball and a half wide and they intersect the zone just a little inside and outside of the corners of the plate. Can you see them? Good. Add that visualization to your strike zone. Yes, it's good to close your eyes for a moment and merge the two images.

"Okay, with every pitch you throw you must see and feel that configuration. Don't consider yourself ready for a pitch unless it's focused and in place. Take your time. From now on you won't be aiming at home plate anymore, you'll be sending your throws down those lanes, high or low, in or out, depending on the signs. Oh, and one more thing. Don't try to throw down those lanes. Just accept the fact that the ball belongs there, that it is part of the nature of things. Let's throw a few."

They continued to warm up with various pitches at various speeds until the fastball began to pop.

"How do you feel?"

"Good," said Jimmy. His eyes were calm, intent.

"All right. Your pitches are gaining accuracy, slowly but surely. Still a little inconsistent, but better than yesterday and they'll be even better tomorrow, won't they?"

"Yeah, they will."

"Yes, they will," said Belteron. "To help it along, we could use more visualization. Let's start with your fastball. Jimmy, look into your Indian heritage. What would be a good symbol for your fastball?"

Jimmy paused and contemplated. He sifted through the myriad images of Apache life and lore, and sights and sounds of the past started to come alive in his mind. Then all of a sudden, it came to him. "Of course, it's obvious. The arrow."

Belteron smiled. " The arrow, the bow and arrow, that's excellent. Have you ever used them?"

"Oh, sure. It's the only other sport I did in school. I was captain of the archery team. And my father and I used to go hunting together. I never used a gun, only the bow and arrow. What about you, are you good with a bow and arrow?"

"No, I'm afraid not," Belteron said, smiling inwardly. "Wasn't very popular back home. But books, I've seen them in books about the Indian. Anyway, the arrow will be the symbol of your fastball. From now on, you'll *think* fastball but *feel* arrow. Every time. Got it?"

"Yeah."

"All right, then loose a few of them at me."

Jimmy reared back, time and again, and threw fastball after fastball, arrow after arrow, up and down the trails to his Medicine Wheel. They zipped straight and true, felling the cougar, the bruin, the deer and the hare.

They went on in this fashion for some time until, finally, Belteron stood up.

"Okay, let's stop for a minute. How's the arm?"

"Great," said Jimmy.

"Good. That's another thing you've got going for you, Jimmy, fluidity of motion. It's a good healthy motion which naturally protects your arm. If at any time, you feel the slightest strain I want you to tell me."

"Oh, sure. No, I feel great." Which was true.

Belteron trotted up.

"Good. Your fastball is looking fantastic. Your control is growing in spite of the fact that your fastball, if anything, is becoming faster."

"I can't believe it, Billy. I've been wild since I can remember."

"Believe it, Jimmy," said Belteron. "You always had the consistent motion, you just lacked a focus. Now you've got it. Look, now would be a good time to work on the change-up. Could you show me your grip?"

Jimmy wrapped three fingers around the ball and pulled it back tightly in his palm.

"Oh, three-fingered grip, huh? Well, try this. Keep the three fingers but pull the index finger down almost off the ball. And shoved back in the palm is perfect. Remember to release it from the knuckles instead of the fingertips. Now, the change-up has to look like your fastball. So choose the symbol of your change-up with that in mind."

Jimmy thought briefly and came right back with a quick answer. "This one's easy. There's a technique in hunting my father taught me called the slack-bow shot. When you're stalking game up close, you slack the string on your bow. That way, if you miss, you don't spend all day looking for the arrow and, if you hit, you sink the arrow just right. It's accurate at short distances only, though."

"Sounds perfect. Let's give it a try. Remember, same motion, different result. And keep the image, the symbol in your mind with every throw."

Jimmy reared back as before, throwing his leg high in the air and his arm blazed toward the plate. The ball that the motion produced, however, was noticeably slower. He liked the effect, and when it hit Belteron's glove he felt as though he had just shot a quail at twenty paces.

After a while, Belteron signaled for them to stop. "I think we should end this workout with one last exercise, Jimmy. Let's alternate the fastball with the change, every other throw. And one more thing. Vary your grips and pressure points. Across the seams, with the seams, off your index finger, and then your middle finger, that sort of thing. Don't be afraid to experiment. And finally, watch the resulting movement on the ball. Get to know the effect each grip produces. Okay?"

Jimmy nodded and went back to work.

Lou Chambers walked into the vast press box that crowned the west side of Candlestick Park. He was looking for John Houser. He wanted to give him a hard time.

Lou had been having a drink with some reporters and friends up at the Stadium Club, enjoying the mood stemming from the winning streak, such as it was. When it came time to leave, he'd gotten the idea of ribbing Houser and had hoped he might still be at work at his desk in the press box. But he must have gone home.

Jeez, I've never been in here when it's empty, Chambers thought as he descended the tiers of desks with their telephones and telecommunications gear. There was a bit of an eerie quality to it, as if the place were unnaturally quiet. I should enjoy it, he joked to himself, the usual mob in here has been saying some pretty bad things about my team.

When he reached the bottom row he stopped and scanned the stadium through the huge panes of glass. He eyes came to rest on the Giants' bullpen. What the hell is that down there?

Strongbow and that other fella, he thought, the new guy that's been talking to my hitters.

Chambers groped around inside the ledge under the front counter and came up with a pair of binoculars. He watched as Strongbow threw pitch after pitch to what's-his-name, Billy. Fastball, change, fastball, change, each had a different speed and movement but all were, more often than not, clipping the corners of the plate.

This is not the Jimmy Strongbow I saw in Arizona. And that Billy hasn't dropped a pitch. This is the weirdest deal I've ever seen.

He sat down and watched throw after throw, until they finally stopped and made the slow, long walk out the center field gate.

8

THE PLAIN DEALER
May 3rd.

Lloyd Cronin

WHO ARE THESE GUYS, ANYWAY?

I'm enjoying the baseball season so far, and I'm sure every fan in Cleveland is as well. I'm also sure that my readers have enjoyed watching me eat my little dish of crow almost as much as they've enjoyed watching the Indians beat up on the American League. As a reporter I'm still waiting for the balloon to burst, but from the point of view of a fan I hope the Tribe never loses another game. Really, I do.

But it's as a reporter that I have to view sports in general and the Indians in particular. And, as a reporter, something has been bothering me which I just can't shake. Ordinarily, I'd just let it go and talk baseball and strategy, who to trade, who to have lead off; you know, basically just do my job, which, naturally, is to tell Jake Conrad how to run his team.

But the question I just can't get off my mind is: who _are_ these guys? Where did they come from? Are they for _real_? It was one thing when they were losing, sure, we're going to see trades and rebuilding and what-not. But now that this bunch of no-names, rookies and Class A ballplayers from the sticks are 19-4, for heaven's sake, I think we all want to know who they are. I've talked to just about all of the team and coaches and, frankly, I haven't got to first base.

Case in point: Warren Evans. Okay, his pitching staff shows that Abe Watkins must have known something I didn't when he hired Evans, and Jake Conrad must have too when he told Evans to start calling the pitches. It's all well and good. So now we all want to know where and why and how Warren Evans learned to be a winner. I've talked to him, to Jake Conrad and to Abe Watkins, and the best I've been able to figure out is that Evans must have been the high school baseball coach in *The Last Picture Show*. For a reporter it's just not good enough.

As for the team, it's no different. Who are these guys? Okay, this isn't the first time a brilliant general manager has turned a team around in a season or two. I won't bore you with the litany from the baseball almanacs. But these players defy belief. They don't play like rookies, they don't act like rookies and they sure as hell don't talk like them. You should visit their dressing room after they pound a team like Detroit. It feels more like a morticians' convention than a bunch of towel-snapping "just happy to be in the majors, yuk yuk" phenoms with their first chaw of tobacco in their cheeks. When this reporter asks any one of them "Where did you come from?" the answer is inevitably "Oh, you wouldn't ever have heard of my little ole bohunk town..." before they vanish into the showers. I might as well be talking to Warren Evans.

Come on guys, and don't say it's sour grapes or an upset stomach because of the crow I've been eating. The fans want to know. With all this mystery, you seem more like the Cleveland Aliens than the Cleveland Indians. You're our hometown

team. We care about you, we want to get to
know you.

I'm a reporter, I know because I
found a press pass in my trousers, and, like
Arnold Schwarzenegger says, I'll be back.

Lloyd Cronin leaned back in his chair and nodded approvingly at the computer screen in front of him. From inside his cubicle on the fourth floor of the Cleveland Plain Dealer Building could be heard all the hustle and bustle of a newspaper in the making, but Cronin wasn't listening. He was all concentration as he proofread his column for tomorrow's paper, smiled with satisfaction and pushed the "send" button on his terminal.

This one ought to do it, he thought. After they read this, they'll be falling all over themselves to talk to me. This time they'll come to me.

Cronin was pleased with the column. The Cleveland "Aliens" was a nice touch. He meant no insult, it was just a way to shake them up a bit, get them to come out of their shell. Sure, they were probably just so into playing baseball and winning that they weren't paying attention to the needs of the fans and the press. But they couldn't ignore this. They can't be that thick-skinned. Throughout his career as a reporter and columnist, he had seen a lot of athletes who wouldn't talk to the press. When he was young, it was a singular pleasure of his to catch that eccentric star halfback as he tried to slip out of the dressing room unnoticed. More recently he had settled into lazy ways and let the story come to him instead of going to the story. That was the beauty of being a columnist. One could sagaciously commentate from the easy chair, and leave the reporting to the cubs. But not this time, and it made him feel young again.

Not that this was that big a deal. It was fun for fans and the press alike to follow a winner, but it grew boring rather quickly. How many different ways could one find to say "Gee, these guys are great" before readers begin to snore? Controversy sells papers and the Indians hadn't left much room for it. That ugly incident when Bertie Thompson had tried to punch out Jimmy Fernandez for taking his job was good juice for the reporters but it hadn't been worth a column. After Bertie served his suspension he just quietly retired and hadn't been heard from since. Life with the Indians had grown too dull.

I'm going to have some fun with this angle, Cronin thought smugly, and I'm not going to let up even if I have to play cub reporter and hot-foot it out to those "bohunk towns" and nose around for myself.

"So, Jake, Sanchez has lost his first game. Do you think some of the magic's begun to fade?"

Jake Conrad, Warren Evans and about a half a dozen reporters were sitting around the media room in the Indians' clubhouse after the game. Boston had beaten them in a tight one, 3-2. As if it weren't obvious, reporters wanted to know why.

"Well, Earl," Conrad replied, "Warren's the pitching coach. He should probably answer that one."

Evans pretended to mull it over before responding. He knew exactly why the team had lost. He had forbidden mind reading for the contest, and Boston had prevailed.

"No, I don't think it's a matter of magic. Emilio Sanchez pitched a beauty of a game for a rookie in his second start. He's obviously got a bright future ahead of him, and it's going to be even brighter after he learns not to groove a fastball to Biff Redman in a 2-2 tie."

That produced a chorus of chuckles from the assemblage. Conspicuously absent from the group was Lloyd Cronin. Someone else spoke up.

"Warren, Bob Hinkley, Cleveland Plain Dealer. I met you at the press breakfast."

"I remember," said Evans, "how're you doing?"

"Fine. Anyway, Lloyd Cronin really took a poke at you in his column today. I presume you read it or heard about it. Any reaction?"

"Yeah, frankly, it cracked me up," responded Evans with a laugh. "Lloyd's got a good sense of humor but, you know, he answered his own question when he said we're more interested in winning ballgames than talking about our own past glories. Maybe we've been too intent and not forthcoming enough. That'll change, and maybe Cronin's done us a favor by lighting a fire under our butts."

Another round of chuckles came from the group, and Jake Conrad visibly relaxed.

"Cronin loves a good fight, always has," said Conrad. "What would we ever do without him, huh? Anyway, that about wraps it up, don't you think so, boys? Warren and I had better go and figure out how to end this one-game losing streak. See you all later."

That seemed good enough for all concerned and the reporters grabbed their notes and headed for the door.

Evans knew well enough to follow Jake Conrad into his office. If Jake didn't want to talk about Sanchez he was sure to have something to say about Cronin.

"Listen, Warren, I'm not going to blame you for this Cronin deal, but the other day I said we've got to start opening up. Whatever you said to Lloyd didn't seem to satisfy him much. This kind of small aggravation can disrupt a ball club. And we're on too good a roll right now."

"Jake, I don't blame you for feeling sore," Evans said. "I've already begun to tackle it. Since you asked me to help out and I let you down, I'm going to personally take charge of the situation and deal with it. I've set up a meeting with Abe Watkins, who should be here in a little while. You just go ahead and take care of the business of managing this team and I'll figure out a way to get Cronin off our backs so we can play baseball. Okay?"

"That'll be a relief," said Conrad. "Frankly, never cared for the man,

Cronin. He's been a pain in the ass to me since my playing days. So, thanks, I know you'll handle it. See you at the Club in a while?"

"Oh, sure, Jake."

Abe Watkins was waiting for Evans when he got back to his office. Watkins' look was one of deep concern.

"Hello, Evan. Have you been talking to the press?"

"Yes," replied Evans. "I've successfully put them off for now. But the situation is dire. We have to formulate a plan for true action, the stalling techniques have failed us. Has Command had anything to say about it?"

"As a matter of fact they have. I spoke to Operation Command up at the orbital station right after I read Cronin's article. Cronin's use of the word "Aliens" has them deeply disturbed. They immediately realized your warnings should have been listened to more carefully, and they were quick to offer blanket authorization to us for action. We're of course to keep them abreast of developments, but they promise to supply support personnel as we deem fit."

"Good. Abakin, I was afraid that events might proceed this way. Ball Fourians avoid controversy but Earthlings thrive on it. It's a prime concern of the press to instigate it. With all the planning that's gone into the Operation, it's a wonder we didn't plan for this as well. But it's hard to foresee every eventuality. However, even if it's not my place, I've been in the center of this little tempest since it began and I've devised a scheme that has a reasonable chance for success."

"I'll be glad to hear it," said Watkins.

"First of all, I wouldn't be too concerned about Cronin's choice of the word 'Aliens.' I'm sure he's not the slightest bit aware of the Operation. It was merely an inadvertent choice in order to agitate us and get our attention, which he most certainly did. Anyway, we can assume, at least for now that we can limit this kind of press interference to the Cleveland area. Other cities in the league are not so interested in the personal lives of other teams' players. So, if we can defuse the immediate situation, we can put this matter to rest. We'll need a mind-disruption team of about six, and I presume we've got that number Earthside already. The sooner we get started the better."

The call Lloyd Cronin was waiting for had come. It had been Evans himself and, if Cronin would come down to Municipal Stadium as soon as possible, he would be only too happy to oblige Cronin on the matter. Details would be forthcoming and Abe Watkins would be present.

What a coup! It was just as he thought it would be, they had come to him. His follow-up column would be juicy indeed, and it should give him a nice bit of prestige. The public respects a man who gets results when he throws his weight around.

He wheeled his car into the stadium parking lot and pulled right up in front of the press gate. There was no need to park in a spot, the place was empty. He jumped out and walked briskly through the untended gate. They would be waiting for him in the media room. This was going to be fun.

Sure enough, there was Abe Watkins, Warren Evans and a couple of other fellows Cronin wasn't familiar with. They stood up as he walked in and took a seat.

"Good evening, Lloyd, you've met Abe Watkins, haven't you?"

"Of course, it's good to see you again, Abe," Cronin said, shaking hands. "I was pleased to hear you'd be here."

"I wouldn't miss it for the world," Watkins said, all smiles. "Warren's in charge of this meeting. I'm only here to help in any way I can."

"And I'd like to get right down to it. Lloyd, you really stuck it to us in that article of yours."

Cronin tried not to appear too smug, but failed.

"Actually, Lloyd, we got a kick out of it. But we do realize that we've been holding back a bit too much and we'd like to make it up to you personally by letting you get the scoop on the whole background of the team."

That was just the music to his ears he'd been hoping for. But alongside the satisfaction he had expected there was a vague unsettling feeling as well. He couldn't quite put his finger on it. It was all a little confusing, he was feeling a small amount of, well, *dread*. It disturbed him. He should be feeling elated.

The sensation of dread grew. He looked up at Evans, who was smiling, gesturing and talking away; but he couldn't seem to make out the words. He looked over at Abe Watkins who was listening with a pleasant, approving smile, occasionally punctuating Evans' speech with a comment or a laugh, but Cronin couldn't make out what Watkins was saying either. Then he glanced up at the two men who stood bracketing Watkins and Evans. They had their arms folded and they were standing there with calm, almost beatific expressions on their faces. Cronin's apprehension grew more intense. The room was starting to spin. Watkins and Evans were laughing at some comment or other, but Cronin couldn't seem to hear anything. All he could hear was a high-pitched squeal. He couldn't actually hear it, it was more like it was inside his head, increasing in intensity. He was quite dizzy. He began to feel something like terror. No, it *was* terror, absolute terror.

"And so, Lloyd, we'll be telling the whole team that it's your scoop and to put off the other media people until your piece comes out. What do you think?"

"What?" Cronin could barely breathe. He had a sense that some time had elapsed, but didn't know how much.

"I said, you'll have the whole scoop and the team will talk only to you. Now, what would be a good time to get started? You know we go on the road in a couple of days."

Cronin could hear again, and the dread was beginning to subside. "Ah, ah, tomorrow? How's that?"

"Perfect," said Watkins. "After the game we'll be expecting you. Well,

Warren, that just about wraps it up. Lloyd, we want to thank you for coming down on such short notice. We're baseball men and sometimes we need a bit of prodding. I guess that's what reporters are for, to keep you honest, eh?"

Cronin was a touch wobbly as he made it out to his car. He had a splitting headache and, in spite of the fact that he was unsure whether or not he could or should drive, he just couldn't wait to get away. By the time he had reached the Shoreway he was feeling a bit better.

As he drove through Edgewater State Park and on along toward Lakewood, his disposition slowly improved. He felt quite able to drive by then and was considering taking a long drive by Lake Erie when it occurred to him that a drink might serve him better. He turned off Clifton Boulevard toward his apartment but pulled over a couple of blocks early and parked in front of Gig's Lakewood Lounge, his favorite watering hole.

"What the devil went on back there?" he muttered to himself as he hurried to the door of the bar. Inside he was greeted by the congregation with the usual warmth and interest accorded him due to his status as a local celebrity. He had penned more than one column sitting in a booth at Gig's.

"Lookin' kinda pale there, old pal," said Henry the bartender, with casual concern. "Need a bracer?"

"Scotch rocks, Henry, better make it a double," Cronin said, grabbing a stool.

Alternately sipping and swizzling his drink, he could feel his old self return. It was good to be among friends. I can't for the life of me imagine what got into me back at the Stadium, he thought, nothing like it has ever happened to me before. I sure hope Evans and Watkins didn't notice. They hadn't seemed to, they were all smiles.

He was working on a second double when a couple of ladies wandered in and sat down next to him at the bar. He hadn't seen them before. They must be new or out-of-towners or something. He was feeling jovial from the booze and relieved to be feeling better, and he was considering whether or not to engage them in conversation when a surge of dread and anxiety hit him again. He fumbled with his drink and drained it in a couple of swift gulps, and looked around uncertain as to what to do. The ladies he'd been eyeing just sat there silently, smiling at him, and apparently unaware of his panic. He tried to shake it but couldn't, as the splitting headache began to return along with the screech in his head. He was vainly trying to figure out what to do when the world started to go black.

When he came to, Henry was standing over him saying something he couldn't make out and another customer he was friendly with named Charlie was offering him a hand up. The two of them helped him over to a booth and, as he sat down, he looked around the bar trying to get a fix on what was happening. Sights and sounds came to him in snatches; he felt as though he were underwater. The neon liquor signs in the bar were waving like flags in the wind and the music of the jukebox seemed to emanate from down the block. The two ladies at the bar were no longer looking at him but wore the same placid smiles. The smiles felt like darts in his eyes and terror flooded his being.

"Lloyd, Lloyd, this is *not* good, do you want us to get a doctor or something?" asked a much less casual Henry.

"What?" said Cronin as his environment gained a more normal shape with a startling rapidity. "A doctor, heavens no, no, I'll be all right...I'm sorry, Henry, I don't know what came over me. I'll be fine, just get me one more of the same."

"Are you sure, Lloyd? Are you driving tonight?"

"Yes, but I'll walk home, believe me, I promise, just get me that drink, I sure as hell could use one right now."

"Okay, pal, you just relax here and I'll bring it over."

A couple of drinks later Cronin was beginning to get looped but the terror was gone, and he could focus on things a little more clearly. With a terrible start, he took a look at his watch. Oh my god, my column, he thought with a shock. It completely slipped my mind. It's deadline in five minutes and I can't write in this state. He shoveled a couple of coins out of his pocket and went over to the pay phone.

"Hey, Louie. Yeah, it's Lloyd. Say, I feel like I got the flu or something. I can't concentrate worth a damn. I'm sorry but I've got nothing for you tonight."

There was silence on the line for a moment. Finally Louie spoke. "Hey, don't worry about it. I know what we can do. I'll just put Hinkley's piece in your spot and run a wire service jobber to cover Hinkley's. Just get some rest, for chrissake, you sound terrible. You got a fever?"

Instinctively Cronin felt his forehead. It was cold and clammy. "Yeah, I feel like crap. Look, I'm going home, but I got a big story brewing for tomorrow. Stay tuned. Sorry about tonight. I'll see you tomorrow, Okay?"

Cronin tossed a tip on his table, emptied his glass and turned to go. As he passed the bar he vaguely noticed that the two smiling ladies were gone.

"Ultimately, it's your decision, Jake. Go ahead and platoon Hunk and Denny at designated hitter. Whoever's not DH is in left. It'll be good for both of them to keep their fielding skills up. It's a fundamentally sound idea, but I'm surprised you're talking to me about this."

"You shouldn't be, Warren," Conrad said. "You've become more than a pitching coach to me. I respect your total knowledge of the game. Last few years I relied a lot on Hal Walker, he's got a good baseball mind. But for some reason you seem to know these players better, and I'll be relying on your judgment in a lot of matters. Oh, by the way, how's that Cronin deal coming along?"

"Just fine," Evans replied. "Abe and I met with him last night. We don't think he'll be a problem, and I'm meeting with another reporter this morning. As a matter of fact, he might even be here now. I'd better go check the media room. Don't worry, Jake, I told you I'd handle it. The press will be happy with us after today."

"That's a relief. See, I do rely on you for a number of things. We'll see you. Give 'em hell."

Bob Hinkley was in fact waiting in the media room when Evans got there. "You wanted to see me?"

"Yeah, thanks for coming," said Evans, taking a seat. "As you know, we're concerned that not enough information about the players' personal history has been made available, so we're making a special effort to open up. All the players have agreed to be a bit more gabby, and they'll be available to you anytime in the next two days before we hit the road. They'll be glad to talk to you before and after the games, and during warm-ups as duties allow. And I thought we might start with me."

"Wait a minute, Warren. Cronin developed this angle with his column. Why are you talking to me and not him?"

"The Cleveland Indians are everybody's business, Bob. You're a reporter. Are you turning down a news story?"

Hinkley considered for a brief moment. "I'm all ears, Warren."

Lloyd Cronin strolled down a quiet path by the river. He'd been in Fairview Park since about eight o'clock and the couple hours of walking in the morning sun had done him a world of good. I haven't been here in years, he reflected, even though my apartment is only a few blocks away. That's what work does to you. You get wrapped up in it and forget to stop and smell the roses. That's probably what's happening to me. Stress from too much work. Not anymore. I'm going to relax. I may be dumb but I'm not stupid.

It was perfect baseball weather and he would have plenty of time to get to the park. The story would be waiting for him, assuming what Watkins and Evans had told him was true. He had no reason to think otherwise. He was looking forward to getting to know the players better and thought there was probably a week's worth of columns in it, possibly two. That suited him just fine, he'd be getting a scoop and a chance to relax at the same time. Maybe he could start writing in the park instead of at Gig's. It would be much healthier.

There were quite a few people in the park with the same idea as his, to stroll and relax, and as he walked he enjoyed seeing their smiling, happy faces. Parents were playing with their kids, young lovers were sitting on the lawns; all in all, they seemed more pleasant than the jaded bastards down at the paper.

A nice young couple in white tennis shorts and sweaters came abreast of him on the path. They were walking a pair of golden retrievers on leashes and, as the three of them strolled side by side, Cronin looked over and smiled. They smiled back. Nice couple, he thought.

Like a bolt out of the pleasant, blue sky, the dread and horror of last night poured over him. He made an effort to continue his pace, hoping it would just *go away*, but his head began to squeal sickeningly and the sun that had been so soothing was now nauseating to him. The blood pounded in his temples as beads of sweat formed on his forehead.

His head began to throb mercilessly. His knees grew weak as he contemplated running, in which direction he couldn't decide. He realized that he was no longer moving at all and, as he looked around, he had trouble focusing on his surroundings. He tried to gain his bearings by looking over at the couple with the dogs, who had apparently stopped and were now kneeling down and stroking their pets. One golden retriever had put his front paws on the young woman's shoulders and was licking her face. The pink tongue appeared huge and terrifying. Cronin turned sharply away and suddenly found the idea of being in a large open space thoroughly horrifying. Everything took on a one-dimensional quality and he felt as though he were being squeezed and twisted. The sweet odors of grass were now putrid and he wanted to vomit.

In pure terror he summoned his last ounce of will and broke into a run. In his weakened state the run quickly dissolved into a trot, then a walk and finally a stagger. No matter, he would move or die.

He didn't die, and after some indeterminable amount of time he was at his apartment door. With difficulty he got his keys out, unlocked the door and entered. He slammed the door shut and, one by one, turned every bolt.

9

It was a travel day for the San Francisco Giants, and a day off for the grounds crew. The crew would be working shorter hours most of the next week and Jimmy and Belteron would be able to train at Candlestick unencumbered by games and team workouts. But today they had to seek other accommodations. Both were new to the city, but a few inquiries quickly revealed the existence of a number of diamonds in the western reaches of Golden Gate Park.

It was unlikely they would find any rivals for the space on a Monday morning, and indeed the diamonds were empty. The baseball area of the park was near Ocean Beach and it was overcast, chilly and damp. Belteron took care to advise Jimmy to warm up slowly and completely. Because of Jimmy's naturally fluid motion there was little chance of his hurting himself, but Belteron wanted to engrain in him the habit of proper warm-up procedure on cold days. Actually, being from Ball Four, Belteron knew next to nothing about weather-related injury. WeatherCon maintained perfect athletic conditions. But luck-ily he had overheard the Giants' pitching coach Ron McIlhenny scolding some of the staff for sloppy procedures last Saturday and Belteron, always a quick study, had absorbed the implications. It would be tragic for Jimmy Strongbow to develop into a fine hurler only to injure himself because of Belteron's igno-rance of climate. Fortunately, that wasn't going to happen.

"Okay, coach, I'm good and loose. What are we working on today?"

Belteron jogged up to the mound. "Jimmy, yesterday we made great strides with your fastball, and the change-up looked good. It's time to move on to some other pitches. You've got a good repertoire of them, but how you learned without any coaching is a mystery to me."

"Oh, that's no mystery," answered Jimmy. "During Christmas vacation when I was a junior in high school I talked my dad into letting me go to a Tom Seaver pitching camp in Phoenix. It was great. If it hadn't been for that camp I'd probably be riding herd on the reservation right now."

"It must have been quite a valuable experience for you. From what I've seen, you've got the basics of most every pitch you'll ever need. I've noticed some problems, though, and we'll try to iron them out. Before we get started there's one thing to keep in mind.

"There's a very simple secret to successful pitching and every pitcher who's ever been in the big leagues knows it: you throw the fastball to set up the other pitches. The fastball is your money pitch and you'll throw it sixty, maybe seventy per cent of the time. You might have the greatest curve in the game, or the meanest slider, but if you can't get them out with your fastball your career will be awfully short. A few pitchers have defied this rule, but they are few and far between and, if they'd had a good fastball in the first place, they wouldn't have had to spend so much time and energy coming up with the junk they needed to survive.

"You've got the good fastball and that's why we focused on it first. Never forget that ninety out of a hundred times the fastball will be your get-'em-out pitch. Keeping that in mind, let's work on the pitches that will make them choke and pull their hair out the *other* ten times. Let's start with the curve.

"Now your curve is already good. With a little visualization we'll make it better. What can you think of in Apache life that would symbolize the curve?"

Jimmy was stumped by this one. Try as he might, nothing came to mind.

"That's okay," said Belteron, "just start throwing before your arm gets cold again. Throw nothing but curveballs and something will come."

Jimmy threw a steady string of curveballs and let his mind loose in the Apache wilds of Arizona and New Mexico. He visualized the painted deserts, canyons and arroyos, and he viewed the buttes, mesas and chimney rocks of that rugged land. He walked the Gila Mountains and the great Sierra Madre of Mexico, and he filled his mind with images of rocks and dust and yellowjack pine. In his imaginary wanderings he looked down at his moccasin-clad feet and saw that from the thongs of his moccasins hung snake rattles. He looked up and, on a nearby rock, a sidewinder lay baking in the sun. He feared no snake bite, his moccasins had good medicine.

"Jimmy, what were you thinking just then?"

"What was I thinking?" asked Jimmy, returning from distant lands.

"Yeah, just then your curve broke three feet, maybe more."

"Well, I...I know, I was thinking about snakes. Would that be it?"

"It appears so. The snake, huh? If that's what you were visualizing during the last throw, it had a profound influence," Belteron said, trying to remember his Earth biology studies. "Let's try a few with that image in mind."

The ball didn't break three feet again on the next throw, or the next. But slowly, toss by toss, the arc widened and deepened until a ball aimed at the batter's head would catch the lower right-hand corner.

Jimmy stopped for a moment, put his hands on his hips and whistled soft and low.

Belteron imitated the pose. "What's the matter? You quitting?"

"Oh, no, not now," replied Jimmy. "Not on your life."

"Okay. But the curveball's hard on your elbow. We should start mixing up the pitches. If you feel a twinge let me know. With each different pitch keep the visualization distinct, but each must flow naturally from your inner vision. Remember? Think curve, feel snake."

It was an eventful week and a half. Jimmy and Belteron continued their daily workouts, and both were encouraged by the steady progress. Jimmy bought a car and together they began to explore the San Francisco Bay Area. It was a new and fascinating place for them (more so for Belteron) and together they roamed, from the streets of the City to the back roads of the coastal mountain range. Being from Arizona, Jimmy was drawn to the sea, and took delight in exploring the beaches and coves of the Pacific. Belteron had been raised on the coast in Seaview and he was endlessly fascinated by the similarities between the two worlds. But what captivated him most of all were the different varieties of cuisine that he could sample. Chinese, French, Greek and Italian, they were all so delicious. He had a substantial amount of money left of the supply he had obtained from the orbital station stores, and Jimmy had to ask him to slow down before he went broke. Belteron sheepishly apologized and treated him to dinner at a Thai restaurant, which only caused Jimmy to wonder all the more about this uncommon new friend.

Belteron was rapidly catching on to the lifestyles and social values in human society, but another inadvertent circumstance nearly caught him off-guard. At the end of a long day of working out, exploring and eating, Jimmy had offered Belteron a ride home. Although he was still staying at the Hotel Meredith downtown, he had come to understand that such an address was considered highly extravagant. He had intended to move but had been too busy with Jimmy's training to accomplish it yet. He didn't want to add to Jimmy's suspicions and averted the close call by claiming that he was looking forward to the exhilaration of walking home. As an athlete, Jimmy could accept the rationale. The next day, Belteron decided, he must find more modest accommodations.

The San Francisco Giants were not having as good a time of it. They were swept by the Mets, lost two out of three in Pittsburgh and split the pair with the Cardinals. Brad O'Nealy had lost his first game of the season and Kiley Upton survived a drubbing at the hands of the Pirates to go 1-1 for the trip. French and Gonzalez had been pounded. The only cause for optimism was the Giants' hitting, which had really caught fire. But the pitchers couldn't hold on to the leads the hitters gave them. The confident mood in which they had departed soon vanished and, in the end, they would limp back to town with a 2-6 record to show for their efforts on the road.

The reports of the continuing decline concerned Belteron and heightened the sense of urgency, but the progress with Jimmy more than offset the overall situation. And the timing of the road trip, disastrous or not, was fortuitous in that it gave Belteron a chance to do valuable research. When he wasn't at work at Candlestick or training with Jimmy, he spent every possible hour at the public library. It was tedious work compared with information systems on Ball Four but, if he combed deeply enough through the endless stacks of books, there was seemingly nothing he could not eventually find. In spite of the years of Operation studies before his deselection, he was constantly confronted with problems of language, social integration and the like. It wasn't that he had missed a lot of training after deselection. He had been trained to be a plausible athletic character in Earthling life, and the Operations support team would have been there to guide him through the infiltration and integration phases. He was not only deprived of that assistance but his set of problems and challenges were quite different, and he was on his own to resolve them.

Every day new gaps in his knowledge of Earth threatened to derail him, and he was constantly feigning understanding of what was no doubt common knowledge among humans. His natural craftiness aided him as he improvised and slithered his way through some tight spots. For instance, Jimmy's reference to snakes caught him off-guard. He had studied basic Earth sciences but he could only conjure up a vague and unsubstantial image to support his understanding of what snakes might mean to Jimmy. Although there were striking similarities among the animal life of each of their worlds, somehow snakes had never evolved on Ball Four. The library provided the answers and, after a couple hours, Belteron was prepared to talk snakes with the best of them.

Belteron knew how to play baseball. He had been trained since birth to play it. But the hows and whys of it on Earth were amazingly different. The moves were the same on both planets but the motivation for each move was often dissimilar, and had a great effect on the psychology and language of the game. At the library he had found a baseball lingo dictionary and the various terms used in Earthling baseball were intrinsically tied to their psychological underpinnings. The concept of a "money pitch" was unintelligible to a Ball Fourian whose motivation was never linked to money. And the idea of a pitcher intentionally hitting a batter, or violently arguing a call with an umpire, was inconceivable. The Operation Universe Series experts had discounted the need for deep understanding of these divergences, but Belteron's position was substantially unique among the Ball Fourians on Earth. It required hours and hours of research just to be an effective coach for Jimmy, and hours more to learn to move around in human society without receiving questioning looks. His progress had been rapid and he couldn't help but think he was becoming both a better person and ballplayer because of it.

The largest question of all was posing the greatest difficulty and necessitating the deepest study. How was he going to offset the mental advantage of the Ball Fourian ballplayer? The answer lay in the relative physiologies of the two species and, though Belteron was no member of the science caste, he had no choice but to find a way to offset this crucial difference. Day after day he leafed through volumes on the subjects of anatomy, neurology and human intelligence. He was astounded by the similarities between the species and he began to grasp how two worlds a galaxy apart could simultaneously evolve the game of baseball. But why the functional dissimilarity of mental processes? Bit by bit, piece by piece, he made critical discoveries; by quantum leaps of both logic and faith he had deduced not only the nature of the divergence of mental processes but the causes of it as well. If he were correct, all was in fact not lost. The breakthrough came with the discovery of one word: biofeedback. From there he crafted a hopeful solution to his dilemma. It remained to be seen if it would work or if he even had the time to make it work. Of course, the obvious and only place to start was with Jimmy Strongbow.

One final area of dismay remained for Belteron. Why had he come to Earth and why had he committed himself to a course of action so opposed to the combined will of his planet? He was alarmed that he could so blithely rebel against every established tenet of his own society; that kind of behavior was common on Earth, which gave him an odd source of solace, but it was unheard of on Ball Four. Of course, there were examples of war and criminal behavior throughout early Ball Fourian history, but advances in psychology and mind discipline had centuries ago put an end to such societal disturbances. Advanced genetics had eliminated the occurrence of biologically-based accidental deviance. So why was he on such a deviant path? In his entire life he had never known of one incidence of such extranormal behavior. Why did he feel so unabashedly righteous about his quest when he had nothing against which to measure his actions?

Back on Ball Four he hadn't questioned his decision to interfere in the united endeavor of his people. He felt compelled to take action, and that compulsion had carried him to Earth. And now he had well embarked on his way and still had found no reason to swerve. The longer he was on Earth the more he relished the idea of championing the cause of the human against the might of his own world. It seemed just, but why he could not know. This was a mystery that would be long in the unravelling. In the meantime he would have to trust that there was some innate wisdom to his quest and that some greater good was being served.

One afternoon after work, it came time to attend to Jimmy's slider. Having the ball club gone gave them greater freedom, and Burt surprisingly agreed to let them practice on the diamond at Candlestick. He seemed honestly to appreciate Jimmy's handiwork with the pitcher's mound, and said that since Jimmy took care of the mound he had a right to throw from it. Burt wasn't such a bad guy after all.

"Okay, Jimmy, let's see what we can do with your slider. Once again, it's basically fine in form but lacking in substance. To be a truly effective pitch it has to perform radically or major league hitters will sit on it and take it downtown.

"The principal weakness I see in most pitchers with their sliders is that they rely too much on snapping the elbow down to create the break. That's bad for two reasons. One, it's hard on your elbow and, two, it robs the pitch of velocity. You're a bit guilty of this but it's probably because you've never faced a hitter who could really challenge your version. But you will soon, and we must be prepared. So, use every part of your motion to add power and break to your slider, with the elbow-snap the second to last aspect and the popping of your fingers off the side of the ball the final aspect of the delivery.

"And, of course, you'll need a symbol to base the pitch upon."

"I'm ahead of you for once," said Jimmy. "I've already given some thought to it, and if my curve is the snake then naturally my slider is the snakebite." He smiled awaiting Belteron's reaction. He was not disappointed.

"You couldn't have done better," said Belteron, with his recently acquired expertise on snakes. "It's about as perfectly appropriate a symbol as you could have chosen. Let's start throwing some, but from the beginning keep in mind that *you* are the snake and *you* are the snakebite."

Jimmy Strongbow was an apt pupil and with comparative ease had improved his slider tenfold in almost no time. The visualization technique was largely responsible, but Belteron had to admit begrudgingly to himself it was more than likely that any good, sound coach could have eventually brought Jimmy up to the level he was now reaching. Belteron was simply glad that he was the one doing it and enjoying it.

It was now time to begin to find out if there was any validity to his theories on mind control. He would start out slowly and bring Jimmy along step-by-step, hoping that he was on the right track.

"Jimmy, I want to introduce a new technique that's essential to success (he hoped) and should help to cement your visualizations more firmly to your every pitch. We've been lucky that things have come so easily to you so far, but this might take a little more work at the beginning and may take longer to bear fruit. Are you ready for it?"

"Too late to stop now," said Jimmy.

"We've been thinking fastball and feeling arrow, thinking slider and feeling snakebite. Now it's time to stop thinking and just start doing. Jimmy, I want you to take your conscious mind and shut it off. You ever heard of meditation?"

"Yeah, sure," said Jimmy. "It's part of eastern religion, right? Well, really it's part of American Indian life too. From what I know about it, there's not a lot of difference between the trance of a yogi and the trance of an Indian on a vision quest. That's something we studied at our high school. I never gave it much thought but, yeah, I know about it."

"You've got the right idea. To take the next step, we've got to split your mind into two parts, the conscious and the subconscious. These aren't exactly accurate terms but they're the ones used most often. Anyway, you think with your conscious mind. We want to stop that thinking. Without working so hard on it that you end up thinking about trying to *stop* thinking, just let that conscious mind go blank as effortlessly as possible. It might not happen right away and completely, but with time you should be able to have it happen at will. Now, finally, I want you to allow your subconscious mind, or feeling mind, to remain alert and in charge. Before, you were thinking fastball and feeling arrow. Now I want you only to feel arrow. When I signal for a fastball, all you will be aware of is the image of an arrow. Your subconscious mind will be in control and you will throw without effort or help from your conscious mind. Do you understand?"

"Yes and no, but I'll give it a try," said Jimmy.

"Don't try," Belteron said. "Just do it."

"Oh, right."

The rest of the workout they threw without speaking. Belteron called them and Jimmy threw them. At first, as Belteron scanned Jimmy's mind, it was nearly wide open but as time went by it began to fog over. What was clearly perceptible in the beginning became less distinct with each ensuing pitch. When Belteron felt that Jimmy was making good progress he dropped into his own "white mind" state on the assumption that it would influence Jimmy's to follow. It did so. Jimmy's conscious mind further clouded over. At no time did it close, but by the end of the workout Belteron was convinced that he indeed had found the link he had sought. It didn't hurt Jimmy's pitching either. In fact, the deeper into the trance he traveled, the closer he got to major league baseball. Jimmy didn't know it yet, but Belteron did; it would soon be time for a fateful step, and Belteron was now convinced he and Jimmy would take it together. When and how were all there remained to discover.

Jimmy Strongbow brought his wheelbarrow full of clay up to the mound and, grabbing his shovel, prepared to fill in the front portion of earth he had dug out. The Giants were due back in a couple of days and he wanted them to find the best mound in the league upon their return. It looked like they might need some cheering up, even Brad. Brad had the final start of the road trip in St. Louis tomorrow, so he had a chance to redeem himself. Jimmy would be listening to the radio and cheering him on.

He couldn't wait to show Brad the progress he had made. He could barely believe it himself, or at least his old self could hardly believe it. More than his pitching had changed. He felt like a new man, a man that two weeks ago he wouldn't have recognized in the mirror. Now he was the man he had dreamt of being as a child. He had come of age. Through his pitching he had begun his vision quest, through his pitching he had begun to unite the inner and outer spheres of his universe; he was becoming whole. Each pitch was part of the journey on the Medicine Wheel Way. The more he became alive as a pitcher, the more he became alive as an Apache, and as a man.

He opened the nozzle of the hose to a fine mist and carefully saturated the mixture of clay and cinder he had finished tamping. Luckily, it was a sunny day at Candlestick Park and the sun would bake the soil like adobe bricks. By the time the home stand began, the pitchers, falling forward after releasing the ball, would have a safe and solid surface on which to land.

As he misted the mound Jimmy looked out to where Billy Icarus was helping with the re-sodding in the outfield. Billy is more than my coach, he thought, he is my shaman, my medicine man. More than that, he is my friend. He gives so freely of himself, without asking anything in return.

Jimmy had stopped wondering why Billy even bothered with him. The results were proof that Billy knew what he was doing and that Jimmy was worth the effort. Yesterday's training session had been another leap forward, another stone added to the Medicine Wheel.

They had tackled the forkball. This was a pitch that Jimmy had always loved to throw. He never had success with it in high school, but it was fun because of its unusual grip and he threw it when he could afford to waste one. It was a natural pitch for a man of Jimmy's physique. Because of his long, slender fingers he could cradle the ball easily between his index and middle fingers without overstretching, and the resulting smooth, snapping release gave it lots of topspin. Thrown as a change-up it floated in temptingly, and hopefully the batter would ground it into a double play. Thrown as a fastball it made it a good strike-out pitch, as the bottom would drop out as the hitter took his cut. Jimmy's problem with it was, as usual, his control combined with a lack of spirit or will in the toss. Yesterday changed all that.

The more Jimmy merged his baseball world with his Indian world, the easier it was to find suitable images for his pitches. For the forkball he had chosen the cougar, the beast that silently stalked the canyons and mountain passes of Apacheria. Jimmy visualized home plate as a rock just beyond which was the cougar's prey. In a lightning flash the cougar pounced from his silent perch above and the hapless prey was his. From this visualization Jimmy got power and spirit, which gave him speed and break, and location, which gave him control. The more he became the cougar the more effective and accurate the pitch. When he broke his concentration and lost the image, the ball tended to drop too soon and bounce in front of the plate. A hungry cougar would never make that mistake.

The final force that propelled Jimmy on his vision quest had been the meditative state Billy had urged him to adopt while throwing. The deeper into the state Jimmy allowed himself to go, the more vibrant his Medicine Wheel-strike zone grew, and the more alive his world of bow and arrow, of snakes and cougars, became. As his thinking mind gave way to his inner vision, the stadium vanished and the colors of the high desert surrounded him. And somewhere above him he could sense the flight of a lone eagle, watching and guiding him. When Billy broke the spell and said it was time to take a break, Jimmy was reticent to leave a world in which he knew he belonged and could not wait until it was again time to return.

The day before the Giants came home was another day off for the grounds crew and Jimmy and Belteron were once again at the diamonds in Golden Gate Park. Belteron was introducing nothing new. All that was needed was work, work, work, and fine tuning for the mind and body. He did have one more pitch, a new one, that he wanted Jimmy to throw; but that could wait. He was already surprised that Jimmy could handle all he'd presented him.

They were taking a break and had walked over to the drinking fountain when Jimmy let out a long, telling sigh. Something was on his mind.

"Billy...," he started, then paused.

"Yeah?"

"How old are you?" asked Jimmy.

"Twenty-eight. Why?"

"Well, look," Jimmy went on, "you obviously know a lot about baseball and you're a hell of a catcher *and* coach. Where'd you learn, and haven't you played pro ball?"

"Lots of people trained me, but it was actually my father that started me out. I grew up around baseball. My father played, and from the time I could walk he was teaching me. We had fabulous fun at it, and we're tremendously close because of it. He's a great man and probably my best friend."

"I see," said Jimmy. "Have you always been a catcher?"

"Actually my father tried to start me out as a pitcher. My first training with him was towards that end. But he was a catcher and I chose to emulate him. Later I trained as both a catcher and a pitcher. But it was only to make me a better catcher."

"You always sidestep around it when I ask questions like this," Jimmy said, "but I'll ask again. Where are you from? What was all this training for? Why aren't you playing in the majors? You're probably a great hitter, knowing you. You say you're twenty-eight. Look, I'm twenty and I *know* why I ended up a groundskeeper. But you, at your age and with your talents, you come out of nowhere and, I guess, without a job. You step out of the stands one day at Candlestick and the next thing I know you're on the grounds crew. You've been great to me and I don't have any right to be pushy but, Billy, what's going on?"

Belteron took a minute to respond. Jimmy waited patiently. "You've been as patient as I ever could have expected a man to be but, just as I asked you before, you've got to trust me on all this. However, I admit, it's time to open up a bit, and time we talked about a couple of things. If I don't answer all your questions, please do me the favor of accepting it for what it's worth. Before this is all over, you'll know everything, I promise.

"Yes, I've played pro ball. And, for reasons I'll explain later, I walked away from it. Yes, I was unemployed when the chance to join the grounds crew came along, but I joined it for a reason. I'm going to play for the Giants. Why are you on the grounds crew, Jimmy?"

That gave Jimmy pause. "I guess for the same reason, in a way. At least I can be around baseball. But what do you mean, you're going to play for the Giants?"

"I mean exactly that. And, Jimmy, so are you."

"So am I *what*?" said Jimmy, stunned.

"What do you think we've been doing all this time? Look, I never antici-pated what's happened between you and me. I wasn't looking around for a pitcher to train. You were just there. Jimmy, I like you, and you've got talent. Not only that, but you're exactly what the Giants need: a good, right-handed pitcher. And I'm another thing they need, and that's a catcher who can hit. You're right, I can hit, I assure you."

"You're strange, Billy," said Jimmy. "Why not just try out for the team? Why did you wait until now?"

"Because I couldn't get here until now."

"Get here from where?" asked Jimmy.

"That'll have to wait."

Jimmy let out a long breath. "Oh, okay. So how're we going to get on the Giants? Seems like a long shot."

"It is, Jimmy. But we will, I assure you."

Jimmy stood there for a moment, hands on hips. He looked up into the sky and, for a second there, thought he saw an eagle. He looked over at Belteron, who stood there with an assured smile on his face. Jimmy shook his head slowly, then smiled back.

"I believe you. Why, I don't know, but I do."

As they walked back to the diamond Jimmy asked yet another question.

"You said that you trained a lot as a pitcher. Can you throw?"

"Sure," Belteron replied.

"Show me," said Jimmy.

Belteron considered for a moment, then chuckled softly. "Okay, let's trade gloves."

Belteron walked slowly up to the mound and turned. He closed his eyes and took a deep breath. He let it out and opened his eyes. Floating over the plate was his strike zone. It was multicolored and composed of Maintenance Man Anti-Grav Constructor blocks, as it had always been since the first day his father had used his young son's toys to teach him where to throw. Criss-cross-ing between the many-colored blocks was a jet-black grid of lines that neatly divided the space into mini-zones. extending from various points in the grid were a complex series of tubular lanes, some straight and some of myriad arcs and slants; each had its own tint and intensity. These all passed through a set of matrices that were placed at various points along the plane to home plate, each also with its own particular hue and luminosity. Behind all this, waiting to receive the pitched ball was not Jimmy Strongbow but Belteron's father. This had always been so, and he couldn't have changed it had he wanted to. His father's sure hands gave him his strength and control.

He began to throw. At first, the movement felt foreign and stiff, but that he tuned out. He turned on the white mind and threw each pitch as though he were giving life, and slowly each ensuing pitch became more alive. He could feel old muscles stretch and loosen, and he sent impulses through his body to nurture them and give them confidence. He launched a curve that seemed to be spinning out of control until suddenly it found form and swung around to intersect home plate, as though it had been sucked through a pneumatic tube. With each pitch that Jimmy called, Belteron sensed a growing joy and freedom, and his universe widened and gathered in planets and moons that spun and arced and orbited and sped through the geometry of Belteron's multicolored construction. The order was given to initiate Time Drive, and Belteron reared back and propelled his ship across parsecs of space with all the sureness and purity of mathematical inevitability.

"Ouch!" cried out Jimmy as the searing fastball stung his fingertips. He stood up, dropped the catcher's mitt to the ground and started to rub the pain out of the offended area. "I wish I could see a speed gun on that one."

Jimmy strode up to mound and said, "Billy, you're the right-hander the Giants need."

Belteron only smiled. He walked to home plate and dusted off his mitt. "Well, shall we get back to it? The Giants come home tomorrow and we're going to be ready for them."

Jimmy started to protest, then shrugged. "If you say so, Coach," he said, picking up his glove. He bent down and peered in for the sign.

10

THE PLAIN DEALER

May 8th.

Bob Hinkley

YOU GOTTA LIKE
THESE GUYS

A lot of mystery has surrounded the upstart Tribe this year. One thing that's no mystery anymore is how they win ballgames. They do it well and often, and they do it the old-fashioned way: pitching, hitting, running and fielding. They're so good at it, who cares where they came from?

A good deal of interest has been stirred up of late about this team of rookies, upstarts, unknown coaches and their mysterious yet sensationally successful general manager, Abe Watkins. The Cleveland Indians have become sensitive to this and, in a move both gracious and unexpected, have made an unprecedented effort to take time out of the business of winning games to let us know more about them. I was the lucky recipient of this gesture, and I've spent the last couple of days visiting with some of the nicest, most genuine guys I've met in a long time. No wonder they win. They're for real, and their story is about as American as apple pie.

Pitching coach Warren Evans took me on a guided tour of this rebuilt and thriving team, and their story is the stuff of novels. Warren's own is a good example. He dreamed since he was a child of pitching in the majors, but never made it past class A ball. The last team he pitched for is as gone as his dreams of major league stardom: the old Wichita Red Birds of the now defunct Midwest League. Instead of giving up and becoming a car salesman he stuck with the game he loved and decided to make a career of helping other kids make it to the big show that had eluded him. He coached for the Cleveland farm club in Akron before making it to the big time with Abe Watkins' surprise moves last year. Coming with him from Akron was rookie Vance Bueller, and we all know his numbers from last season. Abe knew what he was doing. If Evans is responsible in part for shaping Bueller, as I'm sure he no doubt is, then he obviously had the right stuff to direct major league pitching. All in all, it's a great story, and it's understandable that the humble, soft-spoken Evans would rather coach pitchers than gab with the press. The major league uniform he wears is still new and he doesn't want to take it off any time soon. He's worked too hard to earn it.

Another cat out of the bag from Warren Evans is that he's from hockey country. Yes, he was born and raised in Prince Albert, Saskatchewan, Canada. Warrens jokes that he should be coaching the giant slalom instead of the curveball, but he's proud of his American citizenship in his adopted home and equally proud of his role in his adopted sport. And every Cleveland fan should be proud of him as well. Warren, if no one has said so yet, I want to say it for all the skeptics and doomsayers. Welcome to Cleveland.

Over the next few days I'm dedicating my column to the story of the team members themselves. It's no mystery at all. It's a story of the American heartland and I hope you take the trip with me. I'll see you tomorrow.

(Lloyd Cronin is on vacation.)

Warren Evans and Jake Conrad sat side by side in the visitors' dugout at Yankee Stadium. The Indians were batting and Conrad was concentrating on the signs. Evans, for a change, was letting Conrad call them as he saw them. He had reasoned, and Watkins agreed, that Conrad was a sound baseball man and could be relied on to call a reasonable game. Occasionally, the players would, of their own volition, begin to insititute a play uncharacteristic of Conrad's typical strategy, so Evans would have to intervene and send signals to Conrad's mind in order that he be allowed the illusion that he had called the play. But, by and large, the new system made Evans' job decidedly easier and fitted well with the new overall strategy which had recently been adopted. All games against weak teams like New York, Baltimore and Kansas City would be closed to mind reading on a semi-permanent basis. Against contenders like Toronto, Oakland and Detroit, alternating games would be open to any and all mental tactics. Occasionally a game would be manipulated and controlled from beginning to end to tune up mind discipline and to prepare for unforeseen eventualities where such techniques would be required. The entire scheme had an extremely high probability of producing a season record which would not attract too much attention while assuring the taking of the American League East title. It also served as an amusement and diversion for the Ball Fourian players, as it gave them a number of challenges while never allowing them to get into a rut. Actually, the plan hadn't proved itself yet. During the first week of the new scheme the team record had swelled to 22-5 and, at this rate, would end up with a season total of 132-30. That would be unsatisfactory. Operation Command trusted that the record would flatten out over time with the newly adopted system. it would be a shame to have to endure a prolonged losing streak late in the season just to preserve appearances.

With his newly-found leisure Evans sought other amusements to pass the time. A game he enjoyed playing with himself involved the holovision coverage of the Season for the folks back home. As he came into a new stadium he tried to locate the holovision cameras which had been installed by the Holovision One team in every park in the league. Although he'd only been in a few parks as yet, Evans so far had not located a single camera, not even at Municipal Stadium back in Cleveland. He admired the job that the crew had done, but was hopeful he could share a few laughs with them if he could "bust" them with a discovery. So far, no luck.

Conrad had just engineered two runs out of one hit and a walk, and Evans admired the man's ingenuity. He would do well back on Ball Four. This was, in fact, a unique perspective for Evans; watching a human manager lead a Ball Fourian team allowed him to reflect on the merits of human baseball capability. He admired it, generally speaking. It was, in a sense, a shame that his job, and the team's, was to make a mockery of it. Oh, well, that was only natural because of Ball Fourian inherent superiority, which is what the Season was intended to prove. It was to date illustrating it all too well.

By game's end the Indians had indeed illustrated their continuing superiority with a 16-2 trouncing of the thunderstruck New York team. Evans looked forward to hearing from Watkins by phone concerning the on-going project with the Cleveland press. Back in the clubhouse after the game Evans got through to Watkins immediately.

"Hello, Abakin, yes, it's Evan. How are things progressing?"

"Remarkably well, Evan," Watkins replied. "Hinkley's article today makes clear the brilliance of your plan. And he promises a week of "revealing" articles which should satisfy the readers and end the general curiosity. We can also count on other reporters backing off because they won't want to cover old ground or call attention to Hinkley's scoop. I'm very pleased and so is Command."

"That's great news. What of Cronin?"

"He's apparently out of commission for a while. The mind disruption teams did their job, and Hinkley has taken over his column for the foreseeable future. I doubt Cronin could cause us any significant trouble later on in the season should we choose to call off the teams. For now, though, continued discretion would be advised."

"I agree," said Evans. "Anything else I should know?"

"Nothing comes to mind. Just carry on and enjoy. See you when you get back. Bye."

Lloyd Cronin switched off his television set. Another Indian uprising, he thought, the Yankees never saw them coming. Whoever they are, they sure can play baseball. Makes me look silly, with my 81-81 prediction. Maybe they are for real. Time will tell. Not that I'll necessarily be around to cover it.

He tightened the belt on his bathrobe and moseyed over to the refrigerator for another beer. Passing the dining-room table, he spotted the day's paper, opened to Hinkley's column. "He gets my scoop *and* my slot, godammit," Cronin mumbled bitterly. Typical newspaper man. About as ethical as a politician. He chuckled at the irony. When he was young, he'd have sold his mother into slavery for a story. Now, he'd probably put out a contract on her life for same. No, not really, still he couldn't blame Hinkley. We're all scum when it comes down to a story.

He popped the top on his can of beer, walked over and opened the venetian blinds on his front picture window. It looked like a nice day outside. He hadn't left his apartment since Monday and wasn't sure when he would venture out again. He was having his groceries and liquor delivered.

Monday he had tried to walk to the store and he wasn't fifty yards from his apartment when the terror descended on him again. He was fine inside but outside just terrified him. He had raced back and locked his door. When he had calmed down he looked up agoraphobia in the dictionary. Jeez, I'm a reporter who's afraid to leave his apartment. Maybe I could write a column on the mold on my kitchen tile grout. Maybe I could get a shrink who makes house calls. Maybe I should watch some more TV.

He sat back down on the couch and flipped on the tube. He switched to the sports channel. Ah, the Sioux City Rodeo of Superstars. That should be *rich*.

ANCHOR:

> The Councilor for Public Health announced today that sports wagering reached a two-decade low in this month's sampling of planet-wide gaming practices. When viewed with the startling decline that was revealed in a similar sampling of biofashioning establishments released only a few days prior, there is cause for the excitement in First City political circles that First Councilor Tarn's stated goals of reducing both forms of what he calls "decadent behavior" may indeed be reached after all. Councilor Rosten had this to say about the two reports:

ROSTEN:

> We're very enthusiastic about the developments, as is First Councilor Tarn, whose efforts I fully support. I have been authorized to caution, however, that further studies are expected to corroborate our initial consensus that these data are highly prejudiced by unusual and coincidental factors. Firstly, the major league baseball season here on Ball Four is over, which has dampened betting interest. Secondly, it has been estimated that ninety-four per cent of all available gambling credits planet-wide have already been wagered on the Universe Series and any further betting has been seriously discouraged by the complete flattening out of official payoffs to winners of Series bets. These payoffs, by the way, are presently the lowest in history at 1.0001 to 1. The remaining available credits will be wagered in small amounts on the various contests of the Season as it progresses on Earth. This

will have minimal statistical impact. Now, concerning biofashion, the decline seems to be resulting from those Ball Fourians who have wished to emulate Earthlings already having done so, and they will likely keep their present looks until after the end of the Season on Earth. So, while we are happy about the present situation, we cannot, I'm afraid, conclude that the citizenry as a whole have necessarily begun to heed the First Councilor's message.

ANCHOR:

Whatever the causes, First Councilor Tarn is obviously pleased and has stated publicly that he intends to take advantage of this lull to encourage people to reflect on what he calls "more healthy forms of diversion." What he meant by that was not immediately clear, but one can safely assume that the First Councilor's new program will not include a regimen of more work. After factoring out the workload associated with Operation Universe Series, this month's report from the Councilor of Labor contained startling statistics that reflect the success of the new generation of robotics that have in recent months become fully operational. It seems that Ball Fourians are working less than at any time in history, and all indications are that further application of the new technology may indeed lead to the elimination of physical labor entirely. Then perhaps we could all cross over to the baseball caste, couldn't we, Jevv?

SPORTSCASTER:

I don't know about that, but the usual, brief respite from baseball we all experience at season's end isn't taking place this year, as interest in the Season taking place on Earth has reached a fever pitch. The frenzy will culminate in tonight's holographic presentation at all major stadia around the globe. Let's get in on the fun, as Taza is standing by live at First City Stadium...

First Councilor Tarn chatted amiably with a few aides in the plush suite behind his private box at First City Stadium. Across the room Semptor was making a few remarks to a Holovision One reporter. This was a big night for Holovision One as well as for Semptor; the Second Councilor had originally proposed this technological breakthrough. It was left to the ingenuity of Holovision One to make it a reality. In a few minutes the greatest broadcasting feat in the history of the known universe would begin. Tarn retained his usually placid exterior but inwardly he too was caught up in the excitement.

Tarn began to make his way through the throng, pausing here and there to greet the invited dignitaries. *Semptor, it's time.* Semptor reacted to the thought projection almost imperceptibly as he made his excuses to the reporter and gravitated toward the entrance to the First Councilor's private box. He met up with Tarn at the foot of the steps below the box.

"Tarn, my good friend, this is your entrance," Semptor said softly in Tarn's ear. "The crowd awaits you. They have no interest in lesser men."

"I appreciate your modesty, Semptor, but this is your moment too. You, perhaps more than I, are responsible for these glorious events."

"You are, as usual, too kind," said Semptor. "I defer to your judgment. The game must begin. Shall we?"

Tarn nodded, and side by side they ascended the steps. From the top, the playing field came into view but the capacity crowd waiting for a glimpse of their leader would have to wait until he descended to the front of the box. Tarn turned and nodded to an aide, who pressed a button on a column to the left of the entrance. An instant later, the Stadium announcer came over the public address system.

"Ladies and Gentlemen, shall we give welcome to the First Commissioner of Baseball!!"

The crowd rose to its feet and fell silent. Tarn and Semptor, as they slowly descended to the small front balcony, could sense wave after wave of emotional greeting. The silence continued until Tarn stopped and raised his hand. The crowd roared and fell silent again. Tarn would speak. He pressed a button on the railing of the balcony.

"Citizens of First City, I greet you and thank you for your warm welcome. Tonight we are privileged to see our brave men in action on the playing fields of Earth. They, not we, are the heroes of Ball Four. Let the game begin!"

With that the crowd roared again, this time reaching a powerful crescendo as the hitherto empty playing field of First City Stadium came to life. The surface of the diamond shimmered and shifted as the scene of Cleveland Municipal Stadium appeared in front of their eyes in one gigantic holographic display. The Cleveland Indians were taking the field. The crowd roared once more, and the players took their positions. A Detroit Tiger took his warm-up swings in the on-deck circle. Except for a soft, quivering light at the seam where the image of the holograph interfaced with the real edges of the Stadium playing field, the scene in front of the crowd was breathtakingly real. Every Ball Fourian in every seat in every baseball stadium on the planet felt instantaneously transported to Earth. The players before them were *here*, not parsecs away across the galaxy.

Tarn was equally impressed.

"Semptor, my good man, this is the most amazing thing I have ever experienced. And Holovision One has guaranteed the stadia holocasts will continue through the Season and the Universe Series. Issuing tickets to the games must have been a bureaucratic nightmare."

"Not really, Tarn," replied Semptor. "A computer lottery was devised with such utmost fairness that the citizenry has fully embraced it. Each game that Cleveland plays from now through the end of the Series will be holocast five times daily in every major league stadium on Ball Four. Additional transport booths have been installed in all stadia to facilitate turnover. Only a few upper echelon members of the various castes who failed to win seats in good time slots have complained, of course to no avail. And those who cannot attend still have home holocasts to enjoy. The planning was so detailed that, barring technical difficulties in transmission from Earth, the Season has been transported in its entirety to the playing fields of Ball Four."

"The workload must have been a terrific burden for you, Semptor," said Tarn.

"Tarn, you gave me a support team of five thousand technicians for the holocasts alone. There was such enthusiasm for the project that my aides would hardly let me have any of the fun. Don't worry about me, Tarn, worry later when the whole planet collapses into boredom after all this is over."

"You're right, my friend," said Tarn with a warm smile. "There will be time enough to fret about that. But now our attention belongs on our intrepid Indians. Here comes the first pitch."

Interest on Ball Four concerning Belteron had faded, as the First Councilor had predicted. Among the players and management of the Seaview Captains concern had naturally continued. The franchise's search for their former star had continued in hopes that he not only would be found but could also be persuaded to return to salvage the disastrous season. Neither happened, and Seaview lost the championship trophy to First City for the first time in six years. Belteron was not the only star player missing from team rosters, but Seaview's management had thought that Belteron's deselection would be a boon to their continued success. His declining to play after deselection had been a blow, and his disappearance was the final shock.

When Public Safety had announced that Belteron was not only truly missing but presumed dead as well, it was so newsworthy that Tarneen hadn't attempted to suppress the information. She had contacted her father about the issue and he seemed in favor of her decision, including her plans to present a retrospective on Belteron's career. The public was so shocked at the apparent death of its greatest star that attention to events on Earth waned for a brief time. Tarn even proposed a commemorative statue be constructed at Seaview Stadium, but plans were put off for the time being due to the anticipated holographic use of the facilities. Ball Four mourned the loss of the great Belteron, and turned it eyes back to the unfolding drama on Earth.

There was one notable exception: Third Councilor Niver. He seemed obsessed with the issue of Belteron, and used it at every occasion to create disturbances in the Planetary Council meetings. His final move was to call for a plebiscite, assuming his support by the Junior Council was sufficient to garner for him the needed one-third vote. There were two ways the position of First Councilor could be placed before the citizenry for approval by vote. A petition could be circulated which, when signed by sufficient numbers of the general public, would instigate a plebiscite; or, as in Niver's attempt, one third of the Council was required to call for a public vote of confidence.

Such plebiscites had been extremely rare in recent centuries. In fact, the last one to take place had been two hundred years ago when debate over the Technology Anti-proliferation Act raged. The leadership at that time prevailed, as turned out to be the case with Niver's challenge.

Third Councilor Niver was apparently out of touch with his supporters in the Junior Council, who deserted him when the final tally was taken. The Junior Council had then immediately called for a caucus at which Niver was voted out as leader. Niver was, according to custom, stripped of his position as Third Councilor. He was of course entitled to remain on the Council, but his ill-advised blusterings had driven him to the confines of the very back bench. Niver would never again be a force in Ball Fourian politics. His ambition was unfortunately greater than his vision. Tarn was pleased, and barely contained his amusement at the ridiculous affair. It did concern him in one way, however. Breakdowns at this echelon of the political caste were extremely rare, and he could only speculate as to the causes of Niver's collapse. He privately advised Niver to seek psycho-physiological help, which Niver gladly accepted. Tarn was relieved. Even a victor could take no satisfaction when aberrant behavior had led to the victory. It could in no way serve society. It did, however, end the controversy about Belteron.

12

San Francisco Chronicle

May 17th.

Red Henderson

CHAMBERS CAN'T
COACH PITCHING

It's generally considered sacrilegious to criticize our beloved manager Lou Chambers, and I don't relish doing it now. But someone in the Bay Area media has to call it the way they see it and, if it means taking an icon to task, then so be it. I'm of the opinion that managing pitching isn't among Lou's esteemed list of skills. If it were, pitching wouldn't be the Achilles' heel of the Giants, as it has been since Chambers took over eight years ago. And don't tell me that it's Ron McIlhenny's fault. He's primarily a conditioning coach who keeps an eye out for bad habits, like losing. That's a habit all of us couldn't help but notice.

Let's face it. Lou Chambers can't contribute to building a good pitching staff and can't utilize it once he's got it. Brad O'Nealy is a lucky fluke from the draft. Nobody in their right mind drafts Ivy League prospects, and the fact that Chambers and Barnham landed O'Nealy was a mistake in judgment that happened to pay off in spades. But what can you say about the rest of the squad? The short men in the bullpen do their job, but they only have one save apiece because they spend most of their time mopping up disasters instead of saving close ones.

Taking a good look at the rest of the staff doesn't do much for my general disposition. Upton's too inconsistent, French is over the hill and Gonzalez, for heaven's sake, shouldn't even be on the staff and why we invest so much time in a pitcher with an ERA of 11.25 beats the hell out of me. It only tells me that Lou Chambers is incapable of making the hard decisions when it comes to pitching. If he doesn't do something soon, it won't be a matter of replacing the pitching staff, it'll be a matter of changing managers. There, I said it.

Okay, before I get skinned alive, let me at least tell how I would fix it, and save Lou's job in the bargain. It can't be done this year, it appears way too late, but if I had my way I'd...

As things got underway for the Friday night kickoff of the home stand, a somber mood of dismay and discouragement pervaded everyone at Candlestick Park, with a few notable exceptions. Jimmy and Belteron were in fine spirits, although they made an effort to keep it to themselves. Washington, Barker and Renker were buoyant because, in spite of the team's road record, their own personal stats were on a steep up-slope. Brad O'Nealy was unusually quiet out of respect for the veterans, not to mention because of his recently acquired humility stemming from his loss against the Pirates. Lou Chambers wasn't talking to anyone at all. There was at least one local newspaper columnist who would do well to avoid the clubhouse for a few days. All in all, Candlestick Park was not a pleasant place to be. All but 8,254 fans heartily agreed.

Belteron was not so glum, but he was most certainly convinced that the time for action had arrived. If the Giants traded for a catcher or a right-handed starter or both, his and Jimmy's chances of finding a berth any time soon would be sorely limited. Something had to give. A way had to be found.

He thought over his choices. In the present frame of mind of Chambers and the rest of the coaches, he had little prospect of mind-influencing his way onto the team. He'd had luck with weaker, less suspicious minds but these crafty old bastards were another story. He might be able to predispose them to accept him but complete manipulation would take a dangerous amount of time. There were too many to influence all the way up to the General Manager Hal Barnham himself, and though Belteron had his talents, he had to admit that he was no mind disrupter from the political caste. He would probably be wise to go after Chambers alone, perhaps with a straightforward approach. He'd better get to work on a plan.

In the meantime, there was no reason to give up on other areas he could have an impact on. Art French was starting that evening's game. He knew where to find him.

"Hey, Art, how's the arm?"

"Okay, Billy, I'm on to you," said French with surprising abruptness. "Yeah, yeah, half the team has heard about your antics. Let's get it over with. What am I doing wrong?"

"You really want to know?"

"No, but I'm 0-6 and the vultures are circling. Come on, out with it."

"Okay, but I won't bother if you're not ready to listen," Belteron said with a relaxed smile.

French put his hands on his hips. "I'm not going anywhere."

"All right. There's nothing wrong with your pitching. Sure, your fastball ain't what it used to be, but that's to be expected. But you can't use an eighty-three-mile-an-hour fastball for your out pitch anymore. So don't let them keep making you try. It's junk time in your career, Art. You've got a lot of different kinds of junk, I know because I've watched you, but Quigley never calls on it much. Why is that?"

"It's not Quigley, it's Chambers. He calls every pitch."

Belteron shook his head. "Well, it's time you started shaking off the signs until you can throw what you want. Do you have a screwball?"

"Sure," French replied. "Chambers won't let me throw it, though. He doesn't respect the screwball."

"From what I gather it's not thrown much. That's on your side. The hitters aren't used to reacting to it. Listen, Art, here's the whole thing in a nutshell: talk to Quigley, get his cooperation, and mix up your junk as well as your speeds. Save your fastball for spots they wouldn't expect. It won't get any faster but it will get sneakier. And one more thing. Forget the vultures, forget the record, forget Chambers. Go out there tonight and mess with *everybody's* mind. Have a good time. If you win, the old man will pretend he called the whole game. And he will call it that way from now on if you do win. What do you say?"

French shook his head and laughed and laughed. Finally, he said, "You're full of surprises, I'll grant you that, Billy. I thought you were going to tell me to pitch from the stretch the whole game or something. Yeah, I'll try it, you bet I will. And so will Ed Quigley. He's got nothing to lose either."

"I'm glad," said Belteron. "Oh, yeah, one more thing. Don't get discouraged by a couple extra walks. That might happen the first game or two until you learn to spot your junk at the right parts of the plate. Listen, I've got work to do. Give 'em hell, Art, and I hope you catch 'em with their pants down."

Belteron was busy right up to game time. Besides his regular duties, he found time to contact Bob Butterfield. The lanky first baseman was a good-natured country boy with a fine natural swing, but no natural power. His one mistake was believing that he was a switch hitter, feeling the Giants needed more left-handers at the plate. Belteron made a quick comparison of his left- and right-handed stats and Butterfield frowned but, in the end, he agreed to bat right-handed for the game. "Billy Icarus" was getting quite a reputation. Washington, Barker and Renker had apparently seen to that.

As Lou Chambers was walking away from home plate after exchanging line up cards with the umps, he waved Belteron over.

"Billy, things are getting a little out of hand here," he said rather testily. "I saw you with French and Butterfield, you're damned right I did, and I'm ordering you to stay away from my players. You hear me?"

Belteron instinctively began to radiate feelings of friendly equanimity, with overtones of power. "Lou, I know you're feeling harassed and encroached upon from all sides and I don't want to be part of the problem. But, and I mean this, I've done nothing to hurt this ball club. Watch what happens tonight, and if you like what you see, come out and talk to me after the game. No, wait a minute, Lou, if you don't like what you see, I'll promise to leave your boys alone, or even quit the grounds crew if that's your request. Fair?"

Chambers was confused about why he was even considering Belteron's outrageous proposal. He stared at Belteron, then calmly responded in carefully measured words. "I know what you did for Washington and the rest. This is the damndest deal I have *ever* seen, and why I'm even talking to you beats the hell out of me. But we've got a game to play and, yeah, what you said is, I admit, fair. See you after the game." He walked back to the dugout shaking his head.

There was more than mere bravado to Belteron's stance toward Chambers. It was a calculated risk with a high probability of success. The Giants were facing the lowly San Diego Padres who, except for the Giants themselves, had gotten off to the worst start in the majors. And the Giants, coming off the frustrating road trip, were in no mood to lose to the Padres at home. All these factors pointed to an explosion and Belteron was not off the mark in his estimation. The Giants unleashed a vicious attack from the first through the seventh innings, failing only in the fourth to score a run. Bob Butterfield went 2 for 4 with a walk, drove in two runs and scored three.

Art French was staked to an early lead and proceeded to confuse and frustrate the Padre hitters, who wondered why they had ever bothered to study the book on French. This was not the same pitcher. At one point Chambers sent McIlhenny out to see what the hell was going on, and French and Quigley nodded up and down in agreement and continued to ignore the signs from the dugout. When French went into the seventh with a shutout intact, Chambers gave up calling pitches altogether. He came out of the dugout and glanced in Belteron's direction, but Belteron pretended to be occupied with equipment. Chambers shrugged and considered going back to tobacco chewing for the first time in fifteen years but thought better of it. He only hoped that son-of-a-bitch from the Chronicle gave him some credit for the victory, even if he didn't deserve it. When French struck out the last batter of the game with a screwball for the 14-0 triumph, Lou Chambers broke out in a wide grin and was the first out of the dugout to congratulate him. He did not, however relish the idea of talking to that groundskeeper.

But, true to his word, he came out of the clubhouse about an hour after the game and there was Belteron standing around home plate talking to Jimmy Strongbow. As he approached, Belteron looked up and said something to Strongbow, who trotted up toward the Giants' bullpen.

Chambers was the first to speak. "If you're waiting to be thanked, well, wait a little longer. If you're waiting to be chewed out, you're closer to the mark. I haven't made up my mind yet. Tell me, did you convince Art to become a junk man?"

"I might have influenced him a bit," said Belteron, careful not to smirk. "He did throw a lot of garbage out there tonight."

"Uh huh," said Chambers, unconvinced. "And I suppose Butterfield batted right-handed against a lefty for the first time this season by accident."

Belteron didn't bother to answer this time, but did allow himself a bit of a smile.

"Yeah, I thought so," Chambers said. "I don't know whether to kiss you or punch you. But we did win the ballgame and it's obvious I've got to eat a little crow because of French. Maybe I was too conservative or blind to figure out how to bring him around. But I got to ask you, what makes you so damned smart?"

"Lou, don't let this uniform fool you. I've worn a baseball uniform more than this work suit, and that's a fact. But, believe me, it was never my intention to second guess you or show you up, and if I've done that you can count on my laying low from now on. But on the other hand, if you think I can help the Giants win ballgames, then please trust that I, just like you, have the best interests of the club in mind in everything I say or do. Now that things are out in the open, you won't find me sneaking around talking to the players unless I think it's what you wish. Which way's it going to be?"

"I don't know anything about you, Billy, and I'm not so sure I want to. But I saw you working out with that Strongbow fella. Yeah, I saw you catching him the day before we went on the road, and I don't know what you've been doing with him but I will tell you I could see some improvement. That kid can throw. Well, that's all beside the point. The bottom line is you did help me with French, there's no doubt about that, and I guess I owe you one. Just don't blab to the papers. I want a little credit. Sure, you can talk to the players, but if you're going to say anything you think I might not like, at least do me the courtesy of letting me know about it. Will you do that?"

"Absolutely," said Belteron. "I have just one thing to ask of you. Down the road I might have to ask you for a favor, a small one. Just don't turn me down without considering it, okay?"

"What kind of favor?"

"Oh, I don't know, but be open to it if it happens, all right?"

"Okay," Chambers answered after a pause. "This is the most unusual conversation I have *ever* had and I still don't know why I'm talking to you, but for some oddball reason I trust you. Maybe some managers, when their team's having a bad time of it, maybe they start going to see witch doctors and voodoo queens. What do I do? I end up talking to a gardener. So, what's the secret, Billy? Magic dirt?"

They both laughed at that one. "Lou, there's nothing magic about it. I just talked good baseball sense with your boys, that's all. I'm surprised they bothered to listen."

"I like you, Billy," said Chambers. "Well, I'd better go. Oh, listen, don't give any damned advice to O'Nealy. If it ain't broke don't fix it, okay?"

"I wouldn't dream of it, Lou. I'll see you tomorrow morning."

Lou Chambers walked back to the clubhouse door wondering just what kind of favor this character was going to ask of him. Neither he nor Belteron knew just how soon the occasion would arise.

So many of the San Francisco Giants showed up an hour early on Saturday morning that the grounds crew had to scramble to accommodate their request for extra batting practice. Twenty-four hours before, the 9-24 Giants were a sour and somber bunch, but a day later the 10-24 Giants couldn't wait to get to work. Hope springs eternal in baseball, and such was the power of the one-game winning streak. Their 14-0 pounding of the Padres had obliterated the memory of the dismal road trip, and they were ready for more blood. They wanted to take their cuts. They had come to play.

And play they did. They weren't quite as vicious as the day before, but they got to the Padres' pitching early and put together four runs in the second inning. That was all Kiley Upton needed, as he scattered seven hits and went the distance for his third victory. The Giants won 4-2.

Belteron surprised Chambers by staying quiet and unobtrusive all day. He was even less visible on Sunday; Belteron went about the business of caring for the infield and, except for a few greetings, didn't engage any of the players in conversation. Chambers had an eye out, expecting Belteron would think he could coach the players with impunity. When he did no such thing, Chambers didn't know what to think. It did cause him to trust and respect Belteron a bit more; the guy was not a loose cannon.

Sunday, things began to break up a little for the Giants. Julio Gonzalez got the start, and was chased by the third after giving up five runs. A middle reliever named Carl Trumbull slowed the onslaught, and by the eighth the Giants had picked away at the lead until they trailed by a lone run.

In the top of the ninth, the Padres got the first two men on base, but Trumbull struck out the next man he faced. With one out, he got the next batter to fly out to center, but it was deep enough to allow both runners to advance to second and third. If the Giants hoped to stay in it with a chance to win in the bottom of the ninth, the next out was crucial.

Chambers made his move and went with Steve Lafite to get the last man. Lafite got ahead of the hitter 1 and 2, and the crowd was clapping and urging him on for a strikeout. Lafite went into his wind-up and fired a rising fastball. The Padre took a rip at it and sent a wobbling pop foul slicing toward the Giants' dugout. Ed Quigley ripped off his mask and scrambled over. As he reached the dugout he went into a slide, stuck out his glove and grabbed the ball. An instant later the rear spike on his right foot dug into the hard ground, flipping and twisting him at a weird angle. Quigley was catapulted forward and the dugout bench caught him across the bridge of his nose. The cheers of the crowd slowly quieted to a drone of concern as the Giants dashed in and surrounded Quigley. He was motionless, out cold. An umpire, forced to do his job, broke through the circle and verified that the ball was still in Quigley's glove. He threw his thumb up, signaling the third out, then backed off.

The game would not resume for ten minutes. The Padres took the field and stayed loose while the Giants tended to their fallen catcher. A determination was made and, instead of taking him down into the clubhouse, one of the carts usually reserved for use at football games was brought in. Quigley was carried to it on a stretcher, then driven slowly to the centerfield gate where an ambulance waited. He was loaded aboard, the red lights flashed, and the ambulance screamed off into the night.

The shaken Giants failed to pull one off for their injured teammate, and were retired in order in the bottom of the ninth. The Padres prevailed, 6-5.

Belteron was watering down the infield and Jimmy was attending to the mound when Brad O'Nealy came out in civilian dress. He walked over to the mound. Belteron scampered over.

Jimmy looked up at Brad. "Any word on Quigley?"

"Yeah, we got the call from the hospital a few minutes ago. Broken nose and torn ligaments in the ankle. He's scheduled for surgery first thing in the morning. He'll be out for a while, how long is anybody's guess."

"What are they going to do?" asked Belteron.

"Oh, who knows," replied O'Nealy. "Barnham was at the game, and he and Chambers have been sequestered in the office since the end of the game. Butterfield is the back-up at this point, and Simpson will move from right to first. They'll call the kid up from Phoenix for the new back-up spot, but the Giants sure as hell won't plan much of the future around him. They'll probably have to deal for a catcher. I'm sure Barnham and Chambers are already hard at it. Quigley was no jewel, but he called a good game and the guys are pretty down about it. We were actually starting to enjoy ourselves."

With that O'Nealy turned and headed back to the clubhouse. He stopped and rubbed out some of the first base foul line. "What the hell, we'll live. You guys want to go get a pizza?"

At that moment Kiley Upton emerged from the clubhouse. "Hey, Brad, Chambers has called a team meeting. Better get down here."

"Sorry, guys," O'Nealy said with a shrug. "General Chambers is rallying the troops. Rain check on the pizza, okay?"

Whatever Lou Chambers said at the team meeting was not for general consumption and the team was mute about it. One thing that came out of it was an extra two hours of workout on Monday before the last game of the series with the Padres. Apparently Chambers believed hard work would center the team, smooth over the feelings. Once again the grounds crew was called in early.

Belteron of course knew that he had arrived at a cusp, and everything depended on what took place that day or the next. If he failed, he would be unlikely to receive another chance. He wished it hadn't taken an injury to Quigley to open the door, but he also knew there was only one way to go. It was now or never.

Chambers was not passing the time idly. He was active with the extra workout. He played pepper with the infielders, hit fungoes to the outfielders and anxiously observed Bob Butterfield in his new role behind the plate, as he worked out with Ron McIlhenny and made toss after toss to Eddie Renker at second base. Butterfield was solid with the glove but stiff and slow to get the ball to second. The Padres were sure to test him.

A while later the batting cage was in position and Chambers stood with his arms crossed and watched intently as player after player swatted away. He was particularly anxious to see how reserve outfielder Harold DuBois, obtained from Seattle in the off-season, was swinging the bat. He was to play right field that evening.

Belteron waited until DuBois was finished to approach Chambers. He walked up, stood next to Chambers and pretended to be absorbed in watching Eddie Renker in the batting cage.

"Not now, Billy, whatever you got in mind I ain't buying," Chambers said without looking. "Don't think I can't guess something's on your mind. Your timing stinks, so just let it go."

"Lou, I can't let it go, or I would. I'm sorry about Quigley. But the fact is you've got to fill his spot on the roster. I'm your man, Lou, I'm the guy you need."

Chambers spun and faced Belteron. "I might have known it," he said furiously. "I shoulda guessed you were a brick short of a load. I don't have time for this crap!"

The furor attracted Washington and Stokes, who walked up and stood to view the conversation at a distance.

"Lou, I never expected you to react any other way. I know that the whole thing sounds preposterous, but I'm a catcher and a damned good one. You yourself said you've seen me catch. Now, wait a minute, hear me out."

A couple more players drifted over to listen. Belteron continued.

"I asked you a couple of nights ago to do me the favor of giving me a listen," said Belteron, "and the time has come. Take a look at your situation. You've got nobody in the farm system at catcher and, furthermore, nobody worth a damn you can afford to trade, and you know it."

Chambers stared at him and fumed.

"I'm only going to ask one thing, one thing only," Belteron went on. "Let me in that batting cage for ten swings. After that, I'll go to my locker, clear my stuff out and leave if that's your pleasure. Ten swings, Lou, and I'm out of your life forever."

"No way, mister. This is the major leagues, for chrissake!" Chambers was adamant.

"Let 'em hit, Skip," said Willie Washington. "I got a feeling about this guy."

"Absolutely out of the question, and you stay out of this," Chambers responded sternly.

"Let 'em hit, Lou." It was Bob Butterfield, standing in his catching gear. "You got nothing to lose, and lord knows we've got the time. C'mon, it's three hours to game time."

Chambers looked around. By now, half the team had formed a circle around them. He squinted at Belteron, who stood there unblinkingly returning his gaze. Chambers rubbed his whiskers for a couple seconds, then threw his arms up in disgust.

"Ten swings and you're out of my life?"

"Ten swings, that's all I ask," Belteron replied quietly.

"McIlhenny!" Chambers yelled out. "I need you to throw a few!"

Ron McIlhenny, at fifty-two years of age, still threw batting practice from time to time. He trotted over from the bullpen and conferred with Chambers before walking up to the mound. The team dispersed to various vantage points. Jimmy Strongbow, wondering what all the hubbub was about, had come over. Brad O'Nealy, who was scheduled to start, had been loosening up with Jimmy and came over with him. In the meantime Belteron had picked a bat from the pile outside the cage and was swinging and stretching.

"Ten pitches, Ron. You ready or not, Billy?" Chambers inquired.

"I'm ready," Belteron replied, stepping into the cage. He batted right-handed.

McIlhenny went into his wind-up. He unleashed a fastball. Belteron hit a line drive that crashed off the left field fence on the fly. McIlhenny then tried a curve which fell out of the strike zone. Belteron golfed it into the left field bleachers. He then closed up his stance and took the next pitch to center field. it hit the fence under the 410 feet sign on one bounce. The team watched silently and Chambers didn't move a muscle. He stood stoically, with his hands jammed in his back pockets.

Belteron switched over to bat left-handed. Murmurs rose from the Giants, then quieted as McIlhenny wound up to throw. In came an inside fastball. Belteron stepped into the bucket, allowing him to put the sweet part of the wood on the ball. It flew out of the cage and didn't stop until it was rattling around in the empty seats of the upper deck in right field.

"Wait a minute!" ordered Chambers.

"Ah, come on, boss, you said ten swings," said Butterfield, who had been standing next to him.

"Oh, he'll get his cuts, I assure you. O'Nealy! Are you warmed up?"

"Sure, Skipper, good and loose," replied O'Nealy.

"Okay, then. I want to see what he can do with your stuff," Chambers said with challenge in his voice.

O'Nealy smiled as he took the mound. "Okay, Billy, prepare to meet your doom."

"No goddam horsing around, Brad," Chambers called out gruffly. "Give him your best stuff."

"Yessir."

Belteron stayed on the right side of the plate. O'Nealy served up a hopping slider which Belteron took over the center field fence. He put the next pitch in the right field upper deck again, before switching back over to hit right-handed. He stung the next one off the wall in the left field corner. The next two he hit over the fence in left center. Chambers had had enough.

"Okay, side show's over. Everybody back to business. O'Nealy, stay loose but don't overdo it. Billy, I want to see you in my office."

As Belteron followed Chambers toward the dugout he looked over at Jimmy and winked. Jimmy, who had been standing there with his jaw half-way to the ground, recovered and smiled. Belteron grinned back.

"Take a seat, Billy," said Chambers cordially. He folded his hands on his desk and pursed his lips. He still hadn't decided what to do, but if he was going to make a decision he'd need to know more about the man across from him.

"So, Billy, where have you been hiding? A guy with your talent doesn't usually hang out under a rock. Where are you from?"

"No place you'd know," Belteron replied with a pleasant smile.

"That won't do, Billy, and you know it. How old are you?" Chambers asked.

"Twenty-eight."

"Twenty-eight, eh? You ever play major league ball?"

"No," responded Belteron. That wasn't quite true, but it answered the letter of Chambers' question if not the spirit.

"I see. Well, you ever play minor league ball?"

Belteron answered in the negative once again.

"Did you play college ball? No? Well, where in the blazes did you learn to hit like that if you never faced any major league pitching?" Chambers was trying to remain calm, but his temples were beginning to bulge.

"Lou, do yourself a favor. Take my word for a few things. I can hit, field and throw runners out. I am not under contract to any team anywhere. I'm the man you need and, if you let me join the team, I promise I'll tell you about myself before I breathe a word to anyone." Belteron had been avoiding using any mind-influencing but now was a critical moment. *You need me. I'll help you turn the team around. Trust me.*

Chambers scrutinized Belteron with a puzzled look. Finally he said, "From the day I met you, I don't know why, I've sorta just naturally trusted you. My team needs some help if we're going to turn it around this season. I need you, Billy, and I'm going to give you a try. I know Barnham, this might be loony, but he'll go along with me on this one. One thing you said today was right. There's no way we can deal for a catcher right now. Okay, so you're on the team. But we'll sign you to the minimum contract on a game-by-game basis only. Take it or leave it."

"I'll take it, on one condition," said Belteron.

"My hearing's going bad, I'd swear you said *you're* putting conditions on joining the team?" Chambers just stared incredulously.

"You heard right, Lou. I'll join the Giants on one condition. Offer Jimmy Strongbow the same contract as me."

Chambers temples began to bulge again. His lower lip started to quiver as he tried in vain to think of something to say. Belteron jumped in.

"You said you saw Jimmy throw, right? Well, after the game tonight, give him another look. Once again, I'll ask you to withhold judgement until you've given yourself a chance to avoid a rash decision. I haven't lied to you yet, have I?" *Give the kid a look, Lou.*

This time it didn't take Chambers so long. "Well, what the hell, we can't make a roster move until after the game anyway. I'll give the kid another look. I admit I was impressed by what I could see of Strongbow's stuff the other day. But, hell, I was way up in the press box. Okay, are there any more surprises? Tell me now before I go nuts."

"No more surprises," answered Belteron cheerfully. "Lou, Jimmy's a right-hander. I've been working with him every day for two weeks, and every day he gets tougher and tougher. You need another good right-handed starter. If you like what you see after the game, you'll do the right thing. Oh, and save yourself some trouble. Bring Barnham along."

"Good idea," said Chambers, picking up the phone. "Now, you're still a groundskeeper for the time being, aren't you? Go spray some cold water on someone else. I got work to do."

"You won't regret this, Lou," Belteron said as he got up to leave.

"I already do," said Chambers as he started to dial. "Now, give me a break. Yeah, hello Hal, we got problems..."

Belteron closed the door as he left. He was back in baseball. Already his mind began to move ahead. There was much to do. Almost too much. Oh, yeah, he'd better go talk to Jimmy Strongbow.

The San Diego Padres didn't know what hit them. Brad O'Nealy blanked them with a two-hitter, which was just as well. Both baserunners stole off of the rusty Bob Butterfield. He made up for it at the plate, as did the Giants as a whole. For the first time that season, the "Three Musketeers" in the outfield hit homers in the same game. By evening's end the Padres had slipped into the cellar beneath the Giants, who now sported a 12-25 record.

Before the game, Belteron had talked to Jimmy.

"I told you we'd make the team. They offered me a contract."

"That's great," said Jimmy. "You've got a contract. Congratulations. But what do you mean, *we*? They're not beating a path to *my* door."

"I told them I'd only join the team if they offered a contract to you as well," Belteron said. "They're going to give you a tryout after the game."

Jimmy turned white. He was speechless.

"What's the matter?" asked Belteron. "This is what we've been working for. Aren't you ready?"

"I'm not sure, Billy. It's only been a couple of weeks."

"Jimmy, there's a time in everyone's life where you can turn a corner, or go straight. This is your time. Tell me, where's your Medicine Wheel?"

Jimmy looked straight ahead about sixty feet, six inches. There it was, clear as a full moon over the Gila River.

"I'll be ready," he said. And Belteron knew he would be.

As soon as the stands were cleared Lou Chambers was out on the field. With him were General Manager Hal Barnham and Ron McIlhenny, as were Barker, Washington and Simpson, whom Chambers had asked to remain in uniform.

Jimmy was already warming up with Belteron. When the entourage came onto the field, they stopped throwing and waited. Chambers came up to the mound and gave the Indian a hard look. Jimmy's countenance was inscrutable. He seemed to be focusing somewhere out in the distance.

"I'm doing this as part of a deal with Billy here," declared Chambers. "I'll give you a good look, like maybe I should have in Phoenix. But we're not going to be here all night and whatever I say goes. Okay, Strongbow?"

Jimmy focused his eyes. "Sure, Skipper. I appreciate you taking the time."

Belteron loped up and handed Jimmy the ball. "Remember everything we worked on. And stop thinking and just throw. This is going to be good medicine, my friend."

Jimmy smiled. Then he closed his eyes. When he opened them a moment later, he was ready.

"Billy, I'm going to call balls and strikes," said Chambers, "and Rick, Willie and Mitch are going to bat. Barker, you're up."

Rick Barker stepped in. Jimmy read the sign and fired a slider. Barker took a full cut.

"Strike one!"

The next pitch came floating in toward Barker's head, and he fell to the dirt to avoid it.

"Strike two!" Chambers looked down at Barker in the dust, saw the protest forming on his lips and preempted him. "It broke down and in, Rick. Caught the corner. Don't start on me, okay?"

Barker frowned and got back in. Jimmy read the sign, reared way back and kicked his leg high. As he began to move his body forward, there was a moment of apparent stasis; Barker froze in confusion and the screaming fastball was in Belteron's glove before Barker waved at it weakly. Chambers spared him the call. Barker walked away shaking his head. Hal Barnham got up from the seat in the dugout and walked over to the first base coach's box.

Chambers had avoided broadcasting that there was to be a tryout, but slowly the team was slipping onto the field by ones and twos. For a minute he considered ordering them back to the clubhouse but changed his mind. Let the kid feel the pressure of a little crowd. O'Nealy, who had been icing down his arm, came out without his jersey, the bundle of ice still taped to his elbow. A trainer caught up with him and threw a jacket over him.

"Washington, you're up."

Barker hadn't bothered to put his batting gloves on, but Washington thought better of it, went back to his cubby hole in the dugout and came to the plate seriously attired. He gave Jimmy a grim look and settled in.

Striking out Barker had given Jimmy an edge, an intangible something-extra that Jimmy did his best to absorb without breaking his meditative state. He allowed to himself that Washington had stepped in, saw O'Nealy out of the corner of his eye, and his concentration wavered for a moment. Belteron sensed it, and went into the white mind state to help focus his friend. Jimmy, from his mental vantage point, felt his surroundings fall away and saw Belteron hold up a quail at twenty paces.

Willie Washington, on the other hand, felt a fastball and took a mighty blaze of a cut. He was way out in front of the change-up, and pulled it a great distance but sharply foul.

The next pitch came in looking like a hung curve and Washington took a juicy cut. It dropped under his bat and bounced behind the plate. Belteron one-hopped it. Washington turned and stared at Chambers.

"Strike two, Willie."

The crowd, now nearly the entire team plus a modicum of the security and maintenance staff of the park as well, was silent and attentive. Awareness was growing that something of significance was taking place, but the implications remained vague. Only O'Nealy grasped the full picture.

Washington dug in. Jimmy peered at Belteron. He went into his wind-up. Swoosh, *whaap*! Washington stood there like a deer staring at a truck's head-lights. The ball had caught the lower inside corner.

"Strike three!" called Chambers.

A smattering of applause broke out, then died as the team sensed that Washington might not appreciate it. He walked off briskly.

"Okay, Mitch, step up."

Simpson decided to take the first pitch, a fastball that nipped the outside corner.

"Strike one!"

Thinking he had Strongbow measured, Simpson dug his spikes in and got set. The next pitch made for the same spot but tailed down and away as Simpson swung to meet it, and he fouled it off the end of his bat.

A ripple passed through Jimmy's consciousness, and his concentration wavered. He turned his back to the mound and rubbed the ball. He thought of Naiche, Mangus, Victorio, Juh and Geronimo as they mulled over surrender and subjugation. That was not Jimmy Strongbow's struggle, his was a per-sonal one, a Vision Quest. He had only to surrender to the Medicine Wheel Way, and travel freely in the realm of his strength and power. He turned to-ward the plate and embraced his vision. An eagle screamed, but Jimmy didn't hear it. The path was clear, the lanes were straight and vibrant.

Mitch Simpson's bat was poised. He was guessing that Strongbow would challenge him in the same spot, and he was right. His swing was fluid, his arms were fully extended and the bat moved in a perfect arc as the sweet part of the wood passed through the lower outside corner of the plate. The ball would be there. It was, about a tenth of a second before Simpson's bat, and the *whap* in Belteron's glove echoed around the stadium. Simpson raised his bat to throw it in disgust, but halted.

"Strike three..." Chambers voice trailed off. He scanned the dumfounded crowd. "Any takers? Renker, Roberts? No? Okay, boys, let's wrap this up." Nobody budged, and quiet conversation started up. Chambers just let it go.

"Billy, you taught Strongbow to do that?"

"No, Lou," Belteron said quietly as they walked up to Jimmy. "I just taught him to remember to do that."

Chambers smiled and nodded in appreciation. They came up to Jimmy, who was standing motionless on the mound. Belteron handed him the ball. As Jimmy accepted it a shiver ran through him, he let out a long breath and a soft smile crept over his face.

Chambers stuck out his hand. "Welcome to the Giants, Chief."

Part Two

13

THE PLAIN DEALER

May 17th.

Bob Hinkley

THE GENIUS OF JAKE CONRAD

Although much has been made of the fact that our Cleveland Indians are unknowns, no-names and rookies, a lot has been done in recent days to let us feel that we know this ball club, that they are becoming, as they should have been all along, _our_ hometown team. In a celebrity-conscious society like America, we tend to become obsessed with the "who" and to forget the "how." This is doubly true in sport. It's time we paid some attention to this undervalued aspect of the game we profess to know and care so much about. Now that our boys are 27-7 let's start to give credit where credit is due.

When new stars ascend we have a tendency to be dazzled, to forget the old stars that have been burning for so long. We think, "Oh, these new stars are so much brighter than the old ones." That is rarely true and certainly not true now. An old star, gleaming so long above Cleveland, is the reason the Indians are on the ascendancy. That star's name is Jake Conrad.

He's been with us, a part of our story both as a player and a manager for so long that we forget his talents and abilities. He has been given so little to work with for so many years that it is little wonder we have doubted his gifts. But this year has made one thing very clear: give Jake Conrad the right raw materials and he can manage with the best of them. That's exactly what he's doing now.

No team as young and inexperienced as this one could do what it has done so far this season unless it had strong guidance from above. That guidance has come from Jake Conrad; he has kept this train full of wild youthful exuberance from derailing, not only with his strong and mature will but also with his sound grasp of baseball. Even the seemingly innovative play we've been seeing, the daring departure from conventional wisdom, must come from the wellhead of the field boss's vision. Otherwise it would become an unorchestrated disaster. I have never been more impressed by a manager's deft hand than I am now, watching this true master craftsman of the game at work. It is brilliant, and a great testimony not only to the man but to his patience and resolve as well. Jake Conrad had only to wait for the unseasoned ingredients to be provided to demonstrate to the critics and disbelievers what profound talents he has possessed all along.

Sure, Jake is a bit of an anachronism, a dinosaur in an age of college-degree managers. He stomps the dugout with his hands stuffed in the back pockets of his britches, still chewing tobacco and spitting, until the dugout has to be hosed out every night. But his baseball savvy is what has kept these boys on track, and it's what will keep them on track to the end. Let the other teams with their computers and flow charts and highbrow ways, let them eat cake. As for me, give me Jake Conrad and a plug of chaw. I believe in these young Indians because I believe in you, Jake. You're the man. It's only a shame it took us so long to find out.

(Lloyd Cronin is on vacation.)

May 20th, the Indians were hosting the Oakland A's at Municipal Stadium for a night game. Three holovision cameras, secreted at various points in the stadium, were recording the proceedings for the eventual entertainment of the Ball Fourian masses. Having just taken the field to start the game against the Western Division's leading team, the Tribe was looking forward to the contest. As dictated by the new strategy policy rotation, this was to be a no-holds-barred, mind-tactics game. Cy Ellerbach, whose Ball Fourian name was Ellerban, was on the mound. He had been the ace starter for the Spaceport Starmen as well as one of the earliest infiltrators. He had also been the leading strikeout king of Ball Four, and was leading the major leagues on Earth as well.

Oakland lead-off man, Ralph Hudson, was not a man who struck out much. As he stepped in to start the game, he was determined to take the first pitch. Cleveland catcher Eddie Martin scanned Hudson's mind before calling for a fastball down the middle. Hudson took the strike. He was expecting curve on the next pitch, a thought easily perceived by Martin who signaled for another fastball, and the result was another strike. Hudson was surprised, and thought they'd give him a curve out of the strike zone on an 0 and 2 count. Ellerbach and Martin simultaneously projected fastball at Hudson, who altered his expectations and thought, oh, hell, they'll probably try to blow one more by me. He was way out in front of the ensuing change-up.

Curt Langley, next up for the A's, never guessed at pitches. This curtailed almost all mind games the Indian battery could play. Still, Martin projected the opposite pitch into Langley's mind before every throw, but it had little effect. Langley was used to ignoring the hunches that had always run through his brain. They threw him a mix of pitches, the last of which he took to right field for a single. The Ball Fourians never enjoyed pitching to Earthling pure hitters.

Indian third baseman Darvel Nixon, whose real name was Darnix, was closest to the third base coach and first to read the "hit-and-run-third-pitch" sign. He relayed it around the infield. *Hit-and-run, hit-and-run, hit-and-run.* Ellerbach "overheard" it from the infielders and Martin read it from the batter. They wasted two pitches to let the batter go ahead in the count, then served up a sinking fastball with a little taken off it. With the pitch the base runner broke for second, and the batter punched a soft line drive through first and second where the hole would be created by the second baseman moving to cover the bag on the steal. But second baseman Jimmy Fernandez ignored the runner, stayed in position and caught the ball easily on the fly. He flipped to first to double off the runner to end the inning. The entire Oakland team was stunned, wondering why Fernandez had violated the fundamentals of baseball only to be rewarded with a double play. It wasn't fair.

Oakland ace Mike Lester was on the mound and Bob Fusberger was behind the plate. Cleveland's lead-off man, Dizzy Rifkin (whose Ball Fourian name was also Rifkin), focused on Fusberger's mind and read fastball and decided to lay off. The next sign read change-up, same location. He held up a touch and smacked it into left field for a single.

Up to the plate came Buck Nichols. He toyed around with them for a while, taking and fouling off pitches for fun and drama. Then he read inside fastball and lashed it down the third base line for a double. Rifkin held up at third.

Jimmy Fernandez, a man of moderate power, they walked to set up a force at every base. Alan Van De Kirk, strode up to bat with the fans going wild. He stopped to let the excitement build and turned to look at Warren Evans in the dugout. He knew he was free to do as he pleased, but out of respect he gave Warren Evans a chance for input. *Swing for glory, Alvendak.* Van De Kirk smiled and stepped up to the plate. He knew they would throw no fastballs, so he waited for a curve high enough to power. He grabbed a 2 and 1 pitch and took it deep. The right fielder never even moved. 4-0, Indians, and still there were no outs in the bottom of the first.

The rest of the game was an entertainment crafted for the fans in Cleveland as well as those on Ball Four. The team knew well enough without instructions from Evans to hold back from total slaughter. They generously shared with each other the remaining hitting and scoring scripts, and by the end of the day everybody had registered at least one or two hits. Ellerbach struck out a mere eighteen, saving to another day the strikeout record which he knew he would soon enough be allowed. As for the Oakland A's, they managed to score a couple of runs in spite of the mind manipulations. They were too good to control completely. With Langley on base, power hitter Jeff Carter was decoyed with a fastball mind projection, but adjusted and drove the sinker just far enough to clear the fence. It was all for the best. Total invincibility was neither possible nor desirable. The final tally was 10-2.

Jake Conrad sat at his desk in his office, the blinds on the windows which looked out to the dressing room were closed. He was fumbling through some old notebooks when Hal Walker opened the door a crack and stuck his head in.

"You wanted to see me, Jake?"

"Yeah, Hal, come on in," Conrad said in a pensive sort of way. "Please, take a seat. I didn't want to see you, really, just wanted you to, well, visit."

"I can visit," Walker said amiably.

Conrad reached down into the bottom drawer of his desk and came out with a bottle of bourbon and a couple of glasses. "Care to imbibe a little of this twelve-year-old devil juice?"

"Well, Hal, as you know, I never have drunk any, but I sure could use one now!"

"I thought as much," Conrad said with a chuckle. As he poured the whiskey, he grew pensive again.

"Hal, how long have you been coaching third base for me, what is it, seven years?"

"About," replied Walker as he took a draw on the whiskey.

"So, I suppose you know my coaching philosophy about as well as anybody. Tell me, Hal, have you ever seen me call two double steals in one game?"

Walker pulled off his cap and ran his hands through what was left of his hair. "I never have thought about it. No, now that you mention it, no. Look, I know what you're driving at. Yeah, from where I stand every game, you've been calling it rather oddly this year."

"Not badly, just oddly, right?"

"Hell no, Jake, you've been calling some great games."

I know I have, Hal," Conrad said, tilting his glass and staring thoughtfully into the amber fluid. "It's just that I've been calling for plays and strategy that I've never called in my whole managing career. I've been looking through these old abstracts from past seasons. Sure, we've never been known for having a speedy team, but I can't find very many suicide squeeze bunts or double steals or hit-and-runs, It's just never been my style. Hasn't it surprised you?"

"Frankly it has, but it's been working so damned well I just figured you know what you're doing. We sure kicked the A's butts tonight."

"That's just it, Hal, I'm not sure I *do* know what I'm doing. Lately, I just seem to come up with a call, flash the sign over to you and the next thing we know, we got two more runs. Like tonight, what'd we do? Double steal, single up the middle, in the fifth and sixth innings, wasn't it? Identical plays, two runs each, like clockwork. I'm not complaining, mind you, I'm just reflecting on all this. I'm enjoying it and I probably wouldn't even be dwelling on it if it weren't for that Hinkley article that practically called for my sainthood. I don't feel like I'm running this ball club. I feel like it's running me."

"Don't get down on yourself," Walker said. "I think I know what's happening. You've been starved for talent so long that your managing style reflected it. But you're no bozo. You finally got a team that *can do*, so you're letting them do it, helping them do it. If you'd have tried a double steal five years ago, that old team of yours would have figured a way to get triple-played. These kids of ours are just opening up the game for you and you're smart enough to respond. That's what I been figuring as I watch the calls you make. Give yourself some credit."

"I think I will," said Conrad as he polished off his glass. "Care for another? Don't mind if I do. You're right, Hal. That's the same conclusion I've been drawing too. These boys are forcing this old dog to learn new tricks. It's just that I wonder where I get all these new ideas. It's like there's a voice inside of me telling me to go out on a limb with the kind of play I never would have tried, maybe never even tried once in my career, even as a player. I never was a wild man on the base paths."

"Yeah but, Jake, you've got a keen baseball mind. You've watched all the moves over the years. You're just responding to the talent you got now and naturally using it to its potential. I always knew you had it in you. Why do you think I've been putting up with you all these years?"

Conrad laughed and loosened up. "Okay, where do I go to surrender? I believe you, and I'm just going to keep enjoying this season. Maybe they'll coin some phrase for my daring new style of ball. What could they call it, Jake Ball?"

"If you're going to get silly on me," Walker said, "maybe they should call it Jerk Ball!"

The two old friends belly-laughed and smiled at each other. Jake Conrad poured a couple more drinks, leaned back in his chair with a wry grin on his face. He might as well face it. He had a winning team at last, and he might as well enjoy it while it lasted.

Lloyd Cronin stared at his face in the mirror. There were three days of grizzly stubble on his chin, but he'd take care of that later. Right now, his main concern was his hair. Kinda scraggly in back, he thought. I don't know if I can do this. He waved the scissors as he lined them up in the mirror. They always went the opposite way he intended them to go. He gave it a few more weak tries, then gave up. He took another quick look in the mirror, frowned and walked out of the bathroom.

He'd ventured out to get a haircut a couple days back, and the results were disquieting. When is this going to stop, he thought darkly. I truly am going crazy. I can't go one hundred yards from my door without becoming scared to death.

He thought about that young couple in the car. The attack had hit just as he had come abreast of their passenger door. He had frozen with fear, and when it intensified he had looked around wildly, trying to keep his bearings. He saw the couple staring at him blankly. For a moment they looked vaguely familiar, but he couldn't place them. Then all he wanted to do was dash to the safety of his home. He only hoped that he didn't know them. He'd hate to think that anybody could see him like this.

Cronin walked up the hall to the living room. The whole place was littered with beer cans and empty pizza boxes, and newspapers were strewn about. He cleared a spot on the sofa and sat down. He then picked up the day's sports page and let out a long breath that was more of a rattle. He'd taken up smoking again. Something to do.

The greatest baseball season in Cleveland memory was unfolding and he was trapped in his apartment. It just didn't seem right. He wondered if the seeds for this phobia had been there all along. What predisposed him to it, and why now? He couldn't reason it out. His mind had grown as dull and lifeless as his pasty face. He did know one thing, though. He needed help, had to find help. He was too afraid to drive but he didn't want anybody at the paper to see him, so he had few choices of people to call. The boys downtown still thought he had some strange debilitating flu. Or at least he hoped they believed him.

He had the beginnings of a plan. He'd have to clean himself up, swallow his pride and call his ex-wife. Loretta would take a grim satisfaction in helping him, but he could put up with that if he could get out of there. She at least would be discreet. He could count on that much. She'd hate it if any of her friends thought she was connected with a loony.

Cronin got up and began a slow effort to pick up the mess that was his home. I should be ready to break out of here in a couple of days. Just gotta clean things up. And figure out how to cut my hair. If Loretta saw me like this, she'd probably walk out and change her phone number.

He took a stack of pizza boxes and moved them from the coffee table to the dining room table. There, that's a start.

"Greetings, First Commissioner Tarn. Evan reporting as scheduled. My reports no longer need to have so much detail in terms of team performance, as I'm sure you're perfectly capable of evaluating that from the superb holovision coverage. There are, of course, some behind-the-scenes occurrences that you would find of interest.

"First, let me convey the feelings of the team concerning the sad news of Belteron's apparent death. It has cast quite a pall on the happy proceedings of the Season, as so many of our all-star squad had not only great respect for someone who most likely was the greatest player of all time, but many had played with him at Seaview as well. Perhaps now we'll only be able to speculate on what a grand career he would have had if he'd been able to play as long as his celebrated father, and I'm sure the citizens of Ball Four will miss his heroics considerably. It has given me pause to think about my urging his deselection from the challenge team. He was in many ways a rebel, but so many true geniuses who have contributed to the creation of our wonderful life on Ball Four have had some special spark which those of us with smaller abilities cannot always fathom. Perhaps I should have taken advantage of it instead of fearing it. It will be a subject for speculation for some time, and I hope my name will not be linked to it in the history books in a way that displays a lack of judgment. Only time will tell. In the meantime we will honor his memory by dedicating our play on Earth to our fallen comrade. It serves as an example that even in our world where safety and health have been taken for granted, we still can occasionally lose some very prized possessions.

"The good news is that our team, as you undoubtedly have witnessed in the holocasts, is performing brilliantly. They have come together as a unit, loyal not only to the goals of the Operation but to each other and to the entire support staff and management as well. It seems almost unnecessary at this point even to finish the Season to demonstrate our superiority. It has become apparent that our ability and style of baseball far surpasses even the greatest of Earthling teams, and all that remains is for those of us on Earth to enjoy what will continue to be a stunning streak of victories, and for those on Ball Four to enjoy the entertainment of baseball contests spanning a galaxy.

"As I had informed Operation Command, I have recently relaxed my grip on the play-by-play control I had been exerting. I had begun to detect a profound discomfort in the psyche of Jake Conrad. He was undoubtedly beginning to wonder why the team was playing the way it has been, and why he was invoking so many uncharacteristic strategies. Since the team is so strong and Conrad by now has been well-schooled in the possibilities by the play-calling I have done, he would do well to fly solo, if you will, for some time, if not for the rest of the season. I will intervene as little as possible. This in no way detracts from or shares our accomplishments with the Earthlings. They will now be allowed to assist us in carrying out our schemes. This decision will hopefully have the effect of easing the minds of our Earthling cohorts, and thus projecting a more believable team image. We are always on guard to mute any appearance that would alert anyone in the surprisingly active and suspicious media that what we are accomplishing should be subject to undue scrutiny, as in the Lloyd Cronin case.

"I can report that Lloyd Cronin has most assuredly been removed as an investigative threat and by the time you view this report, we will have freed him from disruption. We have not enjoyed subjecting him to discomfort, as necessary as it may have been. We will not only free him, but, as soon as we can be reassured that he is in no way a threat, we will also send a mind soothing team to assist in his recovery. Within a short period of time his health, mental and otherwise, will be restored, hopefully to the extent that he can resume his duties as a columnist. We only wish the best to the Earthlings we encounter. We have two main goals: to proceed without discovery and to soundly defeat them at baseball! So far, we are successful on both accounts.

"I received the news of your intention to join us on Earth in time for the Universe Series with the most profound pleasure. I am only disappointed that you must leave the esteemed Second Councilor Semptor at home to oversee Ball Four in your absence. A great feeling of friendship and admiration has emerged from the work we've done together in this endeavor, and I am saddened that Semptor cannot be here in person to witness his handiwork. In a real sense, I and the team as a whole are merely tools in the hands of the Second Councilor and yourself as well as, in the larger view, all of Ball Four itself.

"Before this baseballer waxes too poetic and pretends even more to be what he is not, I shall terminate this report. I look forward to the time I shall be able to greet your arrival on Earth. A safe and swift journey, I'm sure. Evan off."

Richard Bates turned off the television monitor and clucked thoughtfully as he fingered through the notes he had just taken of the game between the Indians and the Oakland A's. There was absolutely no question about it: what he had just witnessed confirmed his theory once again. He would have a better idea once he'd entered the data in the computer and produced another report, but it was very clear he was on the right track.

A smug smile stretched across his lips. This was turning out to be a very interesting season, and he was glad he had decided to combine his hobby of keeping baseball statistics with his summer internship at WCLV-TV. He was grateful that the Journalism department at the University of Michigan had allowed him to start the internship during the spring quarter. This way he would be able to cover the whole baseball season and save a whole term's tuition while earning up to ten units, as long as he wrote the necessary papers to document his work. No sweat. What he had in mind would more than satisfy the department head, and it wasn't doing his reputation at WCLV-TV any harm either.

Already Ron Osterman, the sportscaster on the evening news, had featured his computer reports on more than one occasion. His computer comparison of the Indians' record after twenty games versus any known team in statistical history with the same average age per player had attracted a lot of attention at the station. It had shown that the present Cleveland team was the greatest in history for its average age, at least for those twenty games. The other report that, although other teams had started a season at a better pace than 19-4, no other team had compiled such an awesome set of team statistics. The success of these reports had caused the management to consider letting Richard arrange statistics graphics for the ninety-odd telecasts of Indian games they were doing, but the fact that it wasn't in his job description (or pay rate!) had helped them decide against it. The additional fact that the present telecast statistician threw a fit might have had something to do with it too. In the end, Richard was encouraged to forward his reports to the statistician, who then would determine if they were of any use. Occasionally Richard would see a stat graphic which he knew was based on his work. It pleased him, even if he wasn't getting the proper credit.

What he was now working on would get him the credit he deserved if data kept piling up in support of his hypothesis. In fact, what he was finding was so startling that he had already decided to go to an outside agency, maybe some paper like *USA Today*, to have it published. He'd be happy as long as he could at least share the by-line.

It was important for more than one reason. He was earning valuable experience at WCLV-TV, but he was getting into quite a financial jam. He had only one more year at the University to get his degree in journalism, but his parents had indicated a possible shortfall of funds to cover his last year's tuition, let alone living expenses. If he could score big on an exclusive expose of this type, he might make enough to make ends meet. Or, at the very least, he might gain enough notoriety to encourage the Ann Arbor paper to give him more than his petty stipend as part-time student reporter. Richard was counting on his scoop to bankroll his last year at school.

He had a lot of work to do and he had to do it fast. Already, some stories had come out in other parts of the country that had called attention to the strange play of the Indians. Some of the California Angels had accused the

Indians of somehow stealing their signs, and the manager of the A's had just a few minutes ago made the same accusation regarding that night's game. Richard had seen the raw footage of the interview on the station feed. But so far no one had put together any data to support the notion that the Indians were doing it on a grand scale, nor had anyone the proof that they were indeed doing it at all. All that had so far emerged was a bunch of spontaneous off-handed accusations. It was the focus of Richard's computer-driven investigation to statistically support the notion that there was signal stealing taking place on a historically unprecedented scale. There were just too many anomalies to explain them away. That night's failure of the Indians to be pulled into the hit-and-run was only one incidence. Richard had seen others, and he intended to collect the data that would demonstrate conclusively that there was a pattern.

Richard Bates had everything a person could possibly need for such an undertaking. He had the game videos that the station kept of its own telecasts, and, in addition, through the sports desk he could access the Major League Baseball footage that included all the other games. It was going to take a lot of work to go through the game tapes play-by-play and swing-by-swing, but he had drafted a couple of his computer hacker buddies who were also baseball stat junkies to help him compile data. Once they'd gone through the game tapes, Richard had programs that he'd personally designed that were powerful enough to crunch the data into lovely bite-size morsels. If his working hypothesis had any merit at all, *USA Today* would be eating out of his hand in no time.

14

San Francisco Chronicle
May 22nd.

Red Henderson

EARTH TO LOU CHAMBERS...

The announcement yesterday of the signings of two new players wouldn't ordinarily cause anyone to bat an eye, but when the press release listed no details of previous teams or experience, I'm sure that more than just this reporter grabbed for his phone. General manager Hal Barnham was very matter-of-fact as he explained that not only did these two new players, catcher Billy Icarus and right-handed pitcher Jimmy Strongbow, have no previous experience in organized ball but also were, at the time of the signings, actually employees of the groundskeeping crew of the San Francisco Giants. Barnham went on to say that he had complete confidence in Lou Chambers' decision to sign the players and suggested that the press give the guys a chance to show what they can do. Well, Hal, I will, I promise, but I've got a suggestion for you as well. It's reality check time. It's time to snap some smelling salts under Lou Chambers' nose and ask him how much patience the fans of San Francisco need to have.

Who is Billy Icarus? No one knows. We all know that Ed Quigley's out for the foreseeable future and that minor league prospects are bleak, but signing someone from the grounds crew can only be viewed as a desperate act, and it's too likely to blow up in their faces.

The other player, Jimmy Strongbow, a twenty-year-old that Chambers apparently checked out at a Phoenix tryout camp and rejected two years ago, is presently the man in charge of preparing the pitcher's mound for the real pitchers. And now, out of the blue, Lou likes what he sees? Sure, the right-handed starter situation is weak, but this strains credulity.

Okay, this is San Francisco, the City that Knows How, a place where the unusual is the usual and the abnormal is the norm, but I've never felt this freewheeling fanciful lifestyle could apply successfully to sports. I don't think so now, and I'm not going to sit idly by and be afraid to let my readers know the truth. This stunt is not only unprecedented in baseball history, but will make a nice sidebar in some writer's future account of the day a whole franchise went up in smoke.

Hal Barnham, I'll give these guys a look because you asked me to and because it's my job. But it's also my job to stay objective and rational in the midst of the emotional storm that a baseball season often becomes. So, Mr. Barnham, I sincerely hope I don't get to say "I told you so," but I seriously recommend you take a cold realistic look around you.

As for your manager, all I can say is, Lou Chambers, phone home.

Tuesday, May 21st, Billy Icarus and Jimmy Strongbow spent getting suited up and working out under the watchful eye of Lou Chambers. The press had not been invited to the stadium and the press gate was locked. The reporters who did show up after the news release of the signings were turned away. Barnham and Chambers were very nervous indeed.

Burt, the grounds crew manager, had lodged a feeble protest and had threatened to quit. Hal Barnham had urged him in no uncertain terms to do so. After that, Burt had stormed off swearing under his breath, but hadn't protested further.

Chambers gradually relaxed during the workout, almost against his will. He had to admit he liked what he saw, liked it a lot. Strongbow continued to impress him and Icarus was completely solid behind the plate. Eddie Renker had graciously agreed to give up part of his day off and stand at second to take throws from Icarus. This part of Icarus' game also looked strong. All in all, the decision to sign the two was appearing less foolhardy all the time. Chambers couldn't wait until these boys proved themselves in a game or two. The press would no doubt be merciless until then. The worst thing about losing or being wrong, Chambers always felt, was reading about it in the paper.

Another strange turn of events took place after the workout. Willie Washington, Mitch Simpson, Rick Barker, Bob Butterfield and Mickey Roberts showed up out of the blue and, along with Renker, had a batting clinic with Billy Icarus. They dragged the batting cage out and Jimmy threw batting practice while Billy talked to the guys as they each took turns in the cage. Chambers wisely stayed out of it, but he was pleased that this sign of teamwork was being evidenced. There certainly was more to this Billy Icarus than met the eye. But Chambers had to acknowledge that it seemed good for the team. He'd seen this kind of team camaraderie before, but it had been a while. The last time he could remember was the time they'd won the pennant some years back. The connection made him smile, even if they were 12-25.

The division-leading Los Angeles Dodgers came into town for a brief, two-game series beginning Wednesday. More than the usual complement of reporters converged on Candlestick, partly because of the Dodgers, but mostly because of the interest piqued by the unusual acquisition of Billy and Jimmy. Many of the stations in the press box were being shared by two reporters, and a lively discussion could be heard as game time approached. The consensus seemed to be that the Giants had gone off the deep end and reporters couldn't wait to see Billy Icarus be thrown to the lions.

Billy himself couldn't wait either, but for distinctly different reasons. He hadn't swung a bat in a game for what seemed like ages, and he suppressed his glee at resuming his beloved sport. He remained rather subdued, and played the part of the humble applicant. Chambers had saved him from undue distractions by banning the press from interviewing Billy. He told them to let Billy's bat do the talking for now. Red Henderson of the Chronicle tried to get around the ban only to be greeted by the icy glare of Lou Chambers.

"I'm surprised you even give a damn after what you said in this morning's rag, Henderson."

"Ah c'mon, Lou, let us at the kid," Henderson pleaded. "Sorry about the column, but the whole thing does look pretty cock-eyed, you gotta admit. Anyway, whaddya got to hide?"

"Not a thing, Red. But after today's column and that crap last week, you better be ready to buy a few rounds at the Stadium Club after the game. Icarus goes hitless and they're on me. Are we on?"

"Okay, but you can't hide him forever."

Billy's bat had to wait until the bottom of the second to voice an opinion. There was no score and two away when Butterfield singled. Chambers had put Billy in the seventh spot not only out of deference to the veterans but also from simple common sense. Billy still had much to prove.

Billy Icarus stepped in right-handed. He took two quick strikes, which prompted sage nods throughout the press box. When he took a pitch wasted outside, the whole stadium quieted and held its breath. Just such a moment, whether on Earth or back home on Ball Four, was what Billy loved best about the game.

On the next pitch, he slammed the challenging fastball far into the left field cheap seats, and pandemonium broke out all over the stadium. Jaws dropped in the press box as dozens of reporters picked up their extensions at the same time. All but a few had to wait for a line to open up. By the time Billy rounded the bases the whole Giants' team was waiting at home plate. Chambers sat alone in the dugout, shaking his head. What the hell, he thought, as he jogged out and joined his boys.

Kiley Upton sailed along through the innings, buoyed by the carnival atmosphere at the Park. Everybody was having fun except the Dodgers who, strong as they were, could not stem the rising tide. Billy's second plate appearance had lit up the fans again, as he drove a slider up the gap in left to drive in two runs. The Dodger center fielder bobbled the ball, and Billy dug for third. As the throw came in, Billy mentally screamed *LOOKOUT!* The third baseman's eyes jerked momentarily toward Billy, and by the time he looked back for the ball, all he could do was stab wildly at it while it sailed past his glove. Billy jumped out of his slide and easily reached home plate ahead of the throw.

Billy stepped to the plate again in the sixth, but by this time the Dodgers has brought in a left-handed reliever. As he came up to the right side of the plate, the crowd buzzed with anticipation. They didn't have to wait long. Billy punched the ball into short right for a single. As he took his lead from first base, he scanned the pitcher's mind only to discover that he was thinking in Spanish. He quickly strained to see what he could pick up from the catcher, and waited for something on the order of an inside curve. On the fourth pitch they obliged him, and he slid into second well ahead of the throw.

The Dodgers tried to mount a threat in the seventh inning, and had gotten one run in already when they decided to challenge the new catcher's arm. Dodger speedster Renaldo Samuel fidgeted off first. Billy could sense the impending attempt, and called for a fastball on the outside corner. Upton missed but missed outside, and Billy's toss got to second well ahead of Samuel. By this time the press corps was caught up in the spirit, and let out a quiet roar of approval. Only Red Henderson frowned noticeably. He knew the shoe would soon be on the other foot.

The Dodgers walked Billy to lead off the seventh inning, and he promptly stole his second base of the game. He reached third on a infield single by Archie Stokes, but was stranded there by a pop out and a double play.

Billy had decided that he'd done enough for the game and would act mortal if he got another chance at the plate. The Giants were comfortably ahead 9-2 when he found himself coming to bat yet again. It was the bottom of the eighth, two out, with Barker, Washington and Butterfield filling the bags. He changed his mind and allowed himself one more bit of fun. It couldn't hurt and, what's more, the fans loved it when the Giants humiliated the rival Dodgers. Billy was getting caught up in the emotions which were so foreign to the Ball Fourian experience, and he liked it, a lot.

He took a ball outside and fouled off the next. He stepped out of the box and pretended to need some pine tar from the on-deck circle. Before heading back to the plate, he looked into the Giants' dugout at Chambers.

"This one's for you, Skipper," he yelled over. Chambers, not guessing what he meant, didn't know how to react. He gave Billy a slight nod.

Billy stood back in, and sent the next pitch on a screaming rope to deep center. It appeared to be still climbing when it cleared the fence. The ball shot into the tunnel leading out of the stadium, and was well through it when it finally touched down. It skipped along the concrete before banging against the fence that separated the stadium from the parking lot. A startled guard standing a few feet away walked over and picked it up. He would discover later what he had found, and wisely decided not to turn it in.

The bedlam that accompanied Billy's lap around the bases echoed around the Park, brought joy to the hearts of the fans and a bit of a throb to Red Henderson's temples. He rummaged through his pockets and quickly reasoned that he would need his charge card to make the gang at the Stadium Club forget his regrettable column. It just as quickly occurred to him that his column tomorrow would do well to center on how enthusiastically he was awaiting Jimmy Strongbow's impending debut.

The team in the dugout, grasping the meaning of Billy's remark, egged Chambers on until he went out alone to greet him at home plate. The crowd loved it, Chambers forgot himself and doffed his cap, overlooking for a second that it hadn't been he who had hit the homer. Billy slapped him on the back and followed suit. This was not a pennant-clinching victory or anything like it, but it was a great moment and the fans wouldn't let go of it until Billy came out for a final bow. Even after Archie Stokes fouled out to end the inning, the crowd continued to stomp its feet in praise of their Giants, their 13-25 Giants.

It hadn't been easy running the gauntlet of reporters after the game, but Billy had wisely gotten dressed in a hurry and pretended to the press that he had an important matter to attend to after the game. He dodged questions with smiles and nods, and did his best to stick to the cliches and hackneyed phrases he'd been taught in his many briefings at home. He was not surprised that they worked. Humans loved humility in their heroes, and this humility was second nature for Billy. He'd been very humble back on Ball Four; it came instinctively to the great ones.

Once Billy managed to get free of the crush of attention, he slipped into the crowd around the bus stops east of the stadium. His face was too new for the fans to recognize, and he boarded a bus for downtown. He enjoyed listening to the banter of the riders as they talked about the game. His name was on everyone's lips. He smiled to himself. He hadn't felt this good since his rookie year.

There were so many things to think about, so much to do, now that he was on the team. Billy didn't know how long he could get away with riding the bus and living in a transient hotel. After he'd moved from the Meredith for appearance's sake, he had taken up lodging in a little hotel a few blocks from the library. It was comfortable enough, but no place for a baseball star, with its ragamuffin, vagabond clientele. He was hampered by the lack of identification cards, bank accounts and such, but it was obvious that he'd have to find a suitable apartment quickly. And he might have to risk getting a car, although he could probably get by with acting the part of an eccentric who didn't like driving. This would fit in with the basic persona he would need to adopt to avoid excessive delving into his personal life. Yes, there was much to think about, much planning to do. He grabbed a transfer downtown and headed for Golden Gate Park. He did his best thinking in parks.

He got off the bus on Stanyan Street. Here the Panhandle merged with the main body of the park. There was still plenty of daylight left and crowds of bicyclists, skateboarders and joggers zig-zagged this way and that. Billy, however, was oblivious to it all, and by the time he found quieter, less traveled paths he'd worked out plans for the day-to-day realities of life in San Francisco. However, one question loomed large and unresolved. It was time he faced it.

His main disagreement with the Operation leadership had been the use of mental tactics against Earthling baseball teams. In fact, it had most certainly led to his deselection. Out of a sense of honor, he had avoided playing mind games against any member of the Giants, who were now his teammates. He had, however, used quite a number of mind manipulations against Lou Chambers and others in order to make the team, even to the extent of reading McIlhenny's and O'Nealy's minds during the tryout. And, at the game that afternoon, he had used every gambit, every trick in the book to make himself look good and to assure his acceptance onto the team. Now that he had reached this goal, he was in a quandary. If he were to continue this use of his mental advantage to guide the Giants to victory, he would be doing the very thing he had taken such a strong stand against for the Ball Fourians. Using every advantage at his disposal, he still had no way of guaranteeing that the Giants would make it to the World Series to challenge the Indians. Must he violate his honor to give himself and the Giants a chance?

There could be but one answer: no. He had made his stand on Ball Four, and it had cost him his slot on the challenge team. He had, for whatever reasons, come to Earth to attempt to prove the point that fairness was more important, more vital, than innate superiority. He had no choice but to play by his own rules. He'd made the team. They'd have a fighting chance. They'd have to win it according to their talent and the breaks. Billy could no longer use the techniques that were allowing the Indians to crush the opposition. If and when the Giants reached the World Series, then it would be another story. He could use any and all methods to oppose the Ball Fourian team. But he would have to remain true to his code until then.

A strong, peaceful feeling washed over him. He knew what he had decided was the only course he could take. As he walked on through the trees and flowers of the park, Billy could sense, under his feelings of honor and conviction, an uncharacteristic atmosphere of wild uncertainty begin to emerge. Perhaps this is what it was like to be human. To challenge the Ball Fourian baseball invasion with humans as his comrades-in-arms required all the integrity and humanity that he could muster. He could live with the doubt. Without it, there could be no challenge. In an instant, he realized what had been wrong with Operation Universe Series from the beginning. The Ball Fourian strategy precluded defeat. Where was the honor in that? It wasn't a matter of honor, it was a matter of domination. With all of the centuries of rapid evolution to the high state of culture on Ball Four, there lacked a deeper sense of universal honor. Billy once again wondered why he presumed to define or defend that sense of honor. Who was he to claim title to such a right?

Billy knew *that* question would have to remain unanswered for the time being. There was one more, however, to consider. Had he brought Jimmy Strongbow to the brink of success only to abandon him now that his major league debut was imminent? No, he owed Jimmy more than that. He would assure Jimmy what he had given himself. Billy had used mental methods to ensure his own spot on the roster. He would give Jimmy the same advantage. But he resolved to use mental means only to the extent that it was needed to support Jimmy's debut performance and strengthen his confidence. After that, Jimmy would have to make it on his own. It had to be. Billy wouldn't be there forever to support Jimmy's talent, and it would be cruel to set Jimmy up for a fall when Billy was no longer there to read batter's minds. Jimmy's talents must be nurtured to allow him to make it on his own. Billy had no doubt that Jimmy had what it took. Jimmy could only discover it through triumph over adversity. It would be a huge disservice to deny him the true test of character that would make him strong.

The next day, Billy's debut as a "human" went well, but not well enough for a victory. Art French pitched a good six innings, yielding two runs. The Dodgers then got to reliever Steve Lafite for two more in the ninth for the win. Billy himself fared well, but his two hits produced a single RBI, and the eighth inning blast by Rick Barker came with no one aboard. The Dodgers won 4-3.

At least Billy could take solace from the fact that he now knew he could hit Earthling pitching without mind reading. The pitching style on Earth was very similar to that on Ball Four, with the exception that humans threw the fastball much more often. Ball Fourians tried to outfox their batting opponents with a greater variety of pitches and speeds, while waiting for one side or the other to stumble mentally. The best teams on Ball Four rarely made such mental errors. Billy's own Seaview Captains were known to go ten games without an "open minder," and did rely more on fastballs for "out" pitches, as they did here on Earth. However, Billy naturally had never faced his own pitchers in competition. But he knew he was going to enjoy this season whatever the outcome, because he loved to hit the fastball.

Attendance at Candlestick Park had steadily grown since the low point around the beginning of May, and the excitement of Billy's debut generated still more. It was no surprise, then, to see over forty thousand fans arrive on Friday night for the debut of Jimmy Strongbow. The press, which had castigated the Giants' management for signing the two nobodies, were now (since Billy's success) turning the debuts into high drama. The fans responded by turning out in droves.

During pregame warm-ups, the mood was festive for everybody except Jimmy Strongbow. He loosened up with a bullpen catcher, with Brad O'Nealy keeping a watchful eye while trying to lighten the mood with jokes and quips. But nothing could ease the tension growing in the pit of Jimmy's stomach. He looked over at Billy, who was busy with the infield workout. Brad sensed the tension and walked over to Jimmy.

"Chief, that I won my major league debut is now in the history books. I'll always remember it. What I hope everybody forgets, though, is that I walked the first two batters I faced. If Archie hadn't turned that double play, who knows, I might be selling shoes by now. All I can tell you is that you've just got to get into the ball game and try to forget everything else. There isn't a player alive that hasn't gotten the heebie-jeebies in his debut."

"I don't know, Brad," Jimmy said in pale tones, "I was okay pitching to the Safford High Bobcats, but the Cincinnati Reds, no, I don't think so."

"Just think of it this way, Chief. The only difference is that it'll be more fun striking out Reds than it was Bobcats, way more fun."

"There is nothing fun about anything right now," Jimmy shot back. "Nothing fun at all."

"Well, time will tell. Oh, by the way, I want to congratulate you for telling Barnham to go to hell about the long hair. That took guts. I like my hair short, but I don't agree with team policies against it. Seems juvenile."

Jimmy shook his head, and the long black hair waved under his cap. It almost reached the top of the numbers on the back of his jersey. "It didn't take any courage, Brad. I had 'em. I told them it was a cultural thing for Indians. They were afraid of racism or something. Anyway, I just can't cut my hair. You know, it really is part of my heritage, at least for me. I wasn't lying."

"Well, nice going anyway, Samson. Say, how do you feel?"

Jimmy paused to reflect. "Actually, much better."

"See," O'Nealy said with a grin, "if you don't think about it, it goes away. You better go back to work."

"Yeah, thanks."

Gametime approached and Jimmy ambled up to the mound, the mound that less than a week ago had been his responsibility to groom, not throw from. He knelt down and patted it, wishing he had a trowel. The slope was a bit uneven. He scraped at it with his spikes, then gave up. He had bigger things to worry about. They were called the Cincinnati Reds.

Billy Icarus came up. "I'm not going to ask you how you feel, Jimmy. I just want to tell you that you're not in this alone. You've got me and seven other players who are very interested in lending you a hand. You can count on them. It's your job to pitch, and theirs to get outs. You aren't doing it alone. You don't have to strike everybody out, and it's really you and I that are pitching this game. Chambers said I could call the whole game because I know you and he doesn't. I spent most of this afternoon reading the scouting reports on the Reds' hitters. I know them like the back of my hand, and I won't let you down. I call 'em and you throw 'em, okay?"

"Okay," Jimmy said, letting out a long breath. "I guess that's all I can do."

"Another thing, Jimmy, the most important thing. Remember this: you've got it. You've got what it takes, and you know it, you've always known it. Focus on your Medicine Wheel, throw down your lanes and, above all, *don't think*. Let me do your thinking for you. If you start to lose your focus, don't pitch. Take your time. Look at me, and we'll help each other. Now, with your warm-up pitches, imagine with each one that you're centering more and more until, by the time the first batter stands in, you've stripped everything away except your power and vision. Let's get 'em, okay?"

Already Jimmy felt the focus coming and the power tingling in his anxious fingertips. With each warm-up toss, the power grew. The colors of his strike-zone Medicine Wheel grew more vibrant, and the brown clay of the infield took on the hues of Apacheria. His last throw hit with a force that echoed off the billboards along the mezzanine level. His stomach was still tight, but he wasn't thinking about it. He was barely thinking at all.

As the lead-off hitter stepped in, Billy stood with his mask off, his mind as white as the face of the moon. Jimmy paused, shuddered, then locked into Billy's eyes. They soothed, nurtured, relaxed. As Billy crouched down, the lanes to Jimmy's strike zone softly glowed. When Billy flashed the first sign, Jimmy was unaware of the crowd, and only barely aware of the shape in gray and red standing at the plate. He was very aware of the arrow and the target and, as he wound up, he felt more like a bow with its string stretched back to its fullest extent than he did a pitcher.

"Strike!"

Jimmy shivered as he realized that he'd barely been aware that he had thrown. He looked at Billy and refocused. The cougar was ready to pounce.

"Strike!" The batter had swung at a ball that had hit the plate.

Billy quickly gave the sign for change-up before the hitter had time to gather his wits, or Jimmy, for that matter, had time to think about the 0-2 count. Jimmy slackened the bowstring, leaned back and blazed a ball that floated at a disturbingly flat pace. The hitter lashed at it and pulled it so sharply foul that it nearly went into his own dugout.

Contact with wood broke the spell and, for a moment, Jimmy felt his vulnerability. Then he thought of the seven men behind him. Billy was right, he must count on them. As Billy called for the curve, Jimmy started to go into his wind-up and stopped. The batter stepped out. When he stepped back in, Jimmy was back in focus, the lanes were bright and the snake ready to slither. The batter watched without moving. Even after the umpire had called him out, he stood frozen. The ball couldn't make the strike zone from where it approached, but it had, and he knew it. He pivoted and slowly walked away.

The crowd roared. Billy stood with the thinnest trace of a smile, and tossed the ball back to Jimmy, who caught it with a snap of the glove. His face was all business, to those who could see it. But deep inside, where he was truly pitching from, the eagle sat high in his mountain aerie. He looked down on the land and was satisfied.

Billy had played no mental tricks on that first batter, but merely spent his energies on nurturing and focusing Jimmy. He reflected that scouting reports were reliable, and Jimmy, who was an unknown commodity, had the edge. Billy decided that all he needed to do was concentrate on calling the right pitches and keep an eye on Jimmy's focus. Jimmy could do the rest.

And he did. As the game progressed, Jimmy threw with increasing control and the natural flow of a veteran. Billy needed to do very little. In fact, he had rarely seen such control by a new pitcher on Ball Four, where the mind component of training was so thorough before a rookie ever took the mound. Billy then knew with a certainty that Jimmy had been, like himself, born to play the game.

Jimmy gave up a smattering of hits, but no groups of them that would yield a run. He struck out ten. The Giants, on the other hand, were beating up on the Reds' staff unmercifully. By the end of the game, five Giants had hit home runs, Billy two of them.

Hal Barnham sat in his box chatting with his staff, trying to expand his role in finding Billy Icarus and Jimmy Strongbow with a few white lies. Lou Chambers passed the time jawing with Ron McIlhenny and enjoying not having to call every pitch. Brad O'Nealy sat at the end of the bullpen bench, yelling "Geronimo!" every time Jimmy brushed a batter back. The rest of the team joked and fooled around in the dugout, and superstitiously gave Jimmy the cold shoulder. The only exception was when Jimmy returned to the dugout after striking out for the fourth time. The team hummed the Chopin funeral march theme. Everybody cracked up and Jimmy smiled for the first time in the game. By game's end it was obvious that Jimmy could pitch in the majors. It was equally obvious that he needed batting practice in the worst way.

When it was all over, Jimmy "Chief" Strongbow had pitched a complete game and won his major league debut by the score of 12-0.

There was a tremendous desire on the part of everyone to go out and celebrate after Jimmy's win. Every man in the organization sensed that a corner had been turned by the franchise. No one understood this more clearly than Lou Chambers, who announced that any one caught even thinking about partying would be fined his life savings. Tomorrow was a day game and everyone was to show up fresh and ready to play. Brad O'Nealy made Jimmy and Billy vow to hold Sunday night open. He wanted to take them out to dinner.

Saturday morning everyone did indeed come to ready to play. A major exception was Julio Gonzalez. To make room for Jimmy on the roster, Chambers had sent him down to Phoenix; the thirty year-old was angered by the move, but at 0-7 he could hardly protest. Chambers believed in a four-man rotation. For now it would be Upton, French, Strongbow and O'Nealy; and no one was more up for the Saturday game than Brad O'Nealy. With all his jocularity, he'd been feeling a lot of pressure to carry the team. Now that Jimmy was aboard, he could relax and throw with abandon.

And throw with abandon he did. He took a no-hitter into the seventh, when he gave up his lone hit, a bloop single to right. It was fortuitous that he was so strong because the Reds' ace, Geoff Pepper, was nearly as miserly with the hits. Billy got two and Eddie Renker one; Renker's lone hit drove in Billy in the eighth inning for the only run O'Nealy would need.

The Cincinnati Reds extracted some degree of revenge on Sunday at the expense of Kiley Upton. They chased him by the fourth, and hung on to beat the Giants, 7-5.

The homestand against Western Division teams was shaping up nicely, however. There'd be no rest until Thursday, as the Atlanta Braves were due in for a three-game series starting Monday night. A sweep could move the Giants past the Braves into fourth place.

Sunday, after the game, Jimmy and Billy met Brad O'Nealy at a small French restaurant on the eastern slope of Telegraph Hill, a mere five minutes' walk from Jimmy's cottage. The atmosphere was relaxed, the view of the Bay charming. And, to Billy's great enjoyment, the food was delicious. They talked about the recent games, Jimmy's successful debut and Brad's own success until it was time for dessert and coffee. Then O'Nealy focused on Billy with his usual directness.

"So what's the deal, Billy," O'Nealy said, spearing a piece of chocolate torte. "How long have you been in San Francisco?"

"Oh, a little over a month," Billy offered amiably.

"And before that?"

"No place a Harvard boy would know," said Billy, in equally light tones.

Brad chuckled. "I can see you're not going to tell me any more than you've told Jimmy. Yes, Billy, we've talked about you. You're quite the mystery man, aren't you?"

"Brad, besides Jimmy, I trust you more than anyone else on the team. I feel I can be very direct with you."

"You can," Brad said simply.

"As I've told Jimmy, and I'll tell you as much, there will come a time when who I am and where I come from will be important. That time hasn't arrived."

"Wow, your candor is shocking," quipped Brad.

"I know you find it strange," Billy countered. "I will share one thing with you. Where I come from is, well, problematical at best."

Jimmy jumped in. "Billy, what could be the problem? Now that we've seen you play, it's obvious that you must have been in baseball all your life. You hit like crazy, run like mad and you've coached me like the best in the business. And I've seen you throw. Yeah, Brad, while we were training Billy threw a little. He's better than I am, I'll tell you."

"Better than *moi*?" Brad said, pointing at himself with both hands.

"This is serious, Brad. Look, Billy, I know you've known us for a short time, but we're your friends. What could you have done that we wouldn't accept?"

"I know this is serious," Brad interjected. "Jimmy's right, Billy. There's a lot of season left. People are going to start pushing you to open up. If you don't, a lot of suspicion is going to build up. It's human nature. You might as well start with us."

Billy leaned back in his chair and took a thoughtful sip of his sherry. He looked at the two friendly, concerned faces in front of him, and considered for a brief moment telling them everything. He wanted to scan their minds to reassure himself, but held back. He would have to trust them. He wanted to wait, but wondered what there was to gain. They would either believe or they wouldn't. They'd be ready to help him or not. It was as simple as that.

He had to answer. "It's just *not* that simple. First and foremost, we're ball players. We've got games to win, and destiny willing, more than that. Yes, I am going to have trouble with the sports press and I'll have to do quite a bit of maneuvering. They can never know who I really am and where I come from. I will have to tell the team eventually, and I'll no doubt be telling you two first. You are going to be my closest allies in the struggle ahead. We've got a lot of ground to gain. Let's get to work, let's play baseball. I've given you a little to chew on, and I'll make a deal with you. If I remember the schedule correctly, we leave after the Braves' series for twelve games on the road. That will put us back in town on the night of June twelfth and we'll have the thirteenth off. Let's meet here, or someplace more private, and I'll reveal all, everything, I'll hold nothing back. Agreed?"

Jimmy and Brad looked at each other, then back at Billy. Brad was finally the one to speak. This time he spoke earnestly.

"I should tell you you're nuts. If you don't mind a little Harvard talk, what you propose is utterly preposterous. However, I like it. I can't imagine why you feel you must deal with the issue of who you are in this circuitous manner, but my interest is truly piqued and, yes, I can wait. There is nothing boring about you, that much I admit. I'll enjoy waiting and speculating about you, Mr. Billy Icarus, but if you don't come clean on the thirteen of June, you're off my dinner list for good. How 'bout it, Chief?"

"I'm used to it by now, Brad. Sure, Billy, I'll go along with you on this one. At least we'll know in a couple of weeks. What'd you do, rob a bank?"

"Of course not, Jimmy. Thanks for giving me a break. I'll need your help with one more thing. Brad, I need to find a better place to live. I'm living at what you might call a dump. If the press finds out, it'll invite too much scrutiny. But I don't have any papers or credit, anything that could help me relocate. Jimmy told me you helped him get his place."

"What am I, a rental agency?" asked Brad. "No, just kidding. Listen, Jimmy's place is small, but I just scored a new pad that's got more room than

I need. It's in Pacific Heights. I chose it for the view, but it's got three bedrooms. What do you say? This way I don't have to keep my eye out for suspicious characters. I'll be living with one."

"That would be great," Billy replied. "And I could ride with you to the 'Stick."

"No car, eh? I am curious about you, Billy. But you are one helluva ball player. Can I get you another sherry, *mon ami*?"

15

The rejuvenated Giants set about their jobs with gusto each game, and Billy was pleased to join in the task without undue curiosity. The rest of the team seemed to accept him at face value and allowed him his anonymity. The agreement with Jimmy and Brad had deferred further inquiry from their direction. The press, fortunately, was satisfied to play up the "Lone Ranger and Tonto" angle that had come into vogue about the two new Giants. How long that might last was anybody's guess, but it did provide some breathing room.

The Giants took two out of three from Atlanta, and began the road trip in Houston to round out the grouping of all-West-Division play. The Astros tried a strange flanking maneuver regarding Billy. Though solidly in third place and a number of games ahead of the Giants, Houston could feel them breathing down their necks and sought to slow them down by obtaining a restraining order to prevent Billy from playing. They claimed that, until it was clear the Astros had no prior claim to his services, Billy should be restrained from play. The judge tossed the motion out as being totally without merit. The Astros could demonstrate neither prior claim nor the potential to suffer loss in the event of Billy's continued play. When the Astros countered that losing to the Giants would constitute such, the judge, though a Texan, laughed and banged his gavel. Case closed.

Whatever the Astros intended, it lit a fire under the Giants, who pulverized them in three straight decisions. Jimmy Strongbow made a particularly strong showing, striking out thirteen and posting his second complete game victory. Billy blasted four home runs in the series. The Giants ended the set of West Division games with a record of 11-4. June second found them at 20-28, still in fourth place but definitely making up for lost time.

The series with the Cubs in Chicago was interesting in several ways. The Cubs altered their rotation to pit the ace of their staff against Jimmy Strongbow, with two decided effects. One, Jimmy lost his first game and, two, Billy went hitless for the first time since joining the Giants. He had hit the ball well, but straight to a Cub everytime. He was tempted to mind read, but knew better. Billy couldn't use such tactics or winning would become too easy for the Giants, and they'd never need to pull together as a team. Only adversity could help them do that. And they would need to be close as a team for Billy's plans to succeed. The Giants lost all three games to the Cubs, and it took all of Billy's resolve not to interfere, especially when Brad got into a jam in the bottom of the ninth and succumbed to a two-out game-winning single by the weakest hitter in the Chicago line-up.

While in Chicago, Billy went into a store called The Self-Made Man, which he discovered while plowing through scientific catalogues back at the San Francisco Public Library. At this store, he spent a good deal of his remaining money from the orbital station on the purchase of six biofeedback machines. Three of them were simple, audio-style machines. The other three were more sophisticated. He had chosen these particular machines because they measured brain waves at alpha, beta and theta frequencies in both left and right brain hemispheres. Another feature was that they registered the wave states through a visual medium, using an array of various colored lights. They were currently available only through this one outlet. Billy had them packed in secure but plain boxes and handed them over to the Giants' equipment manager to see that they returned safely to Candlestick.

In the remaining six contests in New York and Montreal, they fared better than they did in Chicago. Brad O'Nealy lost another game, but Art French was particularly stellar in a game against the Mets. French's new reputation as a junkballer had apparently not yet reached New York, and it was amusing to see confused sluggers waving the stick at seventy-mile-an-hour knuckleballs. Jimmy posted his third victory of the season in a fifteen-strikeout trouncing of the Expos. All in all, the eastern road trip was a success. The Giants returned to San Francisco having improved their record to 27-33. There was every reason to hope for reaching .500 by the All-Star break.

Billy found yet another cause for satisfaction while on the road trip. He had begun to know the team better and better, and strengthened his relationships with those he already had connected with, such as Barker, Washington, Simpson, French and Upton. Eddie Renker was a bit of a hard case, not exactly unfriendly, just a bit of a maverick. He didn't mix with the players and avoided horseplay in the dressing room. Even his road roommate, Bob Butterfield, said that Eddie rarely spoke to him. Butterfield himself went out of his way to make Billy feel at home, and Billy knew that, down the line, this amiable country boy, so guileless and trustworthy, would be someone he could count on. The other surprise was Archie Stokes. The shortstop was also an enigma, so cool and business-like in his ways. He was a short, lean, dark-haired man, and the only Canadian on the team. He smiled broadly most of the time when not on the field, but it always seemed to be at some private joke. He, like Renker, was aloof and rarely had much to say. He was a superb fielder, excellent in execution of the fundamentals of the game, but not much of a hitter. Try as he might, Billy could find no particular way of helping Stokes, which was frustrating because, while in Montreal, Stokes had broken the ice and approached him.

"Say, Billy," Stokes said while waiting for his turn at batting practice, "you're often giving advice to the other players. You've yet to say anything to me. I admit I'm rather a weak hitter and I'm not too proud to take advice. While you were a groundskeeper I wasn't so keen to ask. But now that you're hitting .560 and you've belted six homers, I'm considerably more apt to listen."

Billy looked at the slight man with the plasticine grin, and didn't know which way to go.

"Archie, you puzzle me. I watch you bat, and I can't for the life of me figure it out. It would be easy to dismiss you as a naturally weak hitter, but that's what a lot of unimaginative coaches do and let it go at that. I've drawn a blank but I promise to keep an eye on your at-bats. In the meantime, I'll give you my standard advice. More than one batter I've known has never reached his potential simply for the lack of concentration. When you go to the plate, get all the way into the game."

Stokes nodded and let it go at that.

June thirteenth came at last, and Billy was reasonably assured that the needed cementing of relationships had set the stage for the truth he would now divulge. He and Jimmy had roomed together on the trip and, along with Brad, there had developed a closeness that Billy hoped would support them through the shockwaves he was about to generate. Ball Fourians were of course used to the idea of life throughout the galaxy, even if more than a generation had passed since the time of everyday contact. But it was clear that humans could but hold a different view.

They'd decided to meet for a barbecue at Jimmy's cottage, and the sunny, ambient weather made for quite a pleasant mood under the cover of the wisteria arbor. Steaks sizzled on the grill, the fragrance of flowers fought with the other agreeable aromas for dominance and, with the help of the wine, all were in good humor. Neither Jimmy nor Brad broached the subject, trusting that Billy would be true to his word when he was ready.

After the meal, they sat with their wine glasses, and the talk had fallen off as they relaxed in the cool shade. There would never be a better moment, if there could be a good one for such a revelation.

"Boys," Billy began, "I promised to end the mystery about my background and the time has come. What I've got to say will not be easily believed, so I'll ask one favor of you. Will you listen with whatever open mind you can maintain until I've finished, and then promise not to dismiss it out of hand?"

"Dramatic to the end, eh, my good man," kidded Brad.

"Do you agree?" Billy asked insistently.

"Of course."

"Sure," chimed in Jimmy.

"Okay, here it is," Billy went on. "My real name is Belteron. I'm from a planet called Ball Four, which is thousands of light years away on the other side of the galaxy. Until last season I was catcher and team leader of the Seaview Captains. I was the leader in the Ball Fourian major leagues in nearly all offensive catagories for the past six years. I am indeed twenty-eight and a veteran of eight seasons. I temporarily retired because of a dispute on which I will elaborate in due course."

The pair, sitting across from Billy, looked like a still photograph. Slowly, beginning with a silent chuckle, Brad began to laugh. It took him quite a few seconds to reach a crescendo, just short of a belly laugh, and nearly as long to move from guffaw, to chuckle, to snicker, then finally down to a titter before again falling silent. Jimmy's only movement was turning to watch Brad. They looked at each other, then back at Billy, who wore his usual amiable smile.

Brad broke the spell. "You're not human?"

"No."

"You're an alien?"

"Well, I guess that depends on your point of view," Billy responded. "Since I'm on your world and you're not on mine, then yes, I suppose I'm an alien."

"But, but, you *look* human," said Jimmy, entering the discussion.

"I've been biofashioned. That's a medical procedure whereby an entire body becomes reshaped, restructured, from the genetic level on up. It's vaguely similar to your plastic surgery, only vastly more sophisticated. As a matter of fact, I was biofashioned to resemble a famous baseball player from your past. Jimmy, you've told me you studied the greats of baseball history as a hobby. You should be able to recognize who I look like."

They both stared at Billy, half-trying to recognize who he resembled while, with the other half of their wits, they tried to reckon with what he was telling them. It hit them both at almost exactly the same time.

"I don't believe it!" exclaimed Brad.

"Lou Gehrig?" asked Jimmy.

"Lou Gehrig," replied Billy. "The Iron Horse of the old New York Yankees."

"This is pretty weird, Billy," Jimmy said, shaking his head.

"This is more than weird, Chief," said Brad. "But we promised, I don't know why, to look at this with an open mind. You're telling us you're an alien. We're your friends and, frankly, we've really come to respect you a lot since you've been around, and the last thing we want to do is subject you to an inquisition. But you do realize that what you've told us is basically unbelievable, to put it mildly."

Billy acknowledged him with a smile and a nod. Brad went on. "The only proof you offer us is that you look like Lou Gehrig. It's not only not much proof but, if you don't mind my saying so, not a very bright move for an alien who wants to play baseball on Earth."

"Agreed," said Billy. "It seemed like a good idea at the time and I really didn't have much choice. I had to move quickly. I've thought about it since I've been on Earth and, yes, there might be an arrogant lack of reasoning in that aspect of the plan. But I've come to the conclusion that the worst that can happen is someone might say I look like Lou Gehrig, and the original intent that it would subliminally support my acceptance as a ballplayer may still be valid. But I digress. Yes, it's not much proof, but it wasn't offered exactly as such. I've given it some thought and there are a number of ways to convince you of the truth of my story, not all of them very safe, for me at least. Here's one that will demonstrate quite a bit. Jimmy, could you get us some paper and a pen?"

Without speaking, Jimmy got up and went into the cottage.

"Billy, this is more entertaining than a Star Trek episode," Brad said as they waited for Jimmy to return. "And I'm still trying to keep an open mind. Your story is pretty full of holes. For one thing, how do you manage to speak English so well?"

"Oh, I studied it thoroughly for six years, and I've picked up a lot just since I've been here. Once we Ball Fourians learn something, it's more or less permanently imprinted on our brains, and we learn at a rather accelerated rate, at least compared to humans and other beings."

"Other beings?" said Brad incredulously.

"Forget I said that, please," said Billy as Jimmy came back with a small notebook and a pen.

"I'd be glad to," said Brad, now wearing a considerably dubious expression. "Okay, what have you got for us?"

"A simple little demonstration," Billy said, opening the notebook. He thought for a second, wrote something down on one page, turned to another and wrote something else. He closed the cover. "I want you both to clear your minds as much as possible. Empty yourself of thought to the extent you can. Now, Brad, say the first thing that comes to your mind."

"Christy Mathewson!" blurted Brad.

"Now, Jimmy," Billy said quickly, "say the first thing that comes to your mind."

"Mangas Coloradas!"

Billy tossed the notebook over to where they sat. Brad, grasping Billy's intent, opened the notebook. On the first page was written "Christy Mathewson." Jimmy leaned over, looked at the words and turned the page. There, in bold scrawl, was "Mangas Coloradas."

Brad and Jimmy sat there, this time quite shaken and not sure what to make of what had just occurred. For a change, Jimmy took charge.

"I know I've told you about my ancestors, but how did you make me say that name?"

"I projected it into your mind," Billy replied.

"You can read minds?" asked Brad.

"Not completely, no. Besides, I wasn't reading your mind. I merely projected a strong thought in your direction. You obviously received it."

"I've seen this kind of thing on TV," said Brad, "but I admit you've come a long way toward proving you're at least very unusual. Can you give us another demonstration?"

"Sure, I assumed you'd need more. Let me have that notebook again." He made a couple more entries, and repeated the instructions.

Brad said, "I believe you."

Jimmy said, "You are an alien!"

Billy again tossed the little notebook across the table. And on the next two pages it read, "I believe you" and "You are an alien."

The three sat there in silence for a time. Billy could sense in his two friends a tense sort of resignation. They were coming to believe him, but they'd rather they didn't. Brad picked up the bottle of wine.

"Tomorrow's a game day, but I don't think a little more wine would hurt. Besides, I'm not pitching anyway. Billy, to say I do believe you doesn't quite cover it. But, please, tell us more."

"What I want to know is," Jimmy interjected, "have you been reading our minds all this time?"

"No, Jimmy," said Billy. "Except for this little demonstration, I've never touched Brad's mind and yours I've only examined or interfered with during our training. On Ball Four, it's considered devious and insulting to mind-read or mind-influence, except in baseball, where it's an integral part of the game. I consider it a point of honor not to use mind techniques with teammates, and I've even gone so far as to stop using any against the opposition here on Earth. It's only fair that, when I play against humans, I play like one."

"What do you mean, you examined my mind?" asked Jimmy. He wore a hurt expression.

"Don't be angry with me, Jimmy. All I did was mentally support your training and nurture your self-confidence. And I checked to see the depth of your meditative state while pitching. Your mind and its openness change according to what mental state you're in."

"Can you read minds while you're playing?" Brad asked. "I mean, do you know what pitch someone's about to throw?"

"Of course," Billy answered. "I haven't used it since my first game. As I've said, it's a point of honor with me. I did do a number of things to assure that I'd make the team. I mind-influenced Lou Chambers whenever we spoke, otherwise he'd never have listened to me or let me talk to the players. He'd have had me fired. When I got that batting tryout I knew every pitch you and McIlhenny were going to throw. Yes, Brad, there was one time I read your mind. I should have mentioned that."

"No wonder you pounded me. What am I thinking now?" Brad assumed a look of concentration.

Billy peered at him for a second and quickly responded. "Slider, lower inside corner."

Brad smiled. "Wow. Jimmy, I think what we have here is an alien being. I suppose I should be scared, but that's the furthest thing from my mind. Are you causing that?"

"No," Billy replied, "but I admit I probably could if I wanted to. I don't know all my powers in relation to humans. For that matter, I did a number of things back on Ball Four which I'd only understood in theory. Worked, too."

"The name of your home planet is Ball Four?" asked Jimmy. "That's a very strange name for a planet."

"It's not really the actual name, Jimmy. Originally, its name came from an ancient dialect, which I won't attempt to pronounce for you. The word, however, meant Fourth Orb, since we're the fourth planet from our sun. A few centuries back, when baseball came into prominence, it became stylish to refer to our world as Ball Four. Now it's commonly used. Although official documents and stellar maps do use the old form."

"You say that baseball has been played there for centuries?" asked Brad.

"Oh yes. We've had major leagues for over five hundred years. The game is identical in every way to your own baseball except for the mental component, of course."

Brad was unconvinced. "But isn't that just too much of a coincidence?"

"It was assumed, when the first expeditions embarked, that the search might take centuries, if it could be successful at all. We found a world that played our game in a mere sixteen years. I'm sure I'm not the only Ball Fourian who wonders what deep mystery is behind the unfathomable fact that two worlds across a galaxy could have so many parallels. Not only do we both play exactly the same game, but our gravitational forces are identical. The size of the planets are virtually the same. The comparisons are endless, right down to the basic biology of the dominant, intelligent species of each world. We are, gentlemen, far more alike than dissimilar, I assure you."

"Billy, every thing I know about physics tells me it's impossible to travel across a galaxy without taking several thousand years," Brad said skeptically. "Assuming your world has discovered an advanced form of travel, I still find it inconceivable that you could travel at sufficient speeds to undertake such expeditons."

"Our first attempts at space travel were severely hampered by time constraints. But several centuries ago we discovered the Implied Time Drive. I'm no physicist, but the way it works is based on the relationship between space, speed and time. At high speeds the relationship between space and time gets tremendously warped. The drive was discovered by accident, when an experimental ship went out of control. Its computers recorded the incredible distance that it had traveled in such a short amount of real time. Further experimentation indicated that what had previously been assumed to be impossible rates of speed were in fact possible, and time was so compressed that great distances could be crossed with relatively little time elapsed. All that remained was to create a navigational system that controlled the travel. The drive of the ship propels the ship to the appropriate speed and the navigational system tells it what coordinates to strive for, and what time to arrive there. Hence the name, Implied Time Drive."

"How long did the journey take to Earth?" asked Brad.

"About a week."

Brad shook his head in disbelief. "Wow. And your people spent years searching for a world that played baseball?"

"Yes."

"So you've been changed by plastic surgery, or whatever," Jimmy said. "What do you really look like?"

"From what I've learned about your races, I'd say the closest I could come to a direct comparison, in outward appearance at least, would be with your Eskimos, and some of the races of Lapland and Siberia. They seem interconnected."

"Are there races on Ball Four?" asked Brad.

"There were in ancient times. By now, there isn't the variety there is here on Earth, although different genetic traits surface here and there. But mostly we're rather homogenous. Frankly, one of the things I enjoy on Earth is the diversity provided by the different races. It's fascinating."

"Not everyone feels the way you do," said Brad gravely.

"So I've learned," replied Billy.

Jimmy interrupted the flow of conversation. "Look, Billy, everything you're telling us is interesting and I want to hear more, but I need to know something right now. Is the reason I'm doing so well in the majors because of you? Are you reading the hitters' minds or playing tricks on them?"

"I don't blame you for wondering," said Billy in an assuring voice. "The answer is a simple no. Absolutely not. Oh, I was prepared to do some of it to protect you during your debut, just to build your confidence, but it wasn't necessary. Jimmy, you were born to throw baseballs, I assure you. And I had decided I wouldn't undermine the development of your abilities by making it too easy. Again, it's a point of honor with me. It has to do with why I'm here in the first place. Jimmy, the fact is that all I've done mentally on your behalf is help you focus and strengthen your concentration and visualization during your training, and in the first few innings of your debut. You've been on your own since then."

"You bring up a salient point, Billy," said Brad. "Why, if you are an alien and I believe you are, why are you here? Just to play baseball?"

Billy looked away. He got up and walked to the end of the veranda, where he could look out over the Bay. The white sails of yachts dotted the surface and, here and there larger ships steamed along, leaving large, visible wakes as they passed Alcatraz Island and headed for the Golden Gate. It was a lovely sight. He walked back to the table and sat down.

"I hadn't intended to go into this," he said with a sigh. "I should have expected the question. Since it seems you're leaning towards acceptance of what I can only imagine is an extremely bizarre tale from your perspective, I might as well put all the cards on the table, as we say both here and on Ball Four. The reason I'm here is to defend the honor of my planet by defeating the Cleveland Indians in the World Series."

"The Cleveland Indians, for chrissake!" exclaimed Brad. "How would defeating the Cleveland Indians defend the honor of Ball Four? And how the hell are we going to make it to the Series, anyway? Billy, this is a bit bizarre. Why would you come all the way to Earth to beat the Indians?"

"This is why I wanted to wait until another time to explain. But here it is: the Cleveland Indians are a team completely infiltrated by professional ballplayers from Ball Four. The infiltration began nine years ago, and was completed this year. The entire project has been supported by a staff of one hundred thousand technicians, scholars, linguists, mind-influencing teams and so forth. The whole scheme has dominated the life of Ball Four for years, except for continuing interest in our own major leagues, of course. The point of the project, which is, by the way, called Operation Universe Series, is to have a Ball Fourian team challenge an Earthling team for the championship of the known universe. I was on that challenge team until I was deselected for dissension. I am here now for the purpose of defeating that team."

"Are you buying any of this, Chief?" asked Brad.

"I don't know what to think, Brad. Look, Billy, if you've been studying the Earth, you probably know that we think aliens are gonna come kill us or take us over if they ever come here. That's what usually happens in our science fiction movies and TV, anyway. So, I finally meet an alien and he's here to play baseball? Your planet must be pretty weird."

Billy laughed. "I guess it must appear that way. Yeah, we studied your view of alien life during our training, and since I've been here I've read a couple of novels about space wars and such. But I assure you, we are not a violent race. Ball Four had its violent period like all worlds, but that ended about fifteen hundred years ago. We're very non-violent, in fact we stopped all contact with alien worlds about two hundred years ago because of a war with a violent planet."

"But why would you come all this way to play a game?" asked Brad. "Why baseball?"

"Well, our worlds are very similar biologically and geographically, but we've had a very different history from yours and, culturally speaking, our values are quite different. We've advanced technologically to the point where most of our time is available to us as leisure. So, to pass the time, we play. We have a number of games and amusements, but by far the most popular sport and leisure activity is baseball. Ball Fourians love it, and twenty per cent of the population of Ball Four is involved professionally in it. There are ten major leagues with over two hundred minor leagues, and thousands of amateur leagues as well. I played in the top major league which consists of teams representing the major cities of the historically dominant continent. We occasionally have tournaments against the winners of the major leagues on the other six continents, but it's been over sixty years since any team from another league has been able to defeat our league's representative. I think one of the reasons Operation Universe Series was conceived in the first place was because of the need for another kind of competition and cultural stimulation.

I've also come to realize that the leader of our planet is using our love of baseball to break out of our isolationism. We've been very fearful of contacts with aliens, but this project has propelled us out of it. It's a clever ploy to get around an act of the ruling Council more than two hundred years ago."

"Your planet must be so much older than ours if you're so much more advanced than us," offered Jimmy.

"Not really," Billy replied. "We've paralleled your geological and biological evolution quite closely. Even our early development of primitive culture is similar. Although we haven't been interacting with other beings for a long time, there is quite a science of comparative cultures from previous data, and it's included in the standard course of study in our schools. It constituted a great deal of our cultural studies in the training program for the Operation. There's a prevalent theory concerning the divergence between our two worlds in the areas of technological growth, and biological and social development. Since I've been on Earth I've taken advantage of your libraries to delve into it. And everything I've found confirms the theory."

"What's the theory?" asked Brad.

"It involves the suppression of technical knowledge by the ruling classes, using religion as a tool of that suppression. Between two and three thousand years ago, knowledge of the natural laws of the universe began to be discovered here on Earth. Great breakthroughs in scientific thought were being made in the areas of astronomy, physics, mathematics and so on. Where these discoveries conflicted with prevalent religious beliefs, great fears concerning their implications generated fierce reaction, especially among the ruling classes, in both the political and religious hierarchies. It was very threatening to the power structure of Earth. A king, who depended on the assumption of his divinity as the basis of his power, could not risk the diminishing of that power as a result of newly discovered knowledge of natural laws which offered explanations that challenged his right to rule or his divine nature. The religious cults of power were equally threatened. The high priests and priestesses would use the superstitious beliefs of the people to crush any scientific advance that threatened the belief structure that gave the religious establishment its grip on power. As a result, knowledge and technological advance were continually stymied on Earth for centuries. Many scientists throughout the ages have been imprisoned and even killed because of their discoveries that threatened to upset the balance of power between the ruling political and religious oligarchies. Only as recently as three or four hundred years ago, did science begin to get the upper hand. But valuable time was lost, and even today your world's culture, though becoming scientifically advanced, is still basically in the dark ages where cultural, social and technological levels are concerned.

"Ball Four's experience was quite different. About three thousand years ago there was an emperor of one of the early civilizations who was a brilliant astronomer and mathematician, at least for his day. Many of his discoveries debunked the primitive religious beliefs of his era but, because of his position, he was able to defend them against the religious leaders in his realm. This led to a series of conspiracies and palace revolts, but in the end he prevailed. He set up a state religion based not on myth and superstition but on science. In essence what he did was create a religious hierarchy of priest-scientists, who promoted scientific inquiry rather than suppressing it. This is considered in Ball Fourian history to be the crucial watershed, the point in history to which we can trace the beginnings of our greatness as a civilization. It took over a thousand years, but this original kingdom slowly expanded its dominance until it had colonized the entire planet. The last war of resistance took place about fifteen hundred years ago, and once the planet was united we grew technologically and culturally at a faster pace than any world we have yet discovered."

"Wasn't the ability to communicate telepathically a big factor in your rapid development?" asked Brad.

"Of course, at least in recent centuries," Billy replied. "But this ability was the result of our development, not the original cause. Neurologically speaking, we're not so different from humans, we've only had a significant head start, so to speak. Our knowledge of the brain and how it functions has led to our ability to train it, nurture it and open it up to possibilities which humans presently can't conceive of. We don't have some special organ in the brain which you humans lack. We've merely begun using the brain to its potential. Although it hasn't been tested, of course, It's quite possible that a Ball Fourian raised in an Earth culture would not necessarily develop these abilities and, conversely, an Earthling raised on Ball Four might very well develop them easily.

"Anyway, to finish answering your question, once minds could be linked, teams of scientists could make quantum leaps toward discoveries of all kinds. I haven't been trained to utilize these mind-melding techniques like members of the scientific caste have been, but it's been standard procedure for groups of scientists to link their minds, thus allowing intelligence, insight and creativity to multiply manyfold. Most of the great scientific breakthroughs of the last thousand years have occurred in this way."

Jimmy and Brad listened intently as Billy told them about a world that, until an hour ago, they never would have considered to have existed. Jimmy was satisfied to let Brad, the Harvard graduate, lead the questioning. But now both fell silent as the quantity of information to digest reached somewhat overwhelming proportions. The three sat in silence for a time, with Jimmy and Brad occasionally looking at each other and shaking their heads. Billy waited patiently, knowing how difficult it was for the two humans to fathom the preposterous nature of his revelations. Finally, Jimmy broke the silence.

"Okay, Billy. Where do we go from here? You're obviously working from a plan."

"More or less," Billy replied. "I've been making most of it up along the way. My research has shown that there are possible ways to negate or lessen the advantage that the Indians have over us. I'll need your help and faith to make it all work."

"I don't understand," said Brad. "Why would you come to Earth to defeat your own world's team? Why aren't you on their side? Is it out of revenge for being booted from the team?"

"I don't completely understand it myself, Brad. I've felt compelled to do it. But revenge, I assure you, has nothing to do with it. I was deselected from the team for reasons which, from the point of view of team management, were quite valid concerns. To them, I was an unpredictable factor they chose not to risk. I was disappointed but not bitter. No, I've come to feel that it's a point of honor. To come to Earth merely to prove superiority, using unfair advantage, seems the height of dishonor. I'm here to even the odds, to give the humans a fighting chance, to keep baseball what it should be, a game. Will you help me?"

"I've got to admit, one of the believable elements of your strange tale is that Cleveland team," said Brad. "They've been one of the weakest franchises for the past thirty-odd years, and all of a sudden they're the hottest thing in the majors. And they are all unknown players and rookies. My god, I never looked at it that way before. They're mostly all new players because that's the way it has to be if they're alien infiltrators. But some of them have been around a while and even played in the minors."

"There have been a lot of different paths used to infiltrate the team. The first players began to infiltrate seven years ago, and they've tried to create plausibility as much as possible. They've even sent some players through other franchises and then used mind-influencing techniques to acquire them. I myself was to be one of the last to infiltrate. I was supposed to tryout for the Milwaukee Brewers at their spring camp, make the team and then fizzle out. The Indians were then going to trade one of the humans for me."

"Billy, if all this is true, your timing sucks," said Brad with a chuckle. "I'm a rookie, so's Jimmy, and now, before we can get used to just being in the majors, you've got us involved in a war of the worlds. Thanks a lot."

"Yeah, I see your point and I'm sorry. But look at it this way. You're involved in the greatest epic season in Earth history, even if it'll never make the history books. But you'll know. I myself may be the only Ball Fourian criminal in existence. I haven't totally grasped the ramifications of that yet. In any event, You've got an unparalleled opportunity for an adventure of mythic proportions. I am sorry to mess up your rookie year. But, any way you look at it, we're still going to be playing baseball."

"How do you intend to keep this out of the history books?" asked Brad.

"I don't know, but I doubt you, for example, are willing to try to talk a newspaper reporter into believing you."

"I see what you mean."

"Well, gentlemen," Billy said with an air of finality. "Do you accept the reality of my story and are you prepared to accept the challenge?"

After a little thought, Brad answered. "I don't see that we have any choice. One way or another, you're going for it."

"This is true."

"Okay," said Jimmy resignedly. "I owe you a lot for helping me make the team. I should pay you back in any way you want. But what do you have in mind?"

"That, my friends, can wait. We've been through enough today. Let it sink in. In the meantime, Jimmy, where's that cheesecake I brought?"

16

USA Today

June 15th.

CLEVELAND'S WINNING WAYS:
MODERN MIRACLE
OR MASTER CRIME?

by

Howard Everett

Are the Cleveland Indians the greatest miracle turn-around in decades or the first franchise in history to set up a sign-stealing system so successful that it influences the outcome of a significant number of games? A number of managers and players have, in recent days, maintained that the latter is true, most notably manager Al Hansen of the Oakland A's and California Angels skipper Burt Murphy. But these "gut feeling" accusations pale by comparison to the computer-compiled research provided exclusively to *USA Today* by Richard Bates, an enterprising young intern at WCLV-TV in Cleveland.

With the assistance of fellow computer hackers Bobby Acton and Jason Michalowski, Richard Bates has analyzed the performance of the Indians through June 1st, swing by swing and out by out. When the statistics are computer-analyzed, a startling portrait is revealed.

"The most unusual patterns are right where you would expect them to be if sign stealing was taking place," says Bates, who will be a senior at the University of Michigan next September. "There is an uncanny lack of reaction to opponents' hit-and-run plays, in fact, seventy per cent of the time, the Indians are not lured into reacting. In the case of opponents' base stealing, the Indians have thrown out eighty-two per cent of the attempts. Contrast that with the eighty per cent success rate in their own exploits on the basepaths. And in the critical strikeouts to base-on-balls ratio, the Indians are not even close to historical averages. They strike out once per four walks, with an unbelievable resistance to striking out at all. They've fanned less than 1.6 times per game."

What makes Bates' statistics all the more compelling is the pattern by which they have been changing. Bates goes on to explain:

"In the first twenty-five games of the year, these patterns are unbelievably consistent. Then something significant begins to happen. The patterns begin a very noticeable downward curve against what can be classed as the weaker teams in both divisions, while another, decidedly less downward curve begins against the stronger teams, such as Boston, Oakland, Toronto and Detroit. By June 1st, the Cleveland Indians are presenting a normal picture against the weak teams and are maintaining an enhanced performance level against the stronger clubs. I leave it to others to figure out what that means."

What Bates is reticent to say is that the changing statistics make it appear that the Indians, if they are engaging in sign-stealing, might be reacting to criticism by cutting back on the practice. This would amply explain the pronounced and consistent downward curve.

Bates does allow himself to editorialize on one point. "There was one more area of observation that I couldn't treat statistically, but was so glaringly obvious that I have to mention it. When you watch the swing-by-swing performance of the Indians' hitters, they seem to react perfectly to such a wide variety of pitches. Unlike a lot of hitters, who demonstrate the inability to hit the curveball, for instance, the Indians' hitters don't seem to have any Achilles' heel. I can't quantify it, but when added to the other enhanced statistics, it gives a remarkable appearance that the catcher's signals are being stolen as well as those from the third base coach or the dugout. And, what's more, this ability to hit any pitch appears to diminish about the same time as the downward curves of the stats in general."

When approached for comment, the Cleveland Indians wasted no time in making their feelings known about the charges. Tribe manager Jake Conrad responded that "it's the biggest bunch of bull — — I've ever heard in my life, and to try to take away from the accomplishments of the best bunch of boys I've ever coached is just g — — — — sour grapes." Indians' owner Elliot Edwards was equally livid. "To allow a computer hacker access to the Major League game tapes shows a great deal of irresponsibility on the part of the people who are supposed to be controlling these things," Edwards remarked. "There are copyrights involved, and, besides, just because a team is really hot doesn't mean that anything unethical is going on." Members of the team who were approached issued polite denials without further comment.

The issue of sign stealing is nothing new. As early as 1902...

Jake Conrad was so mad he could spit, as the blotches of tobacco juice up
and down the apron of the dugout could attest. He thought about it over and
over, but could come up with no logical reason they'd want to pick on him,
now that he finally had a winning team. Not just a winning team, a killer
winning team.

The *USA Today* article had been the final straw, but certainly not the only
irritant in a season he'd just like to enjoy. There were constant articles analyzing and probing and accusing. Sure, his boys were a little colorless and didn't
like interviews, but that's their right if they want to concentrate on baseball. Is
this what it's like when you're on top, constant sour grapes and back stabbing?
Hell, I thought Al Hansen was a friend.

"Dammit, Warren, how the hell do they come up with this crap? If there
was sign-stealing I'd sure as hell know about it. I've even tried it over the
years. No percentage in it, waste of time. Everybody knows it."

It was the third inning in a game against the Seattle Mariners at Municipal
Stadium, and Warren Evans was trying to concentrate on the game.

"We've been through all this already, Jake. They're full of crap and you've
just got to let it go. We know we haven't done anything, and it'll fade out, I
promise you. In the meantime, we've got a ballgame going." Evans sent a
projection to Martin, to remind him that the hitter at the plate was weak on the
outside curveball. He was letting Martin call the pitches. Against Seattle,
Martin was more than competent.

"Yeah, I know, Warren, it just sticks in my craw. Is there a way to fight
this thing?"

"Yes, Jake, there is," Evans said as soothingly as possible. "Play baseball,
win the World Series, and tell them if they're worried about their signs, change
them every ten minutes and just admit to the world that the Indians are for real.
Now, let's play baseball. What's going on out there, Sandoval can't hit a
curveball!"

The Mariners' shortstop had just poked a single to right and, with no one
out, Fernandez at second knew what was coming: the hit-and-run. He was
under orders from Evans to allow himself to be lured into it. He further knew
that Ellerbach would not be allowed to sucker pitch. They were under scrutiny, and had to give up the hit-and-run. It was maddening. It didn't even take
mind reading to know what was coming, but now they had to play like mind-
less robots. It was an insult.

The runner took off and the batter smashed a 1 and 1 pitch on the ground
a little too close to second. Fernandez, who had moved towards second to
cover the runner, still had time to move back and field the ball, but elected to
appear to have committed too far. The ball went into right field and both
runners were safe. Every player on the Indians team could sense the collective

mental groan. How long would they have to put up with this?

Back in the dugout, Jake Conrad swore. Warren Evans looked grim, but inside he was satisfied. They'd just have to mute reaction to the accusations in this way. There were other ways to win. *Martane, anything goes. Get these guys out.*

Thank you, Evan.

The next two batters struck out and the third popped out. The Ball Fourians had ways to prevail.

Back in Evans' office, Abe Watkins waited. This had deeply disturbed him. The Cronin thing had long since been forgotten. The season was clicking along, and then some enterprising young Earthling had caught them by surprise. Watkins allowed a smile. He had to admit, these Earthlings were crafty devils. Trying to prevent discovery was harder than winning ballgames.

Evans walked in. "I thought you'd be here. What's the reaction up at Operation Command?"

"Oh, less severe than I anticipated. This kind of thing is not as unusual as you might think. Accusations of sign-stealing and the like are common in all Earthling sports. A research team has already concluded that. We've come up with two options. Ignore the situation and deal with it like Earthlings would, you know, vehement denials, that sort of thing. Or we could remove the threat by other means."

"I'd prefer we find a middle ground," Evans said.

"Again we think alike," responded Watkins. "In fact, that's the conclusion Command has already arrived at. They're sending a technical squad down. These fellows have knowledge of Earthling computers, communications and so forth. They're preparing to undermine the efforts of the boys who came up with the data. We feel if we slow them down they just might not recover until the Season is almost over. And there's the factor that Earthlings lose interest in news stories so rapidly that if they can't keep the interest up in the short term, it'll vanish in the long term. Evan, I'm going to handle this one. You just play baseball. Avoid the kind of thing that's been criticized. You know what to do."

"I've already begun the process. The boys don't like it, but you can't blame them. We're all just tempted to open up to all tactics and beat every team every game. We could, you know. But don't worry. We'll stay in control. It's ironic. I wonder how many of the viewers back on Ball Four realize that it's harder to lose to the Earthlings than it is to beat them."

Watkins smiled broadly. "That is ironic. But you have to take satisfaction from the fact. When it's all over, we'll return to Ball Four as heroes and no one need know how easy it was, except for these minor irritations, of course. You just play ball. I've got to go meet with the technical team. They're transporting down soon. We're going to move fast."

"Good. I know what to do, you can rest assured. If these interfering humans are dealt with, I'll do my best to give no more cause for further accusations."

Watkins got up. "I'm off. You'll hear from me if there's anything else to do. Otherwise, just go about your business."

Richard Bates checked his watch. Five minutes to ten. This morning he and his associates were going to have a computer conference by modem at ten o'clock. He'd better get to his computer and boot up.

The station had let him off to go and see the Indians game last night, and what he witnessed had, to his way of thinking, profound implications indeed. The Indians had obviously reacted to his article in *USA Today*. In every area, from hit-and-run to stealing to strikeouts, they were a different team. It had proved that he was on the right track. If he kept compiling stats, he would no doubt show another interesting change in the curve. He wondered if the Indians were that stupid. They might be playing into his hands.

Bobby Acton rang on. Words began to appear on Richard's computer monitor.

HI. I WATCHED THE GAME ON TV. I SUPPOSE YOU DREW THE SAME CONCLUSION...

YES BOBBY. WE'VE GOT THEM BY THE THROAT. OH, JASON'S COMING ON. HOLD, PLEASE...

Richard threw the toggle on his modem control and the program beeped. Jason Michalowski was on board.

HI JASON. DID YOU COVER THE GAME LAST NIGHT?...

YES RICHARD. I'VE ALREADY CRUNCHED THE NUMBERS. DO YOU WANT ME TO DOWNLOAD?...

YES PLEASE. BOBBY READY? PREPARE TO UPLOAD IN TEN SECONDS FROM ACKNOWLEDGEMENT?...

BOBBY READY...

JASON TO UPLOAD IN TEN SECONDS...

Richard sat back and watched as the modem program downloaded the stat file Jason was sending. They had juiced-up programs that cut transfer time down considerably. The transfer would be finished in no time. It was so much easier having allies in this venture. The amount of numbers involved were so great that one guy just couldn't handle it all. He, Bobby and Jason had been crunching numbers, compiling stats and producing all kinds of analyses since they were in eighth grade. This was the most exciting of all, charting a season swing-by-swing as it progressed.

Suddenly, the screen filled with static, made some quiet popping sounds and went blank. Oh, damn, thought Richard, some transmission error. He wondered about the blank screen, though. He pressed the appropriate keys to reboot up, but nothing happened. His computer acknowledged that it had its ROM and RAM but there was no DOS. His disk operating system was gone. He had utilities programs on disk to run a diagnostic, but no DOS to run them with. He was reaching for the floppy disk with the DOS on it when the phone rang. It was Jason.

"Richard, what the hell happened?"

"What do you mean?" asked Richard with a panicky feeling. "I don't know about you, but my computer might have just crashed. I've got no DOS, but I'm about to reinstall it from floppy."

"My screen went blank too," Jason said. "What's up with Bobby?"

The answer to that came as another line rang. It was Bobby, so Richard toggled him into the conference.

"Bobby, I'm down and so is Jason. What's your status?"

"This is weird," said Bobby. "So am I. How could we crash at the same time? Technically speaking, there's nothing in the modem program that could instigate it. Even a power surge couldn't cause it and, anyway, we're all protected against surges. What happened?"

"I don't know yet," replied Richard. "But hold your horses, I'll know in a second. I'm about to reinstall my DOS."

Richard had slipped the floppy disk containing his disk operating system into the floppy drive. It should have automatically reinstalled but nothing happened. He scratched his head and searched for his back-up disks. He religiously backed up his hard disk all the time and had done it yesterday. He popped the number one disk into the floppy drive. Nothing.

"What's going on, Richard?" said a very anxious Bobby Acton. "I can't hear you."

"Nothing is happening," Richard said frantically. "Either my CPU is fried, or all my back-up disks are blank or unreadable, which is impossible."

"This is not right," said Jason. "I just tried to reinstall DOS, and nothing. What about you, Bobby?"

"Right behind you. Wait a sec. Oh, no, nothing."

"Let's not panic, guys," said Richard. "As weird as this is, there's got to be some kind of logical solution. We just have to find it. We'll go step-by-step until we get everything back. We're all backed-up to the hilt. The only thing we might really have lost is tonight's numbers. We'll live. Let's get to work. I've got duplicates of everything at the station anyway. I'll head there while you guys find somebody to borrow DOS from. We'll be on-line in no time."

Technical Officer Ygarnen sat at a console in his tech group's control module aboard the space station in geosynchronous orbit above North America. Phase One of the clean-up operation had gone better than expected. The group had located Richard Bates' position with relative ease by locking into the communications grid of that sector of Earth. Using scans from the station combined with the schematic of the grid, they had pinpointed Bates' computer system. It was confined to one room in the Bates' family home, and its memory system was of a very primitive electromagnetic design. There were two ways to go: blank the vicinity by scan from space or send electromagnetic "smart" surges through the communications grid. The latter would be more accurate and less prone to needless random damage.

Ygarnen couldn't believe his luck. As he prepared to emit the surge, monitoring of Bates' computer activity had revealed a link-up with his assistants. The tech group hadn't located them yet, but they were next in line to be dealt with. There was no technical reason he couldn't take them out in one pattern. Ygarnen realigned the surge parameters on his console, using the modem connections of the three computers.

Before instigating the surges, he wanted to retrieve all the data from the computers' memories. Command had sensed that if these humans were as clever as they appeared to be, then both the programs and data would be fertile ground for study or, at the very least, an amusement for those on the crew who were interested in the human ways of baseball and computers. Using a retrieval program that had been drawing data from Earthside computers ever since the beginning of the Operation, Ygarnen copied all data from the three humans' computers to the on-board central memory core. The whole process took less than ten seconds. He himself was looking forward to investigating the methods of these so-called "hackers." Crude as the systems were, they were fascinating in the context of human technical growth.

Once done, he instigated the low-level electromagnetic surges and sent them through telephone lines to the three specific locations. A couple of seconds and it was all over. He leaned back with a satisfied smile. He would have gotten them all eventually, but this was so efficient, and it would make a good story at mess hall.

The next order of business was a little trickier. Ygarnen would have to wait for an Earthside team to send him the coordinates of Bates' computer at the TV station. If Bates was using a terminal of the station's mainframe, a team would have to be dispatched to deal with it Earthside. If he was using a PC, it would be far easier. Ygarnen would have to wait for the team to report in.

It was good to finally have something to do. Oh, there were the routine scans and intelligence reports to review, but Ygarnen's job was in the main very routine. He was, of course, gratified that he'd been selected to work in Operation Universe Series. There was something definitely historic about it. But the recreational facilities of a orbital station were rather inhibiting, and the gaming room had such limited opportunities for amusement. Still, he had been allowed a chance to wager gambling credits on the home planet's big board but, by the time his wager had been entered, the odds were prohibitively low. Oh, well, he'd won a bundle in the gaming room on spot bets on Earthside contests. He'd eventually be going home with plenty of play money. He felt a bit guilty that he'd used his computer skills to determine odds. Oh, well, that was a tolerated practice.

A com light lit up on his console. Earthside was reporting.

"Ygarnen here. What have you got for me?"

"It's Investigator Lartrice. We've worked through the station complex and located Bates' computer. We're in luck. He had his own PC in place. We had hoped to erase it Earthside, but the station is in full operation twenty-four hours a day, and we were lucky to get through at all. No way to take equipment in. We had to mind-disrupt a few technicians to get through to Bates' work station. No mind damage, no pain, just hypno-trances. Bates' computer is on and has an open modem connection, ready to receive at any time. His number is 891-3427. You should be able to access and erase. Also, if you design the surge to flood an area of 1.5 cubic meters, you should get all his additional data on disks without damaging any of the station's massive stock of videos."

"Consider it done," said Ygarnen. "What about hard copy?"

"No evidence of it. Bates must have felt that his data was secure, considering the fact that it was in four locations. Of course, the team working on Howard Everett will be expecting to find hard copy. Lartrice off."

Ygarnen had already located Bates' TV station PC before Lartrice had signed off. He logged on to Bates' computer modem, then let go a surge pattern with the additional power to wash the recommended space. That was it. Ygarnen shut off the console. It was time for a little sleep.

The next morning, Howard Everett was at his desk in the Chicago offices of USA Today, sipping hot coffee and eating a Danish. He was reviewing some reporters' notes on the National League pennant race. It didn't seem that there was enough meat for a story. All the excitement was in the American League East at the moment.

He was glad he landed the Cleveland story. He'd wanted some angle into Cleveland and he was pleased this Bates kid had handed him one on a silver platter. He was looking forward to all the follow-up possibilities. Bates had promised him that there was lots more gritty stuff to come. He couldn't wait.

"Howard?"

That was Reggie at reception on the intercom. "Yeah, what is it?"

"A couple of TV guys from Cleveland want to see you. You got time?"

Howard smiled. So rarely did a reporter get to be part of a story rather than just reporting it. "Sure, what the hell, send them in."

Soon two men, one carrying a briefcase and the other holding a video camera, stood in the doorway. They seemed to be amiable types. So many reporters looked so hungry all the time.

"What can I do for you fellas?"

"Hi, Mr. Everett. We're trying to get a handle on the way you and Richard Bates got connected together. We're not trying to horn in on your story, we just want the human interest angle. You know, the story behind the story, that sort of thing."

"What station you with?"

The other reporter with the video camera answered. "We're not with any particular station. We're freelancers and we can go with any station that wants to air our stuff."

Everett sized up the two. Seem like nice guys. Sounds kinda bogus, though, freelancers showing up here. Oh, well, it takes all kinds. These guys are all right. I like the one with the camera. Such sharp eyes. Very compelling. Must be intelligent. Hard to stop looking at them. The beach, warm, salty air. Nothing to do for a change but lie in the sun. Makes you sleepy. Soft, white sand, warm breeze, salty air. So relaxing. Nice to sleep in the sun...

Everett's eyes began to flicker and finally shut. They duplicated the rapid eye movement of sleep, though his head remained erect. The gentleman with the camera nodded, turned around and shut the office door. The other man started to go through the office files quickly, methodically. The cameraman walked over to Everett's desk and checked the computer. It only contained word processing programs, not a lot of file storage. A quick check revealed no file titles related to the Indians.

They found what they were looking for on a back table. There were four notebooks of statistics, backed up with graph after graph. Next to them was a pile of haphazard notes which were obviously used to write the article. Further search revealed nothing else pertinent.

The hard copy was so efficiently compressed that it easily fit, together with the notes, into the briefcase. As soon as the clasp was snapped shut, the cameraman turned to Everett.

"Mr. Everett?"

Everett shivered slightly. "Yes?"

"So, what do you say?"

"What the hell, sounds like an okay deal to me. But now's not the best time. How about later today, say three o'clock. Deadlines, you know."

"Of course. We'll see you back here at three. Thanks, see you then."

The reporters smiled and left. Everett picked up the notes he'd been reading. There's got to be something here, he thought. I need the material.

He pored over the notes, drinking coffee and munching on the Danish, not once turning around to see the now empty table behind him.

Richard Bates was crushed, befuddled and considerably worried. This was all too bizarre.

He had just returned from the TV station. His computer there had been in the same state as his home unit. What's more, all his floppy disks stored in the cabinet next to it were blank. On the way to the station he had stopped off at a computer store where a buddy worked, and borrowed a copy of DOS, intending to use it when he got home. When he discovered the mess at the station, he was relieved that he could reinstall DOS with the borrowed disk. But he was shattered by what it revealed. His hard disk had been blanked, and all his floppies with it. Impossible but true.

He raced home and checked his own computer. Sure enough, it was fully functional when DOS was restored but everything else was blank. Not just the recent work, but everything he'd ever done was gone, gone.

The doorbell rang. That would be Bobby and Jason. He walked from the bedroom to the front door and let them in.

"Hi."

"You do not look happy," said Jason.

"No, I'm not. I hope you can cheer me up."

"No way," said Bobby. "Both Jason and I are wiped out. We've got DOS back but everything's gone."

"Me too," said Richard. "But that's not what's scary. I went to the station and everything's gone there too. I think we're in trouble."

Jason and Bobby stared at each other for a while, feeling rather numb. This was too big for them.

Bobby shook it off. "We've got to face it. Somebody did all this. Do you think your article would shake up whoever was stealing signs enough to make them do this?"

"Maybe so," replied Richard. "But that's to be expected. But who in hell could do all this in twenty-four hours or so? These are baseball people, not James Bond."

"What are we going to do?" asked Jason. "This is very powerful stuff. Whoever can do this kind of stuff is out of our league."

"There's more," said Richard. "Did you guys check your cassette tapes?"

Jason and Bobby looked at each other.

"No."

"No."

"Well, I did," Richard continued. "I was so bummed I put on a tape to chill out, and it was blank. So I checked my collection. Blank. I checked my video collection and they're blank too. My parents' collection in the living room is okay, but everything of magnetic nature in my room has apparently been erased. Nothing I've ever heard of can do that, at least not from a remote position. And there's no sign of entry. Besides, we were all at our keyboards when it apparently happened."

All three were trying to comprehend their situation. Richard's eyes flashed. "We've got one hope! At least we've got the hard copy I gave to Howard Everett. I'll call him, right now."

Richard went back to his room. He dialed Everett's number in Chicago.

"Hi, Howard? Yeah, it's Richard Bates. Do you have all the hard copy data I gave you about the Indians?"

"Hi, Richard. Sure, it's right here behind...What the hell?"

"What is it?" asked Richard.

"It's not here. Nothing's here, my notes, your notebooks, everything's gone. Where could I have put it? This is strange, Richard. Look, I don't remember moving any of this stuff, but I must have. There's got to be a logical explanation. Are you at home?"

"Yeah."

"Okay, I'll find this stuff and call you back. What did you want them for, anyway?"

"Just find them, Howard, if you can. Our computers are down and we want to make sure we've got something to go on."

Everett laughed. "Damned computers. We're so technically advanced that we get screwed every time. Look, I'll find the stuff and call you right back."

By the time Richard reached the living room, he knew that Everett was not going to find anything. He also knew that they were dealing with some incredible organization, maybe the mob. If that was the case, he was losing his interest in baseball very quickly. This was not what he expected from the game he loved.

"Boys, we've got some serious thinking to do."

 17

BUD CUMMINGS:

Welcome back to Candlestick Park. It's time now to speak to our guest, Jimmy "Chief" Strongbow. Chief, the press has been referring to you and your teammate who arrived with you, Billy Icarus, as the Lone Ranger and Tonto, considering the effect you two have had on the team's fortunes since you joined the club. Tell me, do you like the reference to your Indian heritage?

STRONGBOW:

I like everything about being with the Giants, and even though some of my fellow Native Americans think of Tonto as sort of the "Uncle Tom" of Indians, I don't mind. After all, many people maybe don't know this, but Tonto is the name of an Apache tribe, and I'm an Apache and, sure, I'm proud of it.

BUD CUMMINGS:

Well, you and Billy make a great battery, and we've heard that Billy actually had a lot to do with your making the team.

STRONGBOW:

Yeah, I'm very grateful to Billy for the training and encouragement he gave me while we were on the grounds crew together. He's a great catcher and sure knows his pitching too.

BUD CUMMINGS:

There's quite a story in the way you made the team. We know your background in Arizona, but there's sure a lot of mystery so far about Billy Icarus. Can you shed any light on the twenty-eight-year-old rookie?

STRONGBOW:

Er, ah, not really. Billy just seems to want to concentrate on helping the Giants and he said where he's from isn't as important as where he's going. The team respects that and accepts it.

BUD CUMMINGS:

Well, it appears that the only place Billy is going is up, with his .482 average and all. And you're off to a great start with your 3-1 record and...

Starting June 14th, the Giants had an eleven-game homestand that would be a reprise of the eastern swing. They'd be playing the same teams they had just visited on the road. Billy, with his two allies, went to work on molding the team for the future. Brad and Jimmy were willing participants and didn't seem to mind being kept in the dark on details, particularly because everything Billy did had a consistently good effect on them and the rest of the team. Slowly but surely the other players were beginning to get drawn in.

The first thing Billy instituted was a meditative calisthenics program. During pregame workouts, Billy, Jimmy and Brad began to do stretching and toning exercises in the outfield. Billy had instructed them to meditate while executing the movements. To foster this, he drew heavily on T'ai Chi, the spiritually-oriented Chinese martial art, which was yet another library discovery. The slow, dance-like movements were perfectly designed to both strengthen the body and center the mind. Billy would lead and Jimmy and Brad would duplicate his every move. To Lou Chambers and the rest of the team (not to mention the befuddled press), they presented an odd sight. It was a few days before anyone ventured to find out what was going on. Not surprisingly, it was Bob Butterfield.

He came up to them as they were getting started. "What are you guys doing?"

"It's T'ai Chi, with some regular stretching mixed in," replied Billy. "At the same time, we center our minds through meditation, then seek to carry the meditative state into the game with us. This way, we warm up completely and improve our concentration while playing. Care to join us?"

"It sure looks strange," said Butterfield. "Haven't I seen this in Chinatown parks? It's a Chinese thing, right?"

"That's right. Millions of Chinese do this every day around the world."

"What the hell," Butterfield said with a grin. "Can't hurt. I'm always looking to stretch better."

With that he joined in. The next day the whole outfield crew of Washington, Barker and Simpson joined in as well. Over the course of a few days, everyone involved was really enjoying it, and the participants were flourishing at the plate or on the mound. Their batting averages were growing and even Jimmy was getting some hits. His and Brad's pitching remained strong. This was not lost on the rest of the team and, by the end of the homestand, all but a few had joined the sessions. Noticeable among the holdouts were Eddie Renker and the two short relievers, Steve Lafite and Ricky Santiago.

The press had a field day with it, and drove the "only in San Francisco" theme into the ground. Billy, of course, was grateful for San Francisco's reputation for odd values and behavior, because it would serve as a screen for some of the unusual things he must institute if they were to get ready for Cleveland.

Lou Chambers was quite pliant about it, but did wonder at Billy's motives. He didn't mind giving up a bit of leadership as long as he was somehow included. Billy was smart enough to anticipate Chambers' feelings. He approached Chambers before too much time had passed.

"Lou, I appreciate your not interfering with the calisthenics program. You must know that it's good for the health of the team."

"Billy, ever since you've been here, you seem to do something different every other day. We're winning and I got no complaints. But a lot of my old-time buddies are razzing me about my boys dancing in the outfield. It just doesn't look like a baseball thing. However, the team batting average is up to .262 and as long as we're playing the way we are, how can I complain? Just don't get the team wearing tutus or something, okay?"

Billy laughed and agreed. He did his best to forget about Cleveland for the time being, worked on improving and preparing the Giants, and allowed himself to enjoy the task. Regardless of the outcome, the process was its own reward. He especially liked working with the pitching staff. Ron McIlhenny, following Chambers' lead, backed off and gave Billy a wide berth. Again, as long as the staff kept improving, there was nothing to gripe about.

Billy participated as much as possible in warming up the starting pitcher of each game, and sought to encourage them to pitch from the meditative state as he had taught Jimmy. Brad, naturally, had opened up to it right away. Billy allowed himself to scan Brad's mind to check its state and, if anything, it was closer to the white mind than Jimmy's. Brad was a quick study. Kiley Upton and Art French, intent on improvement, tried to utilize the focusing techniques, with mixed results. They weren't very close to the white mind, but their pitching improved and they claimed they liked to throw using the new approach. It was progress any way one viewed it.

Billy had held back one pitch from Jimmy Strongbow's repertoire, and that was a knuckleball his father had taught him. There were a number of different ways to throw it but, more importantly, there was a specific mental place to throw it from. All knuckleballers intuitively understood that. One day between starts, Billy offered it to Jimmy.

"I know you've got plenty of pitches, but there's one more that can be pretty handy. It's a form of knuckleball. Take the ball like this, and palm it tightly between the thumb and little finger. The other three you pull all the way back and hold with the fingertips, like this. You can vary the release points and it'll act differently, and you can also give the ball a slight, gentle twist at release, either left or right, to allow the seams to rotate once during its approach to the plate. That masks the movement of the ball from batters who can perceive seam rotation. Want to try it?"

"Sure," Jimmy replied.

The odd grip made it a difficult pitch to master, but Jimmy practiced it intently and made great progress within a week. After he got the feel for throwing it, Billy offered him the visualization to go along with it.

"Jimmy, your visualizations and symbols for your other pitches are very strong, and it shows, but your visualization for this pitch has got to be your best. While I was researching your tribe's history I discovered the perfect one. One of the warfare tactics that made the Apache so devastating and difficult to fight was his style of ambush."

"Of course," interrupted Jimmy. "At sunrise, with the sun at their backs. It blinded the people being attacked."

"That's right."

Jimmy had learned a lot about the tactics of the Chiricahua Apache. During the final wars led by Geronimo, Naiche and the last holdouts, the Apache was greatly feared because a raiding party of twenty braves could strike and kill virtually at will, with little or no losses, usually against much larger forces than their own. The terror had gone on for years and was a sad if valiant closing chapter to the story of the suppression of the Indian Nation.

"Say no more, Billy," Jimmy said with a grim face. "I understand. With this visualization, I add to the batter's confusion and help myself to decoy the pitch. I'll try it."

Jimmy kept his pitching lanes and strike zone vivid, but superimposed over them a scene of men asleep at dawn. He heard the moccasins glide over rock and sand as the raiders took their final positions. At last the sun glinted from behind a far-off mountain. The waiting raiders brought their rifles to bear on the reclining forms, and Jimmy imagined himself assigned to take out the sentry. As the sun rose enough to bathe the camp in light, the whoop went up and the attack commenced.

Billy watched as Jimmy went into his wind-up. As he released the ball,

Billy at first had trouble picking it up. Just before it reached the plate, Billy spotted the floating orb and positioned his mitt. The ball hit on the thumb of the glove and bounced away a few feet.

Billy stood up and whistled. "If I can barely see that pitch I'd hate to think how the batters will respond." He walked up to the mound where Jimmy stood with the same grim face.

"Jimmy, did I pick too painful a symbol?"

"No, Billy, it's perfect. But now I think I know how the last holdouts felt during the final days of the terror. They were fearless, determined men."

"No doubt," said Billy with respect. "And that's why you must save this pitch for the desperate moments in a game. Use it too much and it loses its power of surprise. It's your secret weapon. Even hitters on Ball Four have trouble with it, though only a few coaches encourage its use. Too inconsistent, unless it's thrown by someone who knows how to use it effectively. And you do, Jimmy."

The entire homestand was very successful and possessed a growing carnival atmosphere which pervaded both the team and the fans in the stands. San Francisco had always needed a winner to galvanize support. Unlike the fans of many cities, here the term "fair-weather fan" often applied. But give them a reason and the people would flock to Candlestick, and flock they did. Attendance was up fifty-five per cent, and it gave yet another boost to the already fired-up Giants. They hit, ran and fielded with consistent grace and power, with near-perfect execution of the fundamentals. This certainly pleased the coaches, who always felt a team won or lost not on pure talent but with discipline and application of the basics as well. The approval from the coaches encouraged the team to give even more, and the energy and dedication they exhibited during workouts was the payback. They posted an 8-3 record during the homestand and, all in all, it was a happy time for the club.

Not everything was sweetness and light. The few players who hadn't joined in the pregame workouts with Billy started to feel excluded and stopped mixing with the other players. Eddie Renker, never much of a mixer, began tossing barbs at some of the workout participants, who responded with some demeaning remarks about Renker's low output at the plate. He was mired in a mini-slump and bristled at the jabs. Billy left it to Chambers to cool off the tensions with a couple of stern, fatherly pronouncements.

The other area of dissension was the bullpen. Lafite and Santiago were good pitchers but, by their very nature as relievers, a bit aloof and apart from the rest of the team. When they took two of the losses during the homestand, they brooded, thinking that the team viewed them as weak links. This was exacerbated again by the fact that they weren't on Billy's program and made them, like Renker, feel like outsiders. This concerned Billy, who watched and waited for a solution to this unwanted complication. It was yet another lesson in human nature for him to absorb.

On June 26th they flew to Atlanta to begin a road trip that would bring them back across the country through almost every West Division town, culminating in Los Angeles. It would be a grueling fourteen games in sixteen days. The Giants, now posting a 35-36 record, were up for it. This was a pivotal point in the season, as the All-Star break would follow. It meant a great deal to the team to reach the .500 mark before the break and, buoyed by the recent high level of play, they were confident of success. Lou Chambers, however, was worried by the slight discord. He'd seen better teams torn apart by pettier problems. He sought out Billy at the hotel in Atlanta. After the team had settled in, he called Billy down to the bar.

"Hi, Billy, thanks for coming. Can I get you a coke or something?"

"That would be fine."

They engaged in small talk until their order arrived.

"Look, Billy, I should be talking to Washington. He's the team captain. So keep this between us, if you don't mind. Besides, you're at the center of the team right now, and Washington can't help me. I'm worried about a small split in the team."

"I know," said Billy. "I am too."

"I'm not surprised," Chambers said with a knowing smile. "You don't miss much, do you? What do you think is the problem?"

"I created some factionalism with my exercise program. You of course know that I never intended it, but it was liable to happen. Not everybody is a joiner, even in team sports where working together is so vital. This is a bit new for me. Where I come from people naturally tend to work well together. So, I'm learning as I go along."

Chambers eyes perked up. "Where *do* you come from? Oh, forget I asked. You won't answer."

"I will someday. What do you want me to do?"

"I've been watching," Chambers replied, "and everyone in your T'ai Chi program has improved their numbers. And, seeing how they're all so tight on the fundamentals, it's obvious that it's good for their concentration too. Frankly, I'm surprised. I've never believed in all that hocus-pocus."

"It's not hocus-pocus, Skip. There is wisdom in the ways of other cultures, and it's setting the stage for further progress as the season develops."

"You talk like you've got more things in mind. I should have guessed."

"I do," Billy responded. "But I'm more interested in the immediate problem. What do you have in mind?"

"I think I should make your calisthenics mandatory."

Billy mulled this over for a while. He swizzled the ice in his coke and pondered the implications.

"The question to be answered, Lou, is what would be the result? We've got Renker, Santiago, Lafite, Ramirez and Powell on one side. Trumbull, DuBois and Ogden are on the fence, and the rest solidly together. See the pattern? Those who are regulars, and feel they are contributing, like to be inside the circle. Those who aren't, don't feel they belong. Except for Renker.

He's a tough cookie. If we make it mandatory, what about morale, and how will they view me? Will they warm up to me that way?"

Chambers shrugged. "I do see your point. Okay, got any ideas?"

"The keys are Renker and Lafite. If I get them, we're set. The rest of the bullpen will follow Lafite. They stick together and he's their leader. I haven't paid enough attention to the bullpen and they undoubtedly resent how much time I spend with Brad and Jimmy. Will you give me some time, Lou?"

Chambers nodded.

"I'm sorry I got us into this mess, Skipper. I'll try to get us out. This is a big trip for us. The boys really want to reach .500 by the break."

"I know you will," Chambers said, getting up. He gave Billy a reassuring pat on the shoulder. "Thanks for seeing me. Listen, I will do one thing. I'll get us out to the ballpark an hour early to give you time to talk to the guys or whatever. Maybe it'll help. See you in the morning."

With that Chambers turned and left.

It was hot and muggy as usual at Atlanta Stadium when the Giants arrived. The team had an extra hour of workout time with no special agenda, so they welcomed the leisurely pace at which they approached the usual routine. They assumed this was the reason Chambers had sent them out early and appreciated it.

The pitching staff was waiting for it to cool down before throwing in earnest, so Billy was free to roam. While looking for a chance to talk to Bob Butterfield, he ran into Archie Stokes.

"I haven't had a chance to thank you, Billy. I'm up to .268 at the plate and it's primarily because of your T'ai Chi. You were probably right about the concentration factor, and that T'ai Chi is great for focusing. I look forward to it every day."

"I'm glad it's working for you. We'll get it going in about fifteen minutes or so. Oh, there's Bob. See you out there."

Butterfield was in the dugout, tightening the webbing on his first baseman's glove.

"Hey, Bob. I want to talk to you about Renker. He's pretty out of sorts, isn't he?"

"Yeah, he's a hard case. We're all doing so well, and he's not. I think he blames us in a way. His fault really. Nothing I can do about it. He's my roommate and he won't even talk to me."

"I was hoping you could," said Billy. There goes that angle, he thought. "Oh, well, let's just leave him alone and hope he gets with it. See you at warm-up?"

"Wouldn't miss it."

A lot of the guys had started to assemble in left field for the warm-up, and were stretching and loosening up. On the way out there Billy swung by the bullpen. Steve Lafite had found a spot in the shade, and was staying cool while Santiago and Trumbull engaged in some low-key throwing. Lafite didn't acknowledge Billy when he walked up.

"How's it going, Steve? Looks like you found your spot."

"It's a hot one," Lafite said blandly.

Billy sat down on the bench next to Lafite. "Steve, I think I owe you an apology."

"Why, what'd you do?" asked Lafite without looking over.

"Well, I think I spend too much time with the starters, you know, since I know them better, especially Jimmy and Brad. I didn't mean to be rude, and I just wanted to say that I admire your skills and, well, I didn't mean to appear unfriendly. I goofed."

Lafite sat up, looked over and took off his sunglasses. "That's not it, but thanks anyway. Some of us think you're a bit too cocky. You're all over the place, in everybody's business. I must admit, a lot of guys say you've helped them. You don't have much to say to us relievers, though, not that we don't like it that way."

Billy sat silently for a moment, reflecting on the progress of the conversation. Dealing with humans was so different from interchanges between Ball Fourians, which were not nearly so complex. Firstly, Billy wondered why, against his natural instincts, he felt compelled to deceive Lafite. He didn't think he'd been rude or unfriendly, nor did he particularly admire Lafite's skills. Perhaps, Billy was getting drawn further into the personal politics of humans. He couldn't be sure if that was a good or a bad sign. It was the human way to deal with conflict, which was the only means available to him at present. With a little mind-influencing the problem would vanish, Billy thought, not failing to see the irony. His choice was between human manipulation or Ball Fourian manipulation. He didn't particularly relish either.

Secondly, Lafite had given him a mixed message. He obviously thought Billy was overstepping his place by acting the coach, but he also, and equally obviously, resented not being offered any help or advice. Strange, Billy thought, but so typically human. It was difficult to decide what Lafite was really trying to say, or what he really wanted.

"Anyway, I'm sorry, and keep up the good work. If I can do anything for you, just let me know. See you later."

With that he left to join the others in the outfield. He was pleasantly surprised to see that reserve outfielder Luis Ramirez had showed up, along with Harold DuBois, the other backup outfielder. DuBois wasn't a regular at the warm-ups, but he had been out there a few times. Things were looking up. Billy reflected on how nice it would be if he could just tell everybody everything and get it over with. All this subterfuge could be unnerving, if it weren't for the fact that he couldn't be unnerved. Billy's mind was a self-tuning apparatus and it served him well in dealing with humans.

Bob Butterfield, at Billy's behest, had taken over the duties of leading the stretching exercises, and led off the session with a series of standard loosening-up movements. When the group was loose, Billy took over. He stood in front of the men, who were assembled in two lines, and paused. He took three long, slow breaths, which most everyone followed, paused again, then went into the T'ai Chi. The slow, sweeping movements of the arms and legs, along with the turning and stepping, had such a powerful and immediate effect on both the mind and body, and were equally captivating to watch. The fans and the press in the stadium stopped what they were doing and became glued to the odd proceedings in left field. Photographers were busy taking pictures and no doubt the Atlanta papers and television would be filled with pictures of the strange brigade at work. Even the Atlanta Braves paused from their workouts to take in the sight. A keen observer would have noticed, however, that the only people not watching were the Giants who weren't participating. They went about their business as if they were in another ballpark. Lou Chambers, always the sharp eye, didn't fail to notice. Yet, with his sharp eye, he was content that things were improving. His head count of participants had showed him that.

When the warm-up was over, Billy went back to the bullpen. Jimmy, who was starting that night, was throwing to McIlhenny; Upton and French were lightheartedly playing catch, and Lafite was still lounging in the shade. Billy walked up to him. During the warm-up, he had reviewed what he'd said to Lafite. He didn't like the way it felt.

"Steve, I owe you another apology," he began. "I wasn't quite honest with you. I *don't* think I've been particularly unfriendly to you, though I admit I haven't spent much time with you. And secondly, although I do recognize your talent, you've got problems which could use a little work. The team needs the contribution only you can give, and, if you're ready for some work, I'm ready to help."

"I'm not particularly interested," answered Lafite curtly.

"I didn't expect that you were," Billy responded. "But I'm ready just the same. When you are, let me know." He let it go at that, and went off to batting practice.

By game time, Billy had decided on a plan to deal with Renker. Renker needed to get out of his slump, it was just that simple, and Billy knew how to help him out of it. It meant that he would have to suspend his decision to avoid mind-manipulation, but he couldn't see a way around it. A bit of rationalization was required, but he could see no harm in helping a teammate. If it affected the outcome of the game, it would be unintentional, and Billy would have to content himself with the slightly twisted ethics.

When Renker came to bat to open the game, Billy positioned himself as close to home plate as he could without leaving the dugout area. He concentrated on the mind of the Braves' catcher. He would read the signs, and relay them quickly to Renker. From that distance, Billy wouldn't be able to prevent his projections from being received equally by Renker, the catcher and umpire. But he assumed the catcher wouldn't notice it because he'd be thinking about that pitch anyway. Knowing Renker, he'd be busy guessing at each pitch and would assume it to be his own instinctive choice. What the umpire might think was anyone's guess.

Fastball!

Renker took the first pitch, as was his habit.

Change-up!

Renker met the pitch with a good match of bat speed and pulled it up the alley for a double. After Mickey Roberts struck out, Rick Barker singled Renker home. Billy grimaced as he realized that his interference had given the Giants an advantage, but he accepted his choice. When he came to bat after Washington had grounded out, he neutralized the situation by intentionally striking out.

As the game progressed, it settled into a pitchers' duel. Jimmy was pitching brilliantly, as was Cedric Smith, the Braves' ace. Each gave up a smattering of hits but, by the sixth, the lone Giants' run was the only one posted. Renker had gotten a single in the fourth but was stranded. Billy was hitless.

Renker came to the plate in the sixth with one out and Archie Stokes on second. He'd walked and Jimmy had bunted him over. Billy positioned himself once again to aid Renker.

Fastball!

Curve!

The umpire abruptly turned and looked around, as though expecting to find someone behind him who might be whispering in his ear. He shook his head and cleaned out an ear with his little finger.

Slider, low and in!

It wasn't Renker's favorite pitch to hit, but he reached down and punched a sharp roller up the middle, past the pitcher and the diving second baseman. The speedy Stokes scored easily.

With Billy's assistance Renker got another double in the eighth, but failed to produce a run. The score remained 2-0 into the bottom of the ninth. Jimmy Strongbow was pitching well and a complete game victory was within his grasp. Things, however, began to unravel after one out. He allowed a single, then got the second out on a fly ball. When he walked the next batter, it brought the Braves' clean-up man, Matt Morton, to the plate. Lou Chambers took one look at the burly left-handed batter as he sauntered to the plate, and decided that Jimmy had had enough. He motioned to the bullpen for the left-handed Lafite.

Lafite barely acknowledged Billy as he took the ball from Chambers. After the warm-up tosses, Billy ran the ball up to Lafite.

"Let's get this guy, Steve."

Lafite nodded stiffly.

Four pitches later, Matt Morton drove the ball over the right field fence. The Braves got the victory, 3-2. Eddie Renker had gone 4 for 4 and had produced both Giant runs. Billy Icarus had gone hitless. Steve Lafite took the loss.

Friday night's game with the Braves didn't go well for the Giants either. Art French was pounded for four runs in the first, Carl Trumbull gave up three more in the third and Rick Santiago surrendered an additional two in the seventh. A young pitcher recently brought up from Phoenix, Jim "Inky" Powell, provided a bright spot by holding the Braves hitless in the last two innings. Maybe Powell had the right stuff for the majors.

The Giants' hitters had the right stuff too as they hit the Braves' pitching with nearly equal abandon. With Billy's surreptitious help, Renker had gone 4 for 4 again, this time including a home run. In the late innings, Billy allowed himself a couple of harmless, bases-empty hits. The Braves triumphed again, 9-7.

Saturday morning, as Bob Butterfield began the stretching portion of the warm-up, Eddie Renker jogged out to left field and quietly took a position in the back row. No one looked at him or acknowledged him, but Billy inwardly beamed. When he took over the direction from Butterfield for the T'ai Chi, he snuck a glance in Renker's direction from time to time, and allowed himself some satisfaction as Renker clumsily but earnestly followed along. Billy knew that Renker would not reverse his decision to join in. Renker was stubborn but not flighty.

When the session was over, Willie Washington asked for everyone's attention. The captain came up and stood in front of the crowd next to Billy.

"Listen up. There's nothing gonna stop us from winning tonight. Brad's pitching and we've got to do for him, and ourselves too. Forget the last two games, they're history, and, like Billy says, take the clarity of this workout into the game. My mind feels good and clear and I'm ready to hit baseballs. How 'bout you, Billy?"

"This whole team's ready, Captain," Billy said with a grin.

"Alright. See you all in the cage!"

It was good to see Washington assert himself. Willie had leadership qualities, and Billy was glad to see them come back out. He would wholeheartedly nurture and support them.

After batting practice, Billy made his way out to the bullpen. It would soon be time for O'Nealy to loosen up.

"Hey, Billy." It was Steve Lafite.

"Hi, Steve, what's up?"

"Look, I'm sorry about the other day," Lafite said, looking at his feet. "I'm digging my own hole here. I got the stuff, but you wouldn't guess it from watching Morton's home run off me. What I'm trying to say is, well, what do you got for me?"

Billy went over, picked up his mitt and walked Lafite over to an empty pitcher's mound. "Steve, you do have good stuff, by and large. There's two problems, though. One, you're holding back on your slider. What are you going to pitch, one, two innings tops each outing? You can afford a little strain on the elbow, more than a starter can, and get the edge when it really counts. Pop that pitch in. And the other thing goes along with it. The batters know you, and you've got to mix your stuff up better. A reliever can be a two-pitch pitcher, but don't be afraid of the change-up. I know you think of yourself as a fireballer. That's great, so do the hitters. If you occasionally throw a change off your fastball *and* slider, you can catch them off guard. But you routinely wave off the change when I call it. Have confidence in it. That home run ball to Morton, what was it?"

Lafite searched back through his memory. "Slider, I think."

"That's right, and you waved off the sign for a change-up just before you threw it."

"You're right," said Lafite resignedly. "I guess I just don't have faith in the change-up."

"I do, Steve. Let's just fine-tune it. You want to work on it?"

"I sure do."

The two of them worked together until it was time to get O'Nealy ready for the game. Before leaving Lafite, Billy gave him a last bit of encouragement.

"You were looking pretty good towards the end there, Steve. The next time you get in a game, remember one point. It's not so important how good your change-up pitch is, it's how much the hitter is expecting fastball. If you believe in your change, the hitter is more likely to buy into it. All you need is an edge. A little edge, no matter how slight, is usually an out."

Saturday's game was a mirror image of the pitching duel in Thursday's contest. O'Nealy was painting the corners of the plate, and gave up next to nothing all day. Renker and Barker put hits together for one run in the third, and Billy drove in Willie Washington with a double in the sixth. Brad carried the 2-0 lead into the bottom of the ninth and, like Jimmy had done on Thursday night, got himself in trouble with a walk and a hit batsman. Again, with two out, Matt Morton came up with a chance to play hero. And again, Chambers called for Lafite.

"Don't screw this one up, Lafite," Chambers said, handing him the ball.

"Thanks for the encouragement," Lafite responded, as soon as Chambers was out of earshot. Billy, standing at the mound, smiled. Lafite didn't return the smile. He was all business.

When play was ready to resume, Morton stepped in. He waved his bat slowly and methodically, and planted a menacing stare on Lafite. Morton ignored the outside fastball and took it for a ball. Lafite followed it by missing with a slider. Chambers grimaced in the dugout. Lafite stepped off the mound and rubbed at the ball.

After he stepped back on the rubber, he proceeded to blaze a fastball past the swinging slugger. The guy on the speedgun whistled at the ninety-three-miles-per-hour reading. Lafite then put everything he had into a slider which

Morton only managed to get a piece of, and it sailed foul behind the screen.

Lafite leaned in for the sign, and nodded grimly at Billy's first offering. He went into his stretch, and when he loosed the ball Morton waved at it so wildly and was so far out in front of the change-up that he lost his grip on the bat, which flew all the way to shortstop. Strike three, game over. Lafite raced off the mound as Billy ran forward. They were shaking hands as the team converged on the mound. Congratulations went all around as they made their way to the clubhouse. Brad O'Nealy's thirteenth victory was secure, and Steve Lafite had saved it for him.

Sunday morning, as the team assembled in left field for calisthenics, Steve Lafite was one of the first to arrive. Upon seeing him there, Rick Santiago joined him. Before Butterfield's part of the session was finished, Carl Trumbull and the new kid, Inky Powell, had gotten in line. Not a single Giant was missing. As Billy led the T'ai Chi, he could sense the extra power generated by the presence of the whole team, and he knew that everyone else could feel it too. The circle was complete, the chain unbroken.

The Atlanta Braves were the unwilling victims of the new unity. Kiley Upton was extremely stingy with the hits, allowing three while walking none on his way to a complete-game shutout. The Giants, on the other hand, were unmerciful as they garnered a season-high twenty-four hits, including six home runs. The seventeen runs they scored were the most in three years.

Lou Chambers called a brief, post-game team meeting. After congratulating them and dealing with some minor details concerning the road trip, he concluded the meeting by declaring that the pregame warm-up sessions were now mandatory. This provoked a hearty round of laughter. Clearly the loudest and longest roar emanated from Eddie Renker.

18

THE PLAIN DEALER

June 30th.

USA TODAY WRITER
DUCKS QUESTIONS
ON INDIANS' EXPOSE

(AP) Howard Everett, a sportswriter for *USA Today*, shocked the baseball world two weeks ago with an expose of what promised to be the biggest scandal since the Black Sox of 1919. In an article published on June 15th, he alleged that unnamed members of the Cleveland Indians' organization were involved in a massive sign-stealing operation, and backed up the claim by citing computer-analyzed data compiled by a team of baseball hobbyists with advanced computer skills. This ignited a firestorm in which accusations and denials were thrown back and forth around the American League, and culminated with the Commissioner of Baseball promising to launch a full investigation.

New questions of the validity of the charges have arisen following Everett's refusal to make public the material on which his story was based. In fact, he has stopped talking to the press entirely, and will not respond to questions involving his own story. In addition, the three young computer hackers said to have compiled the data, identified in the original story as Richard Bates, Bobby Acton and Jason Michalowski, have refused to make public any material used in the story. They have repeatedly refused to be interviewed by members of the press.

Speculation that the entire affair might be a cruel hoax has been offered by a number of sports editorialists around the country. The Cleveland Indians have so far remained relatively calm, demanding only that a retraction of the original claims be printed in *USA Today*. As of this time, no such retraction has been printed and...

Richard Bates had just finished up some video tape editing he had promised to have ready for WCLV's Ten O'clock News. He replayed it and, finding it satisfactory, he slipped the cassette into its sleeve, walked over to the table by the door and dropped it into the "out" bin. He was done for the evening.

Richard was grateful that his internship was still intact, even if the rest of his life was in shambles. His supervisor at the station, who had known Richard long enough to believe in his integrity, had accepted his word that a computer error had wiped out his data; the incident was closed and it was agreed that no comment would be made by anyone at the station. Richard, for his part, agreed to limit his journalistic efforts to his television work.

As he headed down the elevator, he thought about the task that lay waiting at home. In the past two weeks, he'd avoided his computer. It was just too painful. A lifetime of baseball data was gone, not to mention the programs he'd designed. He had entertained hopes of selling those programs someday. But I can't now, he thought, not after two hard drives with eight hundred forty megabytes of disk space were gone, along with cartons of back-up floppies.

However, he knew he could avoid it no longer. It was time to start rebuilding. That night, he would begin the process of redesigning programs, newer and better programs which he hoped would shorten the time it would take to duplicate the work he'd done since he was eleven. He had vowed to do it, even if it took years. It was the only way to put the whole, crazy affair to rest. They weren't going to *get* him, whoever *they* were.

Over at Cleveland Municipal Stadium, Jake Conrad was in a considerably better frame of mind. His boys were beating the stuffing out of the Oakland A's. A's manager Al Hansen had apologized about the sign-stealing allegations before the game, but Conrad wasn't going to feel vindicated until his team had rubbed Al's nose in it. They were doing just that.

Conrad had read the piece in that day's *Plain Dealer* and felt, even without a retraction, that the whole ugly business was over. The Indians' record, after the night's likely victory, would swell to 55-18. They were the hottest thing to hit baseball in years and Conrad was going to settle down and enjoy it, maybe even get a little credit for it.

"Godammit, Ellerbach, throw strikes!"

"Jake, take it easy," Warren Evans said in Conrad's ear. "The count's 2 and 1, for heaven's sake. We got an eight-run lead."

"Yeah, I know, but I'll be satisfied with nothing less than total humiliation for Al Hansen. Then maybe we can be friends again. That's better, Cy!"

Evans shook his head and sat back down on the bench. He couldn't blame Conrad. He had no idea of what was really going on around him, and Evans wished he could let him in on it. The team was trouncing the A's, not because of anything Conrad did, but because, through mind-reading, they knew every move, every pitch the A's were about to make. Of course, it was best Conrad never know. He'd be hurt to know how little he was involved in the season's victories.

Evans was as pleased as Conrad about the apparent demise of the sign-stealing story. He could only wonder, though, if that was to be the last distraction from baseball for the rest of the Season. He, like everyone in the Operation, hoped it would be. There was one good side effect of the sign-stealing business. The whole team had adopted a no-comment policy that could remain in force indefinitely. It could prevent a lot of meddling in many areas of inquiry and, after the recent, discredited press debacle, no one in the media could blame them.

Evans couldn't wait for the All-Star break. He was going to head up to the orbital station for a little visit. There'd be conferences and work sessions, but mostly he looked forward to being surrounded by nothing but Ball Fourians. It would be very relaxing to not worry about letting his guard down for seventy-two hours in a row. Abe Watkins was heading up there with him, along with a few operatives on the Indian's staff. It would be nice. The Ball Fourian food would be wonderful, even if it was all from duplicators.

Out on the mound, Cy Ellerbach, whose Ball Fourian name was Ellerban, peered in for the sign. Of course, catcher Eddie Martin was busy scanning the A's hitter's mind and, once he'd read what pitch he was expecting, Martin would relay it mentally. The signs were just a charade.

Curve, low, inside.

The Athletic at the plate was guessing fastball. Just as the ball left Ellerbach's hand Martin projected *fastball!* toward the hitter, who swung with all his might about a foot above the ball. Strike three. He walked away, dazed and confused, wondering why the ball had broken two feet and he couldn't for the life of him stop thinking it was a fastball.

In the Indians' bottom of the eighth, Evans decided to give Conrad a rush. He told his boys to swing away.

Hit away, team.

Yes, Evan.

The resulting five consecutive home runs were a new major-league record. Al Hansen cringed in the A's dugout. His team was first in the American

League West, but didn't look like it. Conrad, after the fifth homer, yelled across to the visitor's dugout.

"Al, that'll teach you to keep your mouth shut!"

Hansen couldn't make out exactly what Conrad had said, but he got the message all the same.

Up in the orbital station, Ygarnen took a seat at his console. Operation Command had decided on an unusual course, one with which he was in complete agreement. He was charged with carrying it out, and he would do it with pleasure.

After reviewing the data from Richard Bates' hard disks, it was determined that it would be cruel to the human to deprive him of so large a body of work. The Ball Fourians could only admire someone with such a love of and dedication to baseball, and wished no ill toward any human; they only wished to quell suspicion concerning the infiltration, in order that the Season they'd worked so hard for could proceed unhindered. Additionally, the generous act of returning the data to its owner, with all data involving the Indians carefully deleted, would send a mystifying message to Bates that was sure to curtail any further investigation on his part. It was a tidy formulation, and Ygarnen prepared to execute it forthwith.

Restoring the materials which had been blanked on the floppy disks, having been stored outside the computer, was impossible without a physical Earthside operation. Since those materials were, for the most part, duplicates of the hard disk data, Operation Command had decided to forgo that part of the restoration. The important material could be restored to the hard disk electromagnetically from a console chair on the station. It had further been deemed unnecessary to restore the data to Acton and Michalowski's computers, as the three had shared their material so much that they all had each other's on disk.

Ygarnen used the communications circuits to access the computer through its modem link, punched a couple of keys and, in a matter of seconds, had sent the data back to Bates' computer. That was indeed merciful, thought Ygarnen, and it would make a nice story when he returned to Ball Four.

Bates turned into the driveway of his parents' home in Brook Park, just east of the airport. It was only half past ten, but the lights were out. It was typical. His parents were already asleep. They'd worked so hard to get what they had, and to see to it that their only child could get a decent education; but now his senior year at Michigan was in serious jeopardy. The bucks were tight and his antics this summer had done nothing to help.

Not that he'd done a damned thing wrong. As he entered the house and crept through the darkened living room to his bedroom, he wondered what forces had been behind the response to his investigative work. Who was that powerful, and why were they tied to baseball? It was nightmarish.

He sat down in front of his computer, reached around it and turned it on. As he waited for it to boot up, he wondered what to do first. Just because the task was so great and he was so down about school and all, there was no reason to lose his resolve now. Just get to it, maybe start by reprogramming "Stat Cruncher," the program he had the biggest commercial hopes for. He had a long way to go. Since the big crash two weeks ago, he hadn't gone further than restoring his disk operating system. Aside from DOS, his disks were empty. When the computer finished booting up, he sat bolt upright in his chair. What was going on?

This could not be. On the monitor screen in front of him was the root directory of his number one hard drive, just as it appeared two weeks ago. He looked at the DOS clock and calendar and it read 23:56, June 16. That was about the time of the crash. He checked through the directory and everything seemed to be there that used to be. He checked the root directory of the other hard drive and, sure enough, everything was there. What the hell was happening? The DOS clock indicated that it was as though it were two weeks ago and nothing had ever happened. He went into the "Stat Cruncher" program, and all the stat files of the Indians' season were in the subdirectory. He called up the file entitled "hit-run." It was empty. Dammit. He then went through all the files pertaining to the Indians. One by one, they turned up empty.

An hour later, Richard Bates had finished a check of nearly all of the files on the two hard disks. He sat motionless, his face as white as a ghost. He dared not delve too much into the implications. Everything he'd had in memory on disk had been restored, except anything having to do with this year's Cleveland Indians. Who would, or could for that matter, go to all this trouble? Anyone powerful enough or clever enough would never bother to return his data to him after deleting material they didn't want him to have. It was all imponderable.

Wait a minute, he thought, what about my floppy disks? A few minutes later he had verified that they remained blank. Whoever had been responsible was unable or unwilling to restore the data to the floppies. Or was it that they realized it was unnecessary? No more thinking, it just got too scary. Richard reached an abrupt conclusion. What had been done had most certainly been done by extremely capable hands in any amazingly methodical manner. The final act, if indeed it was the final act, was a very kind one. He would not look a gift horse in the mouth. He would take the message for what it was: have fun with your silly baseball toys and stay the hell away from the Cleveland Indians.

"You don't have to tell me twice," Richard said to himself softly. Taking the blank floppy disks, of which he now had an ample supply, he began the very time-consuming task of copying the entire contents of his hard drives to back-up floppy disks. When he finished that, he would repeat the process to produce a second set. Tomorrow he would get a safe deposit box at a bank to keep them in, preferably on the other side of town.

Monday morning, the doorbell rang in the apartment of Lloyd Cronin. That would be Loretta, his ex-wife. Cronin looked around nervously. The apartment was clean enough, he'd spent all of Sunday seeing to that. Loretta could be so critical; it was bad enough that he had to go to her for help.

"Good morning, Lloyd," Loretta said a bit too sincerely.

"Thanks for coming, Loretta," answered Cronin, too casually. "I knew I could count on you." He could too. They'd gotten divorced eight years ago, but, despite the rancor, he still trusted her more than anyone, especially now that he needed somebody to help him get back on his feet. He'd been hiding in his apartment for almost seven weeks and it was time he tried to leave. Whatever was so scary out there wouldn't dare bother him, he thought with a shaky humor. Loretta would bite their heads off.

"We've been through this, Lloyd, but I can't imagine why you didn't call me sooner. Good heavens! This place is a dump."

Lloyd was glad he had cleaned it. If she had seen it before, she would have taken one look and bolted.

"Are you ready?" she asked impatiently.

"Give me a break, Loretta, I haven't been outside for ages."

"As if I couldn't tell," she responded, "you're as pale as the moon. There's no reason to put it off. Your attire looks good enough for those goons down at the paper. Let's just pull ourselves together and face the music. Just get it behind you."

One good thing about Loretta, Cronin thought with tentative amusement: she's cheaper than a therapist. And just as effective. She'll insult me into a cure.

"Okay, okay."

The first few steps were a bit shaky, and the sun was unbearably bright. But by the time he'd gotten into Loretta's car, Cronin felt ever so slightly confident. It hadn't been as bad as he had anticipated.

Driving through the city streets on the way to the office downtown was rather merry after living in a cave all that time. Everywhere, people were hurrying this way and that. They seemed profoundly disinterested in Lloyd Cronin's problem. And, glancing out the window, it appeared most certainly that the sky was not particularly interested in crashing down on his head. It was rather blue and clean for Cleveland in summer.

When they reached the offices of the *Cleveland Plain Dealer*, Loretta wheeled up at the loading zone in front and stopped.

"This is as far as I go, Lloyd," she said. "You're on your own from here."

"But you said you'd make sure I made it to work," Cronin said pleadingly. "It's just a few more steps."

"I've seen you to work and I'm stopping here. After all, it was your association with some of those clowns in there that helped to sink our marriage, or don't you remember? You'll be all right. Best of luck, I look forward to reading your column again."

She waited until he was clear of the car before sliding away from the curb. She vanished quickly into the traffic. Cronin walked across the sidewalk and looked up the steps to the front door. What the hell, I've made it this far, I might as well go the rest.

Once he made it up to his floor, his friends pressed all around him to welcome him back. His editor, Louie Adams, waved everyone back to work. "Give the guy some room, for chrissake!"

Louie walked Cronin back to his cubicle. "What can I get you, anything?"

Cronin looked around. Same old mess, God bless it. "Louie, all I need is a chair, a piece of paper, a typewriter and a slot in tomorrow's paper."

"The slot's yours, and everything else you got already. Welcome back."

Cronin sat down at his desk, took out a piece of paper and fed it into his old trusty Royal. He paused and opened the lower right-hand drawer. There it was, the bottle of twelve-year-old rye whisky he kept for emergencies. He pondered for a second and closed the drawer.

Outside the cubicle, Louie Adams stood listening intently. When the sound of Cronin's typewriter started up he smiled and went about his business. The old bastard was back.

19

After the split with the Atlanta Braves, the San Francisco Giants moved on to a three-game series at Cincinnati, which was to culminate in a special Fourth of July game. Lou Chambers decided to give the pitching rotation an extra day of rest by trying out young Inky Powell with his first major league start. Chambers wanted to know what Powell was made of. It might be important down the stretch when the depth of a team can be a deciding factor.

Inky Powell got his nickname from his jet-black skin. In fact, his skin was so black that Powell believed, correctly or not, that the hitters could see the release of the white baseball better than from other pitchers. To counter this, Powell had created a whirling-dervish sort of wind-up, meant to distract the hitters and mask the ball's release. It was quite effective, and made Powell a very entertaining pitcher to watch.

He made a valiant effort but, unfortunately, it wasn't quite good enough to subdue the Reds, who got to him for three runs by the fourth inning. Carl Trumbull gave up another while closing out the game. The Giants' bats cooled off after the previous game's slugfest in Atlanta and the three runs they produced were not enough to support Powell's debut. The Giants were disappointed to see their record drop to 37-39, and the .500 mark seemed as elusive as ever.

Two starts by Jimmy Strongbow and Brad O'Nealy changed that in a hurry. They threw consecutive shutouts, while the Giants' bats came back to life and brutalized the Reds' pitchers. On the Fourth of July the Giants reached the .500 mark and the fireworks show at Riverfront Stadium after the game seemed, to the Giants, to be for their benefit more than to celebrate America's birthday. Billy enjoyed them immensely, even if they were a bit tame compared to the space-station-generated laser light shows which were prevalent forms of celebration on Ball Four.

Without a travel day, the Giants went straight on to Houston for a four-game series. Still fuming over the outrageous attempt to enjoin Billy and Jimmy from playing, the Giants were relentless in their vengeful dismantling of the Astros. They swept the series as the Giants' pitching gave up only two runs in four games. A sympathetic Houston judge had moved up the final hearing on the Astros' complaint to coincide with the Giants' visit. In spite of Billy's refusal to discuss his life in his affidavit, arguing that it was a constitutionally protected right to privacy, the judge dismissed the unsubstantiated complaint before the Giants left town. By then the Astros quite likely wished they'd never attempted the legal dodge.

The road trip ended with three games against the division-leading Los Angeles Dodgers. The series turned into a pitching duel between the stingy L.A. pitchers and Upton, Strongbow and O'Nealy. They split the first two games, with the Giants winning the rubber match against their traditional rivals. It was always sweet to beat L.A., all the more so as it sent the Giants into the All-Star break with a record of 45-40. It also took them past the Braves into third place, eight games behind the Dodgers. The confident Giants could be satisfied with that.

Players who were selected to the All-Star team were always proud of the honor, but those ignored were nonetheless grateful for the chance to take a rest from the incessant schedule. Brad O'Nealy, with a record of 13-4, was naturally selected to the team. Willie Washington, always a very popular player with the fans, had managed to take the lead in the home run race with twenty-one round-trippers and was chosen to start for the National side. Jimmy Strongbow's 6-3 record was impressive, as was Billy Icarus' .460 batting average, but they were too new to have captured many of the fans's votes or to warrant selection by the manager. Billy was only too happy to have the three days off. He planned a fishing trip with Jimmy, and decided it would be wise to take the opportunity to break the news of his identity to a couple more players. He chose to invite Kiley Upton and Art French. They accepted with pleasure.

Billy was not surprised to hear that the Cleveland team had landed only three on the American League's list of honorees. From what he could gather in the press, the major leagues' most awesome squad had little respect except at home, and even there not much affection had been generated in the hometown fans. The Indians had stayed too distant and aloof to win what was indeed more of a popularity contest than an acknowledgement of true talent. Starters Vance Bueller and Cy Ellerbach were chosen by Al Hansen, the American League skipper, and league-leading home run hitter Alan Van De Kirk couldn't be ignored by the fans. After eighty-five games he had blasted thirty-one homers and people were naturally talking about the possibility of his overtaking Maris' record of sixty-one. Billy was not surprised by the success of Alvendak, as he was known on Ball Four. He was the leading home run hitter of the rival First City Sluggers and had been the only hitter to approach Billy's dominance of Ball Fourian baseball. Alvendak had even won the home run crown away from Billy one year, although Billy had won it six of the last eight years. He was not impressed by Alvendak's success on Earth. It was another example of unfair play.

Art French, a fishing and hunting enthusiast, had a thirty-foot-long motor home which he offered for use on the fishing outing. It had more than enough amenities to serve the foursome's needs. The vehicle had so much fishing equipment on it that the group was able to board it and depart with little or no packing time. As tired as they were, they decided to forgo sleep and got on the road as soon as they could after flying in from L.A. French's favorite fishing area was in the Sierra Nevada mountain range up in Sonora Pass. They took turns driving and napping, and all but Billy drove a shift. It was a four-hour drive from San Francisco, and the sky was just beginning to get light when French announced to the snoozing teammates that they had arrived at his favorite spot on the south fork of the Stanislaus River. It was rugged country, and the tall pine trees and mountain peaks that surrounded them were inspirational as Billy and the others climbed out of the vehicle to such a beautiful sight. That and a pot of coffee soon readied them for the work of fishing the clear mountain stream. Kiley Upton, raised on a constant regimen of Minnesota lake fishing, was drawn into the challenge of finding just the right spot to capture the elusive trout among the boulders and rapids of the rushing stream. Billy, born and raised in the ocean fishing tradition of Seaview, was fascinated by the art of stream fishing. By midday, everyone had caught his limit, including Jimmy, who had opted to make a crude spear following the California coastal Indian traditions. He wasn't that familiar with it, but it had worked just the same. He whittled a razor-sharp point on a stiff manzanita branch and poised himself above a shallow pool. As the occasional fish swam into the pool, he deftly speared the fish with a rapid thrust. He laughed with delight at each triumph.

They retired early that night, and spent the next day fishing and hiking through the remote area. The atmosphere of camping in the mountains, along with the manly pursuits in which they engaged, brought the four men closer together than ever before, and Billy was sure that it would set the stage for revealing the shocking news to Upton and French.

The evening found them roasting the day's catch over an open fire, and the beer, kept ice cold in the mountain stream, had both mellowed and re-freshed them. Jimmy had forgone any imbibing, perhaps sensing that Billy would need Jimmy's head clear to assist him in what he was sure Billy had in mind. Art French, not ordinarily a talkative man, had been opened up by the drink and the camaraderie, and helped Billy by bringing up the central topic.

"Billy, if you weren't such an impressive player," French began, "the press would never let you get away with your evasiveness about your past. As a matter of fact, I don't understand why they haven't lynched you. Those bas-tards are greedy for stories, and mystery always seems to whet their appetites. Why are they so easy on you?"

"It's taken quite an effort," replied Billy.

"My story isn't that interesting," Upton interposed as he tossed a few branches on the fire. "But the reporters squeezed everything they could out of me anyway, I guess because I was a first-round draft pick. But you haven't even told them the name of your hometown. What's the big deal?"

"I've got a lot to hide. The only people I've told are Jimmy and Brad. I wish Brad could be here tonight, then we'd have all the starters together. But he's probably having a ball spoiling the American League's fun even as we speak. Anyway, one of the reasons I suggested this trip was to let you two in on the big mystery. Jimmy, would you do the honors?"

The request startled Jimmy, but he quickly accepted the role he was being asked to play. "Sure, Billy. We might as well get it over with. Art, Kiley, the reason Billy never tells anybody where he's from is because he's an alien from another world."

"I knew it," said French as the two laughed out loud. "Come on, Billy, where are you really from?"

"Jimmy told you the truth. I'm from a planet called Ball Four, and I've come to Earth on a special mission."

"He's telling you the truth, you guys," said Jimmy, "this is no joke. He told Brad and me about a month ago. We had trouble believing it until he proved it."

French continued to chuckle, but Upton could sense that Jimmy spoke in earnest. "Art, these guys are serious. Okay, for the sake of argument, what sort of proof do you offer?"

Billy liked the clear-headed, rational Upton. If convinced, he would likely accept Billy's story at face value. He wasn't so sure about French. He had some of the hard-nosed, pugnacious qualities of Renker. It was what made him such a competitor, but he might remain dubious in spite of proof.

Billy pulled out two envelopes. Jimmy saw that Billy had come prepared.

"Jimmy, you hold these. Each envelope has one of your names on it. Kiley, I want you to say the first two things that pop into your head, okay?"

"Two?"

"Yeah," said Billy.

Upton blurted out, in rapid succession, "fastball" and "Bemidji." That was Upton's hometown in northern Minnesota.

"Give him the envelope that has his name on it, Jimmy. No, Kiley, don't open it yet. Now, Art, please do the same thing. Say the first two things that come to your mind."

"This is ridiculous," snapped French.

"Please, just do it."

French, almost reluctantly, said, "Belteron. Seaview."

"Okay, Jimmy, give him his envelope. Go ahead, both of you open them up."

Each of them ripped at their envelopes, Upton anxiously and French rather defiantly. The defiance turned to amazement as the contents were revealed. In Upton's envelope was a piece of paper on which was written "Two?", "fastball" and "Bemidji." The paper in French's envelope contained the words "This is ridiculous," "Belteron" and "Seaview." After reading them, both Upton and French fell silent. No one spoke for minutes.

Brad O'Nealy, taking the mound for the top of the second inning, looked around at the capacity crowd at Dodger Stadium. In his wildest dreams he had never foreseen this moment. Being chosen to start the All-Star game in his rookie season was enough to humble a player even as cocky as he. But to take the mound in this distinguished ballpark on national prime-time television had shaken his ordinarily steely nerves. His sense of humor was no protection for a moment like this. As the game started Brad had fallen back on the mind-focusing techniques Billy Icarus had been teaching him in recent days. They had served him well. He not only had regained his composure, but he had struck out the American League side in the first inning. Now as the second began, the moment he'd been waiting for arrived. He would face a Cleveland "Alien" in the form of their most ferocious hitter, Alan Van De Kirk. Billy had told Brad everything he knew about Van De Kirk, which was considerable. Now would come an important test. For the first time since the Ball Fourians had arrived on Earth, a human aware of the truth would face one of them.

Van De Kirk strolled to the plate with a composed smile on his face. He, like the rest of the Ball Fourians, would have been content to have avoided the All-Star game. It was not a crucial part of the scheme. But he would enjoy it and learn from the experience as best he could. He looked forward to getting a glimpse of National League pitching, although he couldn't imagine its being very different from what he'd already seen in the American League. This Brad O'Nealy was one of the best, or so it was said, and Van De Kirk anticipated "taking him downtown," as the Earthlings were fond of saying.

Brad knew that the key to dealing with Van De Kirk would be in somehow deceiving him as to the pitch to be thrown. That was next to impossible because, if what Billy said was true, Van De Kirk would know from the catcher's mind what was coming. There was only one door open to Brad, and he would risk angering Vincento Diaz, the National League catcher from Pittsburgh.

This would be a very tight rope to walk.

Van De Kirk stood in. He scanned Diaz' mind and read *fastball, down and in*. Ah, yes, give it to me, he thought as O'Nealy went into his wind-up. Van De Kirk took a mighty cut and pulled the ball sharply foul. What was that, he thought, it was no more than seventy-five miles an hour, that's his fastball?

Diaz got up and ran to the mound to clarify the signs. Brad nodded politely at the gentle reminder. As Diaz squatted behind the plate and gave the next sign, Van De Kirk scanned him and read *change-up*. Yes, this will be too easy, he thought with relish. Brad nodded and blazed a fastball right down the shoot. Caught off-guard, Van De Kirk never really got his bat off his shoulder. His weak effort could hardly be called a swing. Diaz easily caught the pitch because of the location, but gave Brad a brief glare. What was going on?

The same thought occurred to Van De Kirk. Deciding that the catcher's mind must somehow be unreliable, he turned his attention on O'Nealy's. Sensing this from the look in Van De Kirk's eyes, Brad dropped into a meditative state. Van De Kirk was confused by the surprising whiteness of the mind on the mound. He strengthened his attention as O'Nealy looked in. All of a sudden, Brad opened his mind, and the resulting *rising fastball, up!* produced a disconcerting ping in Van De Kirk's brain. He quickly smoothed out his mind and, with practiced determination, prepared to take a hefty swat. He saw the ball clearly as it powered toward him and, with perfect timing, arced a vicious stroke slightly high in anticipation that the ball would rise. Just as the ball neared the plate, it dropped about two inches and made a loud whap! as it hit Diaz' glove. Van De Kirk stood and stared at O'Nealy for a moment before strutting in business-like fashion back to the visitor's dugout. Vincento Diaz threw the ball around the horn, took his mask off and smiled. Whatever this madman who couldn't read signs was up to, it had worked. He had just struck out the most feared hitter in the American League on three pitches.

I wonder if this is how they do it on Ball Four, Brad thought smugly.

Back in the dugout, Alan Van De Kirk was thinking what screwballs these humans could be. This O'Nealy character had accidentally pulled a mind gambit. He must be mentally unstable. Oh, well, he wasn't likely to face that lunatic again.

Back in the high country of the Sierra Nevada, Billy Icarus had spent the last couple of hours answering a series of questions from the stunned pair. Through the long, bright evening of midsummer and well into the mountain twilight, they talked and talked. Over and over, he had to give more demonstrations of his mental gifts. They were by now convinced and fear had first given way to curiosity, then to excitement.

"Now that you've told us, Billy," Upton said, "it all makes sense. You were never an ordinary duck, I'll tell you. Art, he always knew what was going on. And, say, I'm glad you haven't been reading our minds all the time. Under the circumstances, you've apparently been quite fair."

"That's what this whole thing is about, not taking unfair advantage," Billy replied. "Although, against the Indians, anything goes. By now Brad's faced Van De Kirk, and I hope the results were good. It's a little risky, but I doubt they'll draw any conclusions from it. We just need to see if our plans are going in the right direction. You see, boys, the only hope we've got is in preparing our mental game."

"That's the reasoning behind the T'ai Chi," offered Upton.

"Of course," answered Billy. "After a lot of research, I've come to the conclusion that there have been a considerable number of disciplines developed on Earth which, while falling quite short of producing the breakthrough which happened ages ago on Ball Four, still parallel our mental training. Hopefully, we can accomplish something substantial enough by the World Series to narrow the gap. It's a bit daunting, I must confess."

"Aren't we getting ahead of ourselves?" French asked. "We still have to win the pennant. Or do you plan to use your powers to guarantee that?"

"No, I don't. It's another problem for me, for us. If I take unfair advantage, I'm no better than the others. I guess I'd rather fail than triumph through underhanded means. But what about you guys? Would you accept losing while knowing that I had a way, however dishonorable, for us to win?"

"Tough question," said French thoughtfully. "Maybe some of us would. As for me, if I consider it, your way's best. I was brought up with honesty being a point of honor. Kiley?"

"I like the challenge. This is going to be different from what I got into baseball for in the first place but, then again, no, it isn't. The aim is to play well and hopefully prevail. Even against an alien team. It boggles the mind, I gotta say. But I'm with Art, where's the pleasure in winning if you've been underhanded? Sure, the history of baseball has had its moments, with gambling scandals, spitballs and sharpened spikes. But, by and large, it's a more honorable game than most. Mostly because it's hard to cheat, I might add. But what about gambling, Billy? Doesn't all the gambling lead to corruption on Ball Four?"

"It can't, really," said Billy. "We're issued gambling credits which, if we use up, we must wait until we've amassed more. Also, a limited amount of investment credits are allowable for wagering purposes but, again, even investment is a form of entertainment. When all citizens have their needs fulfilled, what is dog-eat-dog on Earth becomes good-humored leisure on our world. Oh, sure, occasionally a citizen goes a little off, but he's treated quickly and quietly by Public Health. No one on Ball Four wants anyone else to suffer."

"Sounds like paradise," said Upton.

"Yes and no," responded Billy. "Since I've been here I realize that life on Ball Four is pretty tame. I love baseball, it's what I live for, naturally, but I've come to think of all that biofashioning and gambling as a bit meaningless, and the imposed isolation had stunted and perhaps halted the development of our species. It can't be good for us. I think some of our leaders have become aware of it. We need to expand our horizons. That's why we're here on Earth."

"You guys plan to take over?" asked French.

"Never," said Billy. "Our concept of individual freedom within the confines of group well-being would preclude it. It was a firmly established principle during our days of contact that to harm or interfere with another sentient species was unethical. It was because of an encounter with a species that used violence against us, with malice and for personal gain, that we chose isolationism. No, from historical precedent, you've nothing to fear. Remember, I'm only a ballplayer, but I've been taught this from birth, and I can't imagine anyone from the political caste as having a different view of it."

"I could ask a million questions, but what else is up for the team?" Upton asked. "Are you going to tell everyone one by one? We got a lot to do. You can't take too much time."

"I can't rush it either. But we'll move as rapidly as possible to bring everybody in. Brad's going to tell Washington tonight."

"Really?" said Jimmy with surprise. "That's news to me."

"Sorry, It was all quickly planned. Brad wanted a shot at it, and I thought it would be good to see Willie's reaction without me around to convince him. I'm anxious to find out."

"Why'd you pick us ahead of the others?" asked French.

"Aside from the fact that you're pitchers, it was just the luck of the draw. I wanted to go fishing and you had an RV."

That provoked a chuckle, followed by pessimistic smirks. "Yeah, right, Billy," said Upton. "No way you do things that haphazardly."

Billy just smiled. "You're right, Kiley. The pitchers are going to need the most training if we're to gain the edge over the Indians. The fiercest mental attacks are going to be against the pitchers. You'll need the most preparation."

Billy paused. "I've got to ask you two a question. Do you accept what I've told you?"

The pair pondered the question for a moment. Upton answered first. "Yes, I do. Who you are and where you came from has always been a mystery and, whatever the truth was going to be, it was bound to be odd. It was odd to see a twenty-eight-year-old rookie. You are twenty-eight, aren't you?"

"Yes. That's always been true."

"But you're not a rookie."

"No. I'm in my ninth professional season, counting the eight on Ball Four."

"So you started at twenty. that's about the same as here on Earth. How long does a, er, what-do-you-call-it, Ball Fourian?, how long can you expect to play? How long do you guys live anyway?

"We live an average of two hundred years. Our careers in baseball average about sixty years, although my father's lasted a record eighty years. I hope to emulate him in longevity, but now that I've gone and done this I don't know what's in store for me."

"Two hundred years?" asked Upton. "I thought you said that our species were mostly alike."

"I did and they are. The reason we live so long is attributable to two basic factors: genetic monitoring and the absence of disease. Through genetic monitoring, all defects and weaknesses are eliminated prior to birth."

"So you build superbabies," French said.

"Not the way you probably mean," replied Billy. "Although it's technically possible, we don't genetically improve embryos. It's against our medical ethics, we consider it tampering with natural law. But we do correct mutations and defects. The result is a basically perfect baby. Nature builds them quite well. We just prevent accidents. We've also enhanced longevity by limiting oxidation through drug implants. And there's no question that our mind training eliminates most stress, which naturally sustains our health. The absence of stress allows our immune systems to prevent most diseases from having a fighting chance. Those other diseases we can't naturally defend against are controlled through drug implants and inoculation. That's one good thing for me. Being away from Ball Four for whatever length of time won't affect my health. In preparation for our infiltration, I had ample drug-implants and inoculations to last quite a while. And, of course, I was inoculated against any Earth diseases, many of which we're not susceptible to in any event. Listen, I'd be glad to answer any and all questions, but we haven't give Art a chance to respond to my original question. How about it, Art, are you accepting any of this?"

"I don't know. I accept your mental powers. But that doesn't prove you're an alien. It only proves that you have special powers. You could still be human, as far as I can see. Either way, it's equally weird."

"Not really, Art. If I'm actually an alien, then everything that I've told you is plausible. If I'm merely a human with telepathic powers, then it follows that I must be quite deluded to propose that I'm an alien and back it up with such a bizarre tale."

"He's got a point, Art," said Upton.

French mulled it over. "I suppose if I had to choose between a sane and honest alien, and a crazy or lying human who can read minds, I'd rather have you turn out to be an alien. It sounds safer. I'll take your word for it, for now anyway."

"Good," said Jimmy, who had been sitting back during the long discussion. "Doubt could eat us up, and that can't be good now that we're winning ballgames."

"That's true, Jimmy," Billy said. "So I'll be glad to stay up all night answering questions if it helps eliminate doubt."

Conversation went on as the endless questions flowed. Billy did his best to answer them all patiently. These guys had a right to know whatever they wished. They were being asked to accept quite a bit of a burden during the days ahead.

Billy and Jimmy sat on the veranda on Telegraph Hill, and waited for the arrival of O'Nealy and Washington. They felt invigorated by their trip to the mountains. They had fished that morning at dawn, had eaten a hearty breakfast before breaking camp, then leisurely drove back across California to the City.

Jimmy walked over to the railing and scanned the long steps down the hillside to the street. O'Nealy and Washington were on their way up.

As they made their way onto the veranda, the two were a study in contrasts. O'Nealy was basking in the glory of the three perfect innings he had thrown the night before, while Washington, who had been held hitless in his two at-bats, wore a sterner, more serious look. Obviously, O'Nealy had broken the news.

After the round of handshakes, Billy went straight to the point. "Willie, what do you think?"

Washington shook his head before speaking. "Frankly, I don't know. It's either the biggest bunch of crap I ever heard or the end of the goddam world."

"It's neither, Willie," said Billy. "It's just the way it is."

"Well, there's no doubt about a couple of things. Cleveland pitching is awesome. if what Brad told me is true, it's no wonder I was fooled so bad."

"You faced Bueller and Ellerbach? Not doubt they fed you misinformation prior to each swing."

"I didn't notice anything, Billy. Look, this is too strange for me. I'm talking to you like this is for real."

"It is," said Billy. "But I can't blame you for being dismayed. Trust me, you just batted against two of the best pitchers from my planet. We'll talk about that later. What can I do to ease your mind?"

"Brad told me how you proved you were an alien by putting stuff into his head. Look here, I don't want you messing with me. This is like voodoo or something."

Billy took a slow, thoughtful breath. "Okay. I've got it. Willie, why don't you give me something to put in Brad and Jimmy's heads? You guys mind?"

"Go for it," said Brad.

Jimmy nodded in assent.

"All right," Billy continued. "Willie, you write something down on this pad of paper and give it to me. Anything you want, but make it a word or a short phrase. Okay. Now, show it to me. Good. Give Jimmy and Brad a piece of paper each. Okay, please split up, go to the ends of the bench."

Jimmy and Brad dutifully slid away from each other. They waited for instructions. Washington looked on dubiously.

"Got pens? All right, write the first thing that comes into your mind."

The pair wrote on the paper in front of them. When they were finished, Washington picked up the pieces of paper. On both of them were written "San Francisco Giants." He tossed them aside and tapped on the table top with his finger tips, then looked over at Billy and shook his head.

After a moment, he spoke. "Okay, just for the hell of it, let's say I believe you. Jimmy and Brad do, so maybe I ought to as well."

"So, it seems do Art and Kiley," added Billy.

"Okay. So why'd you tell me?"

"You're the captain of the team, Willie. I told you out of respect and also because you can be very instrumental in helping the team do what we've got to do."

"Yeah, Brad told me. We gotta get our heads ready to play Cleveland in the Series. Right. If these guys are so hot, how can we possibly stop them? I was swinging at the air against Bueller and Ellerbach."

"You were swinging where they told you to swing," Billy answered. "I know these tactics well. But most mature players on Ball Four have countered the measures. We've got the rest of the season and the playoffs to train ourselves to do the same."

"That's if we even get to the Series. How do you even know we can do that?"

"Think of our team, Willie. Are we winners?"

Washington thought for a second. Then a defiant look came into his eyes. "Yeah, dammit, we are. It's no accident how we've been playing. I don't care what Brad said, have you been messing with the whole team?"

"I assure you that I've just shared with you my knowledge of baseball and started working on our mental game. And, of course, I've been knocking the cover off the ball," he added with a grin.

Washington grinned back. "Yeah, you do smack it a bit. Okay, I admit you've been coaching our team from the sidelines ever since you were on the grounds crew and, frankly, you're more of a captain and manager than me and Lou. Can we keep getting better?"

"I've got a good idea, Willie. You're not comfortable with my being an alien. I don't blame you. In time, you'll come to accept it. In the meantime, let's all help each other by working together to improve the team. Whether or not I'm an alien, it doesn't matter at present. As long as we keep coming together as a team and winning, that's what counts. Let's forget everything else and play good baseball. How about it?"

"I can go with that," said Washington.

"Just one thing," Billy added. "Please cooperate with the things I'll be introducing to improve our mental game. It's our only hope against Cleveland, I assure you."

"All right, but at least tell me something about it."

"Sure. There's a mental state called the white mind. This is the state that Ball Fourian players have to achieve in order to block intrusion or suggestion. Ball Fourians, like humans, have two hemispheres in their brains, and they work in approximately the same way. The left hemisphere controls rational thought and direct action, while the right hemisphere controls images, symbolic thinking and abstract, creative thought. To achieve the white mind, one must place the rational left hemisphere into a meditative state, then utilize the ordinarily subconscious level of the right hemisphere as the center of action. Basically, it's as though you bump the active mind down one floor, if you follow the metaphor. There's a problem and an advantage to this. To achieve this state you have to play the game symbolically, through images rather than rational thought. That's difficult but I'm sure that humans can do it. The advantage is that one must play the game on an instinctive level, which clears the mind of garbage that gets in the way of pure effort. That's why the T'ai Chi has improved our game. We're better at the basics, because the pure game is based on what can be called timeless, unchanging fundamentals."

"That's why you taught me to pitch with all those symbols," said Jimmy with a new awareness. "You skipped a step in my training."

"That's right. I also trained you that way because it's the way I learned originally, and I suspected it would work for you. You had raw talent which needed focus to cure your wildness. Luckily, my system worked for you and, yes, you're a step ahead in your training. I've been working with Brad on this too, and he's doing well. Naturally, he's got an entirely different set of symbols except for the basic framework of his strike zone imaging. His isn't a Medicine Wheel, it's a geometric construct."

"I was always good at math," said Brad professorially.

"I've also worked a bit with Art and Kiley and they should make faster progress now that they're in the know."

"Wait a minute," said Washington. "Won't this screw up the signs? How can you give and receive signs and think about what you're doing if you got this white mind thing going?"

"It's no problem for the pitchers. I'm catching and with my perfectly white mind the hitters can't read me. I flash one finger for fastball and Jimmy thinks arrow. Since arrow is his symbol for fastball, he processes the sign symbolically in his right hemisphere where images are processed. Therefore he naturally functions within the white-mind state. It works too, because I've tried to read him and I can't. If I can't, then no Ball Fourian alive will be able to. And Brad's not far behind."

"You've been working on all this for a long time, haven't you?" Brad asked rhetorically. "Even before you told us the truth, we were well on our way to being trained. You crafty son-of-a-bitch."

"But what about us hitters?" asked Washington, ignoring Brad's levity. "How do we defend against their tricks? I didn't do so well against Bueller and Ellerbach. I struck out twice."

"It can be done, I assure you. But it will be difficult. For one thing, you've got to stop guessing at pitches. So many human ballplayers do it and the Giants are no exception. You'll have to bat instinctively with a quiet mind. You can't be thinking fastball or they'll read you like a book. You'll just have to watch the ball and hit it where they throw it. It'll be good for your game in the long run. The great, really great hitters were the pure hitters with good eyes, like Musial and Williams. Also, the third base coach won't be able to send signs to the plate. That'll kill a little strategy, like hit-and-run. But we can still pull that sort of thing instinctively. And the base coaches will still be useful to us in running the bases and they'll be active in doing a lot of decoying, false signs and the like. That's assuming they go for it, of course, which I'm not sure they will. I worry about how Lou and the coaches are going to take all of this."

"Sounds like an awesome amount of work," said Washington. "And what about the other players? When are you going to tell them?"

"One by one, over the next few weeks. We've got a lot of the work done already. The T'ai Chi workouts have done wonders. I've started monitoring the players' minds from time to time, and all without exception are starting to show signs of the white mind and are guessing less."

"That's true with me," confessed Washington. "I've been trying to take the meditative mind into the game like you've been saying, and I noticed that I don't guess as much as I used to. Been hitting better too. I guess I owe you a lot, whether you're an alien or what. I suppose going along with this whole thing can't hurt the team."

"What's important is that we stay together on it," said Brad. "Did you notice how the whole team became stronger after everyone joined the T'ai Chi workouts? If we stay together, we can win this thing, at least the pennant. What happens after that is up to Billy and what he can accomplish."

"I don't know if we can do it," Billy said quietly. "This is all uncharted territory. We just have to try. Not only do I want to win for the Giants' sake, but I'm very serious about challenging the infiltrators. That's my mission, and I need your help."

"Well, you've got mine," said Washington, standing up. He crossed his arms and planted his feet. "You've been good to me and I'm proud to call you my friend. I could do without this alien invasion business, but we got to do what we got to do to win. I'm with you."

"I knew I could count on you," Billy said. "Boys, let's leave baseball alone for a while. Tomorrow begins the second half of the season and we'll be hard at it, hopefully well into October. Jimmy, let's fire up that barbecue. We've got fish to fry and a little fine white wine to go with it. Let's just relax and forget about work until tomorrow."

"Suits me fine," said Washington. "But I'd like to hear about that planet of yours. Where is it, anyway?"

Billy wondered if he wouldn't have been better off calling a team meeting and getting it over with in one sitting. He was quite likely going to tire of telling his story before too long.

"Willie, it's called Ball Four and..."

20

Tuesday, July 16th, Billy got an early start to Candlestick. There was much to be done. He walked into the clubhouse before eleven, startling the equipment manager, Lester Munro.

"Jeez, Billy, what are you doing here? Team's not due till four."

"Got some business to attend to, Les. Hey, do you remember those packages you brought back for me from Chicago? Didn't you put them in a storage room?"

"Sure, it's back here." Munro walked into the therapy room, past the whirlpool baths. He took out his keys, opened a door and went in. Peering through the opening into the dimly lit storage area, Billy could see another door past the storage cages.

"What's back there, Les?"

"That door?" asked Munro. "Oh, we haven't used it for years. It's sort of an extra storage space. I haven't been in it for a long time. Probably a mess in there."

"Could I look? I'm trying to find some space for a training project."

Munro unlocked a cage, walked in and examined some boxes. "Here are your packages. I suppose I could let you look back there, but you'll have to clear it with Alfie to use it. Gosh, I don't even remember which key goes to it."

Munro rummaged through the couple dozen keys on his chain and selected a likely candidate. He slipped it into the padlock. "By god, got it the first time. How 'bout that?"

Munro found the light. Inside were dusty chairs, tables, boxes full of what-not and a couple of antiquated, disused whirlpools.

"This might work, Les. Do you think that you could leave it open until I find Alfie? Oh, and if I get approval, do you think some of this junk can be moved into the storage cages?"

"Heck, if you're gonna use the room, I don't mind taking advantage of the situation and clearing out this stuff. I got the team's gear all straightened out. I got time. Why don't I start clearing this out while you talk to Alfie? He's probably in his office."

"Thanks."

Alfie Tollman had managed the clubhouse for years. He'd been a young man when he moved with the Giants from New York. Now he was old, but sharp as a tack. He ran the clubhouse like a dictator, but he did it with a sense of humor and took care of the players' needs so well that he was beloved by all.

"That old room? Well, sure, we can spare it, but what do you got in mind?"

"I've got a new training system I'm going to try and introduce to the boys, Alfie. It doesn't require much space. That room would be perfect."

Alfie rubbed his grizzled old chin and tapped his toes. "Sounds pretty fishy to me. Well, okay, but no women, is that understood? You're probably planning some co-ed spa, knowing you guys."

"You're on to us, Alfie," laughed Billy.

"No, seriously, I know how hard you work to help the team, Mr. Icarus. Nothing happens on this team that I don't know about. I have my spies. If you want some space, it's yours. Of course, you'll clear it with the skipper, right?"

"Naturally. But I've got a special request. No one else is to know about this, okay? Special equipment will go in there and if it's meddled with, it could get damaged. And if it gets out to the press, they'll be all over us. We're in a pennant race, we've got serious work to do."

"Sounds fine to me. As long as Chambers gives you the okay, it's all yours. You can get keys from Lester."

Two hours later, the room was in good shape. Munro had gotten a few janitors from upstairs to help him move the junk out and the place had been swept and dusted. Billy kept the tables and chairs, and had the biofeedback machines set up and operational by the time Jimmy and Brad arrived.

"Right on schedule, boys. Thanks for coming out early. The next phase in our training is about to begin. Brad, do you recognize this equipment?"

"A little-known fact is that I majored in pre-med at Harvard," said Brad. "I was on my way to becoming a doctor when I got hooked on the game of ball. Yes, I think I know what these things are. They're biofeedback machines. Look like rather sophisticated ones. We experimented with them in school. There's been some interesting research on applying biofeedback to stroke-victim therapy. Where'd you get these jobs?"

"On our last road trip to Chicago. Had them shipped back. Yes, they're the best I could find."

Jimmy stared at the machines with a quizzical look on his face. "What do they do?"

Brad answered. "They measure various brain waves. These appear to measure alpha, beta and theta waves in both hemispheres. Aha, I'm beginning to see where we're going here."

"I don't," said Jimmy.

"Jimmy, when our minds are engaged in various activities, certain measurable waves are emitted. Beta waves, which oscillate at 13-30 cycles per second, are associated with active thinking and doing. Alpha waves are slower and occur usually when the mind is in an empty, meditative state, although certain great thinkers such as Albert Einstein were reputed to have solved complex problems while in alpha state. Theta waves are even slower, somewhere around 4-7 cycles per second, and are associated with dreaming or half-awake, hypnagogic imagery. One might call it a deep meditative state. Some have associated it with creative inspiration. And slowest of the waves are delta, which basically occur during sleep. These machines don't measure delta waves, primarily because it would serve no purpose for the machine to tell you that you're asleep. How'd I do, Billy?"

"Quite well, Brad, thank you. I can see that I'll need to do little coaching with you, but I should have expected that. Now, there are many more complex activities which are going on in the brain, and these waves are somewhat of a macromeasurement of that complex set of electrochemical activities. But it is unnecessary to understand the underlying activity of the brain to accomplish what we need to do. Also, I might tell you that we Ball Fourians exhibit a number of other measurable, controllable waves other than the three measured by these machines, but they aren't germane to obtaining the white mind. These other waves are helpful in more sophisticated mental operations, and perhaps evolved in the Ball Fourian brain through centuries of discipline.

"Back to the task at hand. As Brad has said, beta waves are associated with active thinking and alpha waves with meditative, nonverbal thought. To make a long story short, we want to train ourselves, using these machines, to place our dominant hemisphere, usually our left, into the alpha state. In the Ball Fourian white-mind state we also force the right hemisphere up into a beta state, but that probably won't be necessary for you humans. If you can achieve alpha while playing baseball, at least for a reasonable percentage of the time or at crucial moments, then you'll duplicate the white mind sufficiently to protect against mind reading and mind manipulation. This is what I hope is the case. I want to use these machines to train us to fall into alpha state at will."

"I follow you, O Wise One of the east," said Brad. "However, it remains to be seen if we can carry our alpha states onto a baseball diamond."

"In a way, it doesn't matter. My theory is that, if we combine work in strengthening our ability to achieve alpha state with the meditative aspects of T'ai Chi, we'll screen our minds sufficiently to block out enough of the Ball Fourian mind game that we'll effectively neutralize their advantage. Of course, it'll take a decidedly team effort. If enough of us fail, the whole team fails. It's that simple. And one other thing, gentlemen. This theory is more or less untested. I imagine we'll know soon enough.

"One of the unusual aspects of using biofeedback is that it's not well understood how it works, just that it indeed works. How we teach our brains to emit alpha is difficult to say. But if we are placed on a machine that informs us that we are in alpha, the great majority of us, with more or less effort, will begin to produce it more and more of the time. On Ball Four, we don't need machines. We learn to control our brains in very much the same way as we learn language: we absorb it from our culture as a natural part of the maturing process. Of course, ballplayers and scientists undergo more intense, specialized training. What members of the political caste undergo, I can only hazard a guess.

"Anyway, that's about it. If we spend time, each and every member of the team, on these machines, then my theory stipulates that we'll strengthen our abilities to at least emulate the white mind."

"This is mostly confusing to me," said Jimmy. "But if I follow what you're saying, it's not important that I understand everything for this to work. Is that right?"

"Basically, yes," answered Brad. "Scientists themselves don't completely understand how the brain can train itself to produce alpha at will when we can't actually feel the waves as they're exhibited. Therefore it follows that understanding isn't a prerequisite of success."

"Brad, you've got such a grasp on this that I'm inclined to assign this project to you. Do you accept?"

"Yes, with pleasure. I've got time between starts, that's more than you do. And it'll take the heat off of you. If you dominate everything we do, the coaches could start to resent you, not to mention the players. At least that will be the case until you've informed everyone of your identity. Then they'll be more inclined to accept you as team leader. That'll be an important eventual step."

"I'm sure you're right. So, let's examine these machines in order to start Jimmy on them today. I've got six machines. Three are audio and three are visual. The audio machines inform the participant that they are in alpha state with a soothing tone in the earphones. That allows the subject to close his eyes, which enhances the likelihood of achieving alpha. When someone achieves alpha with regularity on the audio machines, we'll move them on to the more sophisticated visual machines. These indicate the various wave-states through different colored lights, and in both hemispheres. I'll demonstrate."

Billy picked up the head harness of one of the machines and placed it carefully on his head. "This harness places electrical sensors at key locations on the scalp. They pick up the very faint electrical impulses associated with the brain waves. The machine amplifies these signals to a registerable intensity, and the appropriate light assigned to each wave length comes on. Watch."

He turned the machine on. The array of lights on the face of the machine fluttered for a moment before the green lights of the beta frequency began to glow strongly in both left and right hemispheres. The right hemisphere shifted quickly to the blue light indicating alpha state. A moment later the left side of the light array indicated alpha state as well. After another moment, Billy dropped his left hemisphere into theta state, followed closely by the right. The lavender lights indicating theta activity were maintained on both sides of the array for a minute, and then, step by step, Billy walked his mind up to full beta awareness, following the same pattern he had used to descend. When he was back to beta, Brad whistled.

"If I didn't believe you were from another planet before, I do now! Can you go into any state at will, even theta?"

"Yes. As I said before, there are other wavelengths common to Ball Fourian brains not registered by this machine. Also, I'm capable of instigating a number of internal feedback loops that perform certain operations on the brain. For instance, if a man approached me with a gun, my initial reaction would be very much like a human's. I'd become quite anxious as my fight-or-flight instinct kicked in. However, I can immediately instigate a mind-smoothing loop which allows a rational response. I can also project this loop out to include the brain of a nearby person, and thereby soothe their mind as well. We use that on Ball Four to establish team rapport and build mutual confidence. It works on humans as well, as I've discovered. I used such a technique on Chambers when I wanted him to feel predisposed to have confidence and trust in me. And I've also used it when reporters interview me. So far, it's worked. They accept my refusal to divulge my origins primarily because they feel good about me. They don't know why, they just do. They have no way of knowing I'm bathing them in thoughts of well-being and confidence."

"I read a bit in the papers a while back about the controversy in Cleveland about the no-name Indians," said Brad. "Of course they'd have similar problems. It's more or less faded out. Did they deal with it like you have?"

"I wouldn't want to say. But I do know from my Operation Universe Series training that there's quite a support staff to help the Indians cope with these kinds of difficulties. Do you recall that sign-stealing controversy that surfaced a while back? It came up and as quickly disappeared."

"Of course," interjected Jimmy. "That's the kind of thing a Ball Fourian team would be accused of. It all makes sense now."

"If we're to be ready for those rascals by October, we'd better get started now," said Billy, taking off the head gear. "Brad, show Jimmy how to use the machine. Start yourselves off on the audio models."

"I understand the whole set-up, boss," said Brad confidently.

"Good, I'm off to find the skipper before he finds out about this on his own. Good luck, you two."

Lou Chambers, considerably more dubious about the biofeedback training than the T'ai Chi, nonetheless approved its use. Everything that Billy Icarus had so far introduced to the club, while being out of the mainstream, had produced measurable, positive results; Chambers couldn't argue with success. It irked him that he was surrendering more and more control of the team to Icarus, but he could see no way around it. The rest of the coaching staff, however, were so concerned with the situation that Chambers had to call a staff meeting to cool them off. McIlhenny, who had seen first-hand what Billy had done to improve the pitching, had no problem. But third base coach Sal Donato and first base coach Manny Rincon were concerned that control was slipping away. Hitting coach Wally Walton, though appreciating Billy's work with the hitters, thought things were also going too far. Chambers told them to hold their opinions in abeyance, at least until the value of the newest project could be determined. At Billy's recommendation, Chambers slapped a ban on revealing anything of internal operations to the press. This eased the coaches' minds to a great degree; being older and more in favor of tried-and-true techniques, they greatly feared being ridiculed for the oddball direction the club was taking. The papers would have a field day if this new business with the biofeedback got out.

During the next two weeks, while the Giants were at home, a steady parade of players flowed into the secret confines of the biofeedback training center. After Brad and Jimmy, Willie Washington was next to try out the gear and, not long after, the whole outfield, including reserves, were caught up in the training. Soon, everyone on the team wanted a shot at it. Billy had anticipated difficulty in building interest in biofeedback. It hadn't occurred to him that the novelty of the equipment would attract the players. Before much time had passed, most of the team was hooked on making the machines give them the payoff of the gentle tone that signified alpha, and those that hadn't had much success wanted time to get the hang of it. They envied those who succeeded, and it became a status symbol to join the "Alpha Squad." It was a bit silly and competitive, but if it worked, Billy couldn't see any harm in it.

Not surprisingly, the pitching staff was the quickest to become adept. Without exception, all the pitchers could achieve and sustain the alpha state. Inky Powell had to be asked to give up his chair or he would stay on the machine for hours. Steve Lafite was almost as bad as Powell.

Whether the improved play on the field could be attributed to the biofeedback training was problematical, but the healthy mental state of the team was undoubtedly a direct result; and the level of performance quite likely was a by-product of the good mental health. Chambers accepted it as fact, and the rest of the coaches had to admit it was possible.

And how the team did play. The homestand after the All-Star break lasted twelve games, and the Giants went undefeated from start to finish. No one could touch their pitching, as the staff combined for an ERA during the homestand of 1.21. Brad won both his starts, but the real story was the amazing Jimmy Strongbow. He not only won all three of his starts, but threw three consecutive shutouts. The last was the crowning jewel of the set: a perfect game.

It came against the New York Mets. Jimmy threw with blazing heat and pinpoint control. During the sixth inning of the game, in which he struck out the side, the radar gun recorded one pitch at a staggering one hundred one miles an hour. Though using the fastball predominantly, he mixed in all his other pitches as well, including the knuckleball. He used it on two 0-and-2 counts, striking out both batters. He fanned eighteen in the contest and walked none. By the time it was over Jimmy Strongbow, not Brad O'Nealy, was the acknowledged ace of the team. It was undeniable. In fact, Brad graciously announced it in the locker room by getting down on his knees and repeatedly bowing while proclaiming, "All hail the Chief!" With the whole assemblage cracking up with laughter, an embarrassed Jimmy Strongbow dragged Brad to his feet and gave him a hug.

Art French and Kiley Upton won two contests each. French's new nickname in the press had become "Junkyard Dog," and Upton's consistent ability to craft a way out of jams had earned him the nickname "Wily Kiley." Inky Powell won his first major league game in a brilliant long relief stint, and Steve Lafite picked up two victories and two saves. Rick Santiago saw little action but managed to earn a save.

The hitting had its share of the glory. The team batting average rose to .291, as the Giants' hitting attack went from good to great to lethal. Billy Icarus went on such a tear that his phenomenal batting average climbed back to .452, and the eight home runs he hit during the stand had the press referring to him as "the Fourth Musketeer," going along with the outfield's "Three Musketeers" moniker. The outfield itself smacked a combined ten roundtrippers. Quiet, stoical third baseman Mickey Roberts added three more. With the four others hit during the twelve-game stretch, the total of twenty-five home runs attracted attention around the country. Even the Cleveland Indians considered the idea of scouting the Giants as potential rivals in the Series. They decided to continue to concentrate on Pittsburgh and New York in the East and Los Angeles and Cincinnati in the West. They'd keep a watchful eye on San Francisco and check them out in person if they started to gain on L.A.

The final victory of the homestand swept them into a second-place tie with Cincinnati, but L.A. was so hot during this time that it retained a six-game edge. With the Giants going on the road and the L.A. team returning home, the smart money was on the Giants cooling off and the Dodgers taking off. It wouldn't happen exactly that way.

Billy enjoyed that homestand as much as any time in his career, whether on Ball Four or on Earth. In a sense, baseball was more lively when played by the more vulnerable humans. He admired their wild, competitive spirit. He also was immensely relieved to see with what comparative ease his biofeedback training was being embraced. There was no way to gauge the effect the training was having on the present level of play, but he was content to have the rest of the team and the coaches connect the two. A movement to have the machines accompany them on the road got started but it was quelled when Chambers ruled it out. They would run the danger of discovery, and with it came the danger of controversy which so often disrupted a team on a hot streak.

One bit of controversy did arise and it involved Billy Icarus' appearance. He had begun growing a beard back on the fishing trip and had let it continue. It was strictly against the Giants' policy of no facial hair on the team. Billy wished he could tell Chambers the reason for growing the beard. As the team began to attract more attention in the press, they would eventually draw the scrutiny of Ball Fourian agents. It was possible that someone from the Operation might remember that Belteron had been assigned the Lou Gehrig biofashioning, and recognize him. Billy had no way of knowing that the Operation considered him dead, and he assumed that the beard would disguise him sufficiently to avoid detection. Chambers had no choice but to fine him the required five hundred dollars. Billy didn't shave the beard, but they let it go with that. No one in the Giants' front office wanted their new star to become mired in the regulations.

The road did not cool off the streaking Giants. They carried the sensational level of intensity with them on an eastern swing, and teams that previously had looked forward to a Giants' visit now began to fear and respect the team. As a result, powerhouses like Pittsburgh and New York were now predisposed to lose to San Francisco, and the Giants were more than willing to oblige them. "Chief" Strongbow, as the press was now calling him, won two more games to improve his record to 11-3, and made the cover of *Sports Illustrated*. Billy Icarus had been featured on the cover when the homestand had ended, with a caption that read, "How high can Icarus fly?" After that issue hit the stands more pressure mounted for Billy to divulge his past history, but he dodged it successfully by maintaining that he was the great grandson of the Lone Ranger. The ridiculous ploy had been suggested by O'Nealy, but it had worked. The press ate it up, for it fit with the "Lone Ranger and Tonto" theme they'd been using since he and Jimmy had come to prominence. Still, he didn't know how long he could hold off the incessant requests for real answers.

As they swept series after series on the road, the team grew in confidence and it became easier and easier to win. No one was left out of the fun and every member of the team could boast of contributions to the effort and improvement in their overall numbers. The one exception was Billy. He was concerned his batting average was unreasonably high and sought to dampen interest in himself by getting hits only when absolutely necessary. It was easier said than done. But the pitching was so strong that he found if he could get a home run with a couple aboard in the early innings, he could then lay off and go hitless for the rest of the game. It worked well enough, and he managed to trim his average by some twenty points by the end of the trip.

When the road trip finally came to an end on August 11th, the Giants' win streak stood at twenty-three. The Dodgers went 9-2 during the same period and maintained a four-game edge. Cincinnati had slipped into third, eight games off the pace. A crowd of two thousand strong greeted their 68-40 heroes at San Francisco Airport. Both the fans and the team, including Billy, were beginning to believe that they could go all the way. Only Billy knew the dimensions of the obstacles in front of them. But he had reason to hope.

Whenever possible, Billy would monitor each member of the team for their mental states. In each case, signs of the white mind appeared. Guessing at the plate diminished and, as each hitter's average was on the rise, the general consensus was that the improved mental game was responsible and guessing at pitches became taboo. The progress brightened Billy's outlook, but he was painfully aware of how much remained to be done. Confident that the team was fully capable of winning the division and the playoffs as well, Billy could now concentrate on ways of beating the Indians.

The eyes of all the Giants were on the Cleveland team, whether they knew of their origins or not. Even those uninformed of their alien nature saw the Indians as the team most likely to go all the way. Since the All-Star break the Tribe showed no signs of letting up as they built their record to 82-26. Billy grimly admired the way they manipulated their performances to avoid detection. He had read the *USA Today* article and grasped the implications. The Ball Fourians had some scheme going to create a believable record while assuring a trip to the Series. He wondered what happened to the computer ace who had instigated the story. The way the story had died out worried him. What were the Operation agents willing to do to win? He knew that violence was out of the question, but what tactics did the Operation consider reasonable? It was the first time in his life that he feared another Ball Fourian, and it gave him chills. With the help of a feedback loop, he calmed the disturbance. Fear was not an ally in this quest.

21

ANCHOR:

Acting First Councilor Semptor issued a statement today which will put an end to the speculation concerning the overlapping of the Earthling baseball season with the start of this year's Ball Fourian season. It came as no surprise that the current frenzy over the action on Earth would delay opening day for the first time in two hundred fifty years. In his dual role as Acting First Commisioner of baseball, Semptor held a press conference in the official suite at First City Stadium prior to today's holocast of the game between Ball Four and the Boston Red Sox.

SEMPTOR:

Firstly, let me assure everyone that messages received from First Councilor Tarn's ship indicate that he is having a safe and pleasant journey to Earth. He sends his best wishes to all. I also wish to assure you that the decision reached by the Baseball Commission coincides with Tarn's expressed intentions. Therefore, by my power as Acting First Commissioner of Baseball I announce that, in order that all the people of Ball Four may fully enjoy the coming Universe Series, the start of the new baseball season shall be put off until the Series is complete.

That should delay opening day by approximately twenty days. The season will then be played in its entirety. This decision also reflects the wishes of the managers, coaches and players of the principal leagues of Ball Four. They are as anxious to enjoy the Universe Series as we all are, I'm sure.

ANCHOR:

This announcement was greeted by universal approval across the seven continents of Ball Four, and ended speculation that the baseball caste had ever harbored objections. In a written codicil to the announcement it was assured that all season ticket holders will...

First Councilor Tarn sat comfortably in his suite aboard the transport ship that had been richly appointed for his journey to Earth. He was enjoying the voyage supremely. He had several reasons for wanting to go to Earth for the Universe Series, not the least of which was the opportunity to undertake such a space journey. Because of the space travel ban, he had never been out of the Ball Fourian solar system in his life. Even a First Councilor was powerless to escape the ban. The Operation had changed all that, quasi-legal though it was.

Aside from the standard crew and a few Operation support personnel, the only other person on this extraordinary journey was Dr. Avion, a long-time advisor to Tarn and a member of his Inner Council. His official post was First Scientist. He was rarely able to attend meetings, however, for his researches at the Spaceport Science Center occupied most of his time. When he was available, Dr. Avion had proved himself very valuable to Tarn on numerous occasions. It was imperative that he accompany Tarn on this journey, and Tarn was glad for the stimulating company.

The suite Tarn occupied was actually the ship's captain's, which he had graciously vacated for the First Councilor's comfort. It was equipped in a way which, with the press of a button, allowed the occupant to turn the oval walls, ceiling and floor into a spherical view screen. It was so startlingly realistic that technicians had advised Tarn to mentally cushion himself for the shock he would experience the first time he activated it. And shocking indeed it had been when he first switched on the screen. It was as though the hull had been blown away, revealing the infinity of space in all directions. Even a man of Tarn's mental capacities and training required a moment to settle his nerves and relieve the fear that he was about to drift into forever. After he got used to it, he could sit for hours watching the twinkling effect of the Time Drive, with endless sets of stars blinking on and off as the ship leaped from one set of coordinates to the next. The vision induced a rather pleasant reverie.

He was enjoying just such a reverie when the console in the opposite corner softly chimed. That would be an incoming message, no doubt. Tarn walked across the twinkle of stars and took a seat at the console.

"First Councilor Tarn, greetings from Earth. Evan reporting as scheduled. I assume that you are receiving this in transit to Earth, as I have been informed that you have moved up your arrival time by a month. All members of the team are thrilled and excited that the leader of our world finds our endeavor of such interest that he would come to share so much time with us. I hope your journey has been a pleasant one.

"After the challenging events of the first half of the Season, life here on Earth has settled down to a calm, satisfying passage of time. We are engaged in the pastime of baseball, not in the avoidance of the intrigue which has plagued us until recently. Now the days are full of the stuff of athletic achievement, and the morale of the boys is high.

"You will understand, then, why this transmission will be necessarily brief. There is little to report, except that the team continues to play at a high level of success. A ripple of anticipation has spread among the team that you will be here to observe first-hand our inevitable triumph. We hope it will take nothing away from your enjoyment that our superiority is such that defeat is impossible. In fact, the team looks forward with great relish to the impending play-offs and Universe Series, for I have assured them that finally their play can be completely unrestrained. Their true dominance can then be demonstrated.

"Continued best wishes from all Ball Fourians on Earth, and we await your arrival with great anticipation. Evan off."

Tarn smiled. He wondered if he had concocted this entire scheme merely to provide himself with the opportunity to visit another world. Had he spent nearly twenty-seven years of his life just to plan a good vacation? Absurd, of course, but the thought pleased him. No, great things were afoot across a galaxy, and the life of his planet was alive in a way it hadn't been in his life-time. That he was able to embark on a voyage to a different world was a wonderful side-benefit, even if he had had to get biofashioned again. He hoped the people of Ball Four did not misinterpret his action as a betrayal of his campaign against decadence. He had had no choice, and secretly he was fascinated by assuming the Earthling form. In a few days he would arrive on Earth and mingle with another species, cloaked in their skin. All this, to beat them at their own game. Perhaps the absurdity of the concept was the ultimate basis for its brilliance. He laughed to himself and sat back down into his reverie.

Two days later the transport ship disengaged from Time Drive and came to a halt behind the Earthling moon. Cloaking was impossible as well as un-necessary while engaged in Time Drive, so this tactic of using the moon as a shield had been used during the whole Operation. The ship quickly went into cloaking mode and began the final leg of the journey to the space station. It would take about an hour.

Tarn had been prepared for the sight of Earth from the many pictures from prior missions, but he was fascinated anew to see the incredible resemblance.

It was quite a bit bluer, having substantially more ocean, but in all other respects it could have been Ball Four he was approaching. Parallel evolution required such similarities, but he was nonetheless astonished.

Upon arrival at the station, Tarn would be subjected to the usual pomp required to greet a leader of his stature, and he was prepared to undergo it gracefully. But he hoped it could be kept to a minimum. He would then enjoy a few days of rest and relaxation, combined with a firsthand review of the Operation. Again, this was more a matter of protocol than necessity, as no one was more aware than he of all that had been accomplished in his name. He had personally overseen much of the development of plans and strategies employed in the Operation, but he would be expected to exhibit interest. It was good for morale, and undoubtedly he would gain some insights that would prove useful in future endeavors. He hoped that the station's captain had provided him with a smooth, workable agenda. Tarn was anxious to set foot on Earth.

22

By the end of the road trip, Billy Icarus has come to the conclusion that it was time the whole club, players and coaches alike, were told the truth about himself and the Cleveland Indians. Morale would never be better and his standing on the team was at an all-time high. His credibility was very strong, and he had better seize the opportunity before the vagaries of baseball took it away from him. Besides, he didn't look forward to the time and effort it would take to continue the tactic of revealing the truth in small bunches. It was wearisome, and they could use all the time they could get to prepare for the World Series. It would be a war, albeit a mental one.

On the day off before the new homestand, Billy called Lou Chambers.

"Yes, Billy, what can I do for you?"

"Lou, if I asked you to call a team meeting tomorrow before game time, would you oblige me?"

Chambers took some time to think. When he came back on the line he replied, "Team meetings are rarely useful unless there is some dire need. I know you usually have some method to your madness, but we're on such a hot streak now I can't imagine what it might be."

"Skipper, I wouldn't ask if I didn't think it was absolutely necessary," said Billy. "If you'll call the meeting, I promise I'll meet with you just prior to give you a chance to evaluate its importance. If you decide at that time to cancel, I of course will go along with it."

"Why don't you just tell me now? What's the mystery?"

"Some things are best not discussed on the phone."

"Sounds rather ominous, Billy," said Chambers.

"It is and it isn't," replied Billy. "There's an up and a down side to it. It's important, I promise you."

"Okay, I'll call a meeting. Three o'clock all right?"

"That'll be fine. But it's closed-door, players and coaches only. Okay?"

"Sure. See you tomorrow."

Billy had given a lot of thought to the team meeting, and realized that he had to give an impressive performance in order not to waste the opportunity it afforded for a strong impact. He made a couple of minor preparations, but he planned one demonstration so convincing that it might settle all issues once and for all. There was some small danger to it, but its impact would be unquestionable. It was grandstanding, but it would save a lot of time and effort.

The next day, he arrived well ahead of the team and went to his locker. There he found his toiletries kit. In the bottom, secreted in a soap container, was the control module he had taken from the space station. He slipped it into his pocket.

When Lou Chambers arrived, he found Billy waiting at his office door.

"You look as serious as I've ever seen you," remarked Chambers.

"This is as serious as it gets, Skipper."

Well, come on in, then, let's get this over with."

After they seated themselves, Chambers waited for Billy to speak up.

"Lou, if there were a way to avoid any of this, I'd keep it to myself. But there isn't, as you'll come to realize, so just as I asked you when I was trying to make the club, I'll ask again: keep an open mind until after you've had a chance to consider everything carefully."

"Sure, what gives?"

"It has to do with my identity, and why I'm here."

"It's about time you told me," Chambers said. "Is this what the team meeting is about?"

"Yes. The fact is, sir, I'm not from Earth. I'm from a planet called Ball Four, and we've infiltrated to challenge Earth at the game of baseball."

Chambers didn't move a muscle. "I know," he said simply.

"You know?"

"Yes, I've known for a month now. Was wondering when and if you'd get around to me. Of course, I'm only the manager. And all you are is an alien. Details. Let's play ball."

Of course, thought Billy, I should have expected it. "Willie told you."

"Yep. He's captain, told me out of loyalty. Odd trait."

Billy couldn't gauge Chambers' feelings and was tempted to scan his mind. Don't start now, he warned himself.

"You sound angry, Skip."

Chambers stood up and walked over to the window into the locker room. "No, I'm not angry. But dammit, Billy, why'd I have to find out something like this from Washington?"

"It was never my intention to leave you out of it, Lou. I proceeded step by step as the occasion presented itself. I'm naturally closer to the players and I started with them. It wasn't meant to be an insult, but if it is, then I apologize."

"It's not as simple as that, Billy. First of all, either I got an alien or a complete loony on my team. And if there's any truth at all to your story, then I've had next to nothing to do with one of the most gratifying seasons I've experienced in fifty years of baseball. I can smell a world championship, and then Willie tells me the Indians are invaders from outer space. He also tells me that you've been putting a spell on me. All this is going on behind my back, and, meanwhile, I think I'm in control of my team. Got it running on all eight, a fine oiled machine. Hell, you're damned right I'm angry. I'm furious."

"Putting a spell on you? What's that mean?"

"That's the way Willie put it. I guess he's referring to something you claim to have done to my mind."

This was not what I expected, thought Billy. I thought I had things going smoothly. There are dangerous ripples underneath the surface. He paused to compose himself.

"I can see I've seriously erred here," he started carefully. "You've got every right to be angry with me. But I'm not a loony, and you'll just have to trust me on that one for the sake of the team. I'll do my best to convince you of that. As for your role in our success, it's been major, Lou. It's a manager's job to take talent and keep it on track. They say that good managers don't win pennants, good pitching does. Well, that's simplistic nonsense, and you and I know it. To build a champion it takes everybody, from managing to pitching, hitting, fielding and running. You've done your part admirably.

"Now wait a minute, let me finish. As for doing something to your mind, I admit it. I projected feelings of confidence and credibility into your mind, for the sake of winning a spot on the team. Is that so bad? Here on Earth, from what I've learned in books and watching your television, people do similar things all the time. They smooth-talk their way into the good graces of people, often lying and cheating every step of the way. At least my motives are pure, Lou. I just want to play baseball and win. Those are your goals too."

"Fine," interrupted Chambers. "I can buy a lot of what you're saying. But let's not jump over this claim of being an alien."

"Look, I've come to understand a couple of things," said Billy, "that weren't apparent to me before. They should have been. Firstly, people who claim to be aliens must be crazy. Secondly, aliens are dangerous or at best out to take over. That's what humans think, but neither is true. But it is true I've got capabilities that exceed those of humans. However, I use those capabilities in the pursuit of honorable ends and I've not used them to unfairly excel at baseball. What we need to do is convince you of that as quickly as possible. If we don't, you won't let me near the team again, I know that."

"Why don't you just use your powers to have me believe in you, if that's what you did to get on the ball club?"

"Because, as I'm sure Willie told you, I made a decision to stop doing that. It's dishonorable and insulting."

Chambers sat back down at his desk. "Okay. We've got to stop dancing in circles. What can you do to convince me?"

"Because of what has gone on before, I don't want to enter your mind without your permission."

Chambers eyed Billy thoughtfully. "You have my permission," he said, "if it'll get this behind us."

"Okay, then you devise the test."

"You can read minds?" Chambers asked.

"Not completely. I can sense attitudes, intentions and short, strong bursts of thought. I can also project similar thoughts and feelings toward a receptive mind. Given the right setting, I can merge with another mind in spirit. Others on my planet are trained for merging in abstract thought. Those capabilities remain dormant in me."

Chambers thought a moment. "So if I concentrate on something, you should be able to pick it up?"

"Yes."

"Okay." Chambers closed his eyes in thought. When he opened them he said, "I've gone back and found something I can't imagine anybody in baseball knows. What was the name of my first girl friend?"

Billy peered at Chambers' face, then smiled. "Becky MacLennon. You sure loved her, still do."

Chambers smiled too. The smile faded as his face paled. It struck him what had just taken place. "My god. You just read my mind."

"Yes, Lou, I did."

Chambers walked over to the water cooler and took a drink. He turned around and asked, "What was the name of my first little league coach?"

"Hansford Stoltz, the son-of-a-bitch," Billy replied.

"How'd you know he was a son-of-a-bitch?"

"That's what your mind said, `Hansford Stoltz, the son-of-a-bitch.'"

Chambers laughed. "That's just the way I remember him. By Jesus, you can read minds. But what does that prove? You are the first legitimate mind-reader I've ever met, but it doesn't make you an alien."

"So I've discovered. I'm planning something for the team meeting that I hope will put all doubts to rest. We've got work to do. We can't concentrate on who I am or am not for the rest of the season. We're here to play ball. By the way, did Washington tell anybody else?"

"Not that I know of," answered Chambers. "I know I didn't tell anyone."

"Good. Listen, Lou, I apologize for not thinking of your feelings. We've all got our work to do if we're going to have a chance to win this thing. Your job's one of the toughest."

Chambers got up. "Thanks, I appreciate that. I see through the window that some of the guys are coming in now. This is serious business. The season turns on this meeting, Billy. I give you carte blanche to do whatever you choose, though I know you will anyway. Just don't screw it up."

By three o'clock everyone had assembled in the locker room. Chambers asked the clubhouse personnel to vacate, even the trainers and team doctor. He understood too well why Billy might want a closed meeting.

"Boys, this is a serious meeting. Now, I know we're on the hottest streak any team could ever want, but Icarus here has something he wants to share with the team. Billy?"

"Go ahead, Skipper, you might as well tell them as anyone."

"Okay. Some of you know about this, others don't. There's no easy way to say this. Billy claims to be an alien. How many know about it? Give me a show of hands."

As the few hands went up, the others looked around, not certain at all what was taking place. Steve Lafite was the first to show some awareness.

"Let me get this straight. Skip, did you say Billy's an alien?"

"Nope," answered Chambers matter-of-factly. "Said he claims to be."

"Why," asked Bob Butterfield, "don't you believe him?"

"Don't frankly know. He showed me a few things that make me know he's no regular character, I will admit to that. Billy, you say that you're pre-pared to give some demonstration of proof?"

"That's right, boss."

"Wait just a goddam minute!" It was Eddie Renker. He walked forward. "Are you saying you're a being from another planet?"

"Yes," replied Billy.

"Well, that cinches it. You've been all right till now, even with your weird ways, but this is too much. What are you doing? Pressure too much, you goin' nuts?"

"I take it," Billy said evenly, "that you do not believe me."

"You got the goddam picture, mister," said Renker with a ugly tone to his voice.

"Why not?" asked Billy, advancing a step toward Renker.

"Because *I'm a horse's ass!*" Renker replied abruptly. After he said it he looked around, as though he wasn't sure what he had just heard himself say.

Billy took out a piece of paper from his pocket, unfolded it and showed it around to the players. On it was printed in large, bold letters, "I'M A HORSE'S ASS!" The whole team broke up with laughter as Renker sat down with a confused look on his face. The team quieted down as they came to their senses. O'Nealy stepped forward.

"I'm sure you guys are wondering what the hell is going on," he began. "Well, I suppose Chief and I had a head start on all of you, but we have no trouble believing Billy. He's been serving our best interests since he got here. He's shown us his mental abilities on many an occasion."

"Same goes for us," said Kiley Upton, with Art French nodding agreement.

Washington stood up. "Well, I'm not convinced. Billy, I'm sorry about telling Lou, but it was my duty. I hope you understand. Anyway, what's this demonstration?"

"Willie, I've come to the realization that a lot of humans can believe in ESP before they can believe in beings from other planets. Unfortunately, that's about all I can do to distinguish myself in order to illustrate that I'm not like you. I can't change my form or zap you with death rays or anything like what you've seen in your movies. There is, however one thing else that I can do which may end all your suspicions as to my nature, or my sanity, for that matter."

Billy stepped to the center of the room. "Could everyone move back and sit down? Thanks. Okay, I'll do this only once, so, please, everybody's eyes on me."

He looked around the quiet room and saw that he had everyone's attention. Billy slipped a hand into his pocket and depressed the appropriate button on his control module. His form flickered, then vanished.

A gasp rose up from the astonished witnesses. Washington stepped forward to the spot where Billy had just stood and examined the place, as though he might find some clues. Chambers joined Washington, looked around and, finding nothing, turned to O'Nealy and Strongbow.

"Okay, Brad, Chief, you're in on this. What gives?"

"I swear, boss, we don't know," replied Jimmy. "We're as surprised as you are. Billy just vanished. I've spent a lot of time with him and he's never done this. Has he, Brad?"

"Never," said Brad, shaking his head.

"Okay," Chambers said, in a voice meant to take control. "This is obviously the demonstration he talked about. Any minute he'll probably return. Let's clear out the center of the room."

They stood back and waited for Billy Icarus to reappear.

The moment Billy vanished from the locker room, his form began to reassemble in a transport room aboard the Ball Fourian orbital station, in fact in the very unit he had originally used to transport Earthside months back. To return to the Giants' locker room, he had only to check the coordinates recorded on the display of the control module, then punch them into the control panel of the transport room. It would take a few seconds. Suddenly, an alert sounded. The numbers he had entered were erased. A chime rang and a voice came on the intercom.

"Crew members and Citizens of Ball Four. I am pleased to announce the arrival of our distinguished guest, First Councilor Tarn. A reception will convene on Hangar Deck in exactly one hour. As previously announced, the ban on transport will be in effect during our guest's stay. This will be a period of approximately four days. All will no doubt appreciate the need for heightened security. Captain Argolith off."

Billy was stunned. He composed himself and quickly analyzed his position. Tarn had arrived at the station! It must have occurred nearly simultaneously with his own arrival. What ghastly luck. He was trapped for at least four days. And that depended on his avoiding detection.

He thought back to his last visit. It had been so short that he hadn't needed to eat while on board, let alone find a place to sleep. He had little familiarity with the station. Suddenly he remembered the storage bay where he had found his control module. It had been vacant of personnel at the time. Perhaps it was visited rarely, especially during this part of the Operation. He clearly recalled the way there.

Sure enough, the storage bay was very much the same as it was on his last visit. In fact, it appeared almost as if no one had been there since. Unlikely, but Billy had reason to hope that it was a safe place to pass four days. Where would he obtain food? He walked around the perimeter of the bay, and explored adjacent rooms. Some were small supply rooms, others were control rooms full of various instruments. Apparently this facility could double as a departure bay. In one room there were stored a number of off-ship suits, no doubt used during spacewalks. At last, he found what he was looking for. On an upper level, next to the main control station, there was a break room intended for use by that facility's crew. It was disused with the orbital station's present status. In it were a couple of duplicators. Good. There was the food supply. Now all that was needed was a place to sleep. It occurred to Billy that where a crew might gain refreshment they also might find rest. He was right. Through a door in the back of the break room, he found a compartment full of bunk beds. They were quite narrow, but certainly adequate. He would, with luck, wait out the transport ban. He hoped his teammates wouldn't be too concerned.

"Argolith, this ban on transport, is it absolutely necessary? I hate to think that my visit would be disruptive to the normal flow of operations."

"Do not concern yourself, First Councilor. Very little transport of personnel is taking place at the present time. As for the ban, surely your knowledge of history would tell you why it is wise."

Tarn smiled. "Remind me, Argolith. What you are referring to isn't coming to mind."

"Certainly," replied the Captain with stylized politeness. "You might recall that the war with the Zorkins began after they armed themselves using technology purloined from one of our outposts in their Empire. Hostilities broke out after they infiltrated one of our cruisers, using stolen transport codes. It is highly improbable that Earthlings pose such a threat. But let us err on the side of caution. The only occasion I will ever in my life be able to dictate to you is during this short time when you are my charge and I am captain. Please allow me my overzealousness in guaranteeing your safety."

Tarn laughed out loud. "Semptor warned me of your wry sense of humor. So be it. But do let's not worry too much about me."

Argolith reddened briefly, and as quickly smoothed her mind. She had spoken in earnest. She had no idea what Tarn meant by his reference to a sense of humor.

Some twenty-two thousand miles below, a befuddled Giants team finished its warm-ups and prepared to face the Cincinnati Reds without their starting catcher. Chambers alerted the press that Billy Icarus was "under the weather" and would be sitting the contest out. Butterfield switched to catcher, Simpson went to first and Harold Dubois got a rare start in right. Kiley Upton was on the mound. On the line was the Giants' twenty-three game winning streak, already a new major league record.

Before the evening ended, so had the streak. The dismayed players were held to two hits for the first time since May 20th, and the Reds pounded Upton, Powell and Santiago for fifteen hits and eleven runs. The Giants gave no interviews, but disappeared from Candlestick as quickly as they could shower and dress.

Unfortunately, they had to return to play the Reds the next day. Billy did not. Nor did he return the following day, nor the next. By week's end the Giants had dropped four straight to Cincinnati, who had pulled even with them in second place. The Dodgers, still on a hot streak, were up by six games. And they were coming to town for a three-games series beginning Saturday. The same Lou Chambers who had been mortified by the thought of having an alien on his team only a few days before was now praying for that alien's speedy return. The entire team, confused and in a state of near-total disarray, voiced a similar prayer. Having an alien on the team was one thing, but not having one was worse. What the hell was going on? Where had Billy disappeared to, and what was he trying to prove? Or was he dead?

Though not so agonizing, the time had been difficult for Billy as well. He passed the four days in relative comfort and had avoided detection more or less with ease. The only occasion for fear of discovery had been the cursory tour of the storage bay by the First Councilor. Being disused, it was toured quickly and Billy, alerted by Captain Argolith's voice as she led the party, had stayed out of sight in the bunk room.

After three months of dining in the restaurants of San Francisco, Billy found the duplicator food blander than he recalled, but the living arrangements were satisfactory if a little cramped. What most disturbed Billy about the whole affair was the effect it must be having on his teammates. How confusing and shocking it must be for them. He hoped they were holding up. All he could do was wait for the all-clear to sound so he could be on his way. He was very relieved to have found a safe place to hide. It had made the waiting bearable.

He was finishing off a meal in the break room when the chime sounded. "Attention all. The First Councilor has, only a few minutes ago, transported safely to Earth. The transport ban is hereby rescinded, effective immediately. The emergency rescue teams are now on alert. Check schedules carefully for your team's rotating duty. We must be ready at all times to protect our First Councilor. Argolith off."

Billy wasted no time. He sent the remains of his meal down a disposal chute, and hastily searched the area for any signs he might leave behind that he had been there. Satisfied that he was leaving no evidence of his visit, he carefully made his way to the transport room.

He went around each curve of the corridor leading to the transport room with great caution. His luck had been good so far, and he didn't want it to run out so close to the end. When he arrived at the unit, he smiled broadly. Empty. His greatest concern was that there would be a high demand for transport after a four-day ban. It was not the case.

He stepped into a booth. Pressing the recall button on the control module he was gratified to see the coordinates had been duly retained. He entered the numbers into the booth control panel, then compared them to those on his module. Wait a minute, he thought, that doesn't look right.

Suddenly Billy heard the pad of feet approaching. In the soft acoustics of the corridor they were on him with little warning. As he looked to the left, the knee of the first crewman came into view. In the space of a split second, Billy put on a smile to prepare for the confrontation, thought better of it, then pressed the "Engage" button and was gone.

"Excuse me, what team are you att...?" the lead man said to the fading form in the booth.

"Who was that, Eklorin, another member of the First Councilor's entourage?" asked the team member following close behind.

"I don't know," the team leader said. He looked at the roster on the display next to the booth. "No other teams were scheduled before us. I was certain we were priority one. Could be a late departure with the First Councilor. Yes, that's it, no doubt. They're not so punctual, the political ones."

"Should we inquire?"

"If we worry about their performance, *we* shall be late. No, let's get on with it. We've lost one minute as it is. Stations? Engage."

As Billy rematerialized Earthside, he felt a sudden jolt from behind. Turning around, he reached out in the near darkness and touched what felt very much like the trunk of a tree. He had the odd sensation that, as he had rematerialized, the tree had struck him. He thought back through all he knew about transport functions and remembered that a built-in safety feature provided that rematerialization always took place at surface altitude; further, if another mass occupied your set of coordinates, then your rematerialization took place in the nearest unoccupied space. The jolt he had felt was the instantaneous relocation outside of the body of the tree. In a sense, the tree had pushed him aside as he rematerialized.

A moment of reconnoitering made it amply clear that he was in a forest of large trees. He had calculated that it would be about two a.m. when he transported Earthside, and indeed it was deep night. There was no moon, and visibility was severely restricted. The air was chilly, but still.

Okay, he knew he was not in the locker room at Candlestick, but where was he and why? He scanned back through the moments before transport. Of course. He had entered the wrong coordinates into the transport control and, before he could correct them, he was forced to engage the unit to avoid discovery. He tried to recall the exact numbers he had punched in. Yes, he could recall the numbers but without a map they were meaningless. From his days in the Land Rangers on Ball Four, he knew how to read many forms of maps on land or in space. Assuming the same rules applied, he did a quick calculation which should give him an approximate idea of his location. In all probability, assuming that his recall was correct (of course it was), then he was about two hundred miles northeast of San Francisco. When he had gone on the fishing trip, they'd gone east-southeast to reach the Sierra mountains. They ran north to south along the Nevada border. Chances were very good that he was now in those mountains.

Nothing to do tonight but stay warm, Billy thought, stay warm and out of danger. He didn't recall any talk of dangerous wildlife during the fishing trip, but he would do well to keep ears and eyes open. Working his way through the foliage of the forest floor, he eyes became adjusted to the available starlight. When he was a Ranger, night hiking had held a special fascination for him, and his good vision had been a distinct advantage. It served him well now.

Before long he found a group of trees arranged in a tight circle. There was a depression in the center of the circle, the floor of which was quite sheltered from the elements and thickly padded with a soft bed of needles and peat. Sweeping a pile of the needles into the deepest, most sheltered part of the depression, Billy Icarus settled in for the night. At first light, he would plot a path that would lead back to San Francisco. Nothing more could be done.

Two hundred miles to the southwest, two concerned pitchers talked long into the night. Neither Jimmy Strongbow or Brad O'Nealy were pitching on Saturday, and sleep did not concern them. After the loss to the Reds, they'd come back to Jimmy's place with a take-out pizza.

"Billy would not do this to the team on purpose, we know that," said Jimmy. "I could imagine his being gone for one game, just for effect. But four, possibly more, no, he wouldn't do it. That's what's got me worried."

"We've been over it enough times, Jimmy. I think the theory still stands. Billy grandstanded to end the debate about being a alien and it must have been risky. He's not dead, but more likely he's been discovered. He probably some-how risked discovery to make his point. Remember how many agents he said were employed in the Operation? He ran into some of them and he's been caught. We have to get used to the idea that we'll never see him again. We were ballplayers before he came and we just have to go on without him. He did a lot for the team, and for you, Jimmy. You're a major league pitcher now and a damned good one. Tonight was just a bad dream. You'll get over it."

"Can I win without Billy behind the plate? I don't know. He did more than call a good game, Brad. He knew how to give me confidence, whether he did it in a human way or with mind control. Either way, I feel pretty lost without him. They pounded me tonight."

"Oh, and what did I do the day before?" asked Brad with self-contempt. "I haven't given up six runs in a game all year. But moaning about it isn't going to win ballgames. We're rookies, but the team needs us to show them the way. They're like lost sheep right now. Alien or not, Billy was their shepherd. Let's talk to Bob and Willie. They've got to start leading the T'ai Chi and we've got to start winning games. Billy will come back or he won't."

"Yeah, okay. But I'm really afraid. Baseball's in a world of danger right now, and we can't do anything about it. Did you see what the Indians did last night? Beat Toronto 23-0. They got thirty hits, Brad. Thirty!"

Brad O'Nealy stuck his chin out. "Billy has already given us the tools. We've got to pull it together, we have to do the best we can with what we've got. I'm not saying we can do it, but I for one am ready to try."

"You don't really believe that, do you?" asked Jimmy.

"No, but it sounded good, didn't it?"

"You've got the part, Brad."

The first light of day revealed that Billy was indeed in a mountainous area. The oak, fir and pine trees were further proof that his hypothesis had merit. He'd learned quite a bit on that fishing trip and, as disturbing as the recent turn of events was, he at least had ways to work out of his jam. There was no sense in dwelling on misfortune.

As the sky lightened, the sun remained behind a set of massive peaks. The fact that it was behind the mountains he took as proof that he was on the California side of the summit. Not wishing to wait any longer, he set out a brisk pace, and made good time in spite of the rough terrain. He went up and down two ridges before the sun made it over the tops of the mountains. Taking into account the northern path of the sun, he had estimated quite accurately in which direction he must move, and continued that way until noon. It was time to find food. He was in uncharted territory in that respect. He wouldn't be able to identify edible plants the way he could on Ball Four. It would be risky business to eat berries and mushrooms. Ball Four had its poisonous varieties and so must Earth.

Shortly after noon, Billy made a fortunate find. On a sunny fringe of a small meadow, he ran into a clump of blackberry bushes. Being late August, they were full of ripened fruit, which he could eat without fear. Upton had shown him some on the fishing trip, though at that time they weren't yet ripe. He ate his fill. They were juicy and full of sugar. Their richness made it difficult to eat more than a few, but he forced down all he could stand. The juice would quench his thirst and the sugar would carry him a long way. He had yet to come across water.

After hours of his southwesterly trek, he came to a rushing stream. There were still two good hours or more of daylight remaining, but he couldn't pass up the chance to catch fish and camp by a source of water. He couldn't count on encountering another stream any time soon. It was best that he set up camp for the night and prepared to test his luck with the fish.

Thanks to Jimmy, he knew what to do. He found a straight, stiff branch on a young sapling, snapped it off and stripped it. Up the slope had been a rocky escarpment at the base of which was a crumble of rock shards. He made his way back up to the spot and searched through the rubble. He selected some of the harder, flint-like pieces and went back to the camp. Using the sharp edge of one of the rocks, he fashioned a point on his fishing spear.

A half an hour later, he was perched over a shaded pool in the stream. The first two or three fish escaped his spear, but the next was not so lucky. With childlike glee, Billy passed the next hour in successful pursuit of his dinner. The thrill of the hunt made him forget the dangers of his predicament.

Returning to camp with his catch, a major challenge remained: how to make fire. Again Jimmy Strongbow's Indian heritage came to the rescue. During the fishing trip Jimmy had insisted he be allowed to start the fire using ancient means. He'd notched a fat branch and stuck a sharpened stick into it. Around this he had piled twigs and dried, crumbled leaves. In a matter of minutes, he had a fire started by furiously rotating the stick. Billy's attempt took considerably longer, but by nightfall he too had the blessings of fire.

After dinner, he stared into the embers of his well-banked campfire and meditated on the bizarre events of the past week. How could he have foreseen them? Had he been reckless, and had he destroyed his chances of success in his venture? These questions might have to go unanswered. He had done what he could given his resources and options. What more could he have done?

In all his days he could not recall being in a worse predicament. He was lost in the wilderness on a planet light years upon light years away from home. As he curled up under the pile of leaves and branches at a safe distance from the glowing fire, he could not call to mind a time when he had been happier.

23

San Francisco Chronicle

August 20th.

Red Henderson

FRANCHISE PLAYERS
ARE FOR THE BIRDS

It was not long ago, I regrettably admit, that I openly accused the entire Giants' organization of going off the deep end with the signings of Billy Icarus and his sidekick, Chief Strongbow. I, like so many of my colleagues, choked on my words and have passed many an enjoyable hour at the typewriter singing the praises of the wondrous deeds of Lone Ranger and Tonto. Now, I question again the wisdom of building a team on such a weak foundation.

We've all been enraptured with Billy Icarus. He's a glorious pleasure to watch, his pure swing and tremendous power have sent chills down the spine of the most hardened observer of the game. His throwing arm has gunned down many a baserunner foolish enough to challenge him, and his game-calling (something Lou Chambers admits to having given over to him) has been a clinic. Fine, so Billy Icarus gets the flu and the Giants go down the toilet. Something's terribly rotten here.

When a team has so little going for it that the absence of a solitary player, no matter how great, can cause a complete collapse, then it's time to rethink the whole basis upon which the team has been built.

Are the Giants merely castles in the air, or
are they men? Is Lou Chambers in charge
of this club or a marionette? San Francisco
can't wait around for Billy Icarus to fly back
home, we expect more from the breadth of
talent assembled. Come on Hal Barnham,
you're running the franchise. If that franchise is Billy Icarus, you'd better fire the
team doctor, or get ready for next year's
draft.

I got an ugly feeling that there's
more to it than that. We've given this Billy
Icarus a lot of room. We in the press have
let him dodge question after question about
his mysterious past. Who the hell is he? I
don't like to react to rumors, but the grape-
vine is literally exploding with speculation
that he's flown the coop. Nobody's seen
him in over a week, and in spite of the official story this illness line needs a lot of
shoring up. Lou, what's going on here,
babe?

If you build your house out of
straw, at the least bit of stormy weather it'll
come crashing down on you. If Billy Icarus
is this franchise's gamer, then it's time to
light a candle. Next time, guys, look before you leap. You owe it to the City.

Lou Chambers sat in the corner of the dugout and did his best to appear
inconspicuous. He wanted to show support for his team by attending the pregame workout but, at the same time, he was afraid he'd lose his temper if one
more sportswriter asked where Billy was. The illness charade was apparently
satisfying nobody, but what could he say? Sorry, guys, Billy Icarus just vanished into thin air. We expect him back any minute. So hold yer horses.
Chambers wished he hadn't run out of bromo.

Over in the bullpen Chambers could see Inky Powell warming up. He was
starting Powell in hopes of breathing new life into the team. Losing seven
straight, including three to the Dodgers, had further demoralized an already
shaky team. Maybe Inky could do it. If the Giants couldn't win a couple from
the Astros, for chrissake, then they were in big trouble.

But what was he to do? How do you get a team back on track after your
best player and team leader tells you that he's an alien, and then vanishes in
front of the entire team and its coaches?

I'm never, I mean never, Chambers swore to himself, ever again in my life going to speak to Red Henderson. Makes me feel like telling him the truth. I dare him to put that in his column.

By the 23rd of August, Red Henderson was not the Giants' only problem. The team had been swept by fifth-place Houston, while the Dodgers won their sixth straight. The Giants were now twelve games off the pace and only three games ahead of the surging Atlanta Braves, who were coming to Candlestick Park the next day.

Jimmy Strongbow sat in the small living room of his cottage and fidgeted with the game ball he was given when he won his first game in the majors. Seemed like a million years ago. It seemed almost that long since the Giants had won a game. The losing streak stood at thirteen, and if he couldn't win the last game against the Braves tomorrow, they'd fall into fourth place. It had been painful watching Art and Brad lose the doubleheader earlier that day, and he wondered if he'd get any sleep.

The sudden ringing of the phone gave him a start. It'll probably be Brad trying some useless cheerleading, Jimmy thought as he walked over to pick it up.

"Hello?"

"Hi, Jimmy, it's Billy."

"I don't believe it! We thought you were dead, some of us. Where the hell are you?"

"In a town called Coloma. Do you know where that is?"

"Not really," replied Jimmy. "Is it in California?"

"Oh yeah, it's in the foothills of the Sierras. Do you have a map?"

"In my car. What are you doing there? What's the hell's going on?"

"I'll explain everything later. It was just an unfortunate accident, but I'm back. I need someone to pick me up. I'm at the Flying A gas station, at a phone booth. The whole town's more or less closed up and it's pretty cold. Might take three hours to get here. What time is it?"

"About ten-thirty. I'll leave right now."

"Okay, I'll be right here."

It was a little after one o'clock in the morning when Jimmy pulled into the Flying A gas station in Coloma. He'd made good time. He was lucky he didn't pass a cop on the way. As he looked around, Billy came out of the bushes next to the station, walked over and got into the car.

"Man, am I glad to see you, Billy. You've had us worried sick."

"I've been worried about you guys, too. How's the team?"

"We lost thirteen straight," Jimmy said in an ashamed voice.

"This is not good. I really did it to you guys, didn't I? I'm sorry."

"We lost the games, not you."

"I'm to blame. I tell the team that I'm an alien and then vanish right in front of them. I disrupted the team horribly. I'll try to make it up."

"Don't worry about that right now," said Jimmy. "How are you? Where have you been?"

As the car cut through the darkness of the remote hills and down into the Central Valley, Billy Icarus told his tale.

"So you see, I never would have made it without the Indian skills I learned from you. It was wonderful, exhilarating. Oh, I'm sorry, I don't mean to sound like I was having fun, though I confess that I enjoyed the adventure. But it sure caused you a lot of pain."

"Eight days in the wilderness, huh? How far did you travel?"

"That's the funny thing, actually. About eighty miles as the crow flies, but probably I walked nearly three times that much. It was very rugged terrain. I looked on the map in the window of the gas station back there and I was dumfounded to discover that, if I had gone east or north, I would have reached a town or at least a highway in a day or two. But the summit stood in the way and I just don't know California well enough. Oh well, what's done is done. Is there a game tomorrow?"

"Yes. We play one more against Atlanta and I start."

"Good. We've got a lot of work to do."

"You're too much, Billy," said Jimmy in exasperation. "The team's falling apart, we're thirteen games behind the Dodgers and you act like nothing's happened."

"Something's happened all right, and I'm responsible. It'll take work to set it right. Dwelling on it won't do anybody any good. We're a tough bunch. I like our chances. At least until the World Series."

"If we get that far."

"We'll know in a month or so," said Billy. They fell silent. Stretching out his legs, he leaned back and looked out at the lights of Sacramento as they approached. He felt surprisingly good after his ordeal. In fact, he'd never felt better. The two hundred miles of climbing up and down one ridge after another must have done his body good. He was ready to play baseball, he couldn't wait.

The Giants' players and coaches were assembled in the locker room. The scene was quite reminiscent of the day Billy had disappeared. He was standing in the very spot he had transported from and the team was listening to his explanation. He ended it with an apology.

"So you see, I take full responsibility for what's happened to you. If any of you are angry with me, let me have it now, so we can get on with playing baseball."

Not surprisingly Eddie Renker spoke up. "You're a son-of-a-bitch, if you ask me!"

"I can understand why you'd say that, Eddie," Billy said meekly.

"And I don't see why we should do a single thing you say from now on," Renker continued. "You've jerked this whole team around."

Billy was privately hoping that Washington would speak up. But to his surprise, it was not the captain who rose to his defense. It was Mickey Roberts.

"We don't have any choice, Eddie," said the ordinarily quiet, stoical third baseman. "Look, I haven't been too involved in this whole thing and, for one reason or another, Billy, we don't know each other very well. But I've been watching and, Eddie, there's no doubt we wouldn't even be talking pennant if it weren't for him. He pulls a stunt to convince us once and for all that he's from another world. Some of us have been talking about this since he's been gone, and we've come to the conclusion that if it weren't for mistrust from guys like you, Eddie, Billy wouldn't have had to risk his life. After all, he came here to help us win ballgames. What the hell's wrong with that?"

Renker started to protest, but changed his mind after he saw the look in Roberts' eyes.

"Dammit, Eddie, I don't really blame you," continued Roberts. "But we all know what's going on now and it's time to pull it together. So what if things are wacky? Who cares if Billy's an alien? He's a helluva ballplayer and he's been good to us. I'm willing to put this past two weeks behind me and go for it. If Billy says we got to wear purple underwear to win a World Series, then I say let's go shopping."

Tension was palpably released as the team began to laugh at Roberts' joke. Even Renker smiled. When Roberts sat back down, Renker reached over and gave him a quick high five.

Washington stepped forward. "We can't blame Billy for what happened. And we can't blame him for being from out of town, either. He came here to help us win a championship and I say let's get back to it. What do you say, Lou?"

Chambers looked around the room thoughtfully. He liked this bunch of kids. He liked Billy Icarus. He hated the last two weeks.

"I say, welcome back, Billy. Let's get in some extra batting practice. Hit the field in five. Let's go!"

The team jumped up, eager to get back to it now that there was a chance of winning a ballgame for a change. The room buzzed with excitement, the players jawing with one another as they grabbed for their gloves and straightened out their uniforms. Smiles replaced the frowns of the past two weeks. Renker went over and shook hands with Billy, as did everyone else. As the team went up the corridor to the field, Billy caught up with Mickey Roberts.

"Thanks. I thought it might take a miracle to get things back on track. I never thought you'd be that miracle."

The solidly-built, sandy-haired North Carolinian looked straight ahead modestly. "Billy, how come you never gave me any advice like you're always doing with the other guys?"

"Well, there's a saying I've learned since I got to Earth," said Billy as they emerged from the dugout onto the field. "If it ain't broke, don't fix it."

Roberts broke into a half-grin and headed off to jog around the field.

That night the San Francisco Giants shut out the Braves, 7-0. Jimmy pitched with a fury that even Billy Icarus couldn't contain. He hit two batters and walked three, but struck out nineteen in the process. Brad O'Nealy could be heard all over the field yelling "Geronimo!" every time the ball came near a batter. After the second Brave got hit, the Atlanta first baseman charged O'Nealy and the benches cleared, but nothing serious came of it.

Brad saved some of his bravado for the beginning of the road trip. The team flew down to San Diego for three, the first of which Brad won with a stellar performance, shutting out the Padres and collecting seventeen strikeouts. French and Upton were back on track as they finished off the series sweep. But L.A. loomed.

Chambers had decided to put Inky Powell into the starting rotation. It was not an unusual move during a stretch drive to save the best arms from being worn out. Besides, Powell had shown that he had guts during the losing streak. He had never groused or blamed anyone.

Powell won his start, with the help of Steve Lafite. Jimmy won his, as did Brad. Only French had any trouble with the Dodgers, getting no decision with Carl Trumbull losing the game in relief. But the Giants had the momentum back, and were no longer afraid of the Dodgers.

The short road trip brought them back to Candlestick without a day off to begin a nine-game homestand against St. Louis and Pittsburgh, the teams emerging as the top contenders in the National League East. Billy Icarus spent the homestand getting his program rolling. Chambers acquiesced to Billy's request for a daily team meeting to coordinate the effort to prepare for the Indians. Billy used the meeting before the first game against the Cardinals to set the stage.

"There's a lot of work to do to win the division, and in the next week we'll get a good look at the team we'll have to beat to go to the Series. The way we're playing, I think our chances are good. Every game, though, we've got to play like it's the final, deciding game. Let's have fun, but don't let up.

"I know you guys can do it. In the meantime, we need to accept the spiritual side of the T'ai Chi in a big way. Let's keep the workouts the same length, but those of you who want to stay at it longer, I'll lead it for an extra thirty minutes a day."

Willie Washington spoke up. "A lot of guys are sayin' to me that they don't understand the whole program. Could you lay it out for all of us?"

"Sure," said Billy. "In a way, we might have a big advantage, but it'll last only one game against the Indians. They'll probably come in here thinking that we're pushovers, given their success against the typical human team. It might take them a game to adjust, but that's all we're likely to get. After that they'll be trying every strategy they ever heard of back on Ball Four to get inside our heads and gain the mental advantage. They'll read our minds, project misinformation, try to startle us and decoy us, tell us they're throwing a fastball, then come in with the curve. If I am guessing right, they'll be so surprised that we're not like the rest that they'll try stuff I've never even seen on Ball Four. One thing's for sure, they'll come after us, try to mentally break us.

"Our one chance is the white mind. That's the mental state in which major-league-level players on Ball Four must play in order to dodge the gambits and tactics that are employed to disrupt and steal a player's natural talent. I don't want to brag, but I was, like my father before me, regarded as the premier mental player of my time. I could block all access to my own mind, as well as penetrate all but the whitest minds. I could affect about forty per cent of the major league players to some extent and I definitely was considered a `rookie crusher.' To make a long story short, between the T'ai Chi and the biofeedback we've got a good chance to achieve the white mind, or at least emulate it. With the other advantage of surprise, we just might hold our own. But it'll take hard work and dedication. Otherwise we might just as well give up now."

"What if we just don't get it?" asked Harold Dubois.

"Harold, I know this is heartless, but anyone who can't defense the mental game will have to stay out of the lineup."

"Even starters?" Mitch Simpson asked incredulously.

"Mitch, if you thought you were going to go hitless for an entire Series would you *want* to play?"

"I see what you mean," replied Simpson. "I guess we've got to put in the work if we want to be part of it."

"Unfortunately, yes. Look, these Ball Fourians came to show their dominance. And make no mistake about it, it's possible that in a head-to-head contest without the mental factor, they could win. These are tough ballplayers we're going to face. I know them well. I wish my view concerning fairness had prevailed. The Season would have been a fair contest, I'd be playing with the Indians and we'd know who was best in the galaxy. But I'm enjoying the way it turned out. It's a bigger challenge for me as well as for you."

"Can we do anything mentally to them?" asked Mickey Roberts. "I mean, are we going to be able to get to their heads?"

"It's not likely," answered Billy. "We'll probably just have to find out when we get there. We'd better get going now. Here's the agenda. Bob and I are running the T'ai Chi. Whenever you've got a free moment, report to Brad for biofeedback training. And in the batting cage, work on hitting the ball that's pitched. Stop guessing. Guessing against the Indians will be suicide, I guarantee. If anybody needs help in batting, talk to me or Rick Barker. A lot of you are already pure hitters, but Rick's the best in that department. Maybe he can share his technique or mental approach. Is that okay, Rick?"

"Sure. Whatever you need," acknowledged Barker.

"Okay. See you out there. Oh, and pitchers, keep thinking about the symbols for your pitches. We've got to start throwing imagistically. That'll block the Ball Fourians, and it will do your overall game some good as well. Let's roll."

The next two weeks were a flurry of activity. Teammates watched with amazement the energy displayed by Billy Icarus. He seemed to be everywhere one looked. To the pitchers, Billy was always in the bullpen; to the hitters, he never left the batting cage area; to the coaches, he was constantly in conference with them; to Brad and the players using the biofeedback machines, he was constantly there monitoring their progress. Billy, of course, was only in one place at a time, but gave such personal attention that it felt to each individual that Billy cared especially for him and his individual needs. It was all a matter of heart, and Billy's was growing daily. He marveled at how good he felt. Giving on Earth was exponentially finer than anything he'd ever done in his whole life on Ball Four. He didn't have the time to stop and wonder why.

It took quite an effort to concentrate on the baseball games during this period of intensive training. Billy asked Chambers and the coaching staff to constantly remind the team to be into each game. This they gladly did, for it was their principal job to begin with and made them feel as though they were not becoming insignificant. However, the coaches were reluctant to get on the biofeedback machines, and it took a tremendous amount of urging just to get them to consider it. Chambers broke the deadlock by making it mandatory; Lou was determined not to let the typical conservatism of coaches impede the team's progress. Reminding the coaches what the winning share from the World Series was likely to be didn't hurt either. Just as with the players, once the coaches got the machines to register Alpha, it was more difficult to get them off the machines than on. And, of course, the coaches joined the T'ai Chi. The local press went wild with that.

As consuming as the training had become, it had, nonetheless, a positive effect on their day-to-day play. They took seven out of nine from the Cards and Bucs, and, as they approached mid-September they had reclaimed second place from Cincinnati. Los Angeles still held a six-game lead, but the Giants had seven more to play against the Dodgers. The last four games of the season would find the Dodgers in Candlestick. Conventional wisdom held that the division champion would be determined there and then.

September 11th, the team departed on its last road trip of the season. They would play ten games in nine days against Atlanta and Cincinnati, with two doubleheaders to make up for rainouts. They would finish the trip with three games in L.A. before returning for the final homestand. The equipment manager was instructed to pack up and carry the biofeedback machines wherever they went. Security would be heightened in the road clubhouses.

Morale was high and the team played like a well-oiled machine, taking four out of five in Atlanta. Brad O'Nealy won his twentieth game, a one-hit jewel in which he struck out sixteen. He was on a pace to win the strikeout crown, was leading the league in earned-run average and a Cy Young award was not out of the question. No doubt he had rookie of the year sown up. Jimmy Strongbow's record was a bit better if one took into account the late start and projected the numbers to reflect a complete season, but his limited number of starts would probably keep him out of consideration for the year. Brad lightheartedly brushed it aside, saying that this was the last year he would be first in anything, and he was going to enjoy it. After Jimmy won the last game against the Braves with a seventeen-strikeout performance, Brad started calling him Cy Youngbow.

Billy made a startling announcement before the first game against Cincinnati.

"Boys, I'm going to throw you a curve. After harping on you for days to practice the white mind and stop guessing at the plate, I'm going to ask you to look back at the way you worked at the plate before we started all this training, and re-adopt it for the Cincinnati series. The reason is simple: if the Indians are going to scout us as possible opponents, they're likely to do it here. My guess is that they won't bother because they've grown overconfident, but we can't afford to take that chance."

"Why do we need to do this, Billy?" asked Renker.

"Primarily because we want to appear like any other team. If they scout us, they're likely to check us out mentally. We'll lose our advantage of surprise, and we don't want that to happen. We have little enough going for us as it is."

"What about the pitchers?" asked Lafite.

"Same goes for you guys too, Steve. We need to pitch the old way, without the symbols and images, without the white mind. Just think the way you used to."

Inky Powell asked the obvious. "What about you? How you gonna think human? Oh, and what about Chief? He told me you taught him to throw with the symbols right from the start."

"I've been working on that for a long time. I've got two things to accomplish. First, I've got to play with an open mind, and, second, I've got to think in English. Don't worry about me, I won't blow it. It's my strong suit. As for Chief, if you don't mind, I'll discuss it with him personally."

"What, you think in Ball Fourian?" asked Butterfield.

"Of course, that's my natural inclination, when I think in words, which is not all the time, even for humans. But I've been practicing for a couple months now to expose only English words in my thought processes. So, do we all agree? We suspend the white mind for the Reds' series?"

There were nods throughout the room.

Jimmy caught up with Billy in the bullpen. "Thanks for not saying anything until you talked with me. What have you got in mind?"

"You don't start till the last game of the series, right? Well, the Ball Fourians, if they scout us at all, will most likely be finished and gone by the time you pitch. I don't want to mess with your visualization techniques, they've been too effective. Besides, they'll probably concentrate on the catcher position to observe the mental process of the defensive game in action. That was the practice on Ball Four. So, we have Butterfield catch you in the next start."

"I didn't do so well with him while you were gone, Billy," said Jimmy, dubiously.

"We've recovered from those dark days. I'll be here and I can call the game from first base. Lou and Bob will like that. Besides, It'll be good for you to find out how well you can throw to another catcher. I may not be there for you forever. You've got a long, prosperous career in front of you. I take pride in having gotten you started, but I'm not the secret of your success. You own that."

"You'll be gone after this season, won't you?" asked Jimmy. He'd never thought that far ahead. The idea shocked him. "Of course, you will."

Billy patted him on the shoulder. "We can't always know what's in store for us. But you know you've got a great future."
With that, he turned and trotted off.

Billy had been observing the mind-conditioning of the team as it developed, and was pleased with the progress the players as a whole were making. By the end of the Atlanta series, discipline was good at the plate, with the white mind being exhibited by the starting lineup throughout most of each plate appearance. Reserve players, who weren't getting much playing time anyway, weren't quite as secure. The pitching staff was in great shape. Conversion to imagistic pitching was nearly complete throughout the staff, with the exception of Carl Trumbull and Rick Santiago. That was not too worrisome, because Chambers agreed with Billy that pitching in the World Series could be limited to a core of the best with the whitest minds.

Some of the symbols being employed by the different pitchers were quite humorous. Art French's whole "Junkyard Dog" persona lead him to create such symbols as a rusty bumper for his curve, a truck suspension coil for his screwball and a lunch bucket for his knuckler. His change-up off his change-up was a crushed paper cup. Brad O'Nealy's images were all based on higher mathematics, and fit with his strike-zone grid in a complex pattern of line segments, radii, arcs, all intersecting on various graphs and three-dimensional geometric shapes. Billy loved catching Brad's game. It was like attending a calculus class at Harvard.

Billy had intended to observe the change back to the old ways in the Reds' series, but he realized that it would be far too risky. The Ball Fourian scouts might pick up his own scans of the team and be tipped off. It would be a dead giveaway that something quite peculiar was going on. Billy would just have to trust the Giants' commitment and focus. When the club took three out of five from the Reds, he considered it to have been a mixed success. The performance was uneven and indicated some confusion had existed. Billy hoped that, if they had been observed, the picture presented was convincing enough. The fact that the Ball Fourians weren't anticipating anything unusual would serve to deflect suspicion.

The final game with the Reds brought with it the test of Jimmy Strongbow without Billy's catching. Jimmy was a bit shaky at the beginning, surrendering two runs in the first, but settled down after that. Chambers wisely pulled him in the seventh with a 5-3 lead, and Steve Lafite mopped up to get the save. Jimmy had passed the test, with silent pride and a tinge of sadness.

By the time the Giants reached Los Angeles, the races were down to two teams in each division. In the East, St. Louis was slugging it out with the New York Mets, and the West had come down to a battle between the Dodgers and Giants. The newspapers across the country gave L.A. a decided edge, having a six-game lead with fourteen to play.

Every Giant sensed that these three games would make or break the season, and tension was high as they began their warm-ups in Dodger Stadium. Billy clearly sensed it, and gently focused the team during the T'ai Chi. The whole team, coaches included, were quite adept at an extraordinarily broad range of movements in the ancient art, and the scene in left field before the first game attracted a large number of observers in the stands. Though not as unruly as New York fans, the L.A. bleacher bums could not afford to miss a chance to razz the Giants, especially in a pennant stretch drive. During the workout, the fans lined up in the bleachers in rows and imitated the team, calling out derisively such things as, "Hey, Bruce Lee, don't hit me!" and "Chinaman, after you're done, could you do my laundry? No starchy-starchy, please!" Billy feared the tension on the club might grow, but to his amazement and great satisfaction, the entire team was now so centered that the jeering had an opposite effect. By the time the team finished the T'ai Chi, they were relaxed and quietly but grimly prepared to take on the Dodgers. Billy marveled at the combination of human pride and Ball Fourian discipline. It possessed a compelling power.

Inky Powell took the mound in the opener. It was a crafty move by Chambers; L.A. had never seen Powell and didn't know what to make of his whirling-dervish delivery. The Dodgers' main strength all year had been its pitching. They had led the division almost the entire season in spite of a .247 team batting average. It was a typical Dodger team: pitching, speed and defense. They threw their ace, Harlan Snow, at the Giants in the opener and it backfired. Snow was superb, but lost 3-2. Willie Washington's thirty-seventh home run was the difference. Now, Chambers had O'Nealy and Strongbow to pitch back-to-back in the Sunday doubleheader, and L.A.'s ace was used up. Not that either of the remaining contests were gimmies. But Brad won his, 4-3, with help from Lafite; and Jimmy was unstoppable, giving up two bloop singles as the Giants won, 3-0. All of a sudden, L.A.'s six-game lead was down to three.

The next cover of *Sports Illustrated* featured a photo of Jimmy Strongbow and Billy Icarus conferring on the mound in that last contest of the series. It was a striking picture, with Jimmy's streaming hair almost obliterating the numbers on the back of his uniform and Billy's thick beard making him look like Black Bart in catcher's gear. The caption read, "The Lone Ranger and Tonto ridin' high in L.A."

The whole team was riding high as it returned to San Francisco for the homestand that would end the season. The local reporters couldn't help but notice the effort that the Giants were putting in on and off the field. So far, the biofeedback training, which was going on secretly from early morning until game time, had not been discovered by the press. Billy gave thought to leaking it to the press, but decided he didn't want to give Cleveland any lead time whatsoever to consider what to expect from the Giants. The T'ai Chi could be passed off as "a good stretching system."

At this time, Billy also began to encourage all team members to do some form of meditation as often as possible, whether at home or at the ballpark. Anything that served to empty the left hemisphere of the brain would enhance the acquiring of the white mind. Reporters, observing the Giants sitting around the locker room in various silent poses, speculated with each other about the strange antics. Chambers considered closing the locker room to the press, but Billy suggested openness concerning the meditation. He'd learned enough about San Francisco's reputation as a "New Age" town; and sure enough, the media continued to play up the "only in San Francisco" angle. Pictures of the T'ai Chi sessions became a favorite cover photo in the print medium all over the country. This media-coverage slant would surely be effective in steering Ball Fourian agents away from the real motives behind the Giants' odd behavior.

The rest of the season was composed of three four-game series against San Diego, Houston and Los Angeles. Chambers could not have orchestrated a better set-up for a stretch drive, and Billy couldn't have asked for a better situation for training his Giants while simultaneously building their confidence. In the San Diego series, hitters went to the plate and obliterated the opposing pitchers with pure technique. Billy Icarus put aside all worries of hitting for too high an average (it had begun to hang around .435) and swung at will. The team batting average rose to .302. On the pitcher's mound all the starters without exception pitched from a nearly unreadable place, lapsing only occasionally from time to time. Unfortunately, an unsteady performance by Powell, Trumbull and Santiago in the third game prevented a series sweep.

The meetings against Houston went well except for one tragic incident, which led indirectly to a Giants' loss. Kiley Upton was on the mound and cruising to his eighteenth win with a 9-4 lead in the eighth when a ground ball was hit in the hole between first and second. Butterfield moved over and grabbed the ball and threw it over to Upton, who scrambled over from the mound to cover first base. He made the mistake of approaching the bag out of step, and thrust his foot out too far. He got there just in time for the out, but the Astros' baserunner stepped with all of his weight on Upton's right foot, which was hooked on the corner of the bag. Kiley felt something snap. Later, X-rays would reveal a small break in his pivot foot. It wasn't serious, but he was finished for the year. The Giants, shook up by the cruel blow, gave up six runs in the inning, and failed to help at the plate. Houston won 10-9.

The following day, mercifully, was an off-day for the Giants, who gathered nonetheless at Candlestick Park about mid-morning. The stadium was closed to the media by Chambers, who pleaded that preparing for L.A. was more important than a few useless photo opportunities. The Giants began the day with a team meeting. Chambers opened it.

"I know we're involved in strange doin's this year, but any time you lose someone like Kiley, it's got to upset you. Of course we got to keep working toward being ready for Cleveland, and we'll spend most of today doing chores related to that. But I just want to offer a bit of encouragement about the upcoming series with the damned Dodgers."

Soft hisses and boos filled the room. The team had not completely lost its sense of humor.

"Okay, here's where we stand. Those Dodgers, whether you hate 'em or not, never give up. While we just went six and two against the Padres and Astros, L.A. did the same against the Reds and Braves. So they're still three games up on us. Means only one thing: we gotta sweep or we're history. Now, about Kiley. I know we'll miss him before this is all over, but the fact is he isn't a factor in the L.A. series. He wouldn't have pitched anyway. So, for now, there's no impact on us from his accident. We're the same machine we were before and we got what it takes. Don't forget it. Now, Billy you got anything to say?"

Billy got up to face them. "Not much, only to say that I'm as proud of you guys as any bunch of players I've ever known."

"Even in outer space?" cracked Renker.

"Even there, Eddie. No matter what happens in the next four days I wouldn't have missed it for the world, and I do mean Earth. Now, everybody check with Brad for their time on the biofeedback machines. He's told me everybody's exhibiting alpha. I'm very pleased. In the meantime, Bob and Willie are going to lead T'ai Chi in the outfield and I'm going to run batting practice. The pitchers will rotate throwing to the hitters. I'll be scanning both the pitchers and the hitters to check mind control."

"So don't anybody be daydreaming about their girlfriends!" quipped O'Nealy.

24

THE PLAIN DEALER

October 3rd.

Lloyd Cronin

HISTORIC SEASON
IS ALMOST HISTORY

On April 7th, none of us would have believed it if you had told us. By May we were convinced it was a fluke. In June we were sure something was terribly wrong. But by the All-Star game we were believers. The greatest baseball juggernaut of all time had been assembled in Cleveland, and we finally found the good sense to sit back and enjoy it.

That's the tricky thing about history. When you're inside of it, you can't see it. When you're making it, as the Indians have done this year, of course you have difficulty talking about it. For one thing, most heroes have no idea that they're heroes until someone else tells them, and the first reaction is usually to deny it and try to deflect attention. So many of us, and I include myself, were almost critical of the Tribe's success and their hesitancy to talk about themselves. Now I understand. They were too busy making history to care about discussing it.

Now that the season is almost over and we can look at it in its totality, we can finally grasp some of its meaning. It's been hard to swallow. Our ne'er-do-well Indians changed into a team with so grand a destiny that we almost wouldn't accept them. It wasn't right, not here. It was okay in 1921 for Detroit, it was all right for the 1926 Cardinals or the 1927 Yankees, maybe it was even okay for the '54 Tribe. But that was history, back when baseball was truly great. At some time in the future people will look back at our Cleveland Indians and say, "Now that was when they really played baseball." Friends, history is now. We're the greatest of all time.

I want to say now, before the glory of the World Series swallows up the sweetness of the mere season that got them there, that I am proud, proud beyond measure. I want to remember the names of Vance Bueller, Cy Ellerbach, Alan Van De Kirk, Tony Pantuso. I want to remember them all. They set so many records this year that Guinness, *Sporting News* and Macmillan are scrambling to hire new staff. A team batting average of .325 and a total of 253 homers? A pitching staff with an ERA of 1.84 and two thirty-game winners? This isn't the '20's, this is the '90's. But it's history nonetheless.

Some of us, and I admit I might have been the worst, wouldn't accept such greatness from young, supposedly unseasoned talent. We expect greatness from the great names. But of course they would be young and come from nowhere. Only new blood could breathe this kind of life back into our game, this unique and truly American pastime. It gets me teary-eyed, I'm not too crusty to admit it, to think that this great land of ours can produce this wonderful gang of heroes, who made history come alive for us this year. Those cynics out there need only look at our brave Cleveland Indians to know that America is still alive and well.

Elliot Edwards sat with Jake Conrad in a corner booth in Allie's Steak and Bake at the Lake. The waiter had just brought two of the thickest T-bones ever to grace a plate. A few reporters hung out at the bar and eyed the pair, but they knew better than to bother the Indians' owner during his lunch hour, even at a baseball house like Allie's. They'd wait for a few words to drop as he left.

Conrad was looking down at his steak and wondering where to begin when Edwards cleared his throat. "Jake, I'm glad you could make time for lunch with me today. When the Yankee series is over, the playoffs and Series will occupy all of your time. So, I just want to say here's to you, you did a helluva job."

Jake duly lifted his mug of beer, banged it against Edwards' and took a hefty swig. "Thanks, Elliot, that's mighty kind of you. It's been a helluva year. I wish I could accept your toast, but I didn't run this club this year, it ran me. It's been a great thrill, watching these players, but I can't say I had anything to do with it. It's almost been eerie, the way those boys play within themselves, almost like it didn't matter if I was there or not. A few times late in the season, I'd be daydreaming, and forget to send some signs out. You know, we'd have a big lead and I'd sorta drift off for a minute and, boom, they'd pull a squeeze, hit-and-run or double steal, something like that. I'm sorry but I can't accept any praise. Of course, I won't turn down a new contract, boss."

Edwards chuckled drily, then grew thoughtful. "You know, I've been feeling the same way. I've been hands-on with the running of this club since I bought it, but in the past few years I've felt it just drift away from me. Now, I'm not saying I regret hiring Abe Watkins, not for one minute. And I suppose that it's great to have a general manager that lets you lean back and watch for a change. But he built this club, I didn't have anything to do with it. He made a lot of strange moves and acquired guys I never heard of, and I always approved. He's a pretty compelling guy. Never met anybody like him. And, without exception, every move he made led to some improvement in the team. We were eighty and eighty-two last year. He brought in six new guys and, if we sweep New York, we might even win one hundred thirty games! Dammit, Jake, can you imagine?"

"No, I can't," said Conrad, letting out a long sigh. "Van De Kirk could end up with sixty-five homers. Bueller's got one more start and probably will win thirty-seven. Nixon's stole a hundred and forty-two bases. It's like I said, eerie, but maybe that's what it feels like being part of history. You know who I gotta credit? Warren Evans. A pitching coach, and he's everywhere, talking to the hitters, the other coaches. He's a smooth operator, but a fine baseball man. Helped me out of many a jam this year."

"You know," Edwards said in a low, conspiratorial voice, "Abe and Warren spent a lot of time together all season. In fact, for the past two years, every time I'd look they were together. It gives one pause."

"Yeah, but wait a minute, Elliot, what are we doing? When you're winning, maybe it's supposed to feel easy. If we'd lost ninety this year, you'd be firing Abe and maybe me, and we'd all be in the soup. And guys like Cronin would be calling us dunderheads in the papers. Let's eat these steaks and enjoy ourselves, for chrissake. The papers are calling us heroes and wise old men, and I still got a few more ballgames to win. Let's just sit back and watch, and start planning our vacations with our World Series checks, okay?"

"Yeah, Jake, here's to you, me, Abe and Warren. Maybe we all did something right."

They laughed, took a big swallow of beer and dug in. The reporters at the bar wondered what the two baseball geniuses were talking about now.

Over the next four games, Warren Evans watching with off-handed pride as the boys of Ball Four swept the last four from the Yankees. Ever since First Councilor Tarn had arrived, Evans had been allowing the team to win without restraint. What a pleasure it was, just knowing that Tarn was in the stands; Evans wanted to give him a show. And it was time to gear up for the playoffs and Universe Series, and there was no point in any more forced discipline. The boys, just between themselves, had orchestrated two losses to the better teams, to keep appearances. But the Season would be over soon and they could begin to dismantle the Operation. There was no need for worry. The press was too busy comparing them to the great teams of the past and heaping praise on them. There were no more detractors.

By the last out of the season, the Indians had garnered the records for most wins in a season, highest team batting average, most home runs by a team, most RBI's, most steals, most just about everything. Individual records abounded as well. Van De Kirk finished with sixty-four homers and one hundred ninety-four RBI's, and Tony Pantuso won the batting crown with a .411 batting average, the first time anybody had broken that barrier since Ted Williams did it in 1941. Bueller had thirty-seven wins and Ellerbach thirty-two. The Cleveland Indians had even set a record for setting the most records in a single season.

First Councilor Tarn, Dr. Avion and Abe Watkins sat in a private box during home games for the last month of the season. As First Commissioner of Ball Fourian baseball, Tarn was indeed proud of the team's success. He was all too aware, however, how the use of the mental game detracted from the success. He had agreed with Belteron from the beginning that it would diminish the accomplishment. Unlike Belteron, he had wisely grasped the political implications of such a stand.

On the last day of the season they again looked on as the Indians decimated the hapless New York club. In the presence of the First Commissioner, Abe Watkins was particularly relishing it.

"First Commissioner, these men have performed brilliantly in the service of Ball Four. If I may be so bold, I have hinted that they will be rewarded when they return home. Surely there is some way they can be acknowledged, beyond mere glory."

Tarn contained his desire to laugh. "Abakin, glory should never be described as `mere.' Besides, there is little beyond glory and praise that can be bestowed. Perhaps the gratitude of an entire planet could suffice?"

"Of course," replied Watkins. "It is my own feelings of gratitude that causes me to wish more for my team."

"I understand," countered Tarn, "but we've yet to win the Universe Series. Isn't it a bit early for speculation concerning the triumphal return?"

"I'm afraid there is little I can do to squelch my feeling that it is already over. There is nothing on this Earth that can stop a Ball Fourian team. Nothing."

For the sake of the future history of Ball Four, Tarn thought with a certain scorn, I can only hope you're wrong, my dear Abakin.

Next to Tarn, Dr. Avion appeared to be absorbed by the contest on the field, as though he hadn't been listening to the conversation, let alone scanning Tarn's mind. In a low-level beta-brain area, well-cloaked in theta waves, Avion was a bit shocked by Tarn's scorn. We shall see, he thought, we shall certainly see.

25

By the time of the L.A. series, Lou Chambers had swung the pitching rotation around to reflect his plans for the playoffs. As he had told the team, Kiley Upton's injury wouldn't have an impact. He had O'Nealy, Strongbow, French and Powell ready for the Dodgers, and he hoped it would be enough. It turned out that it was, and there was no doubt in any Giant's mind that what Brad O'Nealy did that October night iced the season for them. He thoroughly demoralized the Dodgers by throwing the first no-hitter of his career.

Billy Icarus was mesmerized by Brad's performance from start to finish. It was obvious that all of the hard work Brad had put in to prepare his mind for Cleveland had paid off ahead of time. His mind was focused, his visualization strong and his fastball off the scale. It wasn't as fast as Jimmy's, probably never would be, but with his concentration he had added another two, maybe three miles to it, even breaking one hundred miles per hour on one throw. Billy knew that, other than Jimmy, Brad was the most prepared on the team to meet the Indians. If it weren't for the one walk he gave up in the eighth inning, it would have been a perfect game. His teammates supported his effort with five runs. Brad would finish the season at 25-5.

The Dodgers must have lost heart, because they didn't mount a threat in the next three contests. Jimmy Strongbow gave up six hits and a run in winning his nineteenth game. He didn't pitch enough of the season to beat Brad in any other categories, but he did manage to qualify for the earned run average title at 2.05. Art French won the third game, 7-5, to finish the year at 16-15. Inky Powell still had the Dodgers' number, winning the final game by blanking them 8-0. The San Francisco Giants ended the season with a record of 101-61, a game ahead of L.A.

Willie Washington took great satisfaction in winning the runs-batted-in and home run crowns. He got his forty-third and forty-fourth homers on that final day of the season. Billy Icarus almost caught him with forty roundtrippers in considerably fewer games. In spite of playing only one hundred thirteen games, in which he hit .433, Billy was awarded the batting crown. After adding the needed number of plate appearances to his record, he still achieved a .418 average; therefore, under the rules, he qualified for the title. Rick Barker came in second at .344. Billy also managed three other titles: he led the league in stolen bases with seventy-seven, and both doubles and triples with fifty and fourteen, respectively. Even with his shortened season, he had put on the greatest display by any catcher in history. It was as good a year, all things considered, as anything Belteron had ever done.

The Giants mugged for the television cameras and sprayed champagne on everyone in sight. Even Hal Barnham and reclusive Giants owner Tom Connolly got soaked. Had anyone been looking, they might have noticed that few Giants drank a drop of the stuff, and that the clubhouse was vacated in an hour. The New York Mets were waiting and Cleveland was never out of their minds. The opening game of the league championship series would be held in two days' time. The Giants would return at eight the next morning.

Later that night, a meeting was held at Brad and Billy's Pacific Heights house, attended by the occupants, as well as Jimmy Strongbow, Willie Washington and Bob Butterfield.

"The team's in great shape," Washington was saying, "and there's no real reason to worry about the Mets. We'll take 'em. That T'ai Chi is a big part of it. I've never seen a team in better physical shape, and it sure makes you feel, well, spiritual. When I go to the plate, I can *see*. The ball's big and fat, it wants to be hit."

"It's the same for me," added Butterfield. "I've never felt this way before. My mind used to go a mile a minute at the plate. I'd be thinking, `Oh, I can't hit this guy, keep your elbow up, next one's gonna be a fastball,' things like that. Now I watch and wait. I sorta climbed inside the game, nothing's going on in the world except that one at-bat."

"I think we're all in agreement that the team's in fine form," said Billy. "We're focused, fit and united as a team. The team unity is a big part of our success. The belief that we can do it is critical. I agree with you, Willie, we will beat the Mets. It's been a great advantage that everything we do to get ready for the Indians helps us to become better ballplayers. And, thanks to the press, we've built a mystique. It intimidates the other clubs. Won't affect the Indians much, I'm afraid."

"That brings up the real problem," responded Washington. "We've been so busy with the preparations and the regular season, we haven't had time to really face up to the fact that in a week we're going to play an alien team. I don't know if the guys will stay tight, or just crumble into nothing."

"It'll be our job to see that they don't," said Billy. "That's why I asked you all here tonight. Willie, I want you to be in charge of the outfielders, see that they're holding up. And don't ignore Harold Dubois. We figure to need at least one reserve before this is all over, and Harold will probably be the designated hitter in the games in Cleveland. Bob, you've got the infield. Brad and Jimmy are to work with the pitching staff. I'm going to see to the coaches and Chambers. Tomorrow, after T'ai Chi, we'll break up into the various groups. We've got to work on everyone's focus and their morale as well. Let's start letting everyone know that Cleveland's around the corner. It's important we stress that they're just ballplayers too, aliens or not. They can be beaten, I know, because I've beaten them."

O'Nealy raised his hand. "Billy, thanks for the pep talk, but that's not going to fly with every player. They've all accepted you, because you seem so human. But I sense that they're all quite intimidated by the Indians."

"Listen, I know how all of you must feel," said Billy. "I'd be lying if I didn't admit that we're up against it. But I've studied your baseball history, and many an underdog has, against all odds, done the impossible. It's all a matter of heart. The message you've got to convey to the team tomorrow is that we've got a plan. They should be made to rely on the plan, focus on the plan. If they're thinking about the plan, believing in it, they might not think about the Ball Fourians so much."

"Great," said Jimmy. "What plan?"

"The one I've been working on for two months," replied Billy. "That's the principal reason for this meeting. Now, we'll need some sleep, but we've got to put in quite a bit of work tonight. I'll explain everything I can about the scheme I've developed. Brad, how about a pot of coffee?"

"Sure."

A few minutes later everyone had stretched, cleared their minds and sat back down to the table with a mug of coffee in front of them.

"Okay," Billy began, "it starts with the first game, which will take place in Cleveland. We've got one advantage, I hope. They have no idea that we're anything but another pushover human team. They'll be expecting more of the same that they've seen all season. But when the game begins, this is what they'll see. We come to the plate first with Eddie Renker and..."

The meeting went long into the night, with all ears on Billy Icarus.

The playoffs against the Mets began on October eighth in Candlestick

Park. Brad O'Nealy took the mound and established dominance from the start.
The Mets, always a powerful hitting team, managed a few scattered hits, and
even did some damage with a two-run blast in the sixth. Against the Four
Musketeers, however, the Mets' pitching did not fare so well. Washington,
Barker and Simpson each hit homers, with Billy collecting two more. With
the 9-2 lead, Chambers rested Brad by bringing in Rick Santiago, who gave up
two meaningless runs in the ninth.

Billy had asked the team to play the entire series with the Mets in the
white mind, as though they were facing the Indians. To support this, each
man, including coaches, was to spend time on the biofeedback units prior to
the game, while registering a minimum of fifteen minutes of alpha activity.
By now, the team was so adept that the request was met without exception. No
doubt it played a part in the merciless treatment of the Mets.

Not every player held the white mind in place throughout each game, but
they did so when it counted. Eddie Renker weakened a few times, but promised to put in extra time on the machines. After the game, Billy was gratified
to see Renker back in the biofeedback room. When he emerged an hour later,
Renker had a serene look on his face.

On Wednesday night, Jimmy Strongbow was warming up with Billy in the
bullpen. Billy sensed something different about Jimmy, but couldn't place it.
He scanned Jimmy's mind, but could see nothing, absolutely nothing. It was
as white a pitcher's mind as any Billy had witnessed on Ball Four. And his
pitches were snapping and humming and hitting all the right spots. Towards
the end of the warm-up, Billy stopped and, with a brilliant smile on his face,
slowly walked up to the mound. Jimmy stood there wearing a face that somehow combined stoicism with serenity.

"Jimmy, something's changed. I see it in your pitching, I feel it in the air.
Is it anything you can share with me?"

Jimmy took a moment to gather himself. He had been back in time, running the trails with his great-great grandfather, Mangas Coloradas. High above,
an eagle flew, always watching, never far from sight. When he finally spoke,
it was as though from a trance. He could speak from another place in his mind,
without disturbing the fabric of his vision.

"I'm there, Billy. I've made the change. I am my own Medicine Wheel,
I am the eagle watching myself."

"Ah, yes, you are there, my friend."

Jimmy came slowly back to a more normal consciousness. "Today, before
I came out here, I was doing my time on the machines. And, for the first time,
I found myself with theta waves in my left hemisphere and beta in my right. I
brought myself up, step by step, then walked back down. I can be in theta
waves at will, keeping my beta brain on a lower level. It was like an explosion
of awareness. For the first time, I merged with who I am. Did you know this
would happen?"

"You describe very much the same mind frame that I achieved with my
father's help. I think the only difference is that I am only a ballplayer, I was

born and raised to play baseball. As an Apache, you have another side to your spirituality. But you've merged it with your baseball mind and heart."

"Thank you, Billy Icarus," Jimmy said soulfully. "As a pitcher, I am ready to throw with all my heart. As an Apache warrior, my vision quest is over. I am home. Let's play ball."

"Yes, indeed, let's," said Billy.

The old timers in the stand said they'd never seen anything like it. The thick-skinned, battle-scarred veteran reporters like Red Henderson called it the greatest pitching performance of all time. The New York Mets, as they marched to the plate one after another to meet their doom, said nothing. Jimmy "Chief" Strongbow had silenced them.

As the game progressed, and Jimmy threw inning after inning of no-hit ball, the Giants' bench was as silent as a church. They didn't even congratulate each other on their plate successes. No one acknowledged Mickey Roberts, Willie Washington and Billy Icarus when they returned after their home runs. This night belonged to Jimmy, and they knew it.

Jimmy, already towering at six feet, six inches, appeared to grow in stature with each inning that went by. As he added out to out and strikeout to strikeout, the cheers of the crowd grew more intense, and the dugout grew seemily more silent, were it possible.

When Jimmy took the mound for the top of the ninth, even the crowd quieted down. All eyes were on him, though one couldn't have told by looking at Jimmy. He was in a world by himself. Billy scanned him, and the same white mind that he saw in warm-ups was still fully intact.

Jimmy had faced twenty-four Mets. He had struck out twenty-one. Now the bottom of the order was, one by one, replaced with Mets' pinch hitters. The first he struck out on three pitches; the second took four. The fastball, which was clocked in the first inning at one hundred two miles per hour, was now recorded at one hundred five.

The tough and rugged veteran Frank Owens was the last chance for New York. At thirty-seven he'd given his best years to four other teams, but he had the distinction of being a man you had to beat, he did not beat himself. He rarely struck out. Against a steady diet of fastballs and hard sliders, Owens fouled off pitch after pitch, staying alive until the count was 3 and 2.

Billy flashed the sign. On the mound, Jimmy Strongbow waited for the sun to come up over the hill. He crept from rock to rock, finally settling in with a clear view of the sleeping camp. With the first glint of sunlight, he charged.

Frank Owens saw the ball clearly. It floated with a big red bow on it. Pulling back for all the power he had, he took a mighty cut. The crowd was on its feet holding its collective breath. Billy was poised behind the plate, watching the seams of the ball as they rotated one precise turn downward. At the moment the ball reached the plate, Owens' bat reached its full extension, perfectly timed. Swoosh. The ball hit just at the base of Billy's mitt and squirted a foot to the right. Owens stared incredulously, frozen by the fact that the ball had seemingly gone through his bat. It must have. Billy picked up the ball, and tagged the befuddled batter out. The crowd, and the Giants, exploded. Jimmy had just thrown a perfect game, striking out twenty-four. As his joyous teammates smothered him on the mound, he looked past them all to Billy, who stood at home plate with his hands on his hips. They were sixty feet, six inches apart, physically, but their minds were one. Nothing need be said. Billy answered Jimmy's faint smile with one of his own, then turned and slowly walked off the field.

Lou Chambers sat on the bench, too astounded to join the celebration on the field. Billy sat down next to him.

"Billy, as long as I live, I'll remember tonight. I don't care what happens next week. I've seen baseball at its best. What was it like catching him? It must have been something."

"Yeah, it was something, all right," answered Billy.

Chambers couldn't avoid asking the next question. "You give him any special help?"

"No, Skip, this was all Jimmy Strongbow tonight. All I had to do was hold on to the ball."

Chambers managed a wry smile. "Struck Owens out on a knuckler, what grit. A goddam knuckler. You called a helluva game, this one's yours too, you know."

Yes, I guess it is, thought Billy. Try as he might, he could not contain his feeling of pride. Before he succeeded in smoothing out his mind, a solitary tear streamed down his cheek.

Jimmy's feat had a more profound effect on the Giants than just the winning of an important game. The whole team took it as a sign that they had passed a hurdle. Each had participated in the accomplishment, even if Jimmy had allowed them only three put-outs. Mentally, they could feel that they had supported his effort. It validated everything that they had been doing to get ready for the Universe Series. They would go to Cleveland undaunted. If they lost, it would not be because of anything they had failed to do to prepare.

First, they had to finish off the Mets. It took them three games in New York to do it. Art French had a strong showing in the third game and, together with Steve Lafite, brought them within one of the pennant. But Inky Powell, though pitching strongly, couldn't contain the meat of the Mets' batting order. It seemed they wanted something to restore their pride. New York won the fourth game, 7-5.

Lou Chambers, who had planned to start Brad in the World Series opener, was forced to use him again in the playoffs. Brad took the assignment with glee, guaranteeing that he would still be ready to open the Series, if need be. He pitched five scoreless innings and was not surprised, with a 6-0 lead, to be asked to give way to Carl Trumbull. Carl surprised Chambers by pitching the best he had all year, giving up only two runs in saving the game for Brad. The Giants were champions of the National League.

Part Three

26

The surprising California Angels had sneaked up on everyone to win the American League West, taking the last two games of the season from the A's. The Angels edged out Oakland by one game in the final standings. Little did they know, it had been Cleveland that had given them their chance. By not regarding them as contenders, the Indians' strategy dictated that they play the Angels without a mental advantage. It was the four victories against the Tribe that gave California confidence against the other teams and, in the end, the edge in the standings.

Having no such advantage in the playoffs, California succumbed in four straight.

Following standard operating procedure, Abe Watkins had sent scouts to check out the competition in the National League. He had indeed sent a Ball Fourian agent to the very series against Cincinnati that Billy Icarus had anticipated, and, of course, the National League playoffs had been well-attended by Cleveland representatives. Other than at the Cincinnati contests, though, all the scouting had been done by Earthling members of the Indians' staff. Thus Jake Conrad got his scouting reports, and Abe Watkins was allowed to have all his agents protecting First Councilor Tarn and the team itself.

Warren Evans had made no particular effort to set up a Series pitching rotation, although for appearance's sake he went along with Conrad's choice of Bueller, Ellerbach and Sanchez, with Bueller coming back for the fourth game. Conrad was prepared to counter with Lefty Pierce in the fifth game, in order to save Ellerbach for a possible sixth; Bueller could then pitch the seventh game if necessary. Evans let Conrad decide. It was all the same to him, and he could not foresee going past the fourth game in any event. Evans was amused by the endless strategy sessions and pretended to view the scouting reports with interest. The players did the same. Only Alan Van De Kirk actually looked at his copy. He wanted to know everything that was available on that oddball Brad O'Nealy. He had to even the score from the All-Star game. With that exception, the Indians made no actual preparations for the Series, other than to suffer through the team meetings called by Conrad.

The San Francisco Giants used every minute of time in preparation. Expecting to fly straight from New York to Cleveland, they had arranged at their hotel to have a conference room available for their use. The day before the first game of the Series, they held a strategy session that was chaired by Billy Icarus.

"Before I talk about strategy," he began, "I'd like to open the floor to questions about the Indians. Ask anything you want. You can't know too much to get ready for them. I've urged you to start viewing them as ballplayers with a definite mental edge, not as aliens to be feared. Let's demystify them if we can. So ask away."

Mitch Simpson held up his hand. "This might be stupid, but what about the blacks and Latinos on the team? How'd they pull that off?"

"Simple. The biofashioning took care of it. Actually, who became blacks and Latinos was decided by lottery, because so many had requested it. It was viewed as prestigious to be biofashioned black or Hispanic. It was very popular in the general Ball Fourian population."

"Oh, *man*," Simpson said with a laugh. "These aliens be very crazy indeed." Everyone erupted in laughter, especially the rest of the blacks on the team.

"I'm glad to see we've kept our sense of humor," said Billy as things quieted down. "There's plenty of work to do, but staying loose can't hurt in the meantime."

"How do we stack up against these guys, Billy?" asked Mickey Roberts. "I mean, man for man. You've played with them, you know them. How tough are they? The numbers they compiled show they're the greatest of all time."

"But they did it with an unfair advantage," countered Billy pointedly. "How do we measure up? I'd be lying if I didn't say that, man for man, it'll be like playing the best human all-star team in history. But sometimes all-star teams don't make the best *team*. We're a united team, we can only hope that it gives us some kind of edge, however small."

Third base coach Sal Donato held up his hand. "I've got a concern. When we all try to use the white mind, how do I give the signs to the hitters?"

"You don't, Sal," replied Billy. "You should keep going through the motions, if only to decoy, but we won't be able to read them. Ball Fourian players can, but that's because our white mind is more advanced, multileveled."

"So I'll be out of it," said Donato.

"You'll still have an important role in our deceptions. We all have our jobs to do."

"Something's been bugging me," said Renker. "Keeping the white mind going is going to wear us out. What happens if we lose it once in a while? It's likely to happen no matter how hard we try."

"You're right, Eddie. But remember, we don't have to keep the white mind going all the time. Hitters need it at the plate, and pitchers, of course, must assume it on the mound. But on the field, you can relax, unless there's a baserunner near you or approaching you. Of course, you have to discipline yourselves as to what kinds of thoughts to allow, but a good portion of the time, you can relax. The real burden, in many ways, is on the pitchers. You guys will all have to be tight. But not in the first game."

"What do you mean?" asked Lou Chambers. "We aren't going to use the white mind?"

"Nope," answered Billy. The room buzzed. What was Billy talking about? "Okay, we might as well get into the first game strategy. No, we're not going to employ the white mind tomorrow night. Brad and Bob, could you help by passing these notebooks out to each player? Their individual names are on the covers. Each of you has a role to play, based on characteristics I've observed in you. If you disagree with anything I've put in any of your files, I'll be glad to hash it out later, after the general meeting. Now, for example, Eddie, let's look at you. You go up to the plate in the top of the first and..."

At game time on Tuesday, October 15th, every available inch of Cleveland Municipal Stadium was draped in red, white and blue bunting. It had been nearly forty years since a World Series game had been played in the park, and the entire city was making the most of it. The stands had been filled since four-thirty, the fans basking in the perfect baseball weather and listening to four strolling bands that zig-zagged up and down the aisles. During the Indians' batting practice, the fans cheered every blast, and an air of confidence and vitality filled every corner of the stadium.

Up in the press box, the talk centered not on who would win, but on how many games it would take Cleveland to finish off the hapless Giants. Five seemed to be the consensus figure. Some talk could be heard that sung the praises of O'Nealy, Strongbow and Icarus, but no one seriously considered the Giants. Nobody thought for a single moment that even those three brave souls could subdue the powerhouse Tribe. It was Cleveland's year, and everybody knew it.

Behind the home team's dugout, First Councilor Tarn and Dr. Avion sat in relative obscurity, dressed in nicely tailored suits and looking to all the world like successful stockbrokers or lawyers. They were surrounded on all sides by a cacophonous mob of what the casual observer would conclude to be everyday people. The nearest fifty of these "everyday people" were in fact Ball Fourian agents. No chances were to be taken, even if Tarn and the good doctor could be transported up to the orbital station with a second's notice. Tarn himself appeared to be enjoying the festivities immensely, which he most certainly was.

Though Abe Watkins would have preferred to sit with Tarn, he was obliged to watch the contest from the owner's booth with Elliot Edwards. Limited language skills prevented the visiting dignitaries from being invited to sit in the booth as friends of the general manager. Tarn had made impressive progress with English, more out of interest than necessity; Dr. Avion shared no such enthusiasm.

The mob in the outfield had heaped a good amount of abuse, most of it good-natured, on the Giants as they went through their now-famous T'ai Chi workout. Even Tarn and Dr. Avion watched with rapt attention; they were particularly curious about Billy Icarus.

After the Indians had finished their workout, Jake Conrad called them back into the clubhouse. He gave them a fatherly lecture on pride and poise, and told them he had ultimate faith in their talent. He closed by telling them to go out there and enjoy themselves. All in all, it was a warm and sentimental speech, and it was a pity no one was listening. To a man, the team was tuned in to the thoughts of their real leader, Warren Evans.

Men, this is just another Earthling team we're about to face. There is one principal difference. This is the big show we've been waiting for all these years, and no doubt the whole of Ball Four will be watching. This is our time, gentlemen. We shall prevail. I shall not coach you, you have complete control. You are free to use every method at you disposal to defeat the Earthling team. Of course, continue to be polite to Conrad's requests. He is only doing his job. Naturally, I will influence his calling of the game, and I will urge him to allow you some free rein. I must rely on you to choose well the gambits and ploys that can only be employed as the need arises. Good luck.

No such meeting was held by the Giants, to the amazement of some of the San Francisco press corps that had come down to the visitors' clubhouse in anticipation of it. There was nothing left to be said. Every Giant knew full well what was required of them. They were working from a script from the moment they had hit the park. That script called for them to act naturally, a near-impossibility under the circumstances. The press chalked it up to nerves. Billy Icarus hoped that in their smugness, the Ball Fourians hadn't taken the step of utilizing agents to observe the Giants. If they had, he reasoned, surely they would uncover his scheme quickly. And he could easily guess what their reaction would be should the Giants win in game one.

Throughout the ritual and pageantry of the pregame ceremonies, Lou Chambers kept a watchful eye on his players. So much of what a manager does on occasions like this had been stolen from him by the unusual circumstances. He tried his best not to resent it, for he realized full well that they would never have gotten this far without the help and inspiration of Billy Icarus. Any remaining doubts as to the veracity of Billy's story would soon be resolved. If a game plan as bizarre as this one could possibly work, it was the ultimate proof that the Indians were alien.

Jimmy Strongbow needed no such proof. As he looked at the faces of the opposing team, it was all he could do to muster some semblance of composure. They were all there: Rogers Hornsby, Mickey Cochrane, Walter Johnson, Jimmie Foxx, Ty Cobb, Jackie Robinson, Cap Anson and more. It was unmitigated gall. Billy was undoubtedly right, no one would consciously recognize them, it was too preposterous. But Jimmy knew. These faces had adorned his bedroom walls most of his life. He'd just have to get over it. It would harm the plan and hurt his own concentration. He was glad he wasn't starting the first game.

Brad O'Nealy, on the other hand, couldn't wait. He recognized many of the great stars from the past, and admired the arrogance of the Ball Fourians. For him, it added spice. The double absurdity of the situation actually relaxed him; how could he worry about the outcome of a game in which he would face an alien who looked like Shoeless Joe Jackson? It was the ultimate practical joke. God, I love my life, he thought, as he turned back to the job of getting into the game plan.

The rest of the Giants, unaware of the biofashioning scheme, had noticed nothing. They were jittery and not a little afraid. They tried to stay loose, and many, as Billy had recommended, used various meditation methods to remain calm, with mixed results. Luckily, Billy's plan required little of them during the early part of the game.

When the national anthem was over, Eddie Renker grabbed his bat, gave it one final swipe with the pine-tar rag and advanced to the plate. The crowd was vibrant with anticipation. Television cameras captured the moment and beamed it into sixty million households. Holocameras secreted throughout the park also gathered images that, seven days later, would be seen by all of the approximately two billion Ball Fourians gathered in stadia around their world. Only the technicians of WeatherCon and the unfortunate robotics supervisors on duty would have to content themselves with viewing the game later on their holocorders. The Universe Series was under way.

Don't swing at the first pitch, thought Renker. Cleveland catcher Eddie Martin read the thought and ordered up a fastball down the middle. Strike one. They'll come back with a curve, thought Renker. Fastball, swing and a miss, strike two. They probably think I'm expecting fastball again so they'll give me another curve, Renker thought. Slider, outside, swing and a miss, strike three.

This will be easy, Vanbellen.
Yes, Martane.

Mickey Roberts stepped in. I don't care what they throw me, he thought, I'm sending one out, right now. Martin understood and called for the change-up. Roberts, way ahead of the pitch, caught it off the end of the bat and sent it softly on the fly to Dizzy Rifkin at short, who gloved it easily.

Next up was Rick Barker. Patience, Ricky my boy, patience. Barker had said this same phrase to himself every at-bat since high school. There was no percentage in guessing.

Pure hitter, Vanbellen. Fastballs and sliders, on the corners.
Yes, it's appropriate.

The first pitch missed and Barker held back. The second pitch, fast and up and in, Barker fouled off getting out of the way. Bueller then served up a hard slider, low and in. Barker laid off. The ball broke at the last instant, and nicked the corner. Bueller continued to work the corners with heat and Barker fouled off three in a row. The next two barely missed, and the count grew to 3 and 2.

Change-up.

Barker missed by a mile, side retired. The crowd screamed its approval.

In the dugout, Billy strapped on his shin guards. Classic Vanbellen and Martane, he thought, if I hadn't known before, I do now. It'll be hard *not* to hit them when my turn comes.

Brad O'Nealy finished his warm-up tosses and watched with disregard as Dizzy Rifkin approached the plate. It was now time, and O'Nealy dropped into the white mind. Rifkin scanned the mind behind him. *Fastball, outside and down.* He swung and missed the high and inside blazer. Billy Icarus, who was holding his mitt on the outside corner, dropped the pitch.

Rifkin settled in, and zeroed in on the catcher's mind. *Curve, high inside.* Let this one go. The fastball that came in caught the inside corner. Surprised, Rifkin had no choice but to watch it go by. Strike two.

In the dugout, Warren Evans was not concerned. He watched as the San Francisco catcher jogged out to the mound, and strained to pick up what he could of the conversation. *Watch signs...wild...settle down...* As Evans expected, the Giants' pitcher, a rookie, was nervous.

Rifkin caught a similar bit of the talk on the mound and drew a similar deduction. As Billy got back into his crouch, Rifkin took great pains to listen to the precise call. *Fastball, down the middle.* Ah, a challenge. O'Nealy went into his wind-up, Rifkin began his swing and as he picked up the pitch he tried but failed to hold up. The ball came in slow, coming for his head, then broke down, inside and clearly a ball. Billy reached in and knocked the ball down, picked it up and appealed to the first base umpire as he tagged out Rifkin. The umpire signaled that Rifkin had gone around. A moment of confusion passed through Rifkin's mind before he walked back to the dugout.

Conrad framed a question, but then thought better of it. It was the first at-bat, for chrissake. Evans, however, did not let it go. "What happened?" he asked quietly as Rifkin sat down next to him.

"This O'Nealy is wild and confused," replied Rifkin.

Next up to the plate was Buck Nichols. As he walked from the on-deck circle, Evans sent a message.

Watch carefully, Bolnici.

Yes, Evan.

Nichols too strained to receive the signs. He too was surprised by the erratic response of O'Nealy to the catcher's calls. Twice, the San Francisco catcher failed to catch the pitches, one rolling to the backstop. Again, Evans listened as Billy Icarus clearly tried to settle down the anxious man on the mound. Once again, the Cleveland batter went down on three pitches, this time swinging.

The hitter in the third spot was Jimmy Fernandez. He strolled to the plate slowly, giving Evans time to project some advice. It was not forthcoming. Evans was busy in the dugout conferring with Van De Kirk.

"I told you O'Nealy was disturbed," Van De Kirk said out of Conrad's hearing. "He doesn't seem to know what he's doing. Perhaps it was nerves in the All-Star game, perhaps it's that now. See how the catcher keeps missing the ball? O'Nealy clearly ignores the signs. He's a madman."

"You're up next, Alvendak. Watch both pitcher and catcher carefully." Van De Kirk hustled out to the on-deck circle and Evans went back down to his seat next to Conrad.

Van De Kirk would have to wait until the next inning. Fernandez' foul pop-up on the second pitch was easily gloved by Butterfield.

When the Giants went down in order in the top of the second, Evans' mind gently smoothed. Watching the feared Billy Icarus go down on three strikes made it clear that there was time to sort this mess out. *Earthlings, they are unpredictable brutes.*

Alan Van De Kirk relished his assignment, and he was resolved to get the best of Brad O'Nealy. When the open-minded Icarus signaled for a slider, in, Van De Kirk quickly diverted his attention to the mound. Nothing there, but as O'Nealy went into his windup Van De Kirk clearly picked up the number "5." Distracted by the unusual message, he could only watch as a change-up nipped the outside corner for a called strike. Van De Kirk duplicated the procedure, this time reading, "fastball, low and away" from Icarus and "3" from O'Nealy. Anticipating his favorite pitch, Van De Kirk put everything into his swing. A fastball arrived, all right, but inside and high. Strike two. Quickly smoothing out his rippled mind, Van De Kirk again scanned the opposing battery's minds. He missed whatever Icarus might have called, but clearly he received the number "5" again from the mound. Having no idea what was coming, he batted instinctively. With an 0 and 2 count, he knew he must swing at anything over the plate. As the pitch arrived, it dropped severely, Van De Kirk only getting a piece of it. As the ball bounced high in front of the plate, Billy settled under it and got Van De Kirk at first by a step.

Evans ran out and greeted Van De Kirk between first base and the dugout. After a few quick words, he ran over to the on-deck circle and conferred with Hunk Jefferson, the Cleveland designated hitter. "Scan the pitcher for numbers. Remember all numbers."

When Evans reached the dugout, Jake Conrad said, "What the hell was that all about, Warren?"

"Sorry, Jake, I saw something in O'Nealy I wanted Hunk to watch for."

"Okay, but leave me something to do," Conrad announced, spitting on the floor.

When O'Nealy took seven pitches to strike out Jefferson and Pantuso, a nervous restlessness came over the stadium. The crowd came back to life as San Francisco went down like lambs in the top of the third. Vance Bueller got Butterfield on strikes, induced Giants' DH Harold Dubois to ground out to second, and put Archie Stokes away on a short fly to right.

From the three batters in the second, Evans had gotten the numbers 5, 3, 5, 8, 9, 7, 9, 3, 2, 3. Was there a pattern here? Not wishing to miss anything, he asked Van De Kirk to pay close attention and scan the mound to see if any additional mind activity could be picked up. He ran back into the clubhouse, but not before issuing orders to the hitters.

Scan catcher for signs and pitcher for numbers. Commit to memory.

Yes, Evan.

When he reached the confines of the clubhouse, Evans hurried to his office. There he unlocked a desk drawer and from the far back pulled out a small rectangular box. Pushing a button, he waited for a response.

"This is Operation Station. Who transmits?"

"Evan. Get me Ygarnen, priority "A" request."

In seconds Ygarnen reported. Evans fed him the number sequence. "Search for pattern recognition. Evan out." He quickly replaced the unit in the drawer.

By the time Evans was back in the dugout, there was one out, one on. Darvel Nixon had managed a bloop single. Denny Smith walked down the dugout aisle casually as though lost in thought. When he passed in front of Evans he sent the message.

846.

Thank you, Denser. Alvendak, anything from O'Nealy?
Numbers only, otherwise blank.

"This O'Nealy sure is lucky," Conrad observed. "Two more wild pitches on Smith's strikeout. Hope he uncorks one now. We could use a break. Hey, where the hell'd you go?"

"Sorry, Jake, nature called."

"Strange timing, Warren. Oh, Jesus!" shouted Conrad as Nixon was thrown out attempting to steal. Icarus had gotten him by two steps. Nixon, who had run with wild abandon against American League catchers, had better be more conservative against San Francisco.

Martin grounded out meekly to end the inning.

Bueller took the mound with confidence in the top of the fourth inning. He was disappointed by the lack of offense, but these Giants were as easy to retire as the American League teams he'd been facing all year. Martin was reading their intentions without hindrance. He would provide his team with time to get runs.

First up was Renker. I want a fastball, he thought. Renker waited three seconds, then blanked his mind. Bueller served up a curve that dropped out of the strike zone. Ball one. Give me that fastball, thought Renker again. After waiting three seconds, he dropped into the white mind. Clearly, he could perceive, almost like an image burned into his retina, the idea of a curve. He set the timing of his swing instinctively for that image and reached down and smacked the duly delivered curve into the gap in left-center. He made second standing up. Fernandez drifted over and scanned his mind. *Come on, Mickey, send me home. Watch pick-off move. Don't screw up.* Satisfied, Fernandez went into position and applied his attention to home.

Next to the plate came Roberts. He followed Renker's thought pattern, telegraphing the pitch that was opposite the one he really wanted, then blanking his mind. It was a hit-and-miss method, and required taking a couple but Bueller and Martin slowly revealed a pattern. Roberts thought inside slider and got a rising fastball. He thought rising fastball and got a sinker. Thinking inside slider on the 0 and 2 count, he pounded a rising fastball straight at

Pantuso in left. One out, and Renker was waiting on second.

Evans walked out to the mound. "They're touching you, Vance. What's up?"

"Mind pattern's the same. Luck is the likely explanation. I feel very strong."

Martin had come up to the mound. "I verify mind pattern. Those two swings were aberrations."

"Keep a close eye, men."

As he walked back to the dugout, he reiterated his message. *Scan carefully, Martane.*

In stepped Rick Barker. He projected, send me anything. Martin received. Bueller shook off the fastball, and sent a change-up. Barker was well out in front. Strike one. *Send anything, I'm ready.* Barker watched the wasted curve out of the zone. *Come on, come on.* Martin recognized again the thought pattern of someone who disdained guessing. They were tough.

Rip it by him, Vanbellen.

With pleasure, Martane.

The man at the speedgun saw it register one hundred one. Barker, without a thought in his mind, swung easily through the pitch and met it solidly but a bit tardy. It went floating to the opposite field, just clearing the outstretched hand of Fernandez. Renker was off like a shot at contact, hesitated for a second as it cleared Fernandez' glove, and scored standing up. Giants up, 1-0.

Buck Nichols scanned Barker's mind as he stood at first. *Steal if possible, steal.* Darvel Nixon at third base scanned third-base coach Sal Donato's mind and read *hit away.* Messages were sent mind-to-mind around the infield. Bueller threw three pitches in a row over to first base, then threw a pitch-out to the plate. Nothing doing. What was going on?

Washington waited to get something to hit. He hated curveballs, so he kept thinking, curveball, curveball. He never got one. Finally he got a good piece of a slider in and down, but not enough of it to elude the glove of Van De Kirk in straight center. Two down, and Billy Icarus was advancing to the plate.

Martane scanned Icarus' mind and clearly heard *hit-and-run, wait for slow pitch.* Billy waited three seconds and dropped into the white mind. Martin sent word to Bueller, who nodded grimly. Bueller delivered a fastball down the middle. Billy met it so cleanly that it was still rising when it cleared the fence in left field. Giants 3, Cleveland 0. It was all Billy could do to keep the wrong words out of his mind as he rounded the bases. He settled on repeating, *yes, yes, YES!* over and over. Rifkin at shortstop was the only Ball Fourian with the presence to scan him. *Yes, yes, YES!* was what he caught.

Bueller and Martin were stunned. Evans was confused; he had monitored the mind-exchange at the plate and was as shocked as the battery when Icarus had swung on the fastball. Conrad swore like a sailor. Abe Watkins got up and walked to the phone to call Evans. First Commissioner Tarn leaned over to Dr. Avion and said, "Icarus is sensational," to which Avion mentally replied, *He is superb.*

Simpson flied out to left to end the inning. When the ball struck Pantuso's glove, Evans was up like a shot and into the clubhouse before Conrad could open his mouth.

"Anything yet, Ygarnen?"

"Nothing to report. Any new data?"

"Yes. Add 846264338 to the sequence. Evan out."

Back on the field, Dizzy Rifkin had just popped up to O'Nealy. When he reached the dugout, Conrad said, "Patience, boys, we'll get 'em yet. It's early." No one was listening. They were all running smoothing loops through their minds. It worked for all except Van De Kirk. He was convinced that O'Nealy was demented, and it was difficult to smooth away the upset that it caused him.

When Evans sat back down, Conrad leaned over and said under his breath, "Dammit, Warren, can you stay put? Abe called for you while you we gone."

"Sorry, Jake, I was grabbing my book on O'Nealy." And, wisely, there was the scouting report on O'Nealy in his hand. He made a show of perusing it, but his mind was out on the mound. He clearly received numbers, one at a time, from O'Nealy, but absolutely no other thoughts were readable. In six years on Earth, he had never experienced a human like this one. He was baffled.

The phone rang. Evans waved the others off, went over and picked it up.

"Warren? What is happening?"

Evans kept his voice low. "Abakin, this O'Nealy is a strange beast. He ignores the catcher's signals. He's thrown a number of wild pitches and when Icarus tries to settle him down, it's to no avail. Meanwhile, all mind scans reveal that his thoughts are empty except for one number per pitch. The numbers appear to be random."

"Have you thought of having Operations do a pattern search?"

"It is underway already. Nothing to report. It is difficult to wait by a trans-receiver for an answer. Oh, no!"

"What is it?" asked Watkins.

"Bolnici has just struck out."

"Evans, use the agreed-upon names. This line may not be secure."

"Sorry, Abe," Evans said in a near-whisper. "Nichols has struck out."

"I will make my excuses to Edwards and work with Operations," said Watkins coolly. "You will then be able to remain in the dugout. I will contact you by phone. Bye."

Evans was off the line in time to watch Fernandez attempt to bunt his way on. O'Nealy was off the mound like a shot, grabbed the ball barehanded, pivoted and threw him out by a step. At the end of four O'Nealy had a one-hitter going, and in their desperation Evans' team was leaving their own game plan to search for a hit. It was time to assert discipline.

Remain calm! There is time. Refrain from disorganized play. A chorus of minds thought, ***Yes, Evan***, as they ran out on to the field.

Bueller retired the Giants in order in the fifth, and Conrad let McTell and Pierce sit down in the bullpen. O'Nealy struck out Van De Kirk to begin the

Indians' half of the inning. The third strike was again dropped by Billy, who tagged the stunned Van De Kirk out. Billy again went to the mound. Once more, all that Evans could pick up was, *Everything's fine...you're fine...watch signs...godammit Brad...can't catch wrong pitch...*

Van De Kirk called Evans to the end of the bench for a quick conference. "The last numbers since I reported are 8, 8, 4, 1, 9, 7, 1. As usual, I can pick up nothing from the mound except numbers. He is somehow twisted, as the Earthlings say."

"That is your theory, Alan," Evans replied. "There must be more to it. Remain calm until more is known."

Hopes were raised on the Cleveland side when Hunk Jefferson doubled up the gap in right. Those hopes were dashed when Pantuso grounded out and Smith struck out to end the brief threat.

While Bueller was making short work of the Giants in the top of the sixth, Evans received a call on the dugout phone. It was Ygarnen. He had patched through to call directly. "This line is secure. We have a match, we have discovered the pattern. We could have done it more quickly, but we were using Ball Fourian mathematics for a period of time. We should have scanned Earth records sooner. The sequence is not a pattern at all. It is various digits from an Earthling formula known as "pi." Using it, one can determine the circumference of a circle by knowing the diameter. We once used it on Ball Four, but..."

"Get on with it, please," said Evans abruptly.

"Certainly. The numbers you provided are the ninth through the twenty-eighth digits of this number. It is an unresolvable number, and proceeds to infinity."

"Give me the first one hundred digits," ordered Evans. He copied them down.

By the time he sat back down he had compared the numbers that had elapsed since his report and, sure enough, O'Nealy had gone correctly through the first fifty-one digits of "pi." What was this madness? It had to stop. When the team sat down for their at-bats in the bottom of the sixth, Evans issued a command.

Do not mind-scan at the plate. Hit with the white mind.
Yes, Evan.

Third baseman Darvel Nixon reached O'Nealy for a single to start the Cleveland side. O'Nealy came back to get Martin on strikes. Rifkin patiently worked his way to a walk. Nichols took a strike, then laced one down the line in right, which Simpson played brilliantly on a hop to allow just the one run. Next up was Fernandez, who smacked a line drive to Butterfield, with the baserunners getting back in time to avoid being doubled off. Now came Alan Van De Kirk with two outs, two on.

O'Nealy wound up and threw. Van De Kirk took a fierce cut at the ball. The swing produced a towering fly to deep, straight-away center. Barker had ample time to get back, back, back until he was up against the fence. All that remained to be seen was whether or not he had ample room to make the catch. At the last second he leaped. The stadium held its breath. The ball hit his glove, then popped out. It took a high arc back toward home plate and Barker, reaching back under it as he fell, caught it before it fell to earth. He ran in holding his glove high. The second-base umpire, who had by this time run half-way out to the fence, signaled out. The Giants trotted off the field, still ahead 3-1.

Evans, relaxed by the improved situation, sat back and went over the events that had transpired. Basically, the Giants as hitters were not unlike the other Earthling teams he had come up against. The fourth inning rally was unusual, but twice this season other teams had scored against them in spite of mental tactics. He had put it up to luck then, he could see no reason to assume anything else now. The mystery centered on O'Nealy. Icarus clearly was attempting to call a rational game and was apparently upset by O'Nealy's performance. Was Alvandek right, was O'Nealy mentally disturbed? More than once he had witnessed mentally distressed Earthling ballplayers, but in every case it had hampered their performance, not improved it. There was more to it. He must find it.

While Evans reasoned through the evidence, Vance Bueller was plowing through the Giants' line-up. Evans watched with satisfaction as Billy Icarus struck out. Perhaps Icarus had used up his luck. When his team came up to bat in the seventh, Evans concentrated his efforts on finding clues to this apparent mystery. There must be something he had missed. He now regretted failing to scout the Giants with Ball Fourian agents. They might have had advanced notice of unusual characteristics. What did he know about the team? There had been the strange warm-up ritual called T'ai Chi. Conrad had made a point of jesting about it. Called them wackos. Wackos. Yes, they were different from other teams. How else were they different? Did it change their mental game?

Whatever O'Nealy was up to, it continued apace in the seventh. He struck out Jefferson, got Pantuso on a grounder to third, and Smith popped out to Icarus. Something was wrong with O'Nealy and his mathematical mind. There Evans would find the answer.

Over in the visitors' dugout, the mood was no less intense. Though possessing a lead, it was too thin for most of the Giants. Still, Billy wouldn't free them up to attempt more scoring. His plan, however, was working. They would trust him. But the pressure was mounting. How long could they maintain their concentration?

It was O'Nealy's concentration that most concerned Billy. When they got back to the dugout, he motioned Brad into the tunnel to the clubhouse.

"Good work, Brad, it's going remarkably well."

"Yes, it is. It's exhilarating."

"I'm glad you can feel that way," said Billy with a smile. "Your special gift for mathematics is tremendously fortuitous."

"It's your plan, I'm just executing it. Are we safe talking like this?"

"Ball Fourians can't think through concrete, Brad. Chances are we're safe in the dugout, at least today. Anyway, there's no sign that they've cracked our code. Six outs to go. Any questions?"

"No, but I'd feel better with more runs. Why so stingy?"

"If we overpower them, they may look deeper. If we barely beat them, they'll be less upset."

"I thought Ball Fourians never got upset," said Brad. "You're so unshakable."

"It's a matter of degree. Let's keep that degree to a minimum, shall we?"

Back out on the field, Bueller continued to throw harder as the night progressed. Butterfield, Dubois and Stokes were no match for the smoke he was throwing. Evans sensed something, but he couldn't zero in on it. The minds of the Giants were too pat. They thought less than other Earthlings he had observed. But still, they were vulnerable to the Ball Fourian mind-game. All except O'Nealy. How was he different?

As O'Nealy took the mound for the bottom of the eighth, Evans walked up to the front of the dugout to get a closer read on this odd Giant pitcher. Jake Conrad came up to stand beside him.

"What are you looking for, Warren? You've hardly said a word to me all game."

"Sorry, Jake, I'm concentrating on O'Nealy."

"Trying to find a chink in the armor, huh?"

"That's right. Let's see if we can find something."

Evans was grateful Conrad let him concentrate. He kept his mind on O'Nealy, trying to pick up every thought possible. All he heard during Darvel Nixon's at-bat were numbers. That's it! No mind chatter, no offhanded thought about who was at the plate or the condition of his arm. There was just mental silence except for the errorless sequence of numbers. It was as though O'Nealy were in the white mind except for the open-minded projection of the next number in the sequence. What could it possibly mean? Was it a focusing technique, or a code?

Nixon grounded out harmlessly to Renker at short. By checking the list of digits in "pi," Evans could compute how many pitches O'Nealy had thrown. Seventy-three. Up came Martin. There was no advice to give, he was on his own, but Evans was gratified that, as a catcher, Martane had the whitest mind on the squad. Perhaps he was less vulnerable to the confusion generated by the odd goings-on on the mound.

Martin took the first pitch for a ball. The second he fouled off. The third he missed to go to 1 and 2. Wait, thought Evans, O'Nealy has left the sequence. He had thought the number "8" twice in a row. That was inconsistent with "pi." O'Nealy threw the next pitch low and Martin laid off. A "2," observed Evans. Is he reversing the sequence?

O'Nealy let the next pitch, a slider that was meant to go up and in, drift ever so slightly out over the plate. Martin swung from his heels and met it cleanly. The crowd rose to its feet with the crack of the bat, and went delirious as it cleared the fence in deep left-center. Billy groaned. O'Nealy knew he had slipped. Evans knew that O'Nealy had doubled back on the "pi" sequence when he reached the seventy-fifth digit, the implications of which were vague. There was nothing vague about Martin's homer, though. O'Nealy was vulnerable, perhaps tiring, and the score was now 3-2.

Chambers felt he had to go to the mound. Billy trotted out. The other players knew better than to interfere.

"How are you, Brad?" Chambers inquired. Getting tired?"

"I've thrown seventy-eight pitches, Skipper. Nah, I just screwed up. What do you think, Billy?"

"Feel good?" asked Billy.

"Feel good." That was enough for Chambers, who ran back to the dugout.

Evans had strained to pick up the conversation, and when O'Nealy had referred to "seventy-eight pitches," he knew it was no coincidence. O'Nealy was perfectly aware of what he was doing. Evans wished he was as aware. Did O'Nealy use this sequence to count his pitches?

O'Nealy went back to work with a vengeance, striking out Rifkin and snaring Nichols' smash grounder to the mound and relaying it on Butterfield to end the inning. That was too close, thought Brad, once in the safer confines of the dugout.

The crowd clapped and yelled, "defense, defense!" as the Giants came up in the top of the ninth. Cleveland was still behind, but back in it as far as the faithful were concerned. The crowd noise was somehow soothing to Willie Washington as he stepped in. The incessant roar made it feel like an extraordinary moment in an ordinary game, like it was supposed to. He cleared his mind as he stepped in.

Back in the dugout Billy resolved to make every effort to hit one out, short of mind gambits. 3-2 was too little support to offer Brad as he went into the bottom of the ninth.

Up at the plate, Washington telegraphed fastball, blanked his mind and swung. He got air as the sinker dropped below his bat. He repeated the thought sequence, swung a little lower and missed as Bueller pulled the string on a high slider. Willie stepped out, smacked his cleats with his bat and shook his head to relax his mind. He stepped back in thinking, all right, all right, throw me junk! I'm ready. The fastball came in low and tight. Washington dropped the bat-head down and golfed at the ball. It had distance as it traveled toward left field, but the slashing golf swing had given it a wicked hook. Would it stay fair? Washington, frozen at the plate, watched and waited. A huge groan was emitted by the crowd when the ball banged into the foul pole and bounced over toward Pantuso in left. Washington made the circuit in a brisk romp. 4-2, Giants.

Billy, waiting on deck, advanced to the plate with determination. Let's give Brad one more. He dug in at the plate. Throw me your best, suckers, he thought, give me your best!

The phrase sounded familiar to Martin. Where have I heard that before?

Vanbellen, challenge him!
With pleasure, Martane.

Billy pulled the ensuing pitch deep but foul. Give me your best, suckers! Martin suddenly shivered. Belteron used to think the very same thoughts. Ah, the unfortunate, departed Belteron. This Icarus fights with the same valor. *Turn up the heat, Vambellen.* The crack of the bat silenced the already stunned crowd. Van De Kirk raced back at full speed, leapt as he hit the warning track and sailed toward the fence. An instant before he struck it, he snared the ball in his outstretched glove.

Billy sat back down in the subdued dugout. He smiled to himself as he thought, Alvendak, you are as brilliant as I remember you. 4-2 must suffice. But you shall have your cuts, my friend.

Billy didn't have long to wait for the face-off. Simpson flew out to Smith in right and Butterfield went down on three fastballs.

Three outs to go. Fernandez, Van De Kirk and Jefferson in the way. O'Nealy was a study of composure. One who studied him was Warren Evans, lounging casually against the railing in the Indians' dugout. There was nothing casual, however, about the attention he was paying O'Nealy. There on the mound was a twenty-three year old rookie, cloaked in a white mind. Why? How? Can mentally imbalanced humans emulate the white mind?

Between them, the three Cleveland hitters who waited had hit over one hundred twenty home runs during the season. If O'Nealy was aware of this, it didn't show in his demeanor. Evans detected not a ripple when Jimmy Fernandez advanced to the plate.

Fernandez caught a piece of the slider that Brad started him off with. It spun uselessly away behind the Giants' dugout and into the crowd. O'Nealy then wasted a couple; Fernandez refused the bait. Ahead of the count, the batter dug in a bit closer to the plate. O'Nealy promptly flattened him with a high, hard one. The crowd erupted into boos and jeers. For the first time of the night, Fernandez had every reason to expect something to hit, something over the plate. The pitch that followed appeared destined for the middle, but broke down and in at the last instant. Fernandez fouled it off his foot.

He hobbled about for a moment or two, as Jake Conrad emerged from the dugout; he was waved back. As Fernandez dug in, he suppressed the urge to scan for the sign. Expecting another fast one, he was way out in front of the change-up, but caught it nonetheless off the end of the bat. It bounced weakly toward Roberts at third who raced in from his deep position. Deftly scooping the erratically hopping ball with his bare hand, he hurled a sidewinder toward Butterfield, pulling him off the bag. The official scorer awarded a single.

Now came the battle with Alan Van De Kirk that Billy had been waiting for. Twice Brad threw speed on the inside corner, and twice Van De Kirk swung mightily but in vain. O'Nealy turned his back to home plate and toyed with the rosin bag. The crowd chanted, "Van de man, Van de man!" Evans watched for mental activity, found none but noted that the number sequence was still traveling on its backward march through the digits of "pi." When

O'Nealy set, looked at the runner and threw, Van De Kirk barely moved a muscle as the change-up drifted outside for a ball. Nor would he reach for the next bit of waste. He thrust his chin out and dug in for the 2 and 2 pitch. The high, outside fastball blazed in so rapidly that Van De Kirk barely got his bat out. But he caught it squarely and pushed it on a rope out above the first base bag. Fernandez was off with the crack of the bat and flew like the wind as the ball made it past Mitch Simpson into the corner. Determining that it was too late to get Fernandez, Simpson shot a strike on one perfect hop to third to try to get Van De Kirk. As he slid in, Van De Kirk mentally screamed *Lookout!*, which caused Roberts to take his eye off the ball for an instant. It bounced off his shin and rolled away behind him. Van De Kirk jumped out of his slide and turned the corner in one motion, but dove back as the alert Archie Stokes had backed up the play. Giants, 4-3, and no one out. Hunk Jefferson advanced to the plate. The press corps up in the box wondered aloud why no one was getting up in the Giants' bullpen.

Billy ran out to the mound. He regarded the grim-faced boy who suddenly looked like the rookie he was.

Billy broke into a broad grin. "Don't you just love this game?"

Brad took the ball from Billy's hand and smiled back. "Yes, I do."

Jefferson, who batted left-handed, gave Billy a clear look at Van De Kirk at third, but also presented a real challenge to the southpaw O'Nealy. Brad's first offering was a curveball so perfectly placed that Jefferson had no choice but to watch it curl in for a strike. It had broken a good two feet. Van De Kirk remained motionless at third. The next pitch, a roaring forkball, zipped under Jefferson's vicious rip. Van De Kirk, who broke toward home when he saw Jefferson begin to swing, was startled by Billy's quick toss to Roberts. The call was close but the umpire gave it to Van De Kirk.

Brad peered in. Billy gave the sign. Jefferson cocked his bat. O'Nealy went into his stretch, checked the runner and threw with all his might at the plate, his left arm a blur. The ball floated in so slowly that Jefferson lost his grip on the bat as he tried to slow it down. Van De Kirk had to leap out of the way to avoid getting hit. The third-base umpire drew a hand from the crowd as he fielded the bat on one bounce.

One out, man on third, bottom of the ninth. The crowd knew, the benches knew and, of course, Tony Pantuso knew as he walked up to bat. A fly ball would tie it, a homer would win it. O'Nealy grabbed the rosin bag, squeezed it and slammed it back down. Evans, still perched on the dugout steps, finally detected an emotion cross the mind of Brad O'Nealy. It flickered so quickly it was unrecognizable, but it caused him to shiver.

O'Nealy fired three straight sliders in three different locations, all of which Pantuso fouled off. He followed with two tosses off the plate, neither to Pantuso's liking. Brad knew he had one last chance to draw Pantuso to a pitch he did not like. Billy knew as well. O'Nealy dropped the stretch, and went into a full wind-up. Brad threw it where Billy waited for it, but it never got there. Pantuso reached out, got under it and pulled the ball toward Washington in left. Willie poised himself under it, then took two steps back. Van De Kirk waited at third. Willie positioned himself perfectly and caught the ball running in, and in one motion hurled it home. Van De Kirk tagged, and Billy Icarus set himself in front of the plate. The crowd bellowed to a crescendo.

The ball and Van De Kirk arrived at the plate so close together that it was impossible to see whether Billy caught it before Van De Kirk crashed into him. Billy had so effectively sealed off home plate that Van De Kirk never reached it. As the two men lay sprawled out in the dust, the umpire circled them to try to make a call. When Billy lifted the ball out of his mitt and held it up above his prostrate body, the umpire's thumb jerked up.

First Commissioner Tarn had been on his feet with the rest of the crowd, but, until the collision, Dr. Avion had remained somewhat disinterested. Only then did he propel himself out of his seat. When Icarus held the ball up and got to his feet, Tarn sent a message. *He appears to be all right.* Dr. Avion sat down.

Billy dusted himself off and walked over to Van De Kirk, who was seated in the dirt. He reached down, offering Van De Kirk a hand. Van De Kirk took it, and Billy pulled him up. "Are you all right?"

A startled Van De Kirk replied, "Yes, I'm fine."

Billy leaned in to say above the crowd noise, "That was a valiant effort, my friend."

Van De Kirk cocked his head with surprise, then smiled. Billy turned and walked toward the dugout.

The Giants poured out onto the field and smothered him in congratulations. He accepted a few before waving his teammates back into the dugout. In less than a minute, there was not a Giant in sight. Evans stared into the empty dugout trying to glean some understanding from what has just taken place. One thing was clear: the Giants had taken the first game of the Series, 4-3.

27

While his team cleaned up and dressed, Warren Evans walked around as discreetly as possible and gathered all the data he could concerning pitches Icarus had called and O'Nealy had thrown. The information was sketchy in the first two innings, but complete from then on. Conrad always had an observer upstairs recording the pitch selection for analysis, and Evans could get a better picture of the beginning of the game from him, though the information was not altogether accurate. He reached the man by phone and recorded the pitch-by-pitch. Once this was done, he went into his office, locked the door and transmitted the data to Ygarnen. He wanted a complete correlation as soon as possible.

Jake Conrad gathered the boys together and gave the "it's only one game" speech, then called the coaches into conference. Evans had anticipated it, and had called a meeting with Abe Watkins in a hour's time. By then the data from the game would be analyzed. He could suffer through this useless conference with the Earthlings until then.

In the visitors' clubhouse, no such meeting was taking place. The Giants dressed as quickly as possible and jumped aboard the team bus to the hotel. All their meetings in Cleveland would be held there, in a more secure setting.

Back in the hotel conference room, members of the Giants' road crew had been busy during the evening. The biofeedback machines had been set up on a bank of tables in a corner, and a security guard had been posted outside the door. By the time the team arrived, everything was ready.

Chambers called them to order. "Boys, you were brilliant tonight. And Brad, I don't know how you and Billy did it, but you pulled it off. Billy, you've got the floor."

"Congratulations, everyone," he said as he walked up to the front. "I'm proud of each and everyone of you. Now the gloating ends. That was the one free game I hoped for. We'll not likely get another."

"How'd you and Brad shut them down at the plate?" asked Steve Lafite.

"Steve, I didn't tell the team before and I can't now after the fact. Each of us has his role to play, and the less we know about the whole plan, the less in our minds there'll be to disturb us. We've got a lot to do, so let's get started. Okay. Tonight's game plan worked because we caught them off-guard. No doubt they were busy analyzing what was going on during the game, and it appears they didn't finish the task in time to affect the outcome. Good. But they will have figured out what took place by game time tomorrow, and we won't be able to use the scheme again. Skipper, did you issue the press release we prepared?"

"Oh, yeah," Chambers responded. "I gave a copy to Red Henderson, one to a network TV guy and another to Lloyd Cronin, a Cleveland columnist who was scrambling for a story. They all licked their chops and said it would be used."

"Thanks, Lou. It should be a great help. Mickey, what happened out there in the ninth when Van De Kirk slid into third?"

"You tell me, Billy," Roberts answered sheepishly. "I had the ball in my sights, and then, I dunno, all of a sudden I got the feeling I had to duck. I guess I took my eye off the ball."

"Don't feel bad, it didn't cost us. Van De Kirk mentally screamed a warning to distract you. It's a classic Ball Fourian move. And it's not your fault,

Mickey. I didn't warn you that such a tactic would be used because I wanted it to work for them, so they would assume we are typically vulnerable. What we can learn from it is that we need the white mind in the field as well, especially when a baserunner is near. Got it?"

"Boy, do I," said Roberts. Others nodded assent.

"Gentlemen, we tried tonight to present the appearance of a team that was fully human in its approach. What they thought of you, Brad, I won't hazard a guess. I only hope they swallow the bait from the news release, and forget about you until your next start. If our job tonight worked, they'll again be taken aback by what we'll present to them tomorrow night."

No one spoke a word. The entire room waited to hear what was in store for them.

"Tonight, and tomorrow during the day, our task will be simple. By shifts, let's stay on the biofeedback machines as long as possible. When not on the machines, rest, relax, meditate, stretch, stay loose. Get inside your minds, feel comfortable there, and tomorrow night, when we arrive on the field..."

In the executive offices of the Cleveland Indians, a midnight gathering was just underway. It was attended by Abe Watkins, two Operation scouts and two security agents. Warren Evans was the last to arrive.

"Where is The First Commissioner?" inquired Evans as he settled into his chair.

"Surprisingly, he declined the invitation to attend. He told me that he was here as an observer of the Universe Series and that he had no intention of interfering with our running of the Earthside Operation. He went on to say that he had complete confidence in our ability. That's all he said, and I let it go at that."

"Very well," said Evans in a muted, dubious tone. "I have the analysis of the data from Ygarnen."

"As do I," said Watkins, "and I can't say that I'm surprised. What is your opinion, Evan?"

"I've only begun to digest it, but one thing is clear. By correlating the pitches called with the number sequence, an obvious code appears. Now, the central question is, why the use of a code?"

"That also should be obvious," answered Watkins.

"The sign-stealing controversy earlier in the year?" offered Evans.

"That was my initial thought."

"Mine as well, Abakin," said Evans. "It is supremely ironic that a meddling, young computer hacker whom we have already dealt with should inadvertently be the cause of our losing the first game of the Universe Series."

"It is indeed. And please accept that I understand there is no blame to be assessed. The team was thrown off and run production stymied until we could discover the nature of the unusual mind-set. But there is a bright side. They have no way of knowing that we have cracked the code. We gave no sign

256

tonight that we are aware of what they were doing. It should give us an edge in tomorrow night's contest, if not for the rest of the Series."

"I anticipate what you will advise next," said Evans with a knowing smile. "We shall distribute copies of the code to all team members. They shall commit them to memory and practice a speedy conversion to the real pitch to be thrown. This is not above their abilities. They should easily master the code and quick response to signals by game time tomorrow. It will be good for morale. Their time will be occupied with valuable endeavor."

"Have we missed anything?" said Watkins, glancing around the room.

"I watched the minds of those in view," replied Evans. "I saw nothing unusual. They are typical Earthlings, with typical foibles. I took particular note of Billy Icarus. Although a supreme batsman, I believe the code was complex enough that he failed to process it completely, causing the muffed catches at the plate. In conversations on the mound, he appeared to be trying to blame O'Nealy. Again, it was the typical Earthling trait of avoiding responsibility for one's shortcomings."

"An interesting and undoubtedly accurate observation. But what of O'Nealy?" Watkins asked.

"He is of a different sort, I must admit," Evans replied.

"If I may be so bold as to offer a theory," interrupted one of the scouts.

"By all means, Dartex," said Watkins.

"I have read the scouting reports on O'Nealy from the Indians' organization, and I spoke with both Alvandek and Martane. The conclusion I have reached is that O'Nealy is unusual in that he is highly educated, having gone to a prestigious Earthling university. His highly evolved mind was suited to the task of the complex code, and exhibited white-mind characteristics because of the deep concentration required while utilizing it."

"Evan, do you concur?"

"Yes, Abakin, I do. I do, however, offer the regret of not realizing until now the value of the Earthling scouting reports. I should have prepared more. I assumed that there were few variances in human personality with which to deal."

"Your successful season lulled you into complacency, and understandably so," responded Watkins with studied forgiveness in his voice. "From tomorrow we shall be better prepared. I suspect we shall easily put this Earthling team away with dispatch."

"I have no doubt," said Evan. "To work?"

"Yes, to work."

The following morning, the phone rang during Abe Watkins' breakfast.

"Abe, It's Warren."

"Good morning, Evan. Don't worry, this line has been secured."

"Excellent. Have you seen this morning's paper?"

"Yes. I am reading it now."

"Have you seen Lloyd Cronin's article?" asked Evans.

"Yes, I have. We surmised correctly. It is again ironic that someone trouble-some in the early season now unwittingly offers us guidance."

"Yes, it is, but it is so. Manager Lou Chambers of the Giants has declared openly that a code was required to assure that no sign-stealing took place during the Series. Now, we can proceed knowing that our efforts won't be in vain. The men have been studying the code since last night. I guarantee that they shall be prepared."

"No doubt. I look forward to tonight's contest. See you at the ballpark. Abakin out."

Jake Conrad and Warren Evans sat side-by-side in the dugout as Cy Ellerbach took his final warm-up tosses prior to the start of the second game of the Universe Series. Conrad was a bit agitated, as the puddle of tobacco juice at his feet indicated.

"God, I hope the boys settle down after last night, Warren."

"Oh, I think they're ready to play," said Evans in a confident voice.

"I almost forgot, Warren. You think I don't notice, but I saw what you did today, and thanks. Making sure that scouting report on Strongbow got out to all the players was real good stuff. I saw them studying it all day."

"It was the least I could do, Jake," Evans replied. The cover story had worked. Conrad was so gullible.

"Well, here it goes," said Conrad as Eddie Renker walked toward the plate. "Hope Cy's got his stuff."

Unceremoniously, Evans got up and walked to the railing to have a closer view.

Behind home plate, Eddie Martin scanned Renker's mind, but to no avail. Nothing there, only strange static. It wasn't exactly the white mind, but it was unreadable. At a loss as to what to call, he recalled that Renker never swung at the first pitch. Fastball, down the middle.

Renker crunched the ball so hard and low that the third base umpire fell over avoiding it. From his seated position on the turf, he indicated that it was fair. As the ball bounced around in the corner in left-field foul territory, Renker never even slowed up until he was well around second base. Being the first inning, he wisely held up.

Up came Mickey Roberts. Evans twitched in the Cleveland dugout and sent the message, Watch minds carefully. Martin shrugged his shoulders toward the dugout before responding, Yes, Evan. He crouched down and took a long, mental look at Roberts. Nothing. Avoid heat and upper zone, Ellerban.

Roberts' at-bat alternated between fouled-off pitches and near-strikes until it reached 3 and 2. Martin had yet to glean a thought from Roberts' mind. He could feel Ellerbach straining on the mound to read Roberts. They chose a cautious pitch.

"Ball four!" yelled the umpire, and Roberts sprinted to first. Only then did Martin call time. Evans beat him to the mound.

"What the hell's he doin'?" said Jake Conrad to no one in particular. It was all he could do to resist running out there himself.

"Martane, what happened in the first two at-bats?" Evans asked as they approached Ellerbach.

"Evan, they have closed minds. These are not the same players we saw last night."

"It's true, Evan," added Ellerbach. "I hear nothing."

"Let's settle down. If we cannot read them, we must attempt mind decoys." He rushed back to the dugout.

"Something wrong with Cy?" asked Conrad.

"No. Just wanted to settle him down before it gets out of hand, Jake," Evans replied.

Rick Barker was up. Martin projected fastball toward him. Barker heard fastball, held up and watched a curve come in for a strike. He stepped out of the batter's box and walked back to the on-deck circle, pretending to need some pine tar. Now it begins, he thought, let it go...

Barker closed his eyes, took a deep breath and stepped back in. Martin signaled slider to Ellerbach, and curve to Barker, who punched the ball into right-center for a single. Roberts held at second, but Renker scored.

Jake Conrad went to the phone and got McTell and Sanchez up in the bullpen. Evans wanted to go out to the mound, but knew he couldn't, or Conrad would panic and send in someone too quickly. Abe Watkins got on the phone in the owner's booth.

"It's for you, Warren," said Conrad, exasperated that Watkins should want Evans. He was tired of being out of the loop.

Evans watched as Washington stepped up to the plate. "Yes?"

"What is happening, Warren?"

Washington took a strike. "They apparently have closed minds tonight. They do not appear to be in the same mind-state. They have changed."

"How is it possible?" asked Watkins.

"It is presently unexplainable. Good! Did you see? Washington has struck out. Ellerbach is settling down. We'll just have to observe and adapt, Abe. Would you suggest another course?"

"No. I only hope the code helps us against Strongbow. Bye."

Billy Icarus came up. Martin scanned him as he approached. Nothing. He continued to scan as he called for the pitch. Still nothing. He automatically decoyed a signal to Icarus, not really expecting an impact. Martin was momentarily without confidence. Evans could feel it in the dugout, but could do nothing. At least Ellerbach was confident on the mound, after the strike out of Washington.

The count went to 1 and 2. Ellerbach tried to slip a slider by on the corner, but it floated a bit. Billy sent it out of the park. Giants, 4-0, one out. Conrad had seen enough. Before Evans could do or say a thing, Conrad was on his way to the mound. He signaled for the left-hander, Spanky McTell. He wanted him against the left-handed Simpson and Butterfield.

No one got up to greet Billy as he walked into the dugout. They were all inside themselves, and were apprehensive, lest they should break the spell. Billy worried for their sake, but admired their efforts. As a team, they were united in the pursuit of the white mind.

McTell made short work of Simpson and Butterfield, striking out the former and inducing the latter into a ground out. The disheartened crowd in the stands breathed a sigh of relief, as did Evans. Now, hopefully, knowing the signal code would produce some quick runs to bring them back into the game.

Dizzy Rifkin was the first to face Jimmy Strongbow and Billy Icarus. After the last warm-up toss, Billy ran the ball out, handed it to Jimmy and said a few words of encouragement. Rifkin took in the unusual sight of Icarus with his thick, black beard and Strongbow with his tall frame and long, dangling hair. Indeed they are an odd pair, he reflected.

As they settled in for the first pitch, Rifkin scanned Icarus' mind. Nothing! Quickly, he scanned the mound. Again, nothing! Strike one. He hadn't had time to set for the pitch.

In the dugout, Evans had taken it all in. The Giants' battery, like their hitters, had white minds! How were they doing it, and how were they signaling? This could not be!

The players on the Cleveland bench watched with dismay as Rifkin went down on three pitches. Immediately, they realized to a man that something was wrong. As Buck Nichols and Jimmy Fernandez took their turns at the plate, they froze at the lack of information to be read from Icarus and Strongbow. They shared the same fate as Rifkin. Side retired on strikeouts.

Evans was also frozen into near-inaction. A conversation with Watkins did nothing to help the situation. The unthinkable, the unpredictable was happening. How did one react? What strategies to employ?

McTell gave them two innings to settle down. He and Martin had dropped into white-minded play with satisfying results, and, once again, the Giants were lambs at the plate. White-minded as well, but nonetheless lambs. Icarus reached base on a single, but was stranded.

Through three innings, Strongbow had held them hitless with seven strikeouts. Evans and Watkins had agreed on a course of action. Walking slowly in front of the bench in the bottom of the third, Evans individually informed his players to search for confidence and to concentrate on individual achievement. *Rifkin, concentrate. Yes, Evan. Denser, Alvandek, Topon, relax your minds, play from within. Yes, Evan. Spantell and Martane, ignore hitters and pitch your game. Yes, Evan. Darnix, Bolnici, Vernanden, attempt to read Icarus and Strongbow, but do not be distracted. Yes, Evan.*

The fourth inning passed, the Indians remained without a baserunner and McTell was having equal success against the Giants' side. Tarn and Dr. Avion watched with interest from their place in the crowd. With their heightened perceptions, they fully grasped the white-minded nature of the Giants. *Avion, it is as though we are witnessing a game on Ball Four, is it not? Yes, Tarn, my friend, it is amazing. What unexpected capacities these Earthlings possess. Indeed, Avion.*

McTell's mastery of the Giants slackened in the fifth, as Butterfield doubled, Dubois sacrificed him to third and Stokes brought him home on a fly to center. Renker ended the inning, a victim of a strikeout. Giants, 5-0.

In the Cleveland half of the fifth, Alan Van De Kirk ended Jimmy's perfect game and shutout with the first pitch, which he parked in deep left. As Van De Kirk rounded the bases, Billy ran to the mound while the crowd noise was still deafening.

"You're doing fine, Jimmy. It was a good pitch. Don't worry." Jimmy gave him a tight smile and nodded.

Only a brilliant, diving catch by Barker in right-center stopped Jefferson from getting on with extra bases. Jimmy was a little shaken, but Billy couldn't risk scanning him. It was clear to him before the game that such action could be deadly. He knew full well that if Evans happened to be concentrating on him at the time, he'd detect it. It wouldn't do to have him know that there was mind-scanning taking place on the Giants' team, most certainly not in this game, at least.

Tony Pantuso was the next Indian to draw blood. On the third pitch, a curve outside the strike zone, he reached down and sent it screaming down the line in right. It barely cleared the fence at the shortest part of the park. Giants, 5-2.

Billy didn't even go to the mound, though Chambers momentarily wished *he* could. If for nothing but show, he got Lafite and Santiago up in the bullpen. It was an unnecessary ploy, as Jimmy dug down deep and blew six strikes past Smith and Nixon.

The Indians never really threatened again. Had Billy been able to take a look, he would have seen, in Jimmy Strongbow's mind, an eagle perched on the railing of the upper deck behind home plate, preening his feathers. He would have sensed the grim determination of Geronimo, Mangus, Juh and Naiche as they refused to knuckle under to General Crook. The arrow was swift, the snake sudden and heartless. Only Van De Kirk managed to reach base again, and that on a bloop single in the seventh.

Spanky McTell pitched the rest of the game, scattering three hits but allowing no more runs. Even Billy, who had faced him countless times on Ball Four, was impressed. McTell gave up a double to him in the sixth, but struck him out to end the Giants' ninth.

The game ended, 5-2, and the Giants had won both games in Cleveland.

The game hadn't been over four minutes when Billy asked Chambers to meet him in his office. "We did it again," said Chambers with a look somewhere between amazement and elation.

"Yes, Lou, but it raises all kinds of concerns."

"Such as?"

"The powers that be among the Ball Fourians are most certainly reacting strongly," said Billy. "We have no way of knowing what their response will be, but there is the possibility of danger."

"Why do you say that? You've made it clear that your people are peaceful. What's there to fear?"

"I know I'm possibly being overcautious, but I think we should get out of here as quickly as possible. Mental tampering is non-violent, but in baseball it could be quite effective."

"Mental tampering?" asked Chambers with a look of shock. "What kind of thing are you talking about?"

"Look, I've never shared this with anyone, but I've had my doubts about certain events since I've been here. Remember the sign-stealing story that surfaced, then quickly disappeared?"

"Sure. We used that against them with the news release last night."

"Well, when I was training with the team before I was deselected, it was made clear that mind-disrupting tactics would be used to assist us in both infiltration and security. Nothing was specific, but I've always suspected that harsh means might be used to avoid detection, and no doubt extraordinary means were used to suppress the sign-stealing story. Do you recall how it came out in *USA Today* and then vanished? There was an article indicating that the charges couldn't be substantiated. The people who made the original claims all of a sudden refused to talk to the press. I think evidence was destroyed. The long and short of it is: we don't know, with the personnel at hand, what the Operation might decide to do.

"Even if agents of the operation choose to do something less diabolical, they'll at least make an effort to discover a way into our heads. While doing that, if they learn that the Giants know they're aliens, or if they learn my identity, they might, well, arrest me. What I've done is unprecedented, so I have no idea how they'll react. Let's get out of town and secure in San Francisco as quickly as possible. Can you help?"

"I don't know," replied Chambers, scratching his head. "I suppose I could call the airport and see if the charter can fly tonight."

"Do it, please. It's for the safety of the club."

"Of course, I'll get right on it."

"Thanks. Hey, Lou, there's one more thing, and I hope I haven't rattled you enough to make it difficult to do. I need you to release something else to the news media."

"Oh, I'm a tough old bastard. This is a very weird year, but I've had worse. What do you need?"

Billy handed him a paper. "I want you to release this statement to the press, now, when the media swamps you."

Chambers looked it over. "You want to make the biofeedback stuff public? Why? Wait a minute, I'm starting to think like you. You released the code business to throw off your alien buddies, and now you want them to think our white minds are because of the biofeedback, right? Don't even answer, I've got you cold."

Billy erupted in a huge smile, which relaxed his mildly perturbed state. "Lou, you'd make a great Ball Fourian. Yes, you've got me cold. Do you agree?"

"You bet. It's the right thing to do. It'll buy some time, at least. And I think you'd make a decent human, too."

"You know, Skip, I like being human, almost feel like one of you. We're not so far apart, we could easily coexist in peace. I want to win, sure, but pardon me if I tell you that I admire my fellow players from Ball Four. They're a courageous bunch, so far from home. They're sportsmen, like ourselves, and they'd be fair-minded if their arrogance would allow them."

"It's their arrogance that's beaten them more than we have, don't you think?"

"Yes," said Billy. "For now, at least. Let's hope we haven't humiliated them into any untoward actions."

Warren Evans didn't even wait to see if Conrad was going to call a meeting. He changed quickly and headed up to talk to Watkins.

"You're alone this time," Evans noted as he walked in.

"Others will be along shortly. What happened, Evan?"

"The Giants were immune to any mind gambits or suggestions. And they were mind-sealed. I hesitate to say they played with the white mind, but for all intents and purposes, they affected the state. The battery, Strongbow and Icarus, most definitely had totally secure minds. We got nothing from them all night. It upset the team, and we never recovered. If we had known from the start, we could have used a classic Ball Fourian attack, as though we were back home, but we're out of practice. For some players, it's been years since we needed our traditional skills and strategies."

"The question is how could they do it, and why?" posed Watkins.

"Let's look at what we have. Last night they appeared to have readable minds and tonight they were closed. O'Nealy pitched employing an obvious code and tonight there was no evidence of a readable code. There is no precedence from our experience on Earth to draw any conclusions. One thing is clear: twice they've played games they needed to play in order to defeat a Ball Fourian team. And yet, there is no possibility of their knowing about our nature."

"We do know they easily could have been reacting to the sign-stealing allegations in last night's contest, but I have great difficulty explaining their actions tonight," said Watkins. "Ah, here is Dartex."

Dartex entered and quickly took a seat. "I have interesting news for us," he said breathlessly, as though he'd been running.

"What do you have?" Watkins inquired.

"I arranged for a scouting team to monitor all post-game statements made by Giants," related Dartex, "and the manager of the team, Lou Chambers, just revealed something of supreme interest. I myself was watching the local news coverage when he spoke."

"What was said?" asked Evans.

"He announced that, for the past two or more months, the Giants have been engaged in a rigorous mental training program, which has included T'ai Chi, meditation and the use of biofeedback technology. Apparently, through the use of machines that monitor brain activity, the players have been trained to emit alpha waves, an indicator of what Earthlings might call a relaxed or creative state. Chambers maintained that the use of these techniques has improved the players' concentration on the field and has been responsible for a general mental wholesomeness for the team. He credits the program for the entire success of the Giants this season."

"There we have it, gentlemen," said Watkins authoritatively.

"I have to agree,"responded Evans. "but what is known about this field of human endeavor?"

"I admit to some ignorance," said Dartex. "But, if I am following the same train of thought as you, Abakin, there is the likelihood that the Giants may have inadvertently emulated the white mind by training themselves to emit these so-called alpha waves. I took the liberty of dispatching agents to investigate this area of human activity. They have been told to report forthwith."

"When can we expect their report?" asked Watkins.

"Momentarily," replied Dartex.

"Good until then, at least we have a working theory. Suffice to say, it is relaxing to know there is a logical explanation for the aberrant behavior of this team. With information, all is not lost. Let's brainstorm strategies, shall we?"

The Giants succeeded in leaving Cleveland by two in the morning. By five o'clock, west coast time, a tired but elated team settled into their hastily arranged quarters at the Hampton Airport Hotel. It would be their home until the Series ended, or they went back to Cleveland.

At noon, the team was aboard a bus to nearby Candlestick Park. It had been sealed to all but members of the team. A security system was set up to check the identity of all grounds crew and concession workers as they entered. By the time the team arrived, their equipment was in place and the biofeedback machines were ready to go. The agenda had been determined and the players busied themselves with T'ai Chi, meditation and time on the machines. With the exception of O'Nealy and Strongbow, Billy had the entire pitching staff working in both bullpens. He ran back and forth between the two as game simulations were taking place. After carefully monitoring their progress for more than two hours, he asked for a meeting with Chambers.

"We have a problem, Lou," Billy began.

"And what would that be?"

"Jimmy and Brad can't pitch every game, but the rest of the staff is a bit weak on the white mind. French is our strongest and best bet, although Inky Powell is physically the most compelling. But mentally, Inky's not there yet. The rest of the staff is shaky at best, although I'd go with Lafite in a pinch."

"They're not ready to face the Indians?" asked Chambers with a worried look.

"Yes and no. Don't get me wrong, they all exhibit white-mind characteristics and they've worked hard on their visualization techniques, but will it hold up under pressure? I can't say. The pitcher's the most vulnerable to the Ball Fourian game, next to the catcher, of course. Jimmy and Brad are very special people. But somebody else has to pitch tomorrow."

"You're the best one to pick," said Chambers.

"I'll work with French and Lafite. They'll have to do."

As game time approached, Candlestick Park was bathed in the glorious autumn weather of the San Francisco Bay Area, and fifty-five thousand adoring fans screamed tributes to their heroes during the endless pregame ceremonies. None but a select few had any idea of the apprehension of both teams on the field. Abe Watkins was well-aware, sitting with Elliot Edwards in their luxury suite on the mezzanine level. Watkins had fortunately been able to purchase a similar suite for the First Commissioner and his guest, who were surrounded by an entourage of agents. Watkins was hoping to avoid any contact between them and humans, but Edwards had asked for an introduction to what Watkins was passing off as "important foreign business associates" from his interests outside of baseball. Edwards won the battle, and the meeting took place without apparent problem. Tarn was masterful in his use of broken English and was totally convincing as a Swiss investment banker. Dr. Avion was equally effective, repeating "sorry, sorry" while smiling and nodding. Edwards was suitably impressed by the twenty bodyguards that surrounded the pair, and acted as though he were in the presence of royalty, which, in a sense, he was.

As the visiting team, the Indians came up to bat in the top of the first. They threatened immediately when the first hitter walked, the second sacrificed, and Jimmy Fernandez singled. With two on and one out, Alan Van De

Kirk drew blood with a sacrifice fly that Barker caught in the deepest part of center field. A shaken Art French managed to get Pantuso to ground out to retire the side.

In the Cleveland dugout, Evans conferred quickly with Van De Kirk.

"This French has a whitened mind, but I could `feel' him think slider at the very end of his delivery. I reacted and hit the pitch for the fly ball. He may be vulnerable."

"Good. I'll relay that to all players," replied Evans to the hopeful news.

Emilio Sanchez, starting for the Indians, looked over at Evans as Renker approached the plate.

Scan deeply, Zaan, but if nothing, stop. Pitch pure game.

Yes, Evan.

Sanchez could read nothing, but his "pure game" was enough to put down the Giants in order.

French was reached for two more runs in the second, as Jefferson, playing in right field for Smith because of the absence of the designated-hitter rule in the National League, homered to start the inning. French allowed the other run on a walk and a hit before putting out the fire.

"What do you think, Billy?" asked a nervous Chambers.

"I can't scan his mind during the game, but three runs are not good. If he doesn't settle down, it's Lafite. You make the call."

Washington worked Sanchez for a walk and Billy advanced to the plate. He contentedly took two strikes, watching and gauging the pitches. The third pitch, a confident, screaming fastball, low and away, was a gift for Billy Icarus. He sent it bouncing around in the upper deck in right field. The Giants were back in it, trailing 3-2.

Sanchez smoothed his mind and easily dispatched the left-handed Simpson and Butterfield on strikes.

"This feels more like a game of baseball than those mysteries we experienced in Cleveland," said a contented Van De Kirk to Evans.

"Yes, let's play baseball," replied Evans with confidence.

And baseball they played. Art French worked his way out of trouble in the third, and Sanchez put the Giants down, one-two-three in his half. But French never survived the fourth. After Pantuso doubled and Nixon singled him home, Lafite was up in the bullpen. Before he could get loose, Martin had doubled Nixon home. French managed to strike out Sanchez, but Chambers had seen enough. Lafite got Rifkin to ground out, but Nichols singled Nixon in before Lafite could end the inning, striking out Fernandez. Cleveland 6-2.

Lafite contained the Indians through the next three innings, giving the Giants time to pick away at the lead. Barker singled to open the fifth, Washington bunted him over and Billy singled him home. Unfortunately, Simpson hit into a rally-ending double play. In the seventh, Sanchez struck out the side, but not before Barker touched him for a solo home run. Cleveland was still up, 6-4.

The Indians put three singles back-to-back to get a run in the eighth, but

Lafite settled down to subdue the threat. When Billy opened the Giants' eighth with his fourth homer of the Series and Simpson quickly followed with his first blast, Conrad brought in McTell, who answered the call. It was 7-6, but the fans in Candlestick Park had every reason to hope.

Those hopes were dashed when the Indians bashed Lafite, Powell and Santiago for seven runs in an endless top of the ninth. Van De Kirk hit a pair of two-run homers, establishing a World Series record. The rattled Giants went down meekly in their half to end the contest. Cleveland finally had a victory, a convincing 14-6 thrashing.

"You warned me, Billy," said a subdued Chambers during the post-mortem.

"I told you all along that the first game or two would be the only free rides. We have to earn it from here on out. Don't blame French and the boys, it's not their fault. I couldn't check for it, but even against white minds those Ball Fourians are capable of this kind of explosiveness."

"Now we miss Kiley Upton, don't we?"

"Yes, we do, Skipper. But tomorrow's another game, and Brad will be ready. No time now to falter. We've leveled the playing field as best we can, now we just have to play on it."

As Billy finished dressing, he looked around for Art French.

"Where's Art?" he asked Stokes.

"He's soaking in the steam room. Been in there since we came off the field."

Billy stripped hastily, grabbed a towel and headed off to the steam room. There, on a corner bench, sat French.

"Sorry, Billy, I sure blew it," said French through the clouds of vapor.

"Ah, don't sweat it, Art."

"Very funny," said French with a half-hearted chuckle. "I just couldn't do it. I won't see action again, will I?"

"Who knows what will happen before it's all over. Everybody got roughed up tonight."

"Don't try to make me feel better. I blew my shot. I'm sorry."

"Art, you had a helluva season. You helped get us here. They can't take that away from you. As Renker would say, those were freaking aliens out there tonight."

French laughed, openly this time. "Yeah, godammit, they were, weren't they? Thanks, Billy. I better get out of here before I shrivel up and die."

"This was much better, Evan," said Watkins. "I feel I can now look Tarn in the face without shame. We were very dominant tonight."

The post-game meeting was being held in Watkins' suite at the team's hotel. Along with Evan, Dartex and Van De Kirk also attended. "Yes, we fared better. Alvandek, what is your evaluation of their mental game tonight?"

"The pitchers we faced tonight are different from O'Nealy and Strongbow. Not only are they less talented, but mentally weaker. We have found their vulnerability. They have two strong pitchers, we have four or five. They cannot win a Series with two pitchers."

"Yes, we have an edge in pitching now," Evans said, "but the hitters, according to Martane, are still mentally strong. Tonight was a good test of head-to-head offense. They are strong, but we are stronger. If O'Nealy and Strongbow tire, we will have the edge again. Do you concur?"

"Yes," Watkins replied. "We should continue to scan for weaknesses in their mental armor, and hope our hitting superiority will prevail. I must say I am relieved. The mind-disruption option is on hold. For now."

"You truly considered it?" Evans was taken aback.

"A disruption team has been in place since yesterday. The Giants' security is tight, but we have been looking for openings. I did not want to use the option, but in front of Tarn, not to mention the whole of the Ball Fourian people, we have an obligation. We must prevail. The Giants coincidentally emulated the white mind with their limited tools and rituals. They cannot be allowed to win by accident."

"Commitment to victory is the creed of our caste," said Van De Kirk reflexively.

"And victory can be ours," affirmed Evans. "Tomorrow's game against O'Nealy will be an important test of our recovered control."

"Yes," said Watkins. "It will determine many things."

29

The fourth game of the Universe Series featured another match-up between Vance Bueller and Brad O'Nealy. Each team had its own overriding question. Could the Giants hit Bueller without the gambits used in the first game? Would the Indians see the code in use by O'Nealy?

Cleveland had its answer in the first inning. There was no code, and O'Nealy's mind was as white as Strongbow's. Information could not be found from that source. Evans had his men prepared to respond to the realization without distraction. They must use their talent to produce runs, while he scanned the Giants for a weak spot. There was little likelihood of finding one, but it was his duty to search.

By the third inning, the answer to the Giants' question was at least partially apparent. They were hitless. Even Billy had struck out. The team was unalarmed, though, since Brad was having equal success against the Indians. Who would break through first? Billy, from the Giants' dugout, and Evans, from his, looked for ways to break the impasse.

During the Giants' fourth, Chambers took Billy into the clubhouse tunnel. "What'll we do?"

"I don't have an answer, Lou," replied Billy. "Great game, huh?"

"It's down to real ball right now, isn't it?"

"That's a fact. Two great pitchers subduing two great teams. This is now truly a Universe Series. You gotta love it, my friend."

Chambers smiled. "Yeah, you know I do. But get a hit, godammit."

"I'll try. I've hit this Vanbellen before. It's a matter of time."

Back out on the field, Bueller was ruthless. Renker, Roberts and Barker went down on nine strikes. O'Nealy, not to be outdone, returned the favor in the Cleveland fifth. When Bueller retired the Giants in order in the bottom of the inning, the entire stadium, from the press box to the ball boys, became simultaneously aware that this was no ordinary game.

Warren Evans was well-aware, but was unrelenting in his search to find a way to get to O'Nealy. Inning followed inning, and he stood at the far end of the dugout, as far forward as allowed, and scanned the Giants ceaselessly. As the Cleveland sixth got under way, he found what he was looking for.

It was Renker. When O'Nealy threw his last pitch to strike out Darvel Nixon, Evans was scanning Renker. He weakly perceived *fastball, down and out*. Was Renker weakening or was Evans imagining things? When Martin went to the plate, Evans concentrated his mind on Renker. First pitch, *inside curve*. Yes! Second pitch, *slider, middle-low*. Renker was indeed weakening! Martin popped the next pitch up, but by the time it settled in Stokes' glove, Evans was already issuing commands. He walked along the length of the dugout, as though he were going to get a drink from the fountain at the other end, but while he went he was sending a steady stream of instructions. Bueller, walking to the plate, was not receiving, but Evan turned and reiterated the instructions for his benefit. *Listen to me for signs. Yes, Evan.*

Icarus called the pitch. Renker telegraphed it. Evans received it. *Fastball, in.* Bueller pulled it foul. *Change-up, inside corner.* Bueller received, timed his swing and sent it deep to right. Simpson settled under it at the fence and hauled it in to end the inning. The sixth was over, the perfect game intact, but Evans smiled to himself. The end was near. The top of the order came to bat in the seventh.

To verify, he called Bueller over before he took the mound.

"The pitches came in as I called them, did they not?" asked Evans in a whisper.

"Yes, Evan, they did. Do we have them?"

"I believe so." *Pitch strongly, Vanbellen.*

Of course, Evan.

The Giants' sixth featured the bottom of their order, which proved an easy task for Bueller, as he quickly dispatched them on a weak fly ball and two strikeouts.

Now came the Cleveland chance. They did not waste it. Rifkin singled, Nichols doubled, Fernandez walked and Van De Kirk hit the first pitch so deep that it cleared the fence in dead center and bounced down the tunnel in very much the same fashion that Billy's had in his debut so long before. Cleveland 4, Giants 0, and the perfect game was so much history. Billy called time and ran into the dugout. "Skip, tell the umpire that a shin-guard strap has broken." With that, he ran back into the clubhouse tunnel. The ploy would gain him perhaps three minutes.

What had just happened? They have our signs, there is no question. How? Billy ran down the list of possibilities as rapidly as possible. He reached the logical conclusion. Stokes or Renker, most likely Renker. What else could it be? His mind reviewing the preceding events, he arrived back at his previous conclusion. He must risk scanning to detect the leak. If it's Renker or Stokes, Evans' mind will be on one of them. I can mind-scan in relative safety.

Billy ran back out on to the field, pausing in front of the dugout to adjust a shin guard for effect, then hustled back to the plate. Hunk Jefferson was waiting for his turn.

It did not take Billy long to verify his hunch. As he flashed O'Nealy the sign, he scanned Renker. *Fastball, outside.*

Jefferson laid off the errant pitch. This time as he gave the sign, he stole a glance at the Cleveland dugout. There was Evans, plainly peering towards Renker. As the pitch came in, Jefferson swung from the heels. He made fabulous contact, but it was too good. Simpson caught the low smash against the right field fence. Billy used the break to run to the mound. He lost no time. "Brad, you're on your own." Before Brad could speak, he waved for Chambers. Chambers trotted out. Two hitters before, he'd gotten Lafite up in the bullpen. Did Billy want him?

"Skipper, Brad's fine. It's a lucky streak. Please don't jerk him."

"How do you feel, Brad, still got it?"

"I think so, but they sure hurt me."

"Don't worry, Skip, I'll settle him down," Billy stated emphatically.

Chambers and O'Nealy looked at him in confusion, then Chambers spoke abruptly. "Okay." He hurried back to the dugout.

While the meeting took place on the mound, Evans scanned the proceedings intently. Ah, they are in complete disarray. The manager seems to have lost control of the players. He shows feelings of indecisiveness. We have them. As O'Nealy prepared to face Pantuso, Evans returned his attention to Renker.

When Brad looked in for the sign, Billy did not give him one, but got into a position to receive. A thought flashed through Brad's mind. You're on your own. He quickly blanked his mind, wound up and blazed a hard slider past

Pantuso, who seemed taken aback.

Equally caught by surprise was Evans. Renker is silent. Ah, perhaps he missed the sign.

On the next pitch, Pantuso again watched motionlessly as a fastball nipped the inside corner. Evans once again noticed that Renker was silent as to the sign, but mentally agitated. Was his mind-state becoming erratic?

Topon, no more signs.

Yes, Evan.

Pantuso missed the forkball for strike three. Billy muffed the catch as it bounced in the dirt, but recovered the ball in time to apply the tag.

Evans abandoned Renker for the moment, but with each pitch to the next batter, Denny Smith, he scanned various players in the infield. All were silent once more. Back to Renker he went, but the tap had been turned off. Smith grounded out to Roberts at third to end the inning. Evans was dismayed but well-satisfied with the four-run lead.

It was all they would need. Bueller lost his perfect game in the bottom of the seventh when Barker doubled, and then lost his shutout when Billy homered to lead off the eighth. But that would be all the Giants would do against him, as he retired the remaining five hitters for his two-hit victory.

Chambers asked Billy for a conference during the Giants' seventh, but Billy begged off, pleading in a whisper that things were under control. Chambers begrudgingly backed off. From across the way, Evans caught the gist of the conversation, and reflected smugly that the Giants' disarray was continuing unabated.

O'Nealy never gave up another hit. He threw four wild pitches and Billy allowed three passed balls, but since there were no more baserunners, it was meaningless, except to the befuddled onlookers, who wondered at the battery's erratic performance.

Evans accepted the turn of events at face value. Renker weakened, then somehow managed to close up his mind. But he would bear constant observation. It might happen again. For the time being, he was satisfied. Cleveland had won, 4-1, and evened the Series at two games apiece. Watkins could look Tarn in the eyes again.

Things were not so cozy in the San Francisco clubhouse. Instinctively, Chambers closed the locker room to reporters. Players wandered around, dazed and dressing at quarter-speed. Chambers waited for Billy to do something, but when he did not he called Brad and Billy into his office.

"All right," Chambers began, "what happened out there?"

O'Nealy, the brashness gone, stood halfheartedly drying his ears. "Beats the hell out of me," he said, looking to Billy.

"Renker was giving them the signs," he said, matter-of-factly.

"*What*?" asked Chambers, leaping to his feet.

"So that's what was going on," said O'Nealy, the light returning to his eyes. "No wonder you stopped giving me signs."

"That explains the wild pitches and passed balls. Why didn't you tell me? It was agony watching the last two innings."

"Sorry, Lou," Billy replied. "The damage was done, and we had a way to stop the bleeding without giving Evans any more to work with. He saw us in collapse and I didn't want him to see us pull it back together. Let him think until tomorrow that they have us on the run."

"God, you never stop thinking, do you?" Chambers said with exasperation. "They do have us on the run. What can we do to pull this together? We got hurt badly tonight. We had three innings, we could have gotten back in it."

"Not the way Bueller was pitching tonight. He had the confidence of a lead. It gave him the will we had stolen from him in the first game. Listen, Skipper, what's done is done. Let's go back to the hotel and share this with everyone. Together we can put it behind us. Tomorrow's another day. This is baseball. It ain't over till..."

"Yeah, yeah, yeah, Yogi," interrupted Chambers. "That's rich, coming from you."

O'Nealy laughed. "Look at you two, you're like an old married couple."

Chambers grinned, and Billy grinned back. "He's got us, Billy."

"I think I get the point," said Billy. "Let's stop bickering and focus our energies. The Indians will show up tomorrow. They're not going away."

"All right, a team meeting will be good. Let's go out and get the boys going. One thing, though, before we go. How do we handle Renker?"

"He's a tough one, Renker is," said Billy. "He'll probably tighten up for the rest of the Series out of pure nastiness. He wouldn't like us to baby him."

"You're right. Okay, let's get going."

An hour later, just before the meeting was to start, Billy pulled Renker off into a corner of the conference room. "Eddie, I'll come straight to the point. Warren Evans, the Ball Fourian leader of the Indians, caught you open-minded on the pitching signs."

"Oh, Jesus, no," said Renker as he reeled back a step. "Is that why they pounded Brad?"

"Yes. You did it unconsciously, probably an old habit from the past. It caught up with you tonight."

"I blew the whole game," Renker said, shaking his head. Tough as he was, he was near tears.

"We don't know that. The way Bueller was pitching, they might have won anyway. You just got used."

"Well, I'm finished. Put Ogden in. Or maybe move me to third. Nah, I don't deserve it."

"That would only start them thinking about why we would do such a thing,"

Billy said. "We can't have them wondering if we suspect that they read minds. And besides, we need your bat." Billy put his hand on Renker's shoulder. "Look, they got you once. Are you going to let them get you twice?"

Renker deliberated for a moment, then drew himself up. "Hell, no."

"Good. We're down, but not out. Don't get mad, get even."

"I like the sound of that," responded Renker with venom.

Fifteen minutes later, what had transpired during the game had been made clear to the entire team.

"Blow it off, Eddie," yelled Roberts from the back.

"It wasn't your fault, we're behind you a hundred per cent," chimed in Washington.

"Now that you know, you'll be solid," said O'Nealy. Hearing it from Brad, who'd paid the price, was enough for Renker.

"I'll be ready tomorrow," he promised.

"Great. That's behind us," said Billy. "What's in front of us is more important. It's come down to real baseball, with some dirty tricks thrown in. I've got some dirty tricks of my own for them, but tomorrow's not the time to play all our cards."

"What's up for tomorrow's game?" asked Butterfield.

"Nothing special," answered Billy. "We got Chief going for us, and also, should I say, a renewed strength of will?"

A chorus of voices affirmed the suggestion.

"And how do we proceed?"

"Time on the machines," offered Barker.

"T'ai Chi and meditation," said Simpson.

"Yes, these methods have worked for us this far, and they'll carry us the rest of the way. That is, unless the Indians can break our will, our unity. I know that won't happen."

Billy got down off the dais and waved everybody closer. "There's something we used to do routinely back on Ball Four before big games. It's called a white-mind meld meeting. It was good for our focus. We can simulate it through meditation. Want to give it a try?"

Heads nodded in agreement. "Close your eyes, meditate. Emit alpha, go willingly into the white mind."

It took some time, but as each player and coach relaxed, the whole of the group, one by one, cleared their minds. If the entire room were one large biofeedback machine, it would have begun to hum louder and louder with the tone signifying alpha, as more and more of the team dropped into the white mind. The music of the spheres seemed to echo back and forth, from mind to mind, effortlessly, and more intensely, as more minds found the state. Billy, who had quickly dropped down into theta waves in both hemispheres, brought his right mind up to active beta and passed from mind to mind, merging with each in turn, opening himself up to each teammate. The action had a focusing effect, which brought the whole of the room into one, resonating mind-set. Anxieties and private concerns melted away, and if there were any emotions among them, it was a unity of purpose, and a shared peace. The hearts and minds of the players, the very air itself, seemed to shimmer. It continued uninterrupted for some incomprehensible period of time, until Billy brought himself back, and the rest of the team with him.

Each member stood there, seemingly vibrating, yet at ease. "If we play from *that* place we just visited," Billy said quietly, "I challenge any team in the universe to defeat us. Now, let's get some sleep. I'll see you in the morning."

30

Jake Conrad and Warren Evans stood in front of the dugout and watched the Giants take the field for the fifth game of the World Series.

"I like our chances one helluva lot better than two days ago, Warren," said Conrad, punctuating the sentence with the usual spit of tobacco juice. "But here comes Chief Strongbow. Suppose our boys will find a way to get to him?"

Evans was scanning the minds of the Giants as they took the field, but roughly followed what Conrad was saying. "That will be the key that we'll all be looking for, Jake." Warren liked the old baseball man, he really did, but right now there was work to do. From the moment they came out for warm-ups, the Giants were a virtual blank on the field. There were random, mechanical thoughts of baseball and communication took place between them about the various drills, but there was nothing indicative of any weakness. It was, Evans realized with dismay, so very Ball Fourian. But someone broke yesterday, and someone will break today, he thought with confidence.

Rifkin, scan for weakness, but focus on the pitch.

Yes, Evan.

Rifkin scanned, but to no avail. He focused on the pitch, but could not put wood on the ball. Nor could Nichols, or Fernandez. Jimmy "Chief" Strongbow was shooting arrows and flinging snakes, and he was not missing. He struck out the side on eleven pitches. Evans, as he worked his way around the diamond, found no crack anywhere. He even looked into the Giants' dugout for what little mind-chatter he could hear at a distance, but it was very quiet. It was an unEarthly quiet, he sensed.

When the Giants came to bat in the first, Eddie Renker presented a stone mind to the Cleveland battery. He carefully picked and chose which pitches he was interested in, and fouled off six pitches on his way to a 3 and 2 count. When Ellerbach finally threw ball four, he had already thrown twelve pitches.

Roberts stepped in. Nichols and Ellerbach scanned Renker for intention, while Martin and Nixon did the same to Sal Donato in the third-base coach's box. Not a sound, not a sign. Not to worry, thought Ellerbach, the Giants were not a running team. They'd yet to attempt a steal. Roberts swung and missed at a fastball. On the next pitch, Ellerbach checked Renker, and came back to Roberts with an off-speed toss on the outside corner. Renker was off like a shot. Roberts swung and missed, and Martin, caught unawares, rushed his throw. It sailed a bit and Renker was able to slide under the tag as it swept down.

Breaking the percentage rules of baseball, Roberts bunted on a two-strike count, and succeeded in laying one down the first-base line. Nichols, playing back, had no play and by the time Ellerbach reached it, it was too late to get Roberts. Men on first and third, no outs.

Here came Rick Barker. Ellerbach smoothed his mind and, concentrating on the edges of the plate, he worked his way to a full count. The crowd buzzed in the stands, wishing for a fly ball, and on the next pitch, Barker delivered. It floated out to left field, a bit high. Renker was poised at third, but he and the crowd watched in disappointment as the wind caught the ball and brought it back towards the infield. Pantuso gloved it in medium-shallow left field and Renker had to hold up.

Willie Washington, now aware that Candlestick Park intended to be tough on right-handers this night, waited for something outside. Ellerbach was foolish enough to provide it on the third pitch and Willie lofted it to reasonably deep right-center. This time Renker tagged and easily scored without a throw.

Conrad had Ellerbach intentionally walk Icarus (a move Evans did not quibble with, considering that it was his idea), and Mitch Simpson hit a fly ball which the winds helped guide into Pantuso's glove to end the inning. Giants, 1-0.

The score would remain that way until the eighth inning. Jimmy was lightning fast and his control was impeccable. He allowed a hit here and there, even letting two men on base in the fifth, but walked none and kept the Indians from touching home plate. Ellerbach gathered himself up and was no less dominating, giving up a few well-spaced hits, but the Giants never mounted a true threat. Billy got two of those hits but never with a man on.

Evans never took his eyes off the Giants, but never did he find that crack in the wall. Dismayed as he was, he couldn't help but admire the incredible focus of his opponents. They were worthy foes and (he hated to admit) would have been a match for most teams on Ball Four. He squelched that train of thought. These were Earthlings, and he must find a clue, some way into their thoughts. He never found it. Watkins could do nothing but wait in the seat next to the anxious Edwards. Tarn and Dr. Avion did nothing in the adjacent suite but watch in silent admiration of both sets of minds on the field. This was baseball at its finest, anywhere in the galaxy.

With two out and nobody on in the Cleveland eighth, Alan Van De Kirk found a way. He did it, not with any mental means, but with sheer power and determination. Against the by-then whipping Candlestick winds, he took a lightning-fast inside fastball of Jimmy Strongbow's and sent it back in the form of a lightning bolt which cut its way through the swirling currents into the cheap seats in left. The score was tied, 1-1.

It was 1-1 after Ellerbach put the Giants away in the eighth, and it was still 1-1 when an unrattled Chief Strongbow struck out the Cleveland side in the top of the ninth. And so it was 1-1 when Eddie Renker walked out carrying his bat to start the bottom of the ninth.

Just moments before, Renker had used the time between innings to rush into the tunnel to the clubhouse. He hurriedly went back through his mind. In his previous at-bats, Ellerbach had always started him off with a shoulder-high inside fastball to push him back off the plate. Would he do it again? He composed his mind and walked back out on the field.

When Renker stepped in, he crowded the plate. Martin scanned his mind, and felt a rippling swirl of anticipation, but no clear clues as to Renker's intentions. As Ellerbach came in with the first pitch, Renker thrust his front foot out, radically opening his stance, and swung tight and shoulder-high. The ball was there to greet the swing. It leapt off Renker's bat and screamed on a rope into the gap between left and center. Van De Kirk was able to cut it off before it reached the wall, but not in time to prevent the determined Renker from reaching second.

Mickey Roberts did not have to think to know that the bunt was the only choice. Ellerbach and Martin, conferring mentally, were of the same frame of mind. They would give him nothing up in the strike zone. Sure enough, Roberts squared to bunt, but let the first go by for a ball. The second, a slashing slider, came in low and inside. Roberts pulled back on the bat to soften the impact, but the ball squirted foul. Ellerbach came back to the same spot, and this time the ball jumped forward toward the right side of the mound. It hung there for an instant during which Ellerbach twisted and dove. His glove hit the ground a split second before the ball did and it slipped into the pocket for an out. Renker hustled back to second.

Ellerbach and Martin talked briefly on the mound. They quickly reasoned that Rick Barker, a good spray hitter, would not rely on the bunt with one out. A single, Barker's forte, could do as well. Barker did not deny their logic. On the first pitch, he whipped a sinking fastball to straight-away right field. Jefferson played it on one hop to hold Renker on third.

Washington leisurely ambled up to the plate, swinging his bat slowly around to stretch his broad shoulders. The crowd was on its feet, shouting "Wil-lie, Wil-lie, Wil-lie!" Watkins, up on the mezzanine, gave up on his mind-smoothing loop and leaned forward anxiously. First Commissioner Tarn smiled as he took in the scene, the moment. *This is baseball, Avion. So I've come to realize, Tarn.*

Washington waited for his pitch. On a 2 and 2 count it came. The incoming slider hung higher than intended and Willie lashed it down the third-base line. Darvel Nixon, playing close to the line against just such a blow, leapt high in the air and snared the smash. Two out, and fifty-five thousand Giants fans sighed with disappointment.

They quickly came back to life as Billy Icarus came forward from the on-deck circle. The new cheer, "Bil-ly, Bil-ly, Bil-ly!" rose from the frenzied crowd. Billy stopped before entering the batter's box and stared down at Renker. Eddie cocked his head in wonder at the meaning. Warren Evans wondered too, and scanned Renker's mind. He picked up confusion, and a single phase, *better stay on my toes*, before Renker's mind dropped back into whiteness.

The crowd's chant turned to boos when Martin brought his arm up to signal the intentional walk. Conrad wondered who the hell had made the call, then thought better of it. It was a good one, but godammit...

Renker danced back and forth on the basepath to distract the catcher, ready to dash home in the unlikely event of a passed ball, as Ellerbach tossed balls to the waiting Martin. On the fourth pitch, Billy suddenly reached broadly across the plate and thrust out his bat with his right hand. The ball popped off the very end of the bat and dribbled out between the mound and the first-base line. A startled Renker froze for a second, then broke for the plate. Martin, from where he stood, was closest to the ball. He sprung like a tiger and was on the ball with amazing speed. He looked to first, but Nichols had also decided to make a play for the ball, leaving first base unguarded. On his knees, Martin whirled to throw home, but no one was there! Ellerbach, completely surprised by the bunt, got a late start off the mound and was only halfway home when Renker crossed the plate standing up. The crowd, momentarily confused as to what had just happened, quieted down for a heartbeat before erupting into celebration. The game was over, Giants 2, Cleveland 1.

In the clubhouse after the game, Billy walked up to Eddie Renker, who sat in front of his locker with a smile glued to his face.

"You scored both our runs. Puts last night pretty far behind you, doesn't it?"

"Yeah, I feel pretty good," Renker replied. "Thanks for your faith in me. And thanks for that totally ridiculous bunt. I froze out there. If they hadn't frozen too, they could have gotten me. Then I'd have really felt like dogmeat."

"I knew you could do it. Besides, I could have popped up to Martin. Then who would have been dogmeat? Got to stick your neck out to win. Just like when you hit the double. I saw you. You had your eyes closed. Guessing all the way, huh?"

"An educated guess," Renker insisted.

"Anyway, between the two of us, we found a way to win. Congratulations again."

O'Nealy walked over, wrapped in a towel. "Bunting on an intentional walk, my dear Billy. Is that how you aliens do it?"

"Actually, I've never done it in my life. It was just an impulse. Why did you shower? You sat down all night."

"As chilly as it was with the wind, I sweated the whole time worrying for the Chief. God, what a masterpiece he threw. He's sure going to make people forget about me."

"I wouldn't worry about that," responded Billy. "You're poised for greatness in Cleveland the day after tomorrow."

"I suppose so," said O'Nealy, the smile vanishing as he spoke. "Either that, or infamy."

The post-game meeting in Abe Watkins' suite was amazingly brief. The First Commissioner had again been invited and again had demurred. Evans, Dartex and a couple of other scouts had offered various opinions, but it all came down to one conclusion: the Giants had simply outplayed them. The San Francisco white minds had held, and no solutions offered themselves.

Now, Watkins sat alone with his thoughts. For the first time in his life, he felt anger and anxiety which no smoothing loop would ease. He was so far from home, and had been charged with the duty of bringing a Universe Series championship back to Ball Four. Was it slipping away?

No, he would not let it. This was too important, too monumental a moment to allow such an eventuality to come to pass. He ran through his options and grimly reached what for him was the logical conclusion.

At six the next morning, under heightened security, the Giants slipped out of San Francisco International Airport aboard their charter. Hours later, under similar security, they reassumed their quarters in Cleveland. After time on the biofeedback machines, Billy once again commenced a team meeting in the hotel conference room. At all entrances, two security guards were posted.

"We're in great shape, boys. We're up three games to two, with a rested Brad O'Nealy and our splendid white minds in fine form for game six tomorrow. I must say I'm very proud of you. You're the finest bunch of ballplayers I've ever known."

"And we're proud of you, Billy," said Lou Chambers. "You won that game for us last night. I've been in baseball for over forty years, I never seen anything like it."

"Eddie and Jimmy won the game last night," said Billy. "I just added my small part. But, as I've said before, now is not the time for speeches or congratulations. We've got the steepest part of the slope ahead of us. We've got two games to put one win together. The Ball Fourians won't lay down. They'll come after us with everything they've got. So maintain the routine, stay within the mind-set we've created. I haven't had the luxury of putting anything down in writing, so you'll all have to take notes of what I'm going to say now. As I told you before, I've saved some good stuff until the end. For tomorrow's game or the next, should it go that far, we're going to be ready with some tricks of our own. To begin with, there are an endless number of gambits that have been used throughout Ball Fourian baseball history, but we'll be limited to those you humans can execute. For instance,..."

They were hard at it for hours in the conference room before ending the day in another white-mind meld meeting. In their rooms later that night, the lights burned on, as they studied their notes, preparing for the final showdown. At the elevators and at all fire exits to the Giants' floor, security guards remained throughout the night and following day.

31

The fans at Cleveland Municipal Stadium spent the pre-game warm-ups chanting, cajoling and imploring their boys to win one for them. The whole stadium buzzed simultaneously with enthusiasm and tension. In seven days' time, the same scene would be reenacted in every ballpark on Ball Four. The hometown boys had to reach down deep. It was crunch time.

While Cleveland was busy with their batting practice, Lou Chambers called his team inside the clubhouse.

"I won't take much of your time, boys," he began. "There's just one thing I've got to say. We're ready, we're a tough team and we can put it away tonight. But remember, we're one game up on 'em, and we're not under the gun. So stay loose, relax. Don't play like it's the end of the world. Let the Indians do the suffering. The pressure's on them. You got anything to say, Billy?"

"Nothing, except to agree wholeheartedly with you. And, may I suggest five minutes of white-mind meld?"

The team easily dropped into the meld. Moments later, when they came out onto the field, they were clear, refreshed and ready to play.

The pitchers went out to the bullpen along the third base line between the stands and left field. Brad O'Nealy took one of the mounds and started throwing to stay loose. Jimmy grabbed a mitt and, just like in the old days, caught for Brad while he threw. It was about five minutes to game time.

Up in the stands next to them, curious fans pressed against the railing. Just opposite O'Nealy, two uniformed Stadium security guards stood by the railing about ten paces apart, casually watching out for trouble and generally keeping an eye on the crowd. In foul territory behind the bullpen, two more guards patrolled, against the possibility of fans jumping onto the field. Nonchalantly, the guards walked out onto the edge of fair territory just beyond the area where O'Nealy was warming up. They watched as Brad threw pitch after pitch to Jimmy.

Suddenly Brad pulled up as he was about to go into his wind-up. He stood still for a moment, then dropped his glove to the ground. Jimmy got out of his crouch and looked at Brad curiously, wondering why he had stopped throwing. The two security guards in the stands and the two on the field watched vacantly as Brad dropped to his knees and grabbed his head. Jimmy yelled, "Brad!" and then yelled at the teammates on the bullpen bench. A couple of them raced toward the Giants' dugout, the rest headed toward Brad. Jimmy got there first just as Brad fell on his side, still clutching his head. The guards stood there with vacant looks on their faces, and Jimmy looked up at them and yelled, "Don't just stand there, this man is hurt!" The guards reacted by walking over, unfastening a gate in the railing and heading up into the stands, presumably going for help.

O'Nealy struggled back up to his knees and Jimmy, with Lafite's help, hoisted him to his feet. By this time Billy and Chambers had dashed out from the dugout. They helped the dizzy O'Nealy back into the dugout, where he sat down and put his head between his legs. It was a minute or so until game time.

"Can you make it into the locker room?" asked Billy.

"Yes, I think so," answered the shaken O'Nealy.

Once inside, they sat him down on a bench. "What happened, Brad?" asked Billy. "How do you feel?"

"Weak and pretty dizzy," he answered. "I was warming up, I felt great, and suddenly the sky just sort of fell in on me. I heard a loud screaming in my head and then I, I don't know, I just felt panic, total fear. God, it was awful. What is going on? I've never felt like this."

"You're white as a ghost, Brad," said Chambers with concern. "We've got a game in one minute. I'll go out and see to the at-bats. Billy, can you see to Brad?"

"Of course. Jimmy, you stay here. Steve, you'd better head back out to the bullpen. See if everybody's all right."

Chambers and Lafite hurried out, and Billy looked back at Brad. "Do you feel like you can pitch?"

O'Nealy held his left hand up. It was shaking like a leaf. "I don't know, I don't know,..I..."

Billy put his hands on his hips and shook his head. Had they gotten to him? Would they really do it? "Jimmy, you were catching him. Did you see anything or anybody strange out there?"

"Not really. We were warming up, and the fans were yelling at us, you know, harmless stuff. Security was there and...wait a minute, there was one thing. A couple of security guards walked out onto the outfield grass next to where we were throwing and, when Brad went down, they just stood there watching with blank expressions on their faces. Like they didn't give a damn!

I yelled at them to find some help and they walked off slowly, like they still didn't care. I know we're the opposing team and all but..."

"Okay, Jimmy. It's very clear what happened. I was afraid of this, but I never seriously thought they would do it."

"Do what?" asked O'Nealy weakly, his head down in his hands.

"They sent a mind-disruption team after you. I guess the thought of Ball Four losing the Series was too much for the Operation to accept. I feel ashamed, it's humiliating. I'm sorry. Look, we've got to decide. Brad, how is your focus?"

"Pretty weak. I feel a little more centered, but still dizzy."

"As bad as you feel now, I'm sure that there's no real harm done. I assume that they wouldn't hurt you permanently. But your ability to use the white mind is no doubt severely inhibited, at least for a while. We'd better not take the chance."

Someone yelled down the tunnel from the dugout. "Hey, we gotta take the field!"

Billy calmly stroked his beard. "Jimmy, my first instinct is to go with you, but I'd rather save you for tomorrow than burn you out today."

"I could go a few, Billy. I'd like to give it a shot."

"He's right, Jimmy," said Brad weakly. "If we lose today, and I can't come back tomorrow, we're screwed."

Jimmy looked down at the floor. "You're right, of course," he said finally. He looked back up at O'Nealy. "You gonna be okay?"

"Yes, he just needs to get some rest," said Billy, answering for O'Nealy. "Let's get out there. Brad, I'm dreadfully sorry about this. I suspected something might happen, but I never thought they'd try it on the field. Makes me feel, oh, I don't know how I feel. I've never in my life..."

"Just go out and get 'em, dammit," O'Nealy said, smiling with effort. "I'll be all right."

When the mind-disruption team had begun its assault on O'Nealy, both First Commissioner Tarn and Dr. Avion were instantly aware that somewhere in the vicinity, potent mind activity was taking place. Tarn scanned the area and within seconds was fully aware of what was taking place. *Avion, against all that is sacred to Ball Four, we have taken a bad turn. Tarn, I sense this disruption clearly.*

Tarn bolted from his seat, went up to one of his agents and whispered in his ear. The agent pointed up to the owner's box. Tarn spoke abruptly to two of the agents, who nodded vigorously. With an agent on each side, Tarn set off up the aisle at a rapid pace.

Just at game time, Tarn arrived at the private box of Elliot Edwards. He stopped in front of the security guard posted at the door, and projected, *Are you Ball Fourian?* The answer came, *Yes, sir.* Tarn answered, *I am Tarn, allow me by.* Leaving his agents behind, he unceremoniously barged into the box.

Abakin!

Watkins looked up to the landing above, excused himself and went up to Tarn. *Yes, First Commissioner?*

You are responsible for the mind disruption of the Earthling player?

Yes, First Commissioner.

It is outrageous! Cease such tactics immediately! I'll speak with you later.

Yes, First Commissioner.

With that, Tarn wheeled and was gone. Watkins, shaken to the core, went back to his seat next to Edwards and ran a mind-smoothing loop over and over as the game got underway.

From his box seat directly behind home plate, Richard Bates sat and stared in wonder at the Cleveland team as they took their places on the field. The sports director of WCLV-TV had given him this ticket to game six as a reward for his hard work during the summer. He had taken a flight down earlier that day from Ann Arbor. Now he wasn't quite sure if he was glad he had come or not. He had noticed the faces of the Indians as he watched the earlier games on television, but now, to see them in the flesh made his skin crawl. Was he crazy, or had the world gone mad?

He had grown up with his nose in books about baseball. When he wasn't leafing through books of statistics, he was reading biography after biography about the stars of the game throughout its long and colorful history. And here they were, out on the field of Cleveland Municipal Stadium tonight.

Was he the only one who realized? Was it because of the frightening events of the summer with his computers that he was looking with open eyes, or had all the United States been terrified into submission? Couldn't they see?

Christy Mathewson, Ty Cobb, Cap Anson, Rogers Hornsby, Jackie Robinson, Satchel Paige. With his binoculars, Richard went one-by-one through the Cleveland roster. They were all there, the greats of baseball. Thinking back at what had happened earlier in the season, he realized anew that powerful forces had interfered with his investigation. And now, as he did then, he would remain silent, and hope that he could sit and watch the game without some deadly result. Or was he really mad?

Up in the press box, Lloyd Cronin straightened his bow tie and grinned while the Indians took the field. It had been a very interesting summer. The illness, whatever it had been, was well behind him and he was enjoying his job as never before.

He looked forward to writing his column for tomorrow. He had a working title in his head. "My, How the Mighty Have Fallen." He liked that. It would serve the bums right.

Cronin wasn't sure why he was so gleeful about the mess Cleveland was in. All he knew was that he could give a damn about their chances in the Series. Maybe it was because bad news was always more exciting than good news. Oh, who cares what it is, this is good, very good.

Cronin took a bite of his hot dog and a sip from his beer, then settled in for the game.

While Billy, Jimmy and Brad conferred in the locker room, Vance Bueller was making short work of the unsettled Giants. Only Rick Barker managed to get wood on the ball with a meek ground out. In the Cleveland dugout, Warren Evans noticed that the minds of the Giant batters were not totally whitened, but none were guessing at pitches, so he sent no instructions. Bueller and Martin needed none. The mind-disruption of O'Nealy obviously had the Giants quite shaken.

For himself, Evans didn't know what to think. When O'Nealy went down, there was no doubt in Evans' mind that Watkins had made good on his veiled threat to use extraordinary means to avoid defeat. Though Evans was stunned, he was relieved to realize that his team would face a weakened opponent. He did not relish returning to Ball Four in disgrace, but, as a baseball man, it flew in the face of everything he had ever cherished about the game to think that such tactics could or would ever be employed, even against aliens. He smoothed his mind against the distracting thoughts and concentrated on the work at hand. His responsibility was the guidance of his team, not the ethics of his planet.

When the Giants' turn at bat was over, Lou Chambers walked slowly over to the home plate umpire to inform him that an injury to the starting pitcher during warm-ups had necessitated an examination and a possible change in the line-up. To buy time while Billy reached a decision, Chambers asked for a clarification of the rules that applied in such cases. This led to a meeting of all umpires on the mound, which prompted a visit by Jake Conrad. Chambers ran the conference out as long as his imagination would allow, inquiring about subtle distinctions in the rules. This led to a few heated words with Conrad. Chambers gladly locked horns with him.

Billy and Jimmy trotted up to the bullpen. "How's everybody out here?"

"Fine, Billy," replied Lafite. "How's Brad?"

"He'll live. Art, can you give me three innings?"

French jumped to his feet. "I'll give you whatever I got."

"Good. Jimmy, you'd better stay in the dugout. It's safer."

Under the rules, French was allowed extra pitches to get ready. As he warmed up Evans walked up and down the front of the Cleveland dugout centering his team. *We know this French. Hit at will, scan at will. He is no threat. Yes, Evan.* Smiles rose on the faces of the gleeful Indian team.

After the last warm-up throw, Billy walked the ball out to French. *I have faith in you, Art. You can get them.*

French suddenly smiled. "I can get them, Billy."

Evans, confident from the turn of events, wasn't even listening.

Three Indian outs later, Evans was still unconcerned. His boys had time to get used to the screwballs, sinkers and knucklers coming from this worn-out pitcher. Vance Bueller would contain the shaken Giants.

Bueller easily contained Willie Washington, getting him on three curves. Martin had scanned him and found him guessing, expecting fastballs. It was child's play.

While Washington batted, Billy scanned the batter's box and perceived Willie's slackened mind. He suspected that all the Giants' minds would be weakened with apprehension. Something must be done.

He did what he could, which was a home run to deep right off of a slider on the outside corner. It gave Evans pause. Who could contain this Icarus? Evans' confidence returned as Bueller dispatched Simpson and Butterfield.

Art French, given the 1-0 lead, pitched with a grim determination that yielded but one hit in the next two innings. Several of the Indians connected solidly against him, but the slowness of his velocity held them to catchable flyballs. Alan Van De Kirk took a mean cut on a sixty-mile-an-hour change-up off a change-up, but the ball stayed within Barker's grasp. More than one Indian grounded out on a sinking knuckleball. But most importantly, French's mind was unreadable.

Bueller gained strength as he plowed through the Giants' line-up, even though their minds began to whiten after Billy's blast. He knew his teammates would eventually hammer the dregs of the San Francisco pitching staff.

Though Inky Powell had begun warming up during the Giants' half of the fourth, French was allowed to stay in. He was pitching too well to remove, and he responded by getting Nichols on strikes and Fernandez on a lazy fly. With two outs, Van De Kirk came to bat. French treated him to a crop of pitches on the perimeter of the plate, two of which Van De Kirk fouled off weakly and three he took for balls. With a full count, French finally made a mistake. It was a screwball which hung in the strike zone instead of breaking inside. Van De Kirk cracked it deep to even the score, 1-1.

"You did fine, you did your job, we're in this one," said Billy. "Thanks, Art, let's see what Inky can do."

French nodded without speaking and handed the ball over to Chambers, who had waved Powell in as he came to the mound.

Perhaps because of the change in velocity from French to Powell, Cleveland didn't manage well against the new Giants pitcher. His whirling-dervish delivery, coupled with a whiter mind than in the third game where they pounded him without restraint, held the Tribe at bay. Through the seventh inning Powell would surrender nothing but a walk and two singles, without allowing a run.

Vance Bueller, but for the one home run, was pitching masterfully. When he faced Billy as he led off the Giants' fifth, Bueller was determined to give Billy nothing, even if it meant walking him. Billy, knowing this, crowded the plate, thereby allowing himself to step out on a brush-back pitch and pull it over the fence in the left field corner. The Giants led, 2-1, and Evans began to scan the field constantly for a weakness. He could find nothing. The Giants had pulled themselves back together. He was disappointed to notice that Eddie Renker averted his eyes every time Icarus called a pitch. What did Renker know?

As Powell stayed out of danger, Bueller continued to remain unshaken by Billy Icarus' homers. When he retired Billy in the seventh on a towering pop-up, Bueller felt he had reached a cusp. With luck, he could finish the game without facing Icarus again.

By the time Eddie Martin came to the plate in the bottom of the eighth, both the Giants and Indians were locked into the contest. The events before the ballgame had faded out of the consciousness of all participants, and the struggle to score had honed the concentration and tightened the stomachs of every player. No one had a thought of anything but the ball itself. Even Warren Evans had stopped scanning minds and had sat down next to Conrad to watch each pitch.

Martin stepped in and Powell delivered. Swing and a miss, strike one. Martin dug in closer and a little forward, and waved his bat in a tight circle of anticipation. The change-up found him overanxious and he was way out in front, strike two. Powell was throwing the best baseball of his young career. Martin backed out of the box, stretched, stepped back in. The crowd was clapping, exhorting its team. Martin caught the next pitch solidly and rapped it into left for a single. For the first time in the game, Cleveland had its leadoff hitter on base.

It proved to be the crack in the seam that the Indians needed. Rifkin, bunting to move Martin over, took advantage of the fact that Powell's odd delivery put him off-balance and made fielding a bunt difficult. From an awkward stance, Powell attempted to pick the ball up with his bare hand, but, in trying to straighten up to throw, he dropped it. Two men on, no outs.

Powell's miscue had cost him his confidence, and Nichols proved it by slamming a double up the gap in right-center. Both runners came in to score, and Chambers was out in a hurry. It was time for Steve Lafite.

Lafite promptly struck out Fernandez and Van De Kirk, but Tony Pantuso singled in Nichols before Barker snared Hunk Jefferson's fly ball to end the inning. But the tide had turned. Cleveland led, 4-2.

The last chance for the Giants came in the ninth, with Roberts, Barker and Washington due up. Bueller, and everyone in the stands, knew that the game hinged on whether on not Bueller had to face Icarus.

Billy never made it to the plate. Roberts struck out, Barker flied out to Van De Kirk, and Washington broke his bat while sending a weak bloop to the shortstop Rifkin. Cleveland won, 4-2. The Series was tied, 3-3, and what had happened so many times on at least two planets had come to pass once again. An entire season of struggle was compressed into nine innings. The meaning of everything that had occurred before was erased, and tomorrow's one game meant everything.

"That was a goddam dirty trick," said Lou Chambers to Billy Icarus after the game. They sat in the manager's office in the visitors' clubhouse. "It was more than that, Billy. It was criminal. If they weren't aliens, I'd turn 'em in. For what, I don't know. But it was, well, evil."

"You may not believe this, Lou, but it may well have been the first Ball Fourian misdeed I can recall in my life, with the possible exception of what I did in coming here."

"There's no comparison," responded Chambers emphatically. "You came here to make things fair, to even up a situation that was never right to begin with. And now, in spite of what you've said about how advanced Ball Four is, the bastards hurt one of our guys on purpose. It stinks."

"You're right, but let's be honest, what's the difference between what they've done and Ty Cobb coming in spikes high back in your old days of baseball? I admit it's unconscionable to use mind disruption, but face it, Skip, humans hurt each other on purpose all the time in sports. Football, I hear, is especially brutal."

"At least when Cobb came in you could get out of the way. How do you duck when they come after your mind? How do we do that?"

"No argument there," replied Billy glumly. "Don't think for a moment that I condone what they did to Brad. For the first time in my life I'm ashamed to be Ball Fourian. I see more than ever now what Tarn has been implying all along. This act, which no doubt was considered by some to be acceptable because only a human, an alien, would be harmed, is another sign of creeping decadence for our planet. When we lose sight of what is right and fair in a small area of Ball Fourian endeavor, the whole of our ethics weakens, becomes suspect. Look, I don't want to talk all night about this, we've got work to do. So, if it helps at all, let me assure you that the actual Indian ballplayers weren't behind the mind disruption. In fact, I doubt they even know it took place. Evan, their real manager, probably didn't authorize it. I know these guys, and they're too good a bunch of ballplayers to do something so unsportsmanlike. They want to win, using the techniques in which they've been trained."

"Fine," said Chambers. "I'll accept that. But we're up the creek here. They know how to get to us."

"Yeah, and we still almost beat them. We were six outs away when they put it together. The weakest part of our team, the bullpen, almost pulled it off. Inky got a bad break. Otherwise, maybe we'd have won. Don't feel bad. We've got a lot going for us. As a matter of fact, in a way, because of what they've tried to do to us tonight, we've got a real edge tomorrow."

"How the hell do you figure that?" asked Chambers curtly.

"I talked to Brad when we came in. He soaked in the Whirlpool during the game, then meditated and did some T'ai Chi. He also spent time on a biofeedback machine. That really did the trick, apparently. Says he feels much better. Almost back to his old self. If that's true, and we can protect him and Jimmy from any more attacks, we've got the edge in pitching. Bueller's spent, and Ellerbach's good but we've got two guys that have beat them. Plus I've got some more surprises for them. If we put together a pitching strategy that throws them off, even just a little bit, we've got at least improved chances. Don't count us out yet."

"Billy, one of the things I like about you is that you never get rattled, never give up," said Chambers with a fatherly smile. "But sometimes you can't win on optimism alone. Don't worry, I'm no quitter, but I'm afraid of what other nasty things your friends are capable of."

"So am I, Lou, but we can't base our strategy on that. We just have to heighten security and play our best game."

"By the way, why didn't you use any of those mind gambits we've been studying?" Chambers asked. "We could have used them in the eighth."

"Maybe you're right, but I didn't want to give away the one secret we've held onto until just the right moment. That moment hasn't arrived. There's still tomorrow and it's another thing we've got going for us. We haven't used up our options. Let's turn our attention to tomorrow. What I've got in mind is unusual, so you and I have to agree totally or we won't do it."

"Why don't you just mind-influence me into agreement?" said Chambers snidely.

Billy glared at him. *Quit the crap!*

Chambers was startled, then looked at Billy suspiciously. Billy smiled back broadly. Chambers broke into knowing chuckles. "Okay, I get the point. What do you have in mind?"

Back in Jimmy and Billy's room at the hotel, the two aces of the San Francisco Giants' pitching staff were looking out of the window past the lights of Cleveland, out to the darkness that was Lake Erie.

"Billy and the Skipper have been at it for two hours now, first at the park and now in Skipper's room," said Jimmy. "I feel kinda left out, like I did today. It was horrible sitting on the bench, watching that lead slip away."

"How do you think I felt," Brad said, staring out into the night. "It was my start. I had to sit in the Whirlpool and listen to the crowd shaking the rafters. That's a tough way to find out the news. Damn it, Jimmy, they stole my chance for glory. I've taken all this year's weirdness by squeezing every last ounce from my sense of humor. They stole that from me today as well. The Indians went from weird dudes to bad guys pretty damned fast."

"Yeah, they took the fun out of it, didn't they? Billy had me convinced that the Ball Fourians were straight shooters except for their mental games. But today was outrageous, totally uncalled for. I had to sit and watch them benefit from it. Why didn't Billy let me at 'em?"

"Aw, he was right and you know it," Brad said gently. "Now we've got you for tomorrow and they've used up Bueller. Billy's smart, don't take it personally."

"It should be your start, Brad, if you're feeling better, you should get your shot. I'd put my money on you."

"I do feel better. In fact, in a way, I feel like I've had my head cleaned out. Maybe they gave me a radio lobotomy."

"And you say they stole your sense of humor?"

"I suppose you think I'm joking," said Brad with a straight face.

When Brad's lips began to curl up into a smile, Jimmy laughed. "You should pitch tomorrow, you've got just enough gall to beat them after what they did to you."

"No, Chief, if I were the Skipper, I'd want you in there." Brad sighed. "We're a long way from Phoenix, aren't we? One thing's for sure. We've had a great year, you and I. We've got Billy to thank for a lot of it, but I'm proud to be on the same staff with you. After this whole crazy season is over, I hope reality sets in and we get to pitch together for a long time."

"Me too, Brad. It's a dream come true, even if it's turned into a nightmare tonight."

"Oh, it's not so bad. We're still in the greatest Series of all time, even if we'll never be able to tell anyone. So they got nasty, we're still in it and maybe we'll find a way to spike *their* punch."

The door suddenly opened behind them and in rushed Billy Icarus. "Hello, boys. I'm glad I caught you before you went to sleep."

"You and Chambers sure have been jawin'," said Jimmy.

"Yeah, we were working on strategy for tomorrow's game."

"Did you decide who's pitching?" Brad asked, trying to sound casual.

"As a matter of fact, we did," said Billy.

"Okay, out with it, Billy," Brad said. "Who's going to pitch tomorrow?"

"We are, gentlemen, we are."

32

On Wednesday, October 23rd, the last game of the Universe Series was about to get under way.

The Giants, complaining about "rude and possibly dangerous behavior" on the part of Cleveland fans, had insisted on warming up their starting pitcher in the center of the field behind second base. Jake Conrad had protested, but the umpires could find no rule that prohibited pitchers from warming up wherever they wanted, as long as it didn't interfere with the ball in play, or unduly distract players involved in the contest.

The Cleveland Indians, except for Conrad, went about their business in a cool and confident way. Warren Evans knew exactly why the Giants were protecting their pitchers, and approved of it one hundred per cent. He had no desire to see a repeat of last night. He did, however, wonder why both O'Nealy and Strongbow were warming up, and why the Giants had not yet announced a starting pitcher. Technically, they had no obligation to announce, at least until the presentation of line-up cards to the home plate umpire just prior to game time. He was further confused by Billy Icarus' odd behavior during warm-ups. Bob Butterfield was warming up O'Nealy, and Icarus was catching for Strongbow. But every five minutes or so Strongbow and Icarus would trade gloves, and Icarus would begin to pitch! What was that absurdity all about? This was no time for horseplay, an important game was about to get under way. Evans wondered if Chambers had lost his ability to maintain discipline.

Abe Watkins was in a better frame of mind than that of the previous evening. It was fairly rough going, watching his team come so close to losing, in spite of the inferior pitching they had to face. And he was still concerned about the First Commissioner's reaction to the mind-disruption of O'Nealy, but he was convinced that, with a victory tonight, all would be smoothed over by the celebration and congratulations.

Tarn himself had already made up his mind about Abakin. There would be no place for him in the world of Ball Fourian baseball back on the home planet. No doubt counseling and ethical mind retraining would cure Abakin of the origins of his folly, but in no way could Tarn allow such a man ever to return to the sport he had disgraced. Such was his outrage that it took all the restraint his otherwise balanced constitution possessed to refrain from having Abakin transported up to the station last night. Tarn must wait, but there must be some public chastisement awaiting Abakin. The moral health of Ball Four required it.

Dr. Avion observed the fury of Tarn with some bemusement. Tarn was ordinarily such a composed person. His view of Tarn's commitment to honor was reaffirmed by the fury of his reaction. It was no wonder Tarn had done what he had with the Operation, and the final chapter was to be played out this very night. Ordinarily quite ambivalent when it came to sports, particularly the planetary obsession with baseball, this night Avion was actually looking forward to observing the contest. It would be quite interesting indeed.

Just before game time the Giants came back into the safety of the locker room for one last conference.

"There's not much to say that we don't already know," said Billy. "We'll not be able to communicate out there, so here's one more reminder. You've had two days to study the tactical plans. We saved them for just such a game. And remember, there are situational gambits which are to be instituted auto-matically and the numbered gambits which I have to call. Hopefully, enough of you will invoke the gambits when appropriate. I know we've all studied hard, and the gambits are sufficiently memory-resident. If I call a numbered play, avoid thinking anything but that number. That way we won't tip our hand. Your minds will most likely automatically perform the gambit at the right time just by the number trigger. Or at least that's the theoretical basis of the plan. It's never been tried by humans, but these are unusual circumstances. Whatever happens, you're all to be commended for your efforts. I wonder if a different bunch of guys could have done what you have. In spite of what happened last night and in spite of how warped a version of baseball this has become for you, let's go out there and have some fun, shall we?"

"Amen to that," said Washington. "It sure ain't boring, is it, guys?"

A ripple of no's and tentative chuckles reverberated throughout the room.

"Brad, Jimmy and Eddie," Billy said more quietly to the three standing in front, "good luck, and concentrate on your individual efforts. Be strong when it comes time to be."

They affirmed Billy's encouragement with silent nods.

Billy then stepped into the center of the room. "For the last time this season, men, let's focus together on the task at hand."

One more time, they dropped into the white-mind meld. Billy quickly passed his mind among his teammates and united with each in turn, coming finally to the mind of Brad O'Nealy, where he lingered. He poured forth as much soothing, confident and healthy energy and trust as he could toward his friend. The mental resonance they struck together felt strong and clear.

When it ended, they walked out to the field without a word.

When Jake Conrad walked back to the dugout after exchanging line-up cards, Evans was quite surprised to hear that O'Nealy was starting the game.

"I'm as surprised as you are, Warren," said Conrad. "It frankly doesn't make any sense. Why go with a hurt guy when your number one pitcher is more or less rested?"

"I don't know, Jake," Evans answered. "But these Giants have been pretty unpredictable in this Series, wouldn't you say?"

"Yes I would. Maybe they didn't like what they saw while Strongbow was warming up, and I gotta admit I like our chances against O'Nealy. We've gotten to him before."

I like our chances too, thought Evans. It will be interesting to see that oddball's mental makeup tonight. I've got to keep a close eye.

The game got underway as Eddie Renker stepped to the plate. The stadium radiated excitement, that rare intense thrill only a seventh game of a World Series can spawn. In spite of the tension, It was obvious to Evans that Renker, at least, was able to maintain the white mind. It was to no avail, as Ellerbach dispatched him on strikes. Roberts and Barker fared no better, although Barker did manage to punch a rope into left, but straight at Pantuso.

Evans intensified his scanning of the Giants' minds from the moment O'Nealy went into his warm-up tosses. Rock solid, he noted with disappointment. Especially this Icarus. Of all the minds throughout the Series, his was as tight as any he'd ever witnessed. How could humans accomplish this? He shouldn't waste his time on Icarus, but he would scan the rest of the team continually throughout the game. Someone out there was sure to weaken under the strain.

From the first pitch to Dizzy Rifkin, it was apparent that O'Nealy was pitching from a numbered sequence again! 3, 1, 4, 1. Yes, that's familiar, thought Evans, as Rifkin grounded out to Stokes at short. He ran back through his mind and brought up the code and fixed it into his active consciousness. *Bolnici, get ready to receive signals. Yes, Evan.*

Evans read the number from O'Nealy's mind, passed it to Nichols, who swung and missed. What happened? It indeed was a fastball, but O'Nealy is wild. Evans flashed the next signal to Nichols, who again swung and missed. Again, it was the correct pitch from the code, but the location was wrong. Was O'Nealy lacking control, or was there a new element to the code? Evans scanned, converted using the code, transmitted to Nichols that it would be a wasted pitch. Nichols watched the ball curve in and nip the outside corner, for a called strike three.

Evans would wait and watch without sending signals. Perhaps the new code would be evident enough without computer help. As Fernandez worked at the plate, O'Nealy employed the "pi" code, but with a twist which was baffling. By the time Fernandez flied out to short center, Evans had computed nothing. Having committed every pitch to memory, he ran inside the clubhouse between innings and transmitted the data to Ygarnen up above at the station, hoping that he could solve the new twist to the code. Such a break might provide the needed advantage.

In the top of the second, Willie Washington tried to hold up on a swing but failed, sending a dying quail into right field for a single. When the Indians played back, showing that they expected Billy Icarus to hit away, Billy promptly bunted for a single, advancing Washington to second. Conrad swore and spit, and Evans wondered anew at the Giants' white minds. Against another Earthling team, his men would have easily read the intention and most likely turned it into a double play. How did the Giants manage it?

Fortunately for Cleveland, Ellerbach pitched around Simpson to load the bases, got Butterfield to pop out, and induced Dubois to hit into a double play. The Indians had really dodged a bullet.

As the Cleveland half of the second commenced, Evans stood by the phone for a direct-line message from Ygarnen and watched and scanned as O'Nealy went to work on Van De Kirk. What? No numbers to the pitches! A second pitch was thrown. Still no numbers. O'Nealy now threw with a blank mind. What is the significance? The phone rang. It was Ygarnen.

"Evan, we have solved the code."

"Thank you, it is not necessary now. Evan off."

A cheer went up from the crowd as Van De Kirk drove a fastball deep into right-center. It bounded rapidly toward the wall as Van De Kirk rounded first. The Giants in the dugout and the bullpen leapt to their feet as one. Van De

Kirk hesitated for a fraction of a second and dug in his spikes, trying for the double. Barker cut the ball off before it reached the wall, then spun and fired a shot to second. Van De Kirk went into his slide. It would be close. The ball arrived, Van De Kirk hit the bag, the umpire signaled safe. Simultaneously with the umpire's call, every Giant, even those in the dugout and the bullpen, mentally screamed *OUT!* Van De Kirk, playing with a wide-open mind, received the message as a resounding *OUT!*, masking his perception of the umpire's call. Shocked, he jumped up, moved toward the umpire with a questioning shrug, and stepped off the bag. Stokes promptly tagged him and the umpire vigorously signaled him out. A confused Van De Kirk, asking the umpire why he called him out twice, was told in reply that he had been called safe but was now out for stepping off the bag and being tagged. Jake Conrad, though having clearly seen the safe call, the stepping off, the tag and the resulting call of out, nonetheless came raging out to protest, attempting to claim that a timeout was implied. The umpire held firm and, after some useless flailing of arms, Conrad retreated to the dugout, with Van De Kirk at his side. Conrad was infuriated by Van De Kirk's attempt at an explanation and kicked the water fountain so hard that it caused a decidedly large dent. After Jefferson and Pantuso struck out to retire the side, Conrad walked back to the water fountain and inflicted further damage.

Up in the stands, Tarn watched with profound interest. *Fascinating, Avion. Tarn, these Earthlings have performed a team gambit, have they not? Most definitely, Avion. Remarkable, is it not?*

Abe Watkins, so high above the field in the owner's box, thought he had sensed some vague mental activity, but it only confused him. It reminded him of the "sound" of a team gambit back on Ball Four, but he could not allow his mind to register that it had just been performed by a human team. He would watch and wait.

Evans, closer to the field of play and by training and practice more mentally adept, had clearly picked up the gambit, as had the players themselves. But all he could muster was a feeling of total astonishment. How this could be? Was it an accident? Could an entire Earthling team, passionately convinced that the call should be "out," could such a team coincidentally emit a "scream" that would accidentally duplicate a gambit? Perhaps it was an unexpected side effect of the Giants' unusual spiritual training regimen. This must be his best working theory, for now. Nothing more plausible could explain such an incongruous episode.

The Indians took the field in the top of the third in a tenuous frame of mind. Van De Kirk was preoccupied in center, Ellerbach stood at the mound running a focusing loop in tandem with Martin at the plate, and the rest of the team attempted to free their minds of speculation, in order to resume play with clear minds.

Ellerbach walked Archie Stokes on four pitches. This elicited a few groans and scattered boos from the crowd. Evans felt he had better do something quickly. *Ellerban, relax, you have control. Yes, Evan.* The Indians anticipated bunt, and Renker obliged, laying down a perfect sacrifice. Mickey Roberts then worked up to a 3 and 2 count before flying out to short left. Stokes could not advance on the play.

Rick Barker came to bat. He could sense that Ellerbach and Martin were being too careful, and would give him nothing in the fat part of the strike zone. On a 3 and 1 count, they obliged him with a favorite pitch of his, inside and low, and he ripped it into left. Though it fell in for a single, Barker had hit it too well and Stokes wisely held up at third.

The Indian battery was equally cautious with Washington, to a fault. They walked him to load the bases. Conrad, still steamed up from the previous inning, cursed and looked around for something to kick. Ellerbach had loaded the bases for Icarus. There would be no pitching around him, they'd have to throw him strikes.

Billy took the first pitch for a ball. Conrad groaned. Evans admonished his pitcher to focus. Ellerbach complied with an excellent slider that caught the corner. The crowd, tense with apprehension, let go a muffled roar. Billy stepped out as though peering toward the third base coach. Instead, shielded from Evans' eyesight, he held up five fingers. Sal Donato in the coach's box at third held up five fingers, a gesture which Manny Rincon, the first base coach, quickly mirrored. Evans wondered at the strange sign. As Billy stepped back in and positioned himself as far back in the batter's box he could, the Giants in the dugout and bullpen slowly stood up and edged forward. Martin signaled an outside-corner curve to Ellerbach. Archie Stokes moved nonchalantly away from the bag at third.

With the bases full, Ellerbach was pitching from a wind-up. Stokes, already well off the bag, broke for home the very instant Ellerbach went into his motion. Simultaneously, Washington broke for second base, then abruptly held up. As the ball came to the plate, every San Francisco Giant mentally yelled *first base, first base, FIRST BASE!* Almost as quickly, Evans and Ellerbach attempted to alert Martin with projections of *Stokes!* and *Home Plate!* By the time the ball reached the plate, the cacophony in Martin's mind was deafening. While swinging deliberately above the pitch, Billy was focusing straight at Martin, projecting *FIRST BASE, FIRST BASE!* Martin, seeing Washington off the bag, caught the pitch, sprang up and cocked his arm to throw to first but held up when he saw Stokes go into his head-first slide. With his throwing arm up and away from home plate, Martin made a desperate twisting motion to get Stokes. The best he could manage was to fall on top of Stokes as he slid across the plate. The umpire signaled safe. Giants led, 1-0.

Evans was thunderstruck. In the course of the three-odd seconds that elapsed during the play, so many mental messages had screamed in his brain that he was unsure what to make of it. There were all the obvious characteristics of an out-dated classic Ball Fourian gambit, but no self-respecting major league manager would expect such a ploy to work. It was strictly moon league stuff. How could Earthlings even conceive of a gambit, let alone attempt to perform it? He must review the events. Surely he had misobserved what had just transpired.

Jake Conrad, by this time almost too stunned to move, belatedly jogged to the mound to calm his players. Evans was glad for the time it would give him to digest the evidence.

First Commissioner Tarn was quicker to analyze the incident. *Avion, do you understand? Yes, Tarn, another gambit? Correct, Avion.*

When play resumed, Billy was still at the plate with a 1 and 2 count. A shaken Martin called the pitch and Ellerbach hurled a whizzing fastball inside to brush Billy back off of the plate. The ball curled inside farther than intended and caught Billy on the shoulder as he fell back attempting to avoid it. Led by Renker, the Giants were unable to contain themselves and came pouring out onto the field. When the Indians did not respond in kind, Billy's teammates slowed their charge and came to a halt at the third base line. Billy got up, turned and waved them back before walking calmly to first. The momentarily dismayed Giants returned one by one to the dugout. Renker stood his ground, giving the evil eye to Ellerbach, then went back and sat down.

Evans scanned the Giants continually through this latest incident and perceived the typical Earthling pattern of fury, suspicion and imminent violence. When the minds of the Giants slowly composed themselves and dropped back into white-mind states, Evans found yet another example of implausible behavior. Had he spent years on Earth only to fail, in the end, to truly know these creatures?

Up in the press box, Lloyd Cronin frowned. What the hell's the matter with these damned Indians? We almost had a good one going there. Gutless jerks!

Down on the field, the damned Indians were preparing to face Mitch Simpson with two out and the bases loaded. Simpson, a bit over-eager, swung at the first pitch and grounded to Nixon at third, who stepped on the bag for the force. All of Cleveland breathed a sigh of relief.

While O'Nealy went to work in the bottom of the third, Evans was furiously trying to absorb the events he had just witnessed. He was pulled out of his train of thought when he detected O'Nealy again pitching with a numbered pattern. By the time Evans had reached the conclusion that O'Nealy was following the same code, only this time backwards from the seventy-fifth place of "pi," Smith and Nixon had struck out. O'Nealy was throwing pure heat, reaching nearly one hundred miles an hour on some pitches, and he was too strong for the distracted Indians. Eddie Martin, still ruffled by the steal of home in spite of his mind-smoothing efforts, easily became the third strike-out victim of the inning. Martin was not aided by the fact that Evans, incorrectly believing that he understood the new code, sent all the wrong signs.

Already having determined that Ellerbach might be mentally spent by the treacherous third inning, Evans had Spanky McTell warmed up and ready to start the Giants' fourth. McTell's fresh mind and arm put down the side in order.

Before the Cleveland half of the fourth got underway, San Francisco had a fresh arm of their own. In to pitch came Jimmy Strongbow! Why would they replace O'Nealy when he was throwing a shutout, wondered a confused Evans. That confusion was enhanced when, instead of leaving the game, O'Nealy replaced Butterfield at first base. Evans' mind, already taxed by all that had occurred, did his best to process data while preparing to observe Strongbow. Jake Conrad, for his part, ran onto the field to confer with the home plate umpire. He wanted to make sure that everyone understood that Dubois was forced out as the designated hitter with Strongbow taking the eighth spot in the order, and that O'Nealy was going in to bat in Butterfield's spot. Of course, that scenario was already apparent to the umpire, who reminded Conrad that he hadn't been born yesterday. Conrad, angered by the remark, nonetheless gleefully ran back to the dugout, savoring the thought that two strong batters had been pulled from the game by this new and seemingly wasteful maneuver. Upon further consideration, he eyed Chambers in the opposing dugout and wondered what vile scheme he had up his sleeve.

Jimmy, who had spent the previous half-inning loosening up in the locker room with the trainer, came out ready to pitch. Three Indians later, Jimmy had run the string of strikeouts to six.

The crowd in the stands could take heart at two things: the score was only 1-0 and Spanky McTell was in no mood to surrender anything to the Giants. The side grounded out in order in the fifth.

Alan Van De Kirk led off the Indians' fifth, and he grimly resolved to avenge the rude treatment he received in the second. He smoothed his mind and tightened it against disturbance. Billy and Jimmy knew well enough to keep the ball away from Van De Kirk, and the count had gone full before Jimmy made a small slip. A forkball did not break down quite as far as intended and Van De Kirk boomed a very high, very deep fly to straight-away center. Barker had time to drift back on it but no space to catch it. It was over the fence. Game tied, 1-1.

Billy ran the new ball out to a deflated Jimmy Strongbow, who was picking at the rubber with his spikes. "Van De Kirk just won't go away, will he, Chief?"

"I blew that one, Billy."

"It was good enough to strike out most of the majors," said Billy, patting Jimmy on the shoulders. "Shall we get back at it?"

Jimmy could feel the soothing strokes rippling through his mind, and sensed his friend bolstering his confidence. He would not let him down. "Sure, Billy, let's get 'em."

And get them he did. Jefferson he finished off in three pitches, the last one a forkball that approached home above the knees and broke down so hard that it skipped off the back edge of the plate. Jefferson fell down trying to reach it. Pantuso went to an 0 and 2 count before hitting a skipping grounder that took a bad bounce off the carpet that Stokes couldn't handle. The official scorer ruled it a single. Jimmy, unconcerned, retired Smith and Nixon on routine fly balls.

Between innings, Billy stepped into the clubhouse tunnel to strip off his catcher's gear and do some relaxed-minded thinking. Jimmy followed him in.

"Billy, should we communicate so openly on the mound? What about that Evans?"

"I just gave him some more to chew on. His mind must be fairly over-worked by now. Got him where we want him, preoccupied and hopefully confused. Sorry, Jimmy, but I've got to get ready to bat."

"Oh, sure."

Billy used the rest of his break reviewing what he knew about McTell back on Ball Four. He did not like to think about it. Spantell, as he was known on the home planet, was one of the few pitchers that had routinely silenced Belteron's bat. Billy could only hope that his hidden identity would prove to be an asset against the former foe.

Billy watched with concern as McTell quickly dispatched Willie Washington on strikes. A few moments later, Billy himself struck out for the first time in the Series. In his turn at the plate Simpson managed to get his bat on the ball, hitting a dribbler back to McTell, who easily threw on to first. Lou Chambers, in spite on his competitive nature, whistled in admiration.

The 1-1 tie and McTell's mastery over the Giants eased Warren Evans' mind back in the Cleveland dugout. In spite of all the confusing moves by the Giants, they had nonetheless succeeded in accomplishing very little. There was plenty of time. A mistake or two might be all that would be needed. He focused and went back to scanning.

Eddie Martin opened the Cleveland sixth. The Indians' catcher, who bat-ted ninth, possessed one considerable talent: he could protect the plate. That talent did not fail him now. He fouled off a series of pitches, carefully working his way to a full count. Martin fouled off two more before Jimmy missed on a slider aimed at the inside corner.

With the crowd buoyed by the lead-off man getting on, Rifkin advanced to the plate amid claps and cheers. Could he sacrifice Martin along? He squared to bunt, and took the fastball for a strike. In the dugout, Evans decided to risk overruling Conrad and sent a message to Rifkin. *Hit away. Yes, Evan.* The maneuver worked. With the infield rushing in to defend against the bunt, Rifkin swatted the next pitch off-field over the incoming O'Nealy. The ball landed in the infield but there was no one there to recover it. By the time Renker got over to it, the lumbering Martin had reached third. Men on first and third, and still there were no outs. In the recesses of Billy's mind, he silently admired Evans' gutsy call. This, in spite of everything, was true base-ball genius. How should it be countered?

Renker walked the ball back to the mound and Billy rushed out to meet him. The three stood there silently while the fans erupted into chants of "Ral-ly, Ral-ly, Ral-ly." Billy smiled at Jimmy and said, "Great call, wasn't it?" Jimmy chuckled and shook his head in dismay at the unflappable Billy Icarus.

Billy turned to Renker and said, "Now, Eddie." Renker nodded and hustled back to his position.

Warren Evans smiled when he perceived the compliment the Giants' catcher paid him. This Icarus was indeed a strange character, if he could enjoy an opponent's good play while in so much danger. He himself enjoyed the situation at hand. They were poised to take the lead. But I must continue to scan, he quickly reminded himself.

Three pitches later, Evans was elated by what he had discovered. Perhaps because of the tough spot the Giants were in, Renker's mind must have weakened again. He was telegraphing the signs!

It was too late to save Nichols, who lined out softly to Stokes, but Evans alerted his team to stay tuned to him for signals. *Slider, inside, high.* Fernandez missed on the outside pitch. Is Strongbow wild? *Fastball, sinking, middle.* Fernandez swung way ahead of the outside curve and barely managed to stay on his feet as he tried to adjust. He looked toward Evans who, preoccupied with the strange calls from Renker, failed to send a signal or alert Fernandez in any way. As a result, Fernandez was unprepared to react to the next pitch and watched it blaze down the middle for strike three. Evans was busy comparing the actual pitch to Renker's call of a change-up. Evans belatedly reached a decision. *No signals will be sent, ignore Renker's mind. Yes, Evan.* Had Evans scanned his players' minds at that moment, he would have been shocked to find that they were suspicious of his judgment for the first time since they came to Earth. Almost as one mind, they ran smoothing loops to quell the mutinous emotions. Van De Kirk, unable to resist his curiosity concerning Renker, read inside slider from him and missed the ensuing curve. His lapse in discipline agitated him and, on the next pitch, the resulting anger caused him to turn the bat over too hard in his swing. He struck the ball low, producing a booming pop fly. O'Nealy drifted over in front of Renker and hauled it in. Side retired.

As the Giants trotted off the field, Billy came abreast of Renker. "Excellent job, Eddie."

"No problem, boss."

In the top of the seventh, McTell remained a mystery to San Francisco, and ran his string of retired batters to twelve. Watching his teammates' futile efforts, Billy reflected that he had miscalculated. Bueller was spent, all right, but the Giants hadn't had a chance to get to Ellerbach before he was pulled. He had never considered McTell in the equation. And that equation was 1-1.

Conrad, Evans and the rest of the Cleveland Indians were dwelling on the same mathematics with some desperation when they were startled by the Giants' sudden change in pitchers. Taking the mound was Billy Icarus and strapping on the catching gear was Chief Strongbow! Conrad quickly conferred with third base coach Hal Walker concerning not only the legality of the move but the wisdom of it as well. Warren Evans wished momentarily that he was back on Ball Four where people were rational, even in sports. Quickly, he ordered his mind to stay as in tune as he could with the everchanging, unpredictable humans.

The Giants in the field had some difficulty as well in absorbing the implications of the move. None had ever seen Billy pitch, and only their overriding confidence in his judgment allowed them to shake the apprehension and refocus. Chambers, who had approved the move in theory the previous evening, still fretted. Earlier that afternoon, he had called Strongbow into his office in the clubhouse and inquired as to Billy's abilities.

"Yeah, Skipper, I caught for him once before we made the club. He's better than me, I'll tell you that right now."

"Better?"

"Better," answered the Chief.

"How much better?"

"A lot better. He's a hell of a pitcher, maybe the best I've ever seen."

"So why doesn't he pitch?" asked Chambers in his dismay.

"Lou, why did Babe Ruth stop pitching?"

Chambers had accepted that at face value, and now a man who had never pitched in professional baseball was taking the mound in the seventh inning of the seventh game of the World Series with the score tied. At least they hadn't burned O'Nealy and Strongbow. They were still technically available to pitch. That part of Billy's scheme was the insurance he needed, in spite of the weakened line-up. Chambers hoped that the baseball history books would not record that it was he who had committed the greatest managerial blunder of all time.

Dozens of reporters in the press box started talking at the same time. Calls went about the room for a rule book, which no one could seem to find. They lumbered steadily through the machinations that were taking place down on the field and eventually came to the conclusion that all was, if not right, at least legal. Reporters from the National League beat reminded everyone of the time the Mets had two pitchers in the game after much of the team had been thrown out in a brawl. Three at one time, it was agreed, was a new one. Red Henderson of the Chronicle changed his working title from "Why the Giants Won" to "Why the Giants Lost." Lyoyd Cronin just sat back and laughed into his sixth beer. He was loving every minute of it.

Back down on the field, Billy was warmed up and ready to face Hunk Jefferson. Jimmy squatted behind the plate. Evans, who had been scanning Icarus since he took the mound, concentrated alternately on both men in the battery. Would Strongbow have as tight a mind as Icarus? It was crucial.

With the first pitch of the seventh, Evans received his answer. Icarus' and Strongbow's minds were the same no matter which was pitching. What is the significance of this unprecedented move? Evans had never witnessed such a thing, even on Ball Four.

Billy, whose arm was loose from all the throwing during the game, sailed past Jefferson on three pitches, two of them fastballs and the last a curve which Jefferson leaned away from and watched in horror as it broke down and in for the called strike three. Chambers' apprehension turned to awe. On the Cleveland side, Conrad and Evans felt their anticipation turn to consternation. Icarus was good, but it didn't make it right.

The next two hitters, Pantuso and Smith, had their guard up and batted defensively. It only served to prolong their misery, as Billy threw a wide mix of pitches and speeds, but only at the corners of the plate. In the end, amidst a spray of foul balls, the Cleveland side succumbed on strikes. The only people in the stands who appreciated the performance were Tarn and Avion. Was there no end to the Giants' surprises?

Spanky McTell took to the mound to face the Giants in the eighth. He smiled to himself. This is what he loved about baseball, and why he had become a relief pitcher. Now the real talent emerged, now the depth of one's character was tested. Icarus was brilliant, but McTell was unruffled. It only heightened the tension and increased his enjoyment. It could not get better than this. Let them try their best.

Eddie Renker did try his best and, mustering all his pugnacity and guile, battled his way to a walk. But Roberts, Barker and Washington were no match for the unshakable Cleveland pitcher; it was child's play for McTell. Like Billy, he seemed to toy with them before dispensing with them. With each wave of the bat, with each swing and a miss, the crowd roared its approval. McTell began to average ninety-eight miles an hour on his fastball, which made his change-up devastating, and his change-up curve impossible to touch. The crowd went berserk as McTell finished them off on strikes.

While Darvel Nixon walked slowly to the plate to begin the bottom of the eighth inning, the fans continued to exhort their team to break through, clapping and chanting. Billy silenced them with his first toss, a blazer that Nixon waved at weakly. The change-up that followed caught Nixon so far ahead that he completed his swing before the ball crossed the plate. The crowd, now hushed and anxious, jumped to its feet when Nixon hit Billy's next pitch, a sinker, deep into the gap between second and first. The ball bounced once, Renker dove to make the stop and, from his knees, fired to the outstretched glove of O'Nealy, a step ahead of Nixon. The crowd sat back in disgust.

Billy started Eddie Martin off with a change-up, which spun off the bat and up behind the plate. Jimmy threw off his mask, turned around and circled, trying to gauge where the ball would come down. It dropped untouched about a foot from his mitt. Chambers winced in the dugout. Billy would have had that one.

Martin missed on a fastball and Billy came back with another change. This time the ball again flipped foul off the end of the bat, but higher, and Jimmy pivoted and pulled it in for the out. He grinned smugly at Billy, who allowed a brief smile in answer.

With two out and the bases empty, Dizzy Rifkin saw nothing but heat. Three hundred-plus-miles-an-hour hurls later, the Cleveland chances in the eighth were over.

Knowing that he would lead off the ninth, Billy once again dashed into the tunnel to think. If only he could risk reading McTell, he might do well against him, but he didn't dare. While at the plate, Evans would scan him continually, and would be sure to observe his mental invasion of McTell on the very first pitch. That would call an abrupt halt to future gambits or mind-reading opportunities, and anything short of a home run on the first pitch would leave the Giants vulnerable to Cleveland in the bottom of the ninth, and without options. No, he'd just have to take his chances, as any human might. He quickly recalled McTell's pitch selection during his last at-bat, and dashed out to the on-deck circle for a bit of stretching before hastening to the plate.

Billy stepped in to bat left-handed. He would lose a little power, but it would take away the outside corner from the right-handed hurling McTell. Any advantage would serve. Evans and Conrad were both stunned. Nothing in the scouting reports said a word about Icarus as a switch hitter. Was there no end? Out at the plate, Billy took the first pitch, a fastball on the inside corner, for a strike. He then swung and missed at a vicious screwball which tailed outside and into the dirt at the last instant. McTell was obviously attempting to counter Billy's move to the other side of the plate. Mental messages were flying back and forth between McTell and Martin, but Billy kept his mind locked tight. He'd take his cuts, like a man. Poised and ready, Billy waited. McTell came back with a brilliant change-up, but Billy was not to be fooled. He held up his bat speed and swatted the ball into the gap in left-center. Only because Van De Kirk had wisely positioned himself for just such a blow did Billy have to hold up with a single. Now was not the time to get thrown out trying to stretch a hit.

McTell's string of hitless innings was halted at five, and the crowd buzzed with dread as Mitch Simpson came to the plate. Was McTell's magic on the wane?

Simpson would not be overanxious this time. He waited, watched and worked his way to a 2 and 2 count. Billy danced off first and McTell checked the runner, then threw to the plate. Simpson got all of the ball and it flew off the bat on a rope. Unfortunately that rope ended in Smith's glove in right, where he didn't have to move a single step to get the putout. The crowd breathed a sigh of relief. O'Nealy and Strongbow were all that were left of the Giants' ninth, a fact not lost on the men in both dugouts. Chambers walked back into the tunnel and swore so loudly even Evans could have perceived it, had his mind been on the location. He, however, was already focusing on O'Nealy.

Brad was no match for McTell. He struck out on three pitches, all of them fastballs. On the third pitch, Billy startled the complacent Indians by breaking for second. Intent on the impending easy outs, they had momentarily forgotten the runner and Billy had crept off first almost without notice. Martin fired a bullet to second, but Billy's hand slipped around the tag. McTell shrugged it off. There were two out and an .068 hitter was coming to the plate. Warren Evans sat back down next to Conrad for the first time since the third inning.

Jimmy took slow, deep breaths as he strolled to the plate, and tried to appear menacing. He gazed around the stadium before stepping in. The eagle was nowhere in sight.

Jimmy took a futile cut at McTell's first pitch, a slider that crossed the plate on a steep diagonal. The next pitch, a similar slider in a different location, was just as effective, with Jimmy missing it by a foot. It gave him a sick feeling in the stomach and he stepped out to regain what composure he could find. McTell stood patiently out on the mound and waited with his hands on his hips. Not really wanting to get back in, Jimmy lingered and stretched and took a couple of loosening-up swings. Just before he stepped back, he looked out plaintively at Billy as though for help. As their eyes met Jimmy heard a distinct *listen!* in his mind. He fought off his anxiety and returned to the batter's box. McTell leaned in for the sign. Jimmy kept his eyes glued to Billy. As McTell went into his stretch, Jimmy heard *low, outside fastball!* rip into his consciousness.

As the ball whizzed in all a blur, he swung in that location with what bat speed he could administer and cuffed the ball on a slice over toward first. It headed on an arc toward Nichols, but the slice drew it away and past his frantically outstretched glove. As Nichols fell in a heap, the ball landed on the outside edge of the foul line, thirty or so feet beyond the bag, kicking up white powder. The umpire gave an animated fair sign. Billy was already digging around third. He slowed up and cruised into home as the ball skidded over into foul territory. Smith would not reach it in time. Had he wanted to, Jimmy might have easily reached second, but he stopped the moment he got to first. He was far too surprised that he had gotten a hit to consider any further action.

Evans, who had already been thinking ahead to the Indians' impending at-bats, was only vaguely scanning the plate when the hit occurred. He had perceived the *low, outside fastball* thought in Strongbow's mind, but could only conclude that Strongbow had somehow managed a correct guess on a pitch. Evans realized with a start that it was the first guess he had observed all evening. That it should result in an RBI for a weak-hitting pitcher was unnerving. It was more than that for Conrad, who swore, spit and then accidentally threw his hat down in the brown puddle. He picked it up, wiped it on his pants, stuffed it back on his head and sat down in a huff.

Jimmy remained on first base until Stokes popped up to end the inning. Giants, 2-1, and the Cleveland ninth loomed.

Jimmy, almost with relief, hustled over to the dugout to don the catching gear. He was surprised to find Billy already putting it on.

"Sensational, Jimmy, absolutely sensational."

Jimmy smiled and then shrugged. "Pure luck. Probably had my eyes closed."

"Looked like it from where I stood. But it wasn't luck. Good job."

"Are you gonna catch?" asked Jimmy.

"Yeah, and Brad's pitching."

"So what do I do, am I done?"

Billy reached over, picked up a first baseman's mitt and tossed it to Jimmy. "Ever use one of these?"

"Nope."

"Well, you're going to now. It's just like catching, only you get to stand up." With that he turned and ran to home plate.

When Conrad saw O'Nealy on the mound, Icarus behind the plate and Strongbow heading for first, he said gruffly, "We'll just see about this..." and headed for the plate.

Evans grabbed his arm and pulled him gently to a halt. "Jake, they can do it and you know it."

Conrad stared at the ground. "Yeah, you're right, they can. But why the hell...wait a minute. Buck is up and he's left-handed. In comes O'Nealy. Those bastards."

Buck Nichols walked slowly to the plate. Throughout the stands there were pockets of clapping, but mostly the crowd hummed like a high tension wire. Abe Watkins and Elliot Edwards sat side by side in a very quiet owner's box. None of the entourage dared utter a sound. Tarn and Avion sat totally absorbed. For the First Commissioner, nearly thirty years of politicking and planning had come down to three outs. For Dr. Avion, baseball was thrilling for the first time in his one hundred twenty-six years. Warren Evans scanned. Jake Conrad chewed furiously.

O'Nealy went into his wind-up and delivered. Nichols missed the rising fastball. The next pitch broke outside and Nichols held up. The next he drove foul into the crowd behind third base. O'Nealy then tried to catch the inside corner with a fastball. The umpire thought otherwise. 2 and 2. On the next two offerings Nichols caught pieces and sent them spinning, foul. O'Nealy tried on the next pitch to sucker him into going after a forkball, but the disciplined Nichols let it fall out of the zone. 3 and 2. O'Nealy turned away from the mound and rubbed for a while at the ball before looking back in. The crowd had ceased its clapping, but the taut hum sizzled around the park. O'Nealy kicked his leg up, came down and threw a hard slider in about knee high. Nichols allowed that it would pass inside. If it caught any of the corner, it wasn't much. But it was enough for the umpire. As Nichols turned to jog to first, the umpire ever so belatedly thrust his left hand across in a furiously called strike three. The tautness of the crowd snapped and erupted into screams of protest and denial.

Billy walked the ball out to the mound. Brad looked at him and said, "Don't ever ask me to do that again." In spite of his jocular intentions, he couldn't muster a smile to go with it.

"Don't worry, Brad, I won't," said Billy, offering the missing smile. He waved the Chief over from first.

The right-handed Strongbow would face the right-handed Fernandez. Conrad didn't even flinch. Nothing surprised him anymore. The gang in the press box weren't surprised either. By now, the move made perfect sense. Chambers was either a genius or a fool.

The home plate umpire begrudgingly allowed the warm-up tosses, but stood glaring at Strongbow to get on with it. Jimmy obliged. He was in no mood to waste time.

Fernandez stood in. Jimmy delivered a blinding fastball which Fernandez missed for strike one. Before giving the next sign, Billy stood up and held up one finger. He crouched back down and gave another signal to Jimmy. As Jimmy wound and delivered, from every place in the park that a Giant stood, various mental calls rang out. What Fernandez perceived in his mind was something like *fastball-curve-slider-curve-knuckeball-fastball-screwball-slider-fastball-change-fastball-fastball*. When Jimmy finally served up the pitch, Fernandez was far too disturbed to know what to do except swing frantically, well ahead of the change-up. In the dugout, Evans finally had had enough. He ordered white minds all around. All complied, except Alan Van De Kirk, who by now was not listening to Warren Evans. He had decided that he was his own best counsel.

When Billy threw the ball back, Jimmy received it, then paused and stood staring at the plate. The thousands in the stands, by now in a cold fury of frustration, began calling for action. Jimmy didn't hear them. He was transfixed by the glowing colors of his Medicine Wheel. It had been there guiding him all season, but now it appeared to have taken real substance. He thought for a moment of fighting the hallucination, then accepted it and backed up slowly to the rubber. He leaned in for Billy's sign. Suddenly the visions of the harsh Sonoran desert flooded his mind. The eagle cried and echoed soundlessly around the park. As the sun peaked over the rim of the mesa, four generations of Chiricahua Apaches merged to deliver the final attack.

Fernandez lashed at the floating orb with confidence, but the knuckleball settled into Billy's glove with a soft pop. Fernandez froze in dismay for a second, then pivoted and walked briskly off.

When Billy came out to the mound, Jimmy looked at him hopefully. "Am I through?"

"Yes, Jimmy, you can relax. It's up to me now."

There on the mound, as the crowd hurled epithets and various abuses, Billy stripped off the catcher's gear and Jimmy strapped it on.

When Billy waved off the warm-up tosses, the umpire yelled out, "Throw a few, godammit. I don't want to be accused of not giving you a chance." Billy obliged him, but it was unnecessary. He was ready.

While Alan Van De Kirk walked with long, slow strides up to the plate, the crowd could no longer contain itself and launched into clapping and stomping of feet. Van De Kirk dug in with determination and slowly waved his bat in preparation. He did not have to wait long.

As the ball came in, Van De Kirk jumped back, convinced that it was aimed squarely at his head. When it broke down into the zone and the umpire screamed out "Stee-riike!" Van De Kirk looked out at Icarus with a confounded look. He stepped out, shook it off and got back in, more determined than ever.

Billy looked in. Van De Kirk cocked his bat. Jimmy assumed his crouch. Every eye in the crowd was riveted. Time stopped for a second, then Billy went into his wind-up. Later, the man on the speed gun would claim that the one-hundred-ten-mile-an-hour reading was not in error. Van De Kirk, though late in his swing, caught every ounce of the ball. It flew off the bat on a straight path down the first base line. The right field umpire turned and straddled the line, poised to make the call. The ball had tremendous distance, and reached the top of its arc well out into right field. As it came down, it tailed off ever so slightly to the right. It smashed into the crowd, twenty rows up. When the umpire signaled foul, the fans were savage in their fury.

Conrad jumped to his feet. Evans calmly projected *let it go!* Conrad sat back down. By now his legs were too wobbly to walk, in any event.

On the 0 and 2 count, Billy stared in for the sign. Jimmy was taking his time. When the call came, Billy smiled in spite of himself. He would not wave it off. Jimmy was in tune.

Van De Kirk, other than Billy the consummate player of Ball Four, dug in once more, unflustered, unconcerned. It was only another pitch.

As Billy got set, he paused. In Ball Fourian, he projected a final challenge. *Hit this pitch, my friend.* Without so much as a quiver of an elbow, Van De Kirk replied instinctively in Ball Fourian, *I will try, my friend.*

The delivery came. As the ball approached it seemed to grow in size. Van De Kirk watched the seams as they slowly rotated a half of a turn. The ball, in Van De Kirk's mind, grew to the size of a moon as the seams began to rotate the other way. This was a gift. Van De Kirk swung his mightiest cut.

When his swing reached the end of its path, he stopped in disbelief. Where was the explosive whaap!, had he impossibly missed? All he heard was a dull thud. He looked back at Strongbow, who was staring down at the ball, which had caromed off his mitt about three feet toward first. They stared at each other and then over at the ball before Van De Kirk suddenly raced to first in a mad dash. Jimmy recovered, picked the ball up, set himself and tossed the ball in a careful arc to O'Nealy. Brad squeezed his glove around the ball two steps ahead of Van De Kirk.

Brad held the gloved ball up to the world and slowly drifted toward Billy and Jimmy, who were also converging. The three met each other with broad smiles and Billy said, "Well done, my friends." Brad, unable to restrain himself, gathered both of his mates up into a tremendous bear hug. Seconds later, the rest of the Giants had reached them, and the celebration was on.

Seven days hence, two billion Ball Fourians, gathered in hundreds of stadia and in front of countless holovision sets, would view the scene and fall into a simultaneous, stunned silence.

Alan Van De Kirk had fallen back slowly as the celebration got under way. He stopped in front of the dugout full of his dazed teammates and looked back at Billy Icarus. What had he said to him? Could it have been?... No, I have been away too long. As the Giants went on with their hugs and handshakes, Billy came into view. He gazed over at Van De Kirk and gave him a smile and a respectful nod. Van De Kirk returned the gesture. Their eyes locked for a moment before Billy's teammates surrounded him and cut him off from view. Could it have been?...

Van De Kirk shook his head. One thing was not in doubt. The Earthlings had just won the Universe Series, four games to three.

33

An hour later, after the trophy presentation was over and the television cameras had been turned off, Billy, Brad and Jimmy sat in front of their lockers talking about the Series.

"I feel like I'm a hundred years old," said Brad, still glowing with victory. "I've forgotten that we're all just rookies." He looked over at Billy. "Well, technically speaking, anyway."

"When I got here last spring," Billy said softly, "I was convinced that I *had* to come to Earth and give it a try. I was equally convinced that it would be in vain. I felt compelled, but doomed. Never could I have imagined that I would find such allies as you."

"Next time you guys decide to invade a planet, pick another galaxy, okay?" said Brad.

They all laughed together. Eddie Renker came over. "You guys were brilliant, totally brilliant."

"Everybody was, Eddie. There isn't a player on this team that didn't play his part."

Lou Chambers called for everyone's attention. "Could you listen up, guys?" The room fell silent. "This won't take long. I hold in my hands the game ball. I hereby present it to Billy Icarus. You damned-well earned it."

Cheers went up around the room. Billy stood up and walked over. "Hey, guys, I think it's more fitting that the Skipper keep this, don't you?"

Another round of cheers went up. Chambers held up his hand. "I can't take it, Billy. It's yours, fair and square. But maybe, now that it's all over, you might let me have my job back. What do you think?"

Billy and Lou smiled at each other as the room erupted into howls.

When the room quieted down, a voice yelled from the back. It was one of the security guards. "Hey Billy, some guy wants to see you. Says it's real important. Says his name is Tarn or something."

Billy momentarily went white, then smoothed his mind and his color began to return. He walked up to the guard. "Where is he?"

"We put him in Therapy Room A. He's with another guy. I didn't know what to do. They friends of yours?"

"Yes," said Billy, already heading down the hall.

When he got to the door of Therapy Room A, Billy stopped. He composed himself. It was inevitable, he thought, and opened the door.

Though in an unfamiliar Earthling form, Tarn was instantly recognizable. Billy would have known those eyes anywhere, in whatever body. The other man he did not know. He looked at the aging man with the wild hair and beard, then back to Tarn. He hopped up onto the examination table and folded his arms. Still looking at Tarn he said simply, "How did you know?"

"Hello, Belteron. It's good to see you. How did I know? I knew, I've always known. This is my good friend, Dr. Avion from the Science Center. He was kind enough to accompany me to Earth. I must say you put on an amazing performance. You must be quite pleased with yourself."

In spite of his efforts, Billy was feeling quite uneasy. He might as well face it. "I suppose I'm in a great deal of trouble."

"On the contrary, my friend," replied Tarn with a warm expression. "You have my profoundest gratitude and congratulations."

Billy was baffled. "What? I took a project you worked on for three decades and brought it to ruin. I used deceit and connivance to come to Earth to interpose myself between Ball Four and victory. How could I have earned your gratitude?"

Tarn smiled. "I'm sorry, Belteron, but I have a confession to make. I've used deceit and connivance as well. Your mission was not only known to me but nurtured by me as well."

Billy was stunned. "Why, that's impossible. I talked to no one. You yourself never broached the subject with me. In all deference to you, First Commissioner, I find this all a bit ludicrous."

"Understandably so. There are a number of things that transpire in the life of our planet that are not common knowledge. The vast majority of Ball Fourians accept the normal perception of history and the evolution of our culture at face value. This is as it should be. However, in extraordinary times, extraordinary efforts by a select few are often the difference between upward development and inevitable decline. Ordinary men occasionally find themselves drafted into the service of their world quite by accident of time and place. You, my friend, though no ordinary man, arrived at such a time and place."

Billy listened without a word. Tarn went on.

"Do you remember all the various meetings held between the two of us prior to your deselection? Yes? During those meetings, two things took place. Firstly, your arguments against unfair play were so compelling that I myself became convinced of the rightness of your views."

"Then why was I deselected?" interrupted Billy.

"It was politically impractical to do otherwise. It would have suggested that the possibility of defeat were a requirement of the Operation. Ball Fourians, however brilliant we are, do not welcome defeat. On the contrary, we presuppose that it is impossible. You used that fact in your victory over the Indians, didn't you?"

"Of course."

"Very insightful of you. As I said, you are no ordinary man from the baseball caste. This I could ascertain from our conversations. To continue. The second thing that took place during our meetings is that I discovered that your outrage was so great you had already begun to consider different options.

One was to go public with your views. This you did, resulting in your deselection. Another option was to appeal to the Planetary Court to obtain an injunction. You dismissed this approach, wisely I might add, because of the unlikelihood of success. The last option you were considering was that of somehow traveling to Earth to defy the Operation. You viewed the idea as fanciful and totally impractical and, though the thought of it was very compelling, it troubled you greatly. It flew in the face of all the values you shared with society."

A shocked expression grew on Billy's face. "It is impossible that you could have known my thoughts so well. I know that inner thoughts are shared in meld meetings in the Science caste, but surely it is a voluntary act. How could you enter my mind in such a way without my cooperation?" All of a sudden, a chilling awareness showed in Billy's eyes.

Tarn smiled grimly. "There are some powers not universally possessed, Belteron. And once I realized the direction in which you were headed, I nurtured those ideas, supported them. I did not compel you to come to Earth, I merely smoothed out the ethical problems that were in your way."

"How ever could you have accomplished that?" asked Billy doubtfully. "I know that I planted ideas in the minds of people on both planets during my quest, but to convince me to go against all the instincts and values I had developed during my lifetime? I find it inconceivable."

"And so you should. Very few people, Dr. Avion here is one of them, know of the mental discipline I have mastered or of the secret brotherhood, if you will, to which I belong. Our mental skills far outdistance those of the rest of the planet."

Billy listened in disbelief.

"Oh, it's not as diabolical as it sounds. Reaching back to days of the Science Emperor himself, is a direct line of leaders and advisors who have always risen above the typical aspirations and talents of those around them. The first of these were the original scientist-high priests of the Science Temple, and their descendants form the generations that have, over time, populated the political caste. At the core of this caste is a group of disciples of the mental discipline to which I refer. At present, I am the carrier of the torch. Our avowed creed is the betterment of society and culture, as well as the nurturing of the highest ethics and values achievable, while safeguarding the greatest possible liberties. You must admit that we have done so?"

"I must admit that it not only sounds plausible," Billy replied, "but I admit further that everything I have witnessed in my life supports the rightness of your efforts. But, I wonder, how do you dare reveal this to me?"

"From the fortuitousness of time and place. And by your own ethical advancement. You have outstripped the ordinary ethics of your race, and now, in a very real sense, you are one of us. In the end you will see our goals and values are the same. I am not afraid of what you might divulge. You do not wish to harm society. On the contrary, you only wish to serve."

Billy reflected for a moment. "Go back to how you sent me to Earth," he said with a wave.

"I did not send you to Earth. It was entirely your idea. However, during our meetings, I subliminally nurtured your feelings of outrage at the injustice we were attempting to inflict on Earthling baseball, and supported your sense of a mission or quest to prevent them from occurring. And, finally, I encouraged your own growing belief that your ethics, far from precluding action, required it of you."

"I'm not sure I even wish to know how you achieved all that mental fine-tuning," Billy said with a frosty snicker. "So, far from outraged at my actions, having provoked them, you are pleased? Have I done nothing on my own?"

"My dear Belteron, you have accomplished *everything* on your own. As a matter of fact, I didn't know that you'd even go through with your mission until you checked into that inn in the desert. You and your strength of character and conviction did the rest. I'm very proud of you. It was a selfless act of the highest order. It was a great service to Ball Four."

At last Billy smiled. "Yes, I thought so as well. And I now hold the humans in the highest regard and affection. Those boys down the hall are as fine as any the galaxy can offer. But tell me, why did you want me to do it, and what if I had failed?"

"Firstly, if you'd have failed, the worst that would have happened is that a glorious entertainment, an amusing diversion, would have been provided to the Ball Fourian world. There is no harm in that. But, that you and your Earthling allies have indeed won, there is in fact the likelihood of profound good coming to our planet. Belteron, we have become isolated, simultaneously superior, contemptuous and fearful of other worlds. In our isolation, we are inevitably becoming complacent, decadent and in grave danger of lapsing into a slow state of devolution. Now, don't you see, if we can *lose* at our premier sport to mere Earthlings, won't all that we stand for and all our superior posturing, won't all of it be called into question? Hopefully, the end result will be that we will, as a race, once again realize there is something to be learned off-world."

Again Billy smiled. "The very conclusion I had reached. Or did you plant that as well?"

"No," replied Tarn. "Again, it is understanding which you have acquired on your own. As I said, you have, by your separate path of excellence in baseball, transcended the norms of consciousness, and become one of the select. It was a natural process."

Billy paused. "Something concerns me. What if you are merely continuing to deceive me?"

"Why should I reveal so much in order to deceive you?" countered Tarn.

"In order to continue to manipulate me?"

"Everything in politics is manipulation, my good friend. We bandy about such words as consensus, compromise and the like but, in the end, these are only achieved when a man more powerful than the rest manipulates, one by one, those less powerful than he. Usually, these manipulations are small, often insignificant, almost imperceptible and, hopefully, kind to all players. Only occasionally are we given the opportunity to do something profound, and this requires more profound manipulations. You were a victim of, or, shall we say, a co-consirator in such a manipulation. My final argument is this: had I wanted to manipulate you further, surely I could have done so without the chicanery of pretending to tell you a preposterous truth."

Billy smiled, then bowed his head. "I submit to your impeccable logic. My apologies."

"It is not necessary," replied Tarn.

Billy's eyes lit up. "I have a question for you, First Councilor." Tarn smiled at the change in title. "I have the most amazing thought. The entire Operation Universe Series was conceived and executed with the single aim of leading to the repeal of the Technology Anti-Proliferation Act, was it not?"

Tarn's eyes also brightened and he smiled knowingly. "How astute of you. Would you like to join my inner council? I could use a mind like yours."

"I don't think so, just now," answered Billy.

"What do you wish to do, return to your grateful planet?"

"I've thought about it. How do they view me now back on Ball Four?"

"They think you are dead," replied Tarn.

"What?"

"When you disappeared from the inn, it was assumed you were on a nature quest in the desert. After a while, people feared for your safety. Some concluded the worst. I, in various ways, supported the adoption of that conclusion."

"How then could I return? Won't I be viewed as a criminal?"

"Not with my help. Should we choose to reveal it, no doubt the planet would be gratified to find out that, in some measure, a Ball Fourian was responsible for the Earthling victory. By my statements, I could support the ethics of your quest. All could be righted, I am sure. You are a very great star."

"And what if I don't wish to return?"

Tarn looked at Dr. Avion, then back to Billy. "Why, Belteron, would you consider otherwise?"

Billy's eyes sparkled. "I have come to love these humans. A man could do worse than stay with these teammates."

"If you had to choose," asked Tarn, again looking toward Avion, "which would it be?"

"I wish to stay," declared Billy. "Would you allow it? Some more years with my comrades would be a rich experience and, if I take your gratitude as sincere, an apt reward as well."

Tarn reflected but an instant, then quickly, without a flinch, dropped Billy into a hypno-trance. Billy's eyes fluttered and closed, and his chin gently settled to his chest.

"This is quite a twist, Avion. What do you think?"

"It is a considerable surprise, I must say," Dr. Avion responded. "But the idea has great merit. He is virtually indestructible, and it would allow the gathering of further valuable data. I wasn't tied to any particular retirement timetable. I am in favor, if it suits you."

"Should he fall into unfavorable hands, what technology breach might we be risking?"

"Minimal, I should think. Magna-cloning is unknown on our world, let alone here on Earth. Their technology is so backward that they wouldn't even know where to begin to comprehend the materials of which he's composed. There is every reason to believe that their medical machines would assume he is human, since he was cloned after biofashioning. No, Tarn, I see no cause for concern. We can only gain. And surely you could leave some of your personal staff to safeguard him."

"I know several that would be delighted," said Tarn. "Very well. I'll awaken him."

"If I might have a moment." With that, Dr. Avion walked over to Billy and placed a device next to his head. He pushed a button and the device pulsed with a soft magenta light for a few seconds. When the light went out, he slipped the device into his pocket, walked over to his chair and struck the same pose he had been in.

Tarn attended to Billy, whose eyes opened and quickly became alert. He looked at Tarn in anticipation.

Tarn smiled. "An apt reward indeed, my friend. I can fully understand the attachments you have created here on Earth, and it is only fitting that you should keep them a while longer. You have my complete support. You will, of course, notify me upon your eventual return?"

"Of course," replied Billy with a look of dismay. "Is it that simple?"

"It's that simple, most honorable Belteron. Well, I won't keep you any longer from your friends. Again, congratulations on your valiant performance and good luck in your future endeavors on Earth. Until we meet again?"

"Thank you, First Councilor," said Billy. "Wait. You will, of course, notify my loved ones?"

"Consider it done. Goodbye, then, for now. Shall we, Dr. Avion?" The doctor nodded assent. They stood up. With a smile and a short, respectful bow, Tarn reached into his own coat pocket and depressed a control module and, together with his friend, dematerialized and was gone.

When Billy walked back into the locker room, Jimmy and Brad were nowhere in sight. Most of the team were still fooling around and toasting one another with what hadn't been spilled of the champagne. Some had headed off to the showers. Lou Chambers was already in street clothes and, with Ron McIlhenny, was standing in a corner out of the fray. Billy came up to them.

"Hi, Lou. Where are Brad and Jimmy?"

"Why, I don't know," answered Chambers. "Must have slipped out while I was dressing."

McIlhenny spoke up. "I thought I saw them head back out to the field."

Billy followed suit and, sure enough, when he came out of the tunnel, there were two Giants standing on the field near the pitcher's mound. The lights were still ablaze, and a good deal of activity was under way.

He came abreast of them. Jimmy was staring down at the mound, which had already been stripped of the pitching rubber. A Caterpillar tractor was slowly rumbling around the outfield warning track.

"What's up, fellas?" asked Billy nonchalantly.

Jimmy just shook his head. He stood with his arms crossed and a deep frown on his face, as his eyes slowly went back and forth between the mound and the advancing tractor.

"They're tearing up the mound," said Brad. "Seems there's a Browns football game Sunday."

Billy, sensing something he was not sure of, waited without speaking. He glanced at Brad, who wasn't much help. Finally Jimmy spoke.

"A while ago we were pitching our hearts out, on this very goddam spot," he said, "and now a bunch of strangers are digging it up. God, when it's over, it's over."

Brad chuckled, opened his mouth to speak, then reconsidered as the poignancy finally struck him. Gently, he said, "Chief, there'll be other games, other mounds. Maybe not as good as the ones you used to tend for us, but you'll be on 'em and we'll be all right. Life goes on. I'm looking forward to it."

Jimmy turned toward Billy. "Yeah, I know, but where are we all going to be when it happens, huh, tell me that? Billy, those people who wanted to talk to you, they were from Ball Four, weren't they? I saw your face, it went white. They're on to you, right?"

"Yes, Jimmy," Billy replied. He looked over at the tractor as it rounded the edge of the outfield and continued on its way to dispatch the mound where the three of them had shared the recent glory.

"You have to go now, don't you? They're calling you back. I knew it, it's just not right, damn it." Jimmy turned and headed away toward the tractor, as though he were thinking of singlehandedly halting the injustice the Cleveland grounds crew intended to perpetrate. The tractor grew louder as it neared.

"I'm not going anywhere," said Billy.

Brad, who had lapsed into a melancholy look, instantly brightened. Jimmy, on the other hand, turned back, still confused. The tractor had drowned out Billy's reply.

"What?"

Brad answered. "He said he's not leaving. Right, Billy?"

"That's right."

Jimmy walked back up to them and said, "But I was sure that if..."

Billy broke into a big smile. "So was I, but it turns out that, well, shall we say I've got some friends in high places?"

Jimmy wiped his cheek where a tear might have been. "You can stay?"

"I wouldn't miss it for the world," replied Billy.

"That's great, Billy," said Jimmy. The three of them stood smiling at each other, oblivious to the tractor's growl. Billy rested his hands on his friends' shoulders.

"We've got a lot of baseball ahead of us, my friends. But right now, I'm starving. Cleveland must have at least one good restaurant."

Brad roared with laughter. Jimmy just smiled and shook his head. Together they turned and headed back in to rejoin their teammates.

34

ANCHOR:

> Last night's presentation of the final game of the Universe Series has left the population of Ball Four in a state of confusion. At different times in the Series itself, there were various reports of an increase of citizens reporting to Public Health with problems of anxiety, but these were easily handled by existing services. After last night's stunning defeat by the Earthlings, however, an unprecedented number of people swamped Public Health facilities all over the globe. We have a live report from Public Health Central in First City.

REPORTER:

> The scramble is on here to cope with what is now being termed a global psychological emergency, as thousands upon thousands of citizens are applying in record numbers for counseling and mental nurturing services. The problem officials here at Central are trying to solve is how to cope with the demand. The first part of their strategy was revealed a few minutes ago, when a statement was released to all news services globally. My understanding is that is was also shown on all holovisions in waiting rooms throughout the planet. Here is an excerpt:

OFFICIAL:

> While we at Public Health appreciate the enormity of the distress caused by the loss suffered by our beloved team, we wish to stress that the resulting mental discomfort is eminently treatable, and that

our entire global staff will be at your disposal around the clock to serve you. Unfortunately, the present heightened demand has necessitated a few advisories of which we hope all citizens will take note. Firstly, do not report to a center without first making an appointment through your consoles. There simply is not enough space available at present in our waiting rooms. Secondly, we advise all citizens to make an effort to enjoy their usual leisure activities, to report to their usual work assignments, and to further realize that the normal course of daily life is essentially unaltered. The one exception is that all gambling establishments have been temporarily closed by order of Acting First Councilor Semptor. He assures us that these shall be opened once the impact of the collapse of the gambling credit system can be examined, and normal operations can be restored.

REPORTER:

The rest of the statement goes on to spell out a number of details relating to the different services and treatments available but, as you just heard, the main thrust of Public Health's position is that life is returning to normal and the necessary services to assure that is does so will eventually be provided to all.

ANCHOR:

One of the principal concerns of the population is the collapse of the gambling credit system. As was reported last night after the game, so many people lost their entire store of gambling credits that an estimated ninety-seven per cent of all credits have been eliminated from circulation. What precipitated the actual collapse was the practice of gambling houses and brokers to wager large amounts against each other, using a margins system which relied upon the health of the gambling credit system itself in order to function. In simple terms, more credits were wagered on the Universe Series than actually existed. When Ball Four lost, all gambling credits in existence virtually vanished, leaving an actual credit deficit. Acting First Councilor Semptor reassured everyone that the Council will sort out the mess quickly, and further promises a rapid enactment of guidelines to avoid such debacles in the future. He also went on to say that, upon First Councilor Tarn's imminent return from Earth, the investment credit system, itself in disarray, will be returned to full use as well.

CO-ANCHOR:

What little joy there is on Ball Four presently centers around the impending return of First Councilor Tarn. He is due to arrive at Spaceport some time during the night of...

When Tarn arrived on Ball Four, he transported immediately to Semptor's residence in First City. There in the rooftop gardens, they had conferred for several hours about the disposition of the planet. From Semptor's console, Tarn had recorded a holographic statement, which reassured the public that all was well on Ball Four and that great days lay ahead. He then transmitted it to his daughter, Tarneen, at Holovision One for immediate transmission.

Now, he was leaving a transport booth in the lobby of the Spaceport Science Center. As he walked along the broad corridors of the facility, he thought to himself how wonderful everything was developing. Far from being depressed by the news of the state of the planet, he was elated. Events are proceeding beyond my wildest expectations, he thought as he entered a lift. Now we can begin the reorientation of our society at a greater pace than I ever anticipated. In the privacy of the lift, he even risked the undignified act of whistling a tune. Hard work well done always elevates the spirit.

At the top story, the lift came to a halt. As this floor was a high-security zone, Tarn had to issue a voice command to open the door to the lift. When the door opened, Dr. Avion was there to greet him.

"Good morning, Dr. Avion. I take it all is well. How is he?"

"Belteron? Oh, he's in splendid shape. We waited, of course, until your coming to revive him. But his readings are simply splendid."

"Good. Where is he?"

Dr. Avion stopped in front of a door. "In here."

They entered. The room in which they stood was filled wall to wall with monitoring equipment, watched over by a pair of technicians. At the back of the room was an observation window into a smaller room. Through that window, one could see Belteron, stretched out on a comfortable bed, as though sleeping.

"Undoubtedly, this is an unnecessary reminder, Tarn," said Avion. "But remember, when you wake him, his first thought will be that he is walking across the lobby of the Desert Rest Inn, seven months ago."

"I understand. Shall we?" They entered the room. Avion looked out through the observation window and nodded to a technician, who then threw a switch.

Within seconds, Belteron stirred. He swung his legs down to the floor and sat rubbing his eyes. When he looked up and focused, he appeared startled. He sat in silence for a moment, then a resigned expression came over his face.

"Hello, First Councilor. This, I take it, is not the Desert Rest Inn."

"No, Belteron, it is not. A team of agents met you there, then you were brought here."

Belteron remained seated. He looked down at the floor and said softly, "I should have known better than to assume I would be allowed to interfere with the Operation. You knew everything?"

"No, but enough," replied Tarn.

"And now the Operation is safe," said Belteron, "and I am in a grave position, am I not?"

"No, my dear friend, you are not. Much has happened since you were taken from the Desert Rest. I want you to listen to a little story, and I suggest that it would behoove you to initiate a smoothing loop while you listen. It will facilitate your adaptation."

Belteron reflected on Tarn's choice of words, then straightened up. "I am ready."

"The last thing you recall is walking across the lobby of the Desert Rest Inn on the outskirts of Spaceport. To you, that was moments ago, yes?"

"Yes," answered Belteron.

"That is not so," continued Tarn. "Time has passed. In that lobby, an agent walked abreast of you and activated a control module which transported you here to the Spaceport Science Center. You rematerialized in a booth on this floor, which had been equipped with an anesthetizing field. The whole process took less than a second and went entirely unobserved."

"And now you have awakened me," said Belteron directly. "I must say, Tarn, you have gone to a lot of trouble to prevent my going to Earth."

"No, Belteron, you *did* go to Earth," responded Tarn.

"What? that is preposterous..." Belteron halted for a moment as the smoothing loop played through his mind.

"If I may be allowed to continue?" asked Tarn gently.
Belteron relaxed and nodded.

"After you were brought here, you remained in an unconscious state. At this point, I'd like to introduce you to Dr. Avion."

They greeted each other politely.

Tarn went on. "Dr. Avion is, as no doubt you are aware, First Scientist of Ball Four. He serves on my inner council as Science Advisor, but most of his time is spent here at the Science Center in research. His work had reached a critical juncture, and he applied to me for help. He had perfected a process of android production called magna-cloning, in which androids can be cloned from a live being."

"If I may say so, First Councilor, I am shocked," interrupted Belteron. "The Anti-Android Manufacturing Act strictly precludes such activity."

"It precludes the introduction of such into the Ball Fourian community, Belteron. It does not impose any restrictions on legitimate research. But Dr. Avion faced a quandary: how to field-test such an android. Having convinced me of both the genuine value of the project and his flawless ability to safely utilize the process, I agreed to search for a means to legally assist him in continuing his work. It was then that I hit upon the plan."

Tarn paused and paced across the room. Belteron waited, with a vague look of discomfort on his face. Tarn turned and continued.

"At this point, it was becoming apparent that you intended to go to Earth. When I was informed that you had checked into the Desert Rest after having been biofashioned into Earthling form, I knew you intended to take the transport ship to Earth. It was obvious. Equally obvious was the fact that a unique opportunity was presenting itself. The chance would not come again. You were our best and only chance. I notified Dr. Avion. He concurred. When you were brought here, all was in readiness. You were then magna-cloned and the resultant android was activated in the lobby of the Desert Rest. That android proceeded to stowaway aboard the transport ship as though he were you, which for all intents and purposes he was."

"And when was that?" asked Belteron as the implications began to sink in.

"That was seven months ago," Tarn answered.

"Seven months ago? What about me?" asked Belteron as he stood up with a start.

Dr. Avion answered. "You have been in biosuspension here at the Center. You have no need to worry. You are in perfect health."

Belteron stroked the sides of his head and paced. He sat back down on the bed and addressed Tarn in an even though acutely angry tone.

"And what did this android do?"

"He went to Earth," replied Tarn. "He found a way to infiltrate an Earthling team called the San Francisco Giants and assisted them in winning the National League pennant. He then guided them to victory over the Ball Fourian Cleveland Indians in the Universe Series."

Belteron was speechless. He sat on the bed for a moment, then slowly walked over to the observation window and looked out at the technicians and ran his eyes across the banks of screens, dials and switches. He walked back, opened his mouth to speak, closed it and again sat down. Tarn and Avion waited patiently. It was fully another three minutes before he spoke.

"This is what you wanted," asked Belteron calmly, "that Ball Four should lose?"

"I could go either way, frankly. The result, however was the best I could have hoped for. The most important thing was that the contest become more even, which it did, with remarkable results."

"So you have done what you wished," concluded Belteron sadly, "and I have done nothing."

"No, no, my friend, quite the contrary," said Tarn sitting next to him on the bed. "You have done everything. That android that went to Earth *was* you, in every way. He had your mind, your values, your insights, your talent and, above all he had your sense of honor, of fair play. In every sense, you have accomplished what you set out to do."

"But I shall never know that I did," said Belteron. "I have only your word for it. I believe you, of course, but I will never have the satisfaction of having done a thing. Only the realization that, while I slept, an android lived out my intentions. It is a dismal feeling. I shall never know."

Tarn rested his hand on Belteron's shoulder. "That is not true. You can know everything."

"What are you talking about?"

"Dr. Avion?" said Tarn, turning to the scientist.

"Belteron, we traveled to Earth, Tarn and I, to witness the Universe Series. When it concluded, we visited with the android you. After a cordial interview, we recorded his entire memory banks. I now make them available to you."

"In what way?" asked Belteron, mystified.

"I can install them in your brain," answered Avion. "They will become your memories."

"It's as simple as that? I will have the memory of an android?"

"No, you will have the memories which another you has acquired. They will be entirely compatible with your own set. In a totally authentic sense, they are memories which are rightfully yours."

"Has this ever been done?" inquired Belteron.

"Of course not," replied Avion. "But the theory is indisputable, I assure you. And, you must realize that you have the added safeguard that you will incorporate these memories with the knowledge of how you received them. They will be yours, but you will know where and how you came by them."

Belteron thought for a moment, then smiled for the first time since awakening. "Tarn, do you agree with the Doctor? Is it a wise course?"

"Yes, my friend."

"Then, when can we proceed, and how long will it take?"

Dr. Avion answered. "We can do it now, and it will take mere seconds."

"Very well then. Doctor?" Belteron tried to offer an assured smile, but the apprehension showed through.

Tarn rose and Avion took his place on the bed. He removed the device he had employed on Earth from his cloak and placed it next to the side of Belteron's head. "Please relax and close your eyes. You will feel nothing."

The magenta light gently pulsed. After a number of seconds, it went out. Belteron remained motionless on the bed. Avion rose and stood by Tarn. Belteron opened his eyes and blinked a few times.

"I was in Therapy Room A talking to you, and now I am here, still talking to you..." He looked about the room in confusion, then closed his eyes again. When he opened them, this time they began to show signs of serenity.

"You are right, Doctor, everything fits, belongs. But I must say it is the most remarkable sensation. Please give me a moment to adjust."

Tarn and Avion smiled. *This is very good, Avion, very good. My mind is greatly eased of the burden I imposed on my good friend. Tarn, I assured you it would work. All is well.*

Suddenly Belteron sprang to his feet. He let out a loud laugh, rather uncharacteristic of a Ball Fourian. "I did it! And you knew! We were working together, and Ball Four thinks I'm dead? Oh, my, this is no problem for me on Earth. I don't even know. But I, that is, the I that is here on Ball Four, I have a considerable problem indeed."

"Do not be concerned," said Tarn. "We have given it much thought on our return voyage. It is relatively simple to solve. You have been declared dead while on a nature quest. It was a very long quest, and you ran into trouble. Scientists from the Center here discovered you near death while on a quest of their own. You were brought here and nurtured back to health. You have had a long and relaxed convalescence and by your request, you were allowed to keep your disposition secret from public eyes until you had regained your full vigor. Now you wish to step back into society, a whole man again. I see no problem."

"Nor do I, Tarn, my friend, nor do I," said Belteron gleefully. "But I must say I'm taken aback by all the mischief you've allowed yourself to be involved in."

Tarn smiled. "Ah, back to our conversation on Earth, I see."

"Yes, but with this new bit of business added," Belteron replied.

"Okay, we've bent some rules, but broken none," said Tarn. "It's gone on throughout the ages. The rightness of our intentions guides us. We are not so different from Earthlings, in a way. The principal difference is that here on Ball Four, power has ceased to corrupt. But the manipulations and fine-tuning of society continue. I must say, Belteron, I've come to have so much regard for you that I almost shock myself with my candor. Perhaps it's because you have been such a loyal servant."

"You are so certain that I will keep all this to myself?" asked Belteron with devilish grin.

"And will you?" Tarn asked with the merest touch of apprehension.

Belteron reflected briefly. "Naturally, I will. You have convinced my of the honorableness of your intentions. You are right. It wouldn't serve to disturb the fabric of the natural order. It proceeds nicely as it is."

"I again welcome you to join my inner circle. You are a natural leader. It wouldn't be the first time a man has jumped from baseball to the political caste."

"Sorry, First Councilor, but I'd rather play baseball," answered Belteron.

"So, my friend, would I," added Tarn with a resigned smile. "So would I."

"Something confounds me, Tarn. Why did you go through so much bother to get me to go to Earth? Why didn't you just ask me? I would have gone, you know."

"Yes, but the purity of your intentions would have been disrupted," answered Tarn. "You had to do it your way, with your honor driving you. Any other way would have impeded your success. The result speaks for itself."

"I suppose you are right." Belteron suddenly stopped, his jaw dropped open. "There are two of me now! This creates a delicate bit of business, does it not?"

"Again, not to worry. Avion and I have also applied ourselves to the problem. You will reassume your place as the great star here on Ball Four, and the other you will continue in a similar capacity on Earth. Once you were the greatest star in all of baseball. Now you are its two greatest stars. I should think you'd like that."

"Yes, but I, that is the I on Earth, intend one day to return. What then?"

Avion answered this time. "Then you shall be reunited with yourself, your further accomplishments on Earth shall be restored to you, and perhaps your android self should then find it appropriate to retire from the game."

"So everything that I shall have done on Earth will become mine?" asked Belteron with a twinkle.

"Yes."

"You are right, Tarn. I am fortunate beyond measure. Thank you."

"Not at all," responded Tarn warmly. "It is I who thanks you."

"Well," said Belteron, standing up and rubbing his hands vigorously together. "When can I return from the dead?"

"Now will be fine," laughed Tarn. "Just fine."

Epilogue

SPORTSCASTER:

> There you have it, ladies and gentlemen, the hectic scene in the Seaview Captains' locker room at First City Stadium. Belteron and his mighty team have reclaimed the Commissioner's Trophy in a devastating four-game sweep over last year's champion, First City. It was a remarkable season, and to see it capped by the emotional scene of First Commissioner Tarn awarding the Most Valuable Player trophy to Belteron was extremely moving. There seems to be a real affection between the Commissioner and the game's greatest star, doesn't there, Jevv?

REPORTER:

> Yes, there is. The gleeful pandemonium here in the clubhouse is a reflection of the feelings all must have toward Belteron, who has had the greatest year of his life. After the distressful events of last year, when all of Ball Four had mourned his loss only to see him recover from his grave injuries, for him to return to finer form than ever, well, it just warms the hearts of every citizen on the planet. It seems also to have made many forget forever the unfortunate developments that took place last year on Earth. Why, just after the game, I interviewed some fans in the stands, and most of them replied, "Earth, where's that?" Yes, Belteron has returned the luster to our beloved game. Back to you in the studio.

ANCHOR:

We now have a retrospective covering the highlights of the season, going back to the time that Belteron returned from his stay in hospital. As you will see, it's quite a story...

*　　*　　*

Associated Press.
November 10th.

BILLY ICARUS
REDEFINES THE GAME

Yesterday, Billy Icarus was announced as this year's winner of the Cy Young Award. Though he has, in the last three years, garnered every other award, this is the first time in history that the Most Valuable Player of the season, the Championship Series and the World Series has also been given the Cy Young Award. The fact that he did this in a season in which he won thirty-seven games while batting .435 and breaking Alan Van De Kirk's single season record with sixty-seven home runs will no doubt serve notice on one and all that baseball has been redefined forever.

It also marked the first time that three different pitchers from the same team have won the trophy in consecutive years. Brad O'Nealy, Jimmy "Chief" Strongbow and Icarus, in that order, have dominated National and Major League pitching for the past three seasons, guiding San Francisco to three straight crowns. O'Nealy, when reached for comment, responded that "It's high time Billy gave us a break. Either that or the least he could do is teach Chief and me how to hit!" Chief Strongbow, presently on a camping outing in the Arizona desert, was not available for comment...

*   *   *

USA Today

March 16th.

CLEVELAND ROSTER DEVOID
OF "MIRACLE TEAM" PLAYERS

With the placing of Indian first baseman Buck Nichols on waivers yesterday, the last member of the "Miracle Team" has departed from the Cleveland roster. In a mere four years, the team that had set a host of modern-era records while driving to a stunning defeat at the hands of then upstart San Francisco has seen every member of that illustrious squad slowly vanish into oblivion.

Indians' ex-manager Jake Conrad offered an explanation for the bizarre turn of fortune. "Losing the Series that year just took the fire out of all of us. I know it did with me. Some players rise out of the ashes of defeat, some are broken by it. Those were fine boys, young too, but I guess their spirit just got stomped out of them."

Cleveland general manager Abe Watkins, who signed Nichols' waiver, sees it another way. "Players come and go, some faster than others. The players on the so-called `Miracle Team' put it together for one glorious year. Maybe that was all they had in them."

Whatever the case, it's unprecedented that a team of such success should vanish so quickly from memory. Added to it is the supreme irony that the team that beat the Indians in the celebrated Series should, one by one, eclipse all of the records the "Miracle Team" set in that one sensational year. Now, the Cleveland roster is empty of its former stars. And their names have been erased from the record books by Billy Icarus and his awesome gang of Giants.